COLLIDE

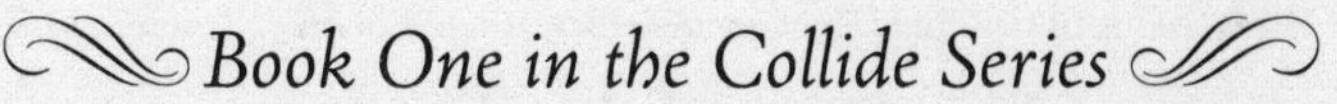
Book One in the Collide Series

GAIL McHUGH

ATRIA PAPERBACK
New York • London • Toronto • Sydney • New Delhi

ATRIA PAPERBACK
A Division of Simon & Schuster, Inc.
1230 Avenue of the Americas
New York, NY 10020

This book is a work of fiction. Any references to historical events, real people, or real places are used fictitiously. Other names, characters, places, and events are products of the author's imagination, and any resemblance to actual events or places or persons, living or dead, is entirely coincidental.

First Atria Paperback edition May 2014

ATRIA PAPERBACK and colophon are trademarks of Simon & Schuster, Inc.

For information about special discounts for bulk purchases, please contact Simon & Schuster Special Sales at 1-866-506-1949 or business@simonandschuster.com.

The Simon & Schuster Speakers Bureau can bring authors to your live event. For more information or to book an event contact the Simon & Schuster Speakers Bureau at 1-866-248-3049 or visit our website at www.simonspeakers.com.

Designed by Dana Sloan

Manufactured in the United States of America

10 9 8 7 6 5 4 3 2 1

Library of Congress Cataloging-in-Publication Data

McHugh, Gail.
Collide / Gail McHugh.—First Atria Paperback Edition.
pages cm.— (The collide series; book 1)
Summary: "A sexy contemporary romance novel set in New York City featuring a love triangle"—Provided by publisher.
1. Young women—New York (State)—New York—Fiction. 2. Man-woman relationships—Fiction. 3. New York (N.Y.)—Fiction. I. Title.
PS3613.C53335C65 2014
813'.6—dc23

2013047310

ISBN 978-1-4767-6534-1
ISBN 978-1-4767-6535-8 (eBook)

To my mother. You were right.

COLLIDE

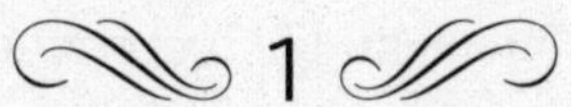

1

Chance Encounters

SHE CALCULATED THE flight from Colorado to New York at three hours and forty-five minutes, after which she knew her life would be forever changed—more so than it already had. Gripping the sides of the seat, palms sweaty, Emily Cooper closed her eyes as the engines prepared for takeoff. She had never been fond of flying; in fact, it scared the living shit out of her. Though she remembered times when the torture of being thirty thousand feet in the air was actually worthwhile: the first time she left home for college, an escape to a tropical island, or a visit to see her beloved family. However, this trip held no enjoyment—it held only feelings of loss and grief.

Looking at her was one of the reasons she still woke up every day—her boyfriend, Dillon. She could tell he noticed the look on her face was filled with the uncertainty of what lay ahead.

As he held her hand, Dillon leaned over and stroked a piece of hair away from her face. "Everything's going to be all right, Em," he whispered. "Before you know it, we'll be on the ground again."

She forced a smile and hesitantly turned, watching the snowcapped mountains disappear beneath the clouds. Her heart sank further as she inwardly said good-bye to the only true home she had ever known. She rested her head against the window and let her mind drift over the past several months.

In late October of her senior year in college, she received the call. Until that moment, life had seemed . . . good. Dillon had come into her world the month before, her grades were where they should be, and her roommate, Olivia Martin, had turned out to be one of the closest friends she would ever have. Picking up the phone that day, she never expected the news she received.

"*The tests came back, Emily,*" her older sister, Lisa, had said. "*Mom has stage-four breast cancer.*"

With those last six words, life as Emily knew it would never be the same. Not even close. Her rock, the woman whom she adored most in her life, and the only parent she had ever known had less than three months to live. She could never have prepared for what followed. Long weekend trips from The Ohio State University to Colorado to aid in her mother's last few months became Emily's norm. She watched her mother wither away from the strong, vibrant soul she had once been to the weak, unrecognizable woman she became before she died.

With sudden turbulence jolting her nerves, Emily gripped Dillon's hand and looked over at him. He gave her a quick smile and nod, essentially letting her know they were fine. Resting her head against his warm shoulder, she started to think about the role he had played through everything: countless flights from New York to Colorado to be with her, beautiful gifts he sent to take her mind off the madness that consumed her life, late-night calls talking with her to make sure she was okay. Even down to arranging the funeral, giving her advice on selling her childhood home, and ultimately moving her out to New York. It was all part of why she adored him.

As the plane descended into New York's LaGuardia Airport, Dillon looked at Emily while her hand was white-knuckling his. He gave a light chuckle and leaned over to kiss her. "See, that wasn't so bad," he said, stroking her cheek. "You're now officially a New Yorker, babe."

After what seemed like forever navigating their way through the airport, Dillon hailed a taxi, and they made their way to the apartment Emily would share with Olivia. That had become a sore topic with Dillon. When he and Emily had spoken about the move, it was his wish to have her live with him. Emily thought it was best, at least for the time being, that she move in with Olivia. Making the trek across the country was a hard enough adjustment by itself, and she didn't want to add more pressure to her situation. Even though she loved Dillon—and she loved him something fierce—a tiny voice in her head told her to wait. Living together would come further down the line for them. He eventually gave in but not without putting up a decent fight.

Once they arrived, Emily stepped out of the taxi. The sounds and sights of the city immediately hit her. Car alarms blaring, brakes grinding, and sirens wailing shattered through the air. People talking and yelling, their footsteps pounding against the busy concrete sidewalks, and the frantic flow of tightly packed cars consisting of a sea of yellow taxis were unlike anything she had ever seen or heard before. Steam billowing from manholes looked like ghosts floating up from the hot pavement.

The sprawling trees and clear lakes in Colorado were now replaced by steel and concrete, loud noises, and a clusterfuck of traffic. This was definitely something she would have to get used to. Drawing in a deep breath, Emily followed Dillon into the building. The doorman tipped his hat and buzzed Olivia, letting her know they were there. They made their way up to the fifteenth floor, thankful for the elevator.

When they entered the apartment, Olivia let out a high-pitched squeal. She raced over and gave Emily a hug. "I'm so happy you're here!" Olivia said, cupping her hands over Emily's cheeks. "How was the flight?"

"I got through it without needing any drugs or alcohol." Emily smiled. "So I would say it went well."

"She was fine." Dillon walked over and snaked his arm around Emily's waist. "I wouldn't have let anything happen to her anyways."

Rolling her brown eyes in Dillon's direction, Olivia crossed her arms. "Right, because you'd be able to stop a plane from crashing, Dill Pickle. I mean—Dillon."

Dillon shot Olivia a hard look and placed Emily's luggage on the floor. "That's right, Oliver Twist. I'm fucking Superman, so don't forget it."

Emily sighed. "It's been a while since I've been around you both at the same time. I forgot how fond you two are of each other."

Olivia smirked and reached for Emily's hand. "Come on, I'll show you around the place." Pulling Emily down the hall, Olivia turned around to Dillon. "Make yourself useful and unpack her belongings or something, Donkey Dick Kong."

Ignoring Olivia, Dillon sank onto the couch and flipped on the television.

"Oh my God, Olivia," Emily giggled, following behind her. "Where the hell do you think up these names for him?"

"Pfft." Olivia waved a dismissive hand. "He makes it easy."

"Well, you both are going to drive me nuts now. I can feel it."

"I make no promises, but I'll try my best to refrain from doing so, friend."

As Olivia gave the grand tour, Emily noticed the sleek, modern apartment included two bedrooms and two bathrooms. Although modest in size, the kitchen held white antique cabinetry, granite countertops, and stainless steel appliances. A large window in the living room paraded the direction of Columbus Avenue, a nice area in New York's Upper West Side. The apartment was breathtakingly beautiful, and without Olivia, Emily could never have afforded it—at least, not without Dillon's help. Although Olivia worked and took care of herself, she came from a well-to-do family, so money was never a problem. Despite growing up on Long Island's North Shore, Olivia and her brother, Trevor, were two of the most down-to-earth people Emily had ever met.

After helping Emily settle in, Dillon left, letting Emily know he would be back later that evening. Promptly grabbing a bottle of red wine and two glasses, Olivia dragged Emily to the couch.

Tossing her champagne-blonde hair to the side, Olivia gave Emily a bittersweet smile. "I know you've been through a ton, but I'm really happy you're here."

Emily's smile matched Olivia's. Her emotions were divided between sadness about the circumstances landing her in New York and happiness from taking a huge leap in her relationship with Dillon by moving out there—even if she wasn't living with him. She took a sip of wine and propped her feet on the ottoman. "I'm happy, too, friend."

Olivia wore a curious expression. "Did Dick give you any more hell about the living arrangements?"

"No, he didn't," she remarked, "but he definitely wants me to move into a place with him by the end of the summer."

"Well, you tell him he's going to have to fight me off during that battle." She huffed. Shaking her head, Emily laughed at Olivia's statement. "I'm serious, Em. He needs to give you some space right now with this move."

"Don't worry. I'm not going anywhere for a while." Emily glanced around the apartment. Her eyes rested on the stacks of moving boxes in the corner. "I'm really not looking forward to that." She gestured toward them with her head.

"I don't have to work tomorrow," Olivia replied, pouring her second glass of wine. "We'll do it then. For now, let's just relax a bit."

Over the next few hours, that's exactly what they did: relaxed. No talks of cancer. No talks of death. No talks of life's expectations. Just two close friends sharing a bottle of wine in their apartment as one began a new chapter in her book of life.

Two weeks later, Emily stood in front of an Italian restaurant located in Midtown Manhattan. She pushed the door open to what would be her new job for the summer. She scanned the place for the man who'd hired her a few days before: Antonio D'Dinato, a native New Yorker in his late twenties.

"There you are, Emily." Antonio smiled as he approached. "Are you ready for your first day?"

Smiling, she took in his dark, shoulder-length hair. "As ready as I'll ever be."

"A little overwhelming for a Colorado country girl, but I'm sure you'll fit right in."

She followed him into the kitchen, where he introduced her to the cooks on the line. Each had a friendly smile, but Emily knew, from waitressing her way through college, that their friendliness would soon come to an end. Eventually, they would yell at her to pick up her orders from the window, and no doubt their faces would be less jovial. She threw on her black apron while Antonio directed her to a waitress around her age. With a smile on her face, Emily studied the other waitress's hair. It was a rainbow fest of every color imaginable streaking through an overlay of bleached blonde.

"Hi, I'm Emily." Emily smiled as she approached her. "Antonio said I'm shadowing you today."

The girl returned the smile and handed Emily an order book and a pen. "So you're the new cat on the block, huh? I'm Fallon; it's nice to meet you."

"Yep, the new cat. It's nice to meet you, too."

"Well, have no worries. I think I started working here straight out of the birth canal." Her laughing gray eyes were wide. "I'll show you the ropes, and before you know it, you'll be able to run around here with a blindfold on."

"Sounds good to me." Emily laughed.

"I heard you're from Colorado?"

"Yes, Fort Collins, actually."

"You drink?" Fallon asked, offering her a cup of coffee.

"One of my addictions." Emily took the cup. "Thank you. Have you lived in New York your whole life?"

"Born and raised." Fallon sat at the coffee bar, gesturing for Emily to join her. "It's early yet. The rush will start within an hour or so."

Emily sat next to her and sipped her coffee. She glanced around the restaurant, watching the busboys set up the tables. Antonio spoke to them in what Emily assumed was Spanish. His voice rose anxiously as he motioned out to the streets of New York.

"So what brings you across the country to the city that never sleeps?" Fallon asked. "Are you an actress or a model? Which is it?"

"Nah, neither," she replied, trying to ignore the pain anchoring itself in her chest. The fresh wound still felt as if salt had been sprinkled over it. "My, uh, mother passed away in January. There was really no reason to stay out there after she died."

Fallon's face softened. "I'm sorry to hear that. Death definitely fucking sucks, that's for sure. My dad died a few years ago from a heart attack, so I know how you feel." Fallon sighed and looked away for a moment. "No matter what age, race, or economic status we hold, death touches us all at one time or another."

Emily found her comment wise beyond her age, but then again, she knew death seemed to bring out a completely different way of looking at life once someone was gone. "It does. I'm sorry to hear about your dad."

"Thanks. Not a day goes by that I don't think of him." Fallon paused. "What about your dad? Did he move out here with you?"

Another sore topic, but sore topics had become plentiful and unavoidable. "Nope. I haven't had any contact with him or his family since I was five. I really don't remember him."

"I'm batting zero here with you," Fallon joked. "Sorry. Maybe I should ask about puppies or something?"

Shaking her head, Emily smiled. "Don't worry about it. It's cool. Besides, I don't have any puppies, so that would be a dead end."

"Neither do I. They're cute, but I don't do the shitting all over the place that well." Fallon laughed, tossing her hair into a ponytail. "So what made you come to New York specifically? Do you have any other family here?"

"Not here. I have an older sister in California." Emily sipped her coffee. "But my boyfriend, Dillon, lives here. We started dating during my last year of college."

Fallon smiled. "College sweethearts, huh?"

"No, actually, he was already living here when we met. My roommate's brother visited her one weekend, and Dillon went with him."

"Isn't it amazing—the paths that bring people together?" Fallon stared into Emily's eyes. "I mean, had your Dillon not taken the trip with your roommate's brother, you two would've never met. Life is all kinds of weird like that."

Emily knew she instantly liked Fallon. "I totally agree. Fate and the roads that get placed in front of us. It's like one huge puzzle that ultimately fits in the end."

"Exactly." Fallon smiled. "So, what did you study in school?"

"I graduated with a teaching degree. I've started to put out some résumés, hoping to land something for this fall."

Fallon frowned, her lip ring shimmering in the light. "So you'll be leaving us by the end of the summer?"

"Nah, I'll probably work part-time then."

"Cool beans." She stood, her tall, lengthy frame towering over Emily's. "So, do you club?"

Emily wrinkled her brows. "Club?"

"Yeah, go out clubbing," Fallon replied, shaking her hips from side to side.

"Oh, you mean dancing." Emily laughed. "Yes, in Colorado I did, but I have yet to do it here."

"Killer. I love breaking in newbies to the club scene."

"Well, I'm down for getting broken in. Let me know when."

"I will. I'm dating this guy in his forties, and he gets me into some of New York's hottest clubs with no cover charge at all."

Emily nodded and sipped her coffee.

"The sex is just a bonus," Fallon added.

Emily nearly choked on said coffee. "Oh, that would definitely be a bonus for sure."

"Yeah, that's what I figured." She smiled. "Okay, new girl, let's get going."

Throughout the day, Emily followed Fallon. She showed her how to use the computer and introduced her to quite a few of the restaurant's regulars. They varied from upscale business-suit types to your "Average Joe" construction worker. A heavy lunch rush came around noon, and one of the waiters called in sick, so Emily took a few tables. Even though she wasn't familiar with the menu and felt shaky on the computer, she made it through without any major problems. By the end of her shift, Fallon had Emily's head buzzing with which guests tipped the best to which servers were the cutthroat types. For the most part, considering it was her first day, Emily thought it went well.

On her way out the door, Antonio stopped her with a to-go box. "Emily, my delivery boy quit," he said, his eyes thick with worry. "Do you head toward the Chrysler Building?"

"I don't, but it's only a few blocks away, right?"

"Yeah, it's right on Lexington and Forty-Second."

"Do you need me to take that there?" Emily asked, pointing to the box.

"Yes, please."

Emily shrugged. "Not a problem. I'll walk it over and just take a cab home from there."

"Thank you so much." He handed her the box, sighing with relief. "I'll throw a little extra cash into your pay next week."

"No need, Antonio. I like sightseeing anyway."

"Nah, nah, nah, I insist. We'll see you tomorrow, Country."

Laughing, Emily shook her head, amused at her new nickname. She rocked onto the rounded heels of her waitressing shoes and stepped out into the hot, humid air. June in New York was undoubtedly warmer than Colorado. She made her way through the city wide-eyed, still in awe that she lived there.

The air was thick with the bustle of traffic and the aromas from food vendors' carts. She was adjusting to New York better than she had anticipated. From the subway vibrating underneath her feet to the mixed array of faces, everything about the city intoxicated her mind. It was sensory overload at its finest. Three short blocks later, quite sweaty from the walk, she arrived at her destination.

Though his father had told him stories about it, until that fateful afternoon, Gavin Blake believed love at first sight didn't exist. He had the full attention of the blonde at the information desk, but his eyes locked on to Emily when she walked in. He took in the way she smiled at the security guard. Her beauty instantly hit him. But more so, he felt drawn to her as if a rope bound his waist and she was on the other end, pulling him to her. Blinking twice, he shook his head at the magnetic connection.

"Miss, can I help you with something?" the security guard asked her.

"Hi, I'm making a delivery," Emily replied, glancing at the receipt. "Floor sixty-two."

Before the security guard could answer, Gavin called out from across the lobby. "I can take her up, Larry."

The receptionist, who had gained Gavin's attention prior to Emily walking in, pouted her lips as he walked away.

Emily's gaze slid over to where the voice came from. Her breath hitched at the sight of the tall, devastatingly beautiful man making his way toward her. She felt thrown off-kilter, as though her equilibrium had skewed itself all over the building. Her eyes raked across his inky black hair, cut short and styled in a slightly haphazard way. He had breathtakingly chiseled features; his mouth seemed to have been painstakingly carved to perfection by an expert sculptor. Her eyes flicked down to what appeared to be a toned body hidden beneath a gray three-piece suit. Trying to seem unbewildered by his insane male hotness, she turned her attention to the beefy-looking security guard.

"Are you sure, Mr. Blake? I can show her up."

"I'm very sure, Larry. I was on my way up anyway." Gavin turned to Emily. "Let me help you with that." He gestured to the box.

His voice was as smooth as brandy and made Emily's stomach flutter. She tried to find her words. "It's all right, really. I'm okay holding it."

"I insist." Gavin smiled. "Besides, it's an old Boy Scout thing."

Forget about his piercing blue eyes or the charm bleeding from his pores; his dimpled smile alone had Emily instantly convinced that countless women dropped their panties for him on his command.

Daily.

Reluctantly, she handed him the box and tried to play it cool. "Okay, well, since you put it that way, you've earned your merit badge for the good deed."

"Why, thank you. It's been a while since I've earned one." He laughed. Turning in a leisurely pivot, he led the way to the elevators.

Emily followed and caught a glimpse of herself in the brushed-aluminum doors. She knew she looked like a sweaty mess just coming from work, and all she wanted to do was run away when the doors opened.

"After you," Gavin said with a smile.

As Emily walked in, Gavin's eyes devoured her silky auburn hair, which fell just above her waist. He had never favored a woman in a ponytail—nonetheless one who looked as though she had just been in a food fight—but in that moment, she was the most magnificent creature he'd ever laid eyes on. Between her heart-shaped face, petite Coke-bottle physique, and her perfume wafting around them, Gavin found it hard to catch a decent breath. He stepped in and tried in vain to ignore his heightened awareness of her—but it was no use.

"Looks like Armando's been replaced?" he said, pressing the button for the sixty-second floor.

Emily tried not to fidget as she met his gaze. Being so close to him only made her realize exactly how gorgeous he really was. He was a potent force in such a small, confined space. Her lips parted to accommodate her fast breathing. "Armando?"

"Yeah, Armando." Gavin smirked, looking down at the box of food. "Bella Lucina. My office orders from there almost weekly. Armando's usually the delivery boy."

"Oh, of course, but I'm not the new delivery boy. I mean, I work there. Well, obviously, I do, since I have the uniform on, and obviously, I'm a girl, not a boy." Emily cringed, knowing just how asinine she sounded. Drawing in a deep breath, she started over. "I waitress there. My boss asked me to drop off the food on my way home because the delivery boy quit." She started to blush and wanted to drop dead right there. Literally. Drop. Dead. "Really, I *can* articulate complete sentences."

"Long day at work? I can sympathize." Gavin chuckled, studying her face. She had the greenest eyes he had ever seen and a tiny beauty mark perfectly positioned above her lip.

She smiled. "Yeah, a very long day at work."

A ding sounded on the thirty-ninth floor. The doors opened and in walked a woman. She was as tall as Gavin in her black stiletto heels. She wore a white business suit and her crimson hair was twisted into a bun.

"Well, hello there, Mr. Blake," she rasped, pressing the button for the forty-second floor. An alluring smile ran across her lips as she leaned toward Gavin's ear. "I'm hoping we can pick up where we left off the last time I saw you."

Gavin took an easy step back, his face smoothing into an unreadable impassivity. He simply nodded. The woman smiled and turned to face the elevator doors.

Gavin glanced at Emily again, embarrassed that a one-night stand was unexpectedly in the elevator with them. "So, have you worked at Bella Lucina for a while?"

Emily bit her lip and smiled. "No, today was my first day."

"A new job. That can be stressful." Gavin returned the smile, shifting on his feet. "I hope it went well."

"It did, actually, thanks."

When the elevator doors opened, the woman stepped out and turned to Gavin. "Call me."

He gave a curt nod, and she walked away. The doors closed, leaving him and Emily alone again. "She's not my girlfriend, if that's what you're wondering."

Emily shot him a look, bemused by his remark. "And who's to say I was?"

Her unexpected, sexy feistiness prickled across his skin. He shrugged noncommittally, trying to get a feel for her. "And who's to say you weren't?"

"You don't know me well enough to assume much of anything I'd be thinking," she scoffed, a laugh escaping her lips.

"That you are correct about." He smirked, sidestepping to be closer to her. "But I must admit, I'd like to get to know you."

Great. He wasn't just hot in his urbane, outrageously expensive suit. He was conceited, too. Emily blinked out of her semidaze, trying to ignore how enticing he smelled up close.

"Well, I can't. I'm sorry." She tucked a piece of hair behind her ear.

Before he could respond, the elevator doors opened on the sixty-second floor.

"This is where I get off." Emily turned to grab the box from him. "I appreciate your help carrying it up for me."

"Not a problem. This is also where I get off."

"You work on this floor?" Emily asked, noticeably confused.

Not wanting to tell her he owned the company located on that floor, he decided on a partial truth. A boyish grin slid across his mouth. "Yes. I'm the one guilty of placing the order."

Emily's eyes flicked to his luscious lips. "So you knew when I walked in that I was on my way up here?"

"I had a few minutes to spare. I was waiting downstairs in the lobby for you." He flashed a smile. "Well, I was waiting downstairs in the lobby for *Armando,* but instead I was graced with the beautiful woman before me. I decided to be a gentleman and help you with the box." He stepped out of the elevator, his stride strong and graceful. "Care to join me for dinner? There's more than enough here for you."

"I . . . I can't. I'm sorry," Emily replied, hitting the button for the lobby.

"Wait!" Gavin swiftly leaned in and held the door open. He'd come on too strong and felt like an asshole at that point, but he tried to recover as best as he could. "That was rude of me, and I apologize; my mother raised me better than that." He tossed a nervous hand through his hair. "I'd love to take you out to dinner sometime. I know an office setting like this isn't romantic by any means. I just work a lot. But like I said, I'd love to take you out one night."

Before Emily could reply, a svelte dark-haired woman spoke up from behind a desk. "Mr. Blake, you have a call on line two."

Smiling, he turned to face the woman. "Please take a message for me, Natalie."

With trembling fingers, Emily quickly hit the button to close the door. It shut completely before Gavin could turn around. Leaning against the wall, she grabbed the brass railing, trying to compose herself. The effect the stranger had on her was unnerving. She shook her head, regretting that she'd agreed to drop off the food. Nonetheless, she made her way out of the building and went home.

"He was that good looking?" Olivia asked, sitting at the kitchen table.

Emily placed a finger over her mouth. "Jesus, Olivia, Dillon's in my room. Keep your voice down." Her eyes darted to her door and then back to Olivia. "Yes, he was *that* good-looking. Take-your-breath-away good looking. Want-to-strip-your-body-naked-and-let-him-devour-you-alive good-looking. Certified-eye-candy good looking."

Olivia laughed and then quickly covered her mouth. "Sounds very fuckable," she whispered. Emily nodded and giggled. "I think you need to take the delivery boy's position instead."

"I don't know. It was just the strangest reaction I've ever had with someone. And talk about embarrassed at the way I handled myself. A preschooler would've done better."

Smirking, Olivia took a sip from her glass of wine, her brown eyes sparkling. "It may make for some great sex tonight with Douche if you keep Mr. Tall, Dark, and Fuckable Handsome in mind."

Emily lightly slapped her arm. "Stop. No more Mr. Tall, Dark, and Fuckable Handsome thoughts for me." Emily took her hair out of her ponytail. "Besides, I love Dillon. Mr. Tall, Dark, and Fuckable Handsome will be a gift for some other woman, believe me."

"Okay, okay." Olivia laughed quietly. "But at least you know you have a backup."

Before Emily could discuss her newfound fuckable eye candy any further, Dillon strolled out of the bedroom dressed in his finest suit and tie. Emily instantly forgot about the sexy stranger when her eyes feasted upon his dampened dirty blond hair and handsome face. To her, he was all the fuckable eye candy she needed.

"I thought we were hanging here tonight?" Emily asked, walking over and circling her arms around his waist. "I rented a movie."

He placed his arms on her shoulders. It was easy enough for him since he was much taller than Emily's tiny frame. "I'm having dinner with a potential client." He sauntered over to the refrigerator and took out a bottle of water. "It was an unexpected call. We'll watch it another night."

Emily frowned at his nonchalance. "How many unexpected dinners can you have in one week, Dillon?"

After letting out an audible sigh, Olivia pushed to her feet and made her way out of the room.

Dillon sighed. "You know it goes with the territory, Emily. I'm a stockbroker. I need to wine and dine a client a little in order to gain the account."

"I get that, Dillon. I really do." Emily walked into the kitchen and pressed her body against his. "But I've been here less than a month, and I'm constantly being left alone when you have these meetings." She playfully pulled at his tie. "I saw you more when I was living in Colorado than I do now."

He backed away, his brown eyes narrowing. "You sound

like a whiny sorority girl." He twisted the cap off the bottle of water and took a sip. "Just relax. I shouldn't be back too late."

A frown marred the space between her brows. "A whiny sorority girl? What's that supposed to mean? Why did you even come here to shower, then?"

"I got the call *after* I got here, that's why."

"Maybe you need to go sleep at your place tonight." She undid her apron and threw it on the table. "You're out wining and dining these *so-called* clients at least five nights a week."

His voice rose as he eyed her. "What are you trying to say, Emily? Do you think I'm lying to you?"

"I have no idea. I just thought you'd be here a little more than you have been," she answered, tossing her hand through her hair. "Maybe help me adjust a bit?"

After taking a sip of his water, he cocked his head to the side. "I moved you out here on my dime. What more do you want from me?"

"That was low, Dillon," she breathed, her green eyes narrowed. "I didn't ask you to do that. I could've stayed in Colorado, and we could've continued a long-distance relationship."

Dillon stepped closer, lifted his hand, and gently brushed her cheek. "No, you couldn't. You love me, and you needed to be here with me after everything that happened." He slid his thumb against her chin. "And I love and need you here, too. Now stop the bullshit, let me go take care of this client, and I'll be back later, okay?"

Assessing and reevaluating the situation on the fly, Emily pushed up on her tiptoes and pressed her lips against his. He eagerly accepted her advance and he groaned into their kiss. Fisting his hands in her hair, he drew her closer, pulling her into his chest.

Emily spoke against his mouth. "All right. Go do your thing, and I'll see you later."

"So I'm not being forced back to my apartment tonight?" He smiled against her lips. "If you really insist, I guess I can sleep at my place."

"Stop being a wiseass, Dillon. I'll be waiting for you when you get back."

"I promise you'll have my undivided attention then."

Dillon laced his fingers in hers, and she followed him to the door. After giving him one last kiss, Emily watched him walk out.

When the door snapped shut, Olivia reemerged from her room. Sinking onto the couch, she patted it. "Okay, spill it. What's the deal, woman?"

"He just seems distant, you know?" Emily replied, sitting next to her.

"Look, you know I can't stand Dillon." Olivia paused for a second and tapped her chin. "Actually, I hate him." Emily rolled her eyes, and Olivia laughed. "But in his defense, and *only* because my brother works in the same office, they really do have to take care of potential accounts."

"Yeah, but is Trevor out five nights a week taking care of these people?"

"No, but I guess Dillweed's more of an aggressive broker. Considering he's an asshole, I wouldn't be surprised."

"Okay, friend, enough cutting him down," she said, shaking her head. Olivia laughed, and Emily contemplated her words. "Maybe I'm overreacting. I don't know. I guess between trying to adjust to my mom's death and the move, my brain's short-circuiting."

Olivia placed her hand on Emily's shoulder, her eyes softening with sympathy. "It's a shitload to take in all at once. I couldn't imagine going through it." Olivia pulled her close and gave her a tight hug. "You're a strong woman, and you'll get through this. I know you will."

"Thank you, Olivia, really. I don't know what I would've done without you. I was blessed having you as a roommate in college, and now living here with you, I'm forever indebted, honestly."

Olivia laughed. "Now you're getting overdramatic, girl." She stood and grabbed the movie Emily rented. After popping it into the DVD player, she settled back onto the couch. "Tonight's a certified ladies' night."

2

Cream or Sugar

EMILY WOKE THE next morning, her slumberous gaze mesmerized by Dillon's sleeping body. She rested her head against his warm chest and her mind drifted over their relationship. As with anyone, he was full of quirks. She knew she would get used to them, but in the meantime, his fast-paced lifestyle was a big challenge for her. At first, their differences hadn't seemed so big because their relationship grew and blossomed in *her* world. Now that she was coexisting in *his,* there was a lot she needed to accept.

Being a trophy girlfriend wasn't on her top-ten list of goals. However, since she'd moved to New York, Dillon seemed to push her into that role. When she'd gone out with him, he paraded her around to the few friends of his she'd met. She'd also noticed a possessive shift in his demeanor. Sometimes it was cute—in a boyfriend kind of way—but most of the time, it was overbearing and confusing. Nonetheless, in that moment, as her senses soaked him in and all of the good he had done for her, Emily accepted their relationship for what it was. She curled closer to him, moving a wayward strand of hair away from his forehead.

Letting out a yawn, he smiled at her. "You're up early." His voice was husky from just waking. "I must not have done a good job sexing you into a coma last night."

Playfully nuzzling her nose in the crook of his arm, she smiled. "If you had sexed me into a coma, you would never be able to be with me again, sir."

"Ah, you are incorrect, my love. I'd still take it from you—coma or not."

"That's just sick," she giggled, sitting up.

A predatory glimmer sparkled in his brown eyes. "Ready for round two?"

"Aren't you taking me to breakfast this morning like you promised?"

"Of course I am."

"Well, I have to be at work by ten o'clock, and I still need to shower."

"You know I'm good for a quickie if need be," he said, rising to his feet and pulling her up.

Unable to say no, she followed without a fight as he undressed them both before they reached the bathroom. She propped herself on the vanity and watched him turn on the water. She felt the edgy energy radiating from his body as he strolled over to her, wearing a boyish grin that got her every time. He pulled her to him and kissed her so softly she felt her lips shiver against his. She couldn't free herself from the hypnotic spell of his kiss if she wanted to. With his hands smoothing everywhere, branding his hot touch against her skin, fervor fueled in her blood, making her body strain for more. He shifted his mouth to the valley between her breasts and slid his tongue across her nipple. It drove her wild.

Staring up at her, he sucked and swirled his tongue around its taut peak. "You like that, don't you?"

"Yes," she breathed as her hands gripped his hair.

With a slow, maddening pace, he tunneled his fingers inside her wet pussy. The pressure was excruciatingly wonderful and correlated with the sudden tightening sensation between her legs. He pushed harder against her mouth while she dug her nails into his back. Dillon groaned when she ran her hands across his chest, her fingers slowly sliding down every muscled ridge on his abdomen. She wrapped her legs around his waist, and he carried her into the shower. He backed her against the wall, and she let out a gasp of pleasure when he sank perfectly deep inside her. Her every nerve ending lit on fire as their bodies melded together as one.

"Ah Christ, you feel so good, Em," he hissed, his voice thick with desire.

Emily clung to his shoulders as hot water trickled down their bodies. Her ache for him increased with every pulse and thrust. With their lips locked, Emily clenched her legs tighter around his waist and arched her body against his, taking everything he had to give. Dillon's eyes dilated when he felt her hot, slick flesh contract around him. Emily moaned out in satisfied completion when she felt Dillon jerk, shudder, and tremble against her. Burying his face in her neck, he let out a guttural groan as he climaxed. When he pulled back, their gazes met and locked, holding steady as their breathing slowed.

"I love you, Emily," he said as he gently placed her down and pulled her into him. "I'm happy you're here with me."

"I love you, too. I'm sorry for the way I acted last night before you left." She feathered kisses across his chest, her hands framing his face. "I'll try to be more understanding about your wacky schedules from now on."

He gave her a soft grin. "I know you will."

They spent the next half hour washing each other. Dillon playfully ran soap over her body, and Emily returned the gesture when she cleaned his back. She realized what he'd said the night before was correct. She needed to be in New York with Dillon. She loved him. There wasn't a fiber in her soul that thought she could live so far away from him again.

Considering they didn't have time to go out to eat breakfast, Emily wound up cooking for them. After cleaning up, Dillon left for work. Emily got ready for her shift and called her sister, Lisa, who lived in California. Emily missed her tremendously. Older than Emily by ten years, Lisa was like a second mother. She'd married her high school sweetheart, Michael, six years ago. Because of their absentee father, Emily looked to Michael for the help that she would've sought from her own father had he been there. Lisa and Michael meant the world to Emily. Seeing them before her mom died had been difficult, but literally being on opposite sides of the continent meant their visits would be less frequent. However, they made a tentative date to try to see each other in a few months.

Once finished with the call, Emily jumped in a taxi and headed to work. As she settled in for the ride, she found herself remembering how much her mom had wanted to visit New York. She had gone as far as booking tickets to a show on Broadway, but she fell ill shortly after. The rapid-fire progress of her illness prevented her from going. The thought was bittersweet. Here she was in the city her mother longed to visit, but they weren't there together. As she made her way into the restaurant, Emily tried to push the sorrow invading her thoughts to the side.

"Hey! You no gonna say hi to me?" Roberto, the Spanish cook, asked. "Me like you, Emmy. Me like you a lot."

"Hi, Roberto." She laughed. "I like you, too."

He blushed as Emily punched her card through the time clock. Fallon told her that since she'd pulled her weight during the rush the day before, they felt she was strong enough to have her own station. Her first customers were a few New York City police officers. Antonio watched her closely as she approached them.

"Hello, my name's Emily. I'll be taking care of you today." Smiling, she pulled her pen and pad out of her apron. "Would you gentlemen like to place your drink orders, or do you know what you want?"

The oldest officer, a man with salt-and-pepper hair, smiled back. "You're not our regular waitress."

"No, sir, I'm not. I just started working here yesterday, so you gentlemen need to take it easy on me, okay?" Emily gestured over her shoulder to Antonio. "My boss is watching."

With warm faces, they chuckled, clearly amused at her remark.

The youngest cop chimed in, "Who? Antonio? Nah, he's harmless."

The middle-aged cop smirked. "Don't worry. We'll try to be nice, but sometimes we can be a pain in the ass."

"Well, don't be too hard on me, boys." Emily smiled, happy they all had a sense of humor. "What can I get you gentlemen to drink?"

Emily took their orders and sent them back to the kitchen. She had a few more tables come in before the lunch rush really picked up. The place went from being pretty calm to a madhouse layered with every type of customer she could've imagined.

As Emily walked out with one table's orders, Antonio called

out to her and motioned to one of her booths in the corner. "Hey, Country, you just got sat again. Are you okay to take another?"

She adjusted the tray on her shoulder. "Yeah, I'm cool. I'll be right there."

He nodded and whisked off to the front door to greet more customers.

She reached for a tray stand, set the food down, and handed out the plates to a party of five. "Does anyone need anything else?"

An attractive brunette in a summer dress held up an empty glass of soda. "I need a refill, please."

Emily gave a hurried smile and grabbed the glass. "I'll be right back." She headed over to the soda fountain, glancing at the table where she could barely see the lone gentleman she had yet to greet. "Shit," she mumbled to herself.

Quickly returning to the party of five, Emily handed the woman her drink. "Sorry about that. Does anyone need anything else?" she asked, inwardly praying no one did. They all shook their heads no.

Emily let out a soft sigh of relief and let them know she'd be back to check on them. Walking away, she pulled her order pad from her apron and rounded the corner. Sliding her hand across her sweaty forehead, she approached the table and accidentally dropped her pen in front of the booth. She knelt down to pick it up, but before she could, the stranger's hand reached for it.

"Thank you," Emily said, still crouched on the floor. "I appreciate that. Can I . . ." Her voice trailed off when she made eye contact with the customer.

It was Mr. Tall, Dark, and Fuckable Handsome from the elevator. Her breath caught at the sight of him casually sitting there. She literally had to hold on to the table for balance as she slowly stood up. He was even better looking than she remembered. Not that less than twenty-four hours could erase his image from her memory, but now he was just *so there, so male,* and *so enthralling.* He sparked that all-too-familiar tingle across her skin. He had his suit jacket off, hung neatly on a hook next to the booth. He wore a crisp, white button-down shirt, and the stark absence of color only emphasized his clear blue eyes.

Gavin's lips curled into a smile. "You don't look too happy to see me."

"I'm just a little . . . I . . ." Emily struggled to find her words.

Gavin wasn't about to admit that his need to see her again was intense—so fucking intense he had actually canceled a meeting with a large account in hopes of catching her at work. Nor would he tell her that when the elevator doors closed last night, he was left feeling oddly robbed by her departure.

"You ran off so quickly last night that I didn't get a chance to give you a tip for delivering the food."

"Ooohhh," Emily elongated the word, trying to think of something to say since he seemed to wipe her clear of any thoughts. "Right . . . About the way I left . . . I'm sorry about that. Can I get you something to drink?" She bit down on the pen cap.

Gavin flicked his gaze to her beautiful lips and smiled at her nervous reaction. "Yes, I'll take a coffee, please."

"Do you take cream or sugar in that?"

He cocked his head to the side. "Do you?"

"Do I what?"

"Take cream or sugar in your coffee?"

Thrown by his question, she shifted on her feet. "Why do you want to know?"

Gavin paused, a grin softening his mouth. "Well, I'm trying to find out as much as I can about you. I figured coffee was an easy enough topic to conquer. I may be wrong, though."

A light laugh escaped Emily's lips. "Seems a little stalkerish. Wouldn't you agree?"

"Mmm . . . a stalker. That's a new one and pretty brutal." He laughed, and his amusement lit up his eyes. "I'd like to call it *curiosity*."

She shook her head and smiled. "Okay, so you haven't answered my question. Would you like cream or sugar?"

"You haven't answered *my* question." He arched one perfect brow. "Do you take cream or sugar with your coffee?"

Certain she would lose the battle, she gave in. "Yes."

"Ah, opposites do attract. Perfect." He leaned back in his seat and crossed his arms. "I'll take mine black, please."

Emily blinked, taking in his sensual face for a few more seconds. She turned away and strode back to the party of five, asking if they needed anything else, and dropped their check when they declined. She made her way to the coffee bar, feeling breathless by this stranger. As Emily prepared his java, Fallon promptly made her way over.

With her hair dyed jet-black today, her mouth dropped open as she snuck a glance in Gavin's direction. "Country, do you know that guy?"

Emily drew in a deep breath and looked at Gavin. His attention was on a newspaper in his hand. "No . . . well . . . kind of, I guess." She placed his coffee on a tray.

Fallon yanked Emily's pad from her apron, scribbled her name and number on it, and handed it back. "Puh-lease give this to him. My eyes have never feasted on such extreme fucking hotness in my life."

"That would be an understatement." Emily started to walk away and then turned back. "Wait, what about your father-aged boyfriend?"

Fallon placed her hands on her hips and smirked. "I make

myself available to any age, race, or gender if given the right opportunity."

Shaking her head, Emily laughed and made her way back to his table. Trying to control her pounding heart, she tried to guess his age. He didn't look a day over twenty-five. With a shaky hand, she set the coffee down in front of Gavin. He gave her a wide-eyed smile and placed the newspaper beside him.

"Have you decided what you want to eat?" she asked, glancing down at his onyx cuff links and expensive-looking watch.

"Actually, I haven't even looked at the menu yet," he replied, picking it up to scan it.

"Okay, I'll be right back, then."

"Wait," he said with a grin. "Can you recommend anything in particular?"

"The only thing I've eaten here is the Asiago cheese and portabella mushroom panini sandwich."

"Good suggestion. I'll take that, then."

She went to write down his order but stopped. "It has spinach on it, too. Is that all right?"

Slowly dragging his bottom lip between his teeth, Gavin smiled. "Does it include your name and number as well?"

Damn him and those lips, Emily thought.

Trying to act as if she was unriveted by his question, she pulled out Fallon's number and handed it to him. "No, not mine, but she wanted me to give you hers." Emily crooked her head in Fallon's direction. She stood at the host station watching them. "Hope she's your type."

Gavin didn't take his eyes off Emily, not even for a second. "I'm not interested in her," he answered evenly, sliding the piece of paper to the edge of the table.

"How do you know you're not interested? You haven't turned around to look at her."

Resting his elbow on the table, a smile softened his perfectly sinful mouth. "I know I'm not interested in her because the only woman in Manhattan whose name and number I want is standing right here."

Emily shifted, her breath catching in the back of her throat. "Well, I'm sorry. I have a boyfriend."

"I assumed you did," he replied, casually crossing his legs. "It would seem almost impossible for you not to have one."

"You assumed I did, yet you're still asking me for my number?"

With the stroke of his gaze shifting to her left hand, he smiled. "Yes, but I don't see a ring on your finger, and while there's *not* a ring on your finger, there still may be hope for me."

"So you're basically saying you're a cheater?" she stated, eyeing him incredulously.

"I've said no such thing." He laughed.

Smiling, she tilted her head to the side. "Well, you're assuming I would cheat on my boyfriend to go out on a date with you, so that right there makes you a cheater."

"I'm hoping you'll *break up* with your boyfriend and go out on a date with me," he quickly countered with a wry curving of his lips. "That right there makes me an honest man."

She wrote down his order. "Honest, no. Conceited, yes."

"I prefer to use the term *hopeful*," he replied, studying the way she nervously bit her lip. "Can I at least get the name of the beautiful waitress taking care of me?"

Heated by his words but not wanting to reveal her real name, Emily simply replied, "Molly. My name's Molly."

Gavin opened his mouth to speak when Antonio called out from across the restaurant.

"Country, you have a phone call."

Emily unwillingly tore her attention from Gavin. She sauntered over to the host station on her way to get the phone.

"Well, what did he say?" Fallon asked.

Emily frowned. "He has a girlfriend."

"Fuck, and I waited, too." Fallon picked up her purse and headed out the door. "Guess the old man will have to do for now. I'll see you tomorrow."

With a wave good-bye, Emily reached for the phone and found it was Dillon calling to make plans for the evening. After they hung up, she was glad he had called and brought her thoughts back to where she knew they should be. Drawing in a deep breath, she strolled over to the computer and entered Gavin's order. She greeted a family of three and completed her side work.

Eventually, she risked a glance over to Gavin when she took a seat at the coffee bar to wait for his order. She felt inordinately overwhelmed when their eyes met and locked. She was confused. She didn't know why she was shaken by his gaze, and she hated the fact that she actually *liked* the way he stared at her. Emily snapped from her coma-like daze when she heard one of the cooks call her. She went into the kitchen, picked up Gavin's food, and grabbed a coffeepot.

"One Asiago cheese and portabella mushroom panini sandwich with spinach," she said, placing it down in front of him. "And here's a little more coffee for you."

"Thank you." Gavin's eyes flicked to her neck as she leaned over to pour the coffee. The sweet scent of her body teased his nose. Picturing his lips sliding against her beautiful skin, he brought his attention back to her face and smiled. He cleared his throat, trying to rid himself of the vision.

Emily's heart thumped erratically as he stared at her. "Can I get you anything else?"

"Actually, yes. I'm sorry," he said, trying to pull himself from the odd spell she'd cast on him. "I received a call notifying me that I need to get back to the office. Can I get this to go?"

"Oh . . . I'm sorry it took so long," she said, picking up the plate. "I'll just put it in a box for you."

"Don't worry about it. I should've said something earlier." He rose to his feet and shrugged into his suit jacket.

Emily turned away, striding toward the kitchen door.

After throwing a twenty on the table, Gavin took out a business card and two one-hundred-dollar bills. He wrapped them around the card and covered them up with a five-dollar bill.

Emily returned with the box and handed it to him. "Again, I'm sorry it took so long." She stared into his eyes. Her senses automatically became heated again.

Gavin leaned in, inches from her face. He reached for her hand and placed the money-wrapped card in her palm, his breath soft against her ear. "And I told you not to worry about it."

Emily froze as her breathing became as ragged as her heartbeat. His warm breath so close to her body almost sent her over the edge. He radiated an intense sexual energy she couldn't deny—and she was pretty damn sure no other warm-blooded female could either. Unable to form a sentence, she didn't answer as she looked up into his eyes.

His mouth curved into an alluring smile. "Call me if you change your mind, Molly." With that, he turned and walked out the door. The eyes of every woman in the restaurant followed him.

Emily let out a breath she didn't know she was holding. She thumbed through the cash, shocked not only by how much he'd tipped her, but that he'd left his card, too. Blank side up. She fought with herself to not turn it over. She sighed, furious at herself, as she tried to brush thoughts of him out of her head. It was no use. He invaded every corner of her mind.

She couldn't deny she found him beyond attractive; she'd

been startled into staring the first time she saw him. There was something mysterious about his eyes, which were a shade of blue so light they almost begged her to submit to him, obey him, and do some of the naughtiest things with him that her mind could conjure up. Maybe it was the curve of his cheekbones, which fell slightly short of being too high. Possibly it was the smooth, raspy tone of his voice, which basically disarmed her every cognitive thought the first time he spoke.

Of course he has a bedroom voice to go with those bedroom eyes.

He was definitely a fuckable, bedroom-voice-and-eyes-bearing specimen. Fuckable or not, Emily knew she'd have to resist as long as her sanity ruled over her subconscious. It took everything in her to walk to the kitchen without looking at his name and contact number. Against every sexual demon in her head screaming to go for it, she threw the card into the garbage, her fingers tingling from its absence.

Deep Breaths

OVER THE NEXT few days, Emily reluctantly unpacked the rest of her belongings. A holdup at the shipping company had made them arrive late. Tonight, if it killed her, she would clear out the last of the items. Olivia helped her sift through years of memories. Those memories were all Emily had left, and she clung to them as if they were her last heartbeats. The final item in the last box took her breath away, tightening her chest and spinning her emotions out of control. Sighing, Emily slumped on her bed and clung to a photo showcasing her mother's proud smile at her high school graduation. The barrier Emily had fought so hard to build over the last few months broke, and the tears tumbled down. The reality of what had happened—the unwavering fact she would never see her mother again—hit her hard.

Sadness clouded Olivia's eyes as she watched her friend crumble. "I don't know what to say, Emily. I wish I could take your pain away."

Emily reached out and took Olivia's hand, thankful she was there. The two friends shared a few minutes, neither saying a word, knowing nothing more could be said. Standing, Emily gave Olivia a slight smile and hastily wiped the tears from both their cheeks. She gave her a hug and sauntered to the bathroom. She was exhausted, mentally and physically. The last few days of working three doubles in a row had caught up with her, and she looked forward to a relaxing evening on the couch with Dillon. Making her way into the shower, she purged her mind of anything to do with her mom. It was difficult, but nonetheless, she did it. Once out, she slid into a pair of comfortable pajamas and set herself up on the couch with a much-needed glass of wine.

After a while, Olivia walked into the living room wearing a red summer dress with her hair pinned up and a clutch in her hand. She eyed Emily hopefully. "Come out with Tina and me tonight. It'll do justice to your mood."

Giving Olivia a smile, Emily thought about her friend's new lover, Tina Reed, a twenty-four-year-old Columbia University graduate. After being burned by too many men, Olivia had sworn them off, deciding women might suit her better.

Sighing, Emily tossed her hand through her hair. "I really just want to relax the night away." She picked up the bottle of red wine and smiled. "I plan on polishing this off, too."

Olivia placed a kiss on top of her head. "Okay, but if for some reason you change your mind, just call my cell."

Emily nodded, and Olivia walked out the door.

Glancing at the clock, Emily noted it was a quarter past ten. Dillon should've been there already. She wondered if another late-night meeting had held him up. Her thoughts didn't stray too far when her phone rang a half hour later. Dillon was calling to announce that he was out at a club in SoHo, celebrating a new account. He insisted she meet him. Emily tried to argue that she was exhausted and had already settled in for the night, but he wouldn't relent. His dissatisfaction traveled through the phone. Sighing, Emily succumbed to his demand, dragged herself into her room, and prepared for an evening out despite her emotional and physical state.

It can't be her, Gavin thought. He rubbed his palm over his face, staring across the dimly lit club in her direction. It was, though. Molly—the waitress who'd never called him. Molly—the waitress who tugged at his every sense, fiber, and male instinct. Molly—the waitress who looked more ravishing than he could've ever imagined. Gavin watched her move across the club through the endless bodies pressed against one another.

His eyes feasted upon her long auburn hair spilling over her shoulders onto a tight black dress that fell just above her knees. The perfect amount of cleavage and neck burned a hole into his mind, awakening his undeniable, primal urge to claim her. His eyes devoured her legs—sleek, long, and shapely—which came to a rest in black heels. Raking his hands through his hair, Gavin couldn't help but feel a quickening in his heart as she approached. He went to move toward her, talk to her, breathe in her scent, but a modest cough from Dillon broke his gaze from hers.

"I see you looking, Blake, but she's mine," Dillon remarked, a crooked smile twisting his lips.

Gavin's mouth fell open as if to speak, but nothing came out. His blue eyes swung over to the beautiful woman who had invaded his world a few days ago and then shifted back to Dillon.

"Wait, that's . . . *Emily*?" Gavin asked, confusion peppering his expression.

"Yeah, man. I told you she was fucking gorgeous." Dillon motioned for Emily to hurry up. She was frozen and rooted in one spot a few feet away and Gavin knew why.

Gavin took a long pull from his beer, a lump forming in his throat as he leaned against the bar. Unable to look away, he maintained eye contact with the woman his friend had just proclaimed was his.

Chewing on her lip, Emily tried to keep her panic at bay when she saw Mr. Tall, Dark, and Fuckable Handsome with Dillon. The air seemed to thicken. Her balance was knocked askew with every step.

There's no way they could possibly know each other. This is Manhattan, for Christ's sake, Emily thought.

Her heart seemed to pound harder the closer she got. A curious yet boyish smile rounded Gavin's lips and a kiss of a dimple indented his cheek. His piercing blue eyes were intense and unblinking. Emily's gaze flicked down to his chest. The planes of his pectorals were visible under his shirt. If it was possible, he looked even more handsome while relaxed in his casual attire of a black V-neck T-shirt and jeans that hung perfectly on his waist. His eyes seemed to delve into her and smother every bit of oxygen from her lungs. Taking a long, cleansing breath, Emily approached the two men, trying to focus solely on Dillon.

Dillon pulled her by the waist into his body and placed an exaggerated kiss on her lips. After ordering her a drink, Dillon shifted her in front of him, positioning her back against his chest. She had a close-up view of the stranger when Dillon finally spoke. "Gavin, this is my girlfriend, Emily Cooper. Emily, Gavin Blake."

Unable to pull his eyes from hers, Gavin reached down tentatively and drew her hand to his lips. Kissing it softly, he hesitated, almost absorbing the heat radiating from her skin. Reluctantly, he finally let go. "The pleasure's most definitely all mine, *Emily*."

Inwardly marveling at the way Gavin's slight stubble felt against her knuckles, Emily gave a curt nod and smiled. "It's nice to finally meet you."

"She's beautiful, isn't she?" Dillon asked Gavin.

Averting her gaze to the floor, Emily flushed, embarrassed by the comment. Nonetheless, she grinned, trying to regain her bearings from the shock coursing through her body.

Gavin's gaze dropped to her mouth, her ruby-red lips fascinating every inch of him. He shifted his eyes back to hers, which were a variation of green melting into gold. *Beautiful*, he thought. Drawing his lower lip roughly through his teeth, Gavin let his words hang. "You're a very lucky man, Dillon."

Dillon nodded, tossing back the last of his whiskey on the rocks. "Come dance with me, babe." He caught Emily by her hips and dragged her out to the dance floor. Knowing she shouldn't, Emily risked a glance back at Gavin as they walked away.

Gavin tried to maintain his cool when she peered over her shoulder to look back at him. He watched the way Dillon held her close and the irrefutably loving way she responded. He watched the way she stared into Dillon's eyes, giving him her undivided attention. Ordering another beer, Gavin fought back the urge to walk onto the dance floor, knock his friend out, and pull her into his arms.

As if his mind couldn't register anyone else, Gavin brushed off countless women who approached him. He knew he was in uncharted territory and his thoughts were irrational, considering Dillon was a close friend, but he felt as if Emily had a sick pull on him. These new emotions had him at odds with his body and mind.

And Gavin didn't like it one bit.

Eventually, Dillon walked up to Gavin when Emily disappeared into the restroom. He leaned against the bar, an irreverent smile breaking out across his face. "Wishing you were me, buddy?"

Gavin couldn't help feeling a stab of jealousy, but this wasn't something he was about to confess. "I'm just wondering how you pulled that one off."

It wasn't a question but a statement on Gavin's part. Dillon usually hung with crowds of women that were far wilder than Emily seemed to be.

Dillon threw his head back and laughed as he ordered a shot of tequila. "You seem to think you're the only god in this city."

"I'm no god, Dillon, and you're certainly not either," Gavin remarked, propping his arm on the rolled leather edge of the bar. "But I do know you need to take care of a woman like that."

Dillon started flexing his hips back and forth. "Oh, I'm taking care of it. She has no complaints whatsoever in that department."

"I didn't mean it like that," Gavin snapped, trying to rid the thought from his mind. He smoothed his voice out to a calmer tone. "Be good to her, seriously."

Cocking his head to the side, Dillon furrowed his brows. "Since when did you become so worried about how I treat a woman, Mr. Noncommitment? You fuck anything that throws itself at you, and they're lucky if they get a call the next day."

"We're not talking about me. Like I said, take care of her."

"Gavin Blake's trying to teach me how to treat a woman. This is hysterical." Dillon swallowed his drink and slammed the glass down. "I'm marrying this one. You'll see. Just to torture you, you're going to be in the wedding party." Dillon shook his head and laughed but recovered quickly as his expression tightened. "Like I said earlier, she's mine. You get enough everywhere you go."

Before Gavin could respond, Emily approached. Dillon handed her a beer, and she smiled. "Thanks. So, what are you guys talking about?"

Gavin figured he would play a little game since Dillon was taunting him. His eyes concentrated on the curve of Emily's jaw before locking on to hers. "I'm just wondering how my friend here landed such a beautiful woman. He's obviously out of his league."

Emily felt the way Gavin stared. His eyes seemed to sink into her, making her want to bare every emotion and every secret. *What a dangerous talent for a man's eyes to possess,* she thought.

She started to speak, but Dillon's voice broke through the deafening music. "Fuck you and your comment. Out of my league?"

Gavin casually sank into a seat at the bar. "Yes, *very* out of your league."

A grin curled Dillon's lips. "Whatever makes you sleep better tonight, man, but she's leaving with me." Dillon glanced at an incoming text and turned to where Emily stood, mortified at the conversation taking place. "Trevor's on his way, babe. I need to use the restroom, but don't let this clown fool you while I'm gone. He's a player." He dropped a chaste kiss on her cheek and walked away.

Gavin watched Emily carefully, silence stretching between them as she sipped her beer. He felt her eyes on him, nervous little looks that tugged at every rational instinct he had left. Each time her gaze met his, he wanted to own it and live in it forever. He wondered if she'd felt the connection between them when he'd kissed her hand. He took a long pull from his beer, trying to ease the dryness in his mouth. "So, *Molly,* are you enjoying New York?"

Knowing that one was coming, Emily laughed. "Yes, I am, actually, stalker boy. Thanks for asking."

"I'm really not a stalker or a player, honestly," he said, chuckling at the nickname.

"The stalker part may be questionable, but I have to be honest, I've heard otherwise about you being a player." Emily bit her lip, realizing how horribly offensive those last words must've sounded. Even so, it was the truth. Olivia had told her stories of Dillon's rich friend Gavin, who was a ladies' man. She also warned Emily that once she met him, it would take everything in her not to rip off his shirt and watch the buttons scatter on the floor, along with her every sexual inhibition.

Yep, completely fuckable.

Shifting in his seat, Gavin flashed a smile. "And who did you hear that from?"

"Olivia Martin."

"Mmm, you must not know her that well, then," he replied, motioning for the bartender to bring them another round.

"Let's see. She was my roommate in college, and I live with her now. I consider her a pretty reliable source, but hey, to each his own."

"Forgive me and my horrible memory. That's right; that's right. You're Emily and not Molly." He smirked, tossing a hand through his hair. "Of course you know Olivia."

She smiled. "Yes, my real name is Emily. We've established that, but how come I have a feeling you'll never let me live that down?"

A delicious grin slid across his lips. "Ah-ha, I may or may not. But that's for me to know, and you to find out." They both laughed, relaxing a bit. "So, what else did Olivia say about me?"

"Ah-ha, that's for *me* to know, and you to find out."

Amused by her quick-witted response, Gavin hung his head and laughed. His features softened as he stared into her eyes. "But in my defense, the whole player thing's a misconception. I just haven't found the right woman yet."

"Well, there seem to be an awful lot of ladies trying to get your attention right now." With a sweep of her hand, Emily gestured toward a group of women at the end of the bar noticeably glancing in his direction. "Pretty decent pick, if you ask me."

Although he tried, he couldn't pull his eyes away from her. He stared at Emily, wanting to let her know—again—the only woman he wanted was already taken. "Unfortunately, most of them are only interested in one thing."

Confusion knitted her brows. "Isn't that what all guys want anyway?"

"Not quite, but I like the way you think." He studied the way she nervously tucked her hair behind her ear. He liked it more than he should. "No, seriously, though, I don't want to come off like a conceited ass, but there's a fine line between me and my money."

His remark struck an odd cord with Emily. She knew he had money—the whole damn city did. However, to assume women were after him strictly for his cash was indicative of some sort of insecurity.

"Oh, so in your eyes, every woman's a gold digger?" she remarked, drawing the bottle to her mouth as she leaned casually into her seat.

Gavin tried hard to focus on her eyes instead of her lips. "No, it's not that at all. That came out the wrong way; I apologize." He placed his empty drink on the bar. "It's just hard to tell who's real and who's not. I want a woman who wants me with or without my money." He flashed a sheepish grin. "And, for some reason, I seem to attract the all-beauty-and-no-brains type, too."

"Oh." Emily shifted in her seat, embarrassed by her assumption. She tried to deflect her earlier statement. "Sounds like you're trolling the wrong places, buddy."

The bartender put their refills down. Gavin laughed, immensely enjoying her honesty. "Apparently I do." An infectious smile ran across his mouth. "Where is it you said you hang out these days, other than Bella Lucina?"

"Dillon's apartment, but thanks for trying again," she quipped. She tilted her beer to her lips, allowing herself to hold his gaze a little longer. "Maybe you should search for women at the library? That would take care of the no-brains problem you seem to attract."

"You're a pretty funny girl, Emily," he remarked, shifting his body to face hers. "I'm *really* starting to regret Dillon getting his hands on you first."

Emily's heart skidded across her chest at his declaration. Before she could answer, she felt a warm hand on her shoulder and assumed it was Dillon.

She turned and found Trevor flashing his winning smile, his thick blond hair falling onto his forehead. "I'm here. Let the party begin!" he hooted, slapping his hand on Gavin's shoulder. He gave Emily a hug and inched his way between them to order a drink. "It's going to be a bender tonight!"

Emily smiled, happy to see Trevor. She'd grown close to him over the last few months. Besides the fact that he was Olivia's brother, he was an all-around good guy. Even before she'd moved to New York, he called to check up on her to make sure she was doing okay.

Trevor glanced around the club from behind his glasses.

"Where's Dillon?" he asked, accepting his drink from the bartender.

"Think he fell in." Gavin smirked, motioning toward the restrooms.

"That sounds like something he would do, especially if he's drunk enough," Trevor joked. "So, how've you been, man? Feels like I haven't seen you in forever."

"Good. Had to do some traveling. You know how it is. I should be in the city for most of the summer, though."

"Having your annual Fourth of July party at your house in the Hamptons, right?"

"Absolutely," Gavin answered. "I'm actually heading out there this week to open up the place."

Trevor turned to Emily, who wasn't paying attention to the conversation. His laughing brown eyes were wide with excitement. "Yoo-hoo, Emily. You're going, right?"

She looked puzzled as she scanned the club, knowing Dillon had been gone for a while. "Going where?" Her voice trailed off as she looked away from Trevor.

"Gavin's party in the Hamptons on the Fourth of July. Dillon told you about it, right?"

She shrugged, bringing her attention back to Trevor. "He hasn't mentioned it yet, but it sounds like fun. I'm sure we'll be there."

Dillon's voice broke through the conversation. "Be where?" He leaned in to kiss Emily's neck. "I hope these guys weren't trying to proposition you while I was gone."

Twisting her body to face his, Emily smiled. "No worries; they were entertaining me. You took a while. Are you okay?"

"I had to make a quick phone call."

A mischievous smile tugged at Gavin's lips. "We thought you fell in, and we were actually about to assemble a search party. But don't get high on yourself, though; we weren't going to look too hard."

"Wow, you two are brutal." Emily giggled.

Trevor took a swig of beer. "You haven't seen anything yet, Em. They're just getting warmed up."

Dillon shook his head and eyed Gavin. "Once a wiseass, always a wiseass, Blake. Never fails."

Gavin hung his head and laughed. He took a long pull from his beer, swung his eyes over to Emily, and then reluctantly looked at Dillon. "So, how's about it? Are you two coming to the party?"

"I totally forgot about it," Dillon replied. "But of course we'll be there."

Trevor cocked his head to the side. "What do you mean you forgot? Dude, you've been coming for the last couple of years."

Dillon pulled Emily close, anchoring her body in front of his. He wrapped his arms around her shoulders. "I've been distracted by my lady here. I can't seem to think of anything else."

Emily smiled and noticed a beautifully groomed blonde approach. She snaked her arm around Gavin's waist and planted a kiss on the corner of his mouth. "I *thought* it was you, Gavin." She ordered a drink and let the bartender know to put it on his tab. "Where have you been hiding lately?" Her words slurred as she clung tighter, trying to keep her balance.

"Obviously not far enough," Trevor mumbled under his breath. The woman didn't hear his remark, but she didn't need to. His expression told all. Dillon's eyes narrowed on the blonde.

Gavin knew who she was and tried to play it cool. His smile was relaxed as he curled his arm around her waist, trying to hold her steady. "I've been away on business. How've you been?"

"Oh, I've been doing great. Thanks for asking," she replied, shifting her weight closer to Gavin. She glanced in Emily's direction. "Who do we have here? I don't think we've met. You're so cute. Are you one of Gavin's newest playmates?"

Emily's mouth dropped open, but she said nothing, not wanting to severely insult the woman. She thought the comment was ridiculous, considering Dillon had his arms around her.

Gavin smirked, gazing in Emily's direction. "No, she's Dillon's girlfriend. I'm trying my hardest to make a play for a girl named Molly, but unfortunately, she's already taken."

Emily nervously bit her lip and looked away.

The pleasant expression left the woman's face as she shot Dillon a hard look. "Oh really? I didn't know you were seeing anyone, Dillon."

Gavin stood up and caught the blonde by her arm. "Come on, sweets. We have a lot to catch up on. Take a walk with me." He led her out of the club, and Emily watched the way the woman stared back at her while she tried to release Gavin's hold.

"Who the heck was that?" Emily asked, turning to face Dillon.

"No one," he replied, giving Emily a wide-eyed smile. He dragged a hand through his hair. "Just some girl he went to college with."

"One of his ex-girlfriends?" Emily probed.

Trevor looked at Dillon but didn't say a word.

"Yeah, just some girl he used to screw around with," Dillon replied after ordering a few shots. "Come on, let's get hammered, babe."

Gavin made his way through the crowd of sweaty bodies. Walking the woman out of the club, he cornered her against a wall, propping his hand against it. Looking down to her, his expression tightened. "What are you doing, Monica?"

She lifted her chin in defiance, and her hazel eyes glassed

over. "What do you mean, Gavin?" She pushed her hands through her hair. "He thinks he can just fuck me like that and then go off and start fucking someone else so quickly?"

Sighing, a muscle tensed in his jaw. "You and Dillon were exactly that and nothing more. Fuck buddies. Get over it."

Her gaze narrowed. "No, Gavin. If that's what I was looking for, then I would've just fucked you." She trailed her finger across his chest. "Want to take me home tonight? I could add another notch in your bedpost."

"Not a chance and you know it," he quickly said, grabbing her wrist. "The two of you have been over for a while. Now stop the bullshit."

"What a joke! We never stopped!" she snapped. "I was just fucking around with him upstairs."

Dipping his head, Gavin forced her to stare into his eyes. "Upstairs, huh?"

"Yeah, maybe I should tell the goody two-shoes he's here with," she replied, trying to push past him.

"Don't even think about it," he growled. "So help me, if I find out you got within five feet of her . . ."

Widening her eyes, her voice rose as a curious grin stretched across her mouth. "What? Do you have a thing for her?" She paused for a moment and continued when he didn't answer. "You do, don't you? Some friend you are, Gavin Blake." She laughed, tossing her hands through her hair again. "All of you guys—every one of you in your rich little group—are a bunch of fucked-up assholes! I'm just sorry our parents are friends!"

Gritting his teeth, Gavin stared at her for a second. He signaled for the bouncer. "Here's a hundred bucks. Call her a cab and get her out of here—now."

"No problem, Mr. Blake." He reached for the money and

Monica. She struggled against the beefy man, causing a further spectacle as she called Gavin every name in the book. Finally, she was put into a cab and sent on her way.

Letting out a weighted breath, Gavin headed into the club. He would have to do some damage control in the morning, considering Monica Lemay was indeed the daughter of one of his father's closest friends. Making his way back to the bar, Gavin wondered how true her statement was. He didn't put it past Dillon. Dillon was known for cheating, God knew he was. On the other hand, Gavin didn't dismiss Monica lying to try to make her way back to Dillon. It wouldn't be the first desperate move she'd made to get back together with him.

Dillon spotted Gavin approaching. He let Emily know he'd be right back and stalked over to Gavin, tossing his arm around his neck. "Everything taken care of?"

Crossing his arms, Gavin stepped back. "Yeah, she's gone. What the fuck are you doing? Are you still messing around with her?"

Dillon shrugged nonchalantly. "I was, but I'm done with her now. She kept calling and harassing me. You know how she gets."

Dillon went to walk away, but Gavin grabbed his arm. "Man, seriously, you have a pretty cool woman now. What the fuck is wrong with you?"

Dillon pulled his arm away. "There you go again, getting concerned about what I'm doing. You just worry about yourself. I told you that I'm done with the whore." He tossed his shot down his throat. "Come on, I don't want to waste any more of my night on her." He started to walk away and then turned back. "Oh, I told Emily *you* used to fuck around with her."

Before Gavin could say a word, Dillon walked back to

Emily, a smile twisting his lips as he kissed her. Gavin watched his friend play the smooth Jekyll and Hyde he'd come to know over the years. Gavin couldn't help but notice the way Emily stared at him as he lounged back into his seat.

"You really do know how to pick them, Gavin," Emily teased, tilting her beer to her mouth. "The library—don't forget the library."

Gavin finished his beer before leveling an icy look at Dillon. He then flicked his eyes over to Emily as he contemplated her words. "Yeah, I've had my share of troubled women, I guess." He motioned for the bartender to bring him another. "I'll definitely start with the library as you've suggested, Emily."

Over the next few hours, Dillon became mindlessly hammered. The many beers and shots of tequila caught up with him. By the end of the night, both Trevor and Gavin had to help him out to Trevor's SUV. Having lost all his patience by that point, Gavin tossed him in the backseat and closed the door. Trevor shook Gavin's hand and got into the vehicle.

Emily stood in the parking lot, embarrassed by Dillon's drunken stupor. "I'm sorry about this. He gets a little out of hand when he celebrates a new account."

Gavin leaned against the vehicle, his eyes resting on her lips. "There's no need for you to apologize on his behalf." His eyes shifted to meet hers. "I've known him long enough to know how he gets."

Drawing in a deep breath, Emily held out her hand. She tried hard to appear relaxed, but her voice sounded unnatural and shaky. "Well, it was good officially meeting you, Gavin. I guess I'll see you around."

Closing the space between them, he reached for her hand. He felt momentarily frozen as he stared deeply into her green eyes. He simply shook her hand and gave her a smile. "It was good to have finally met you, too, Emily. I guess I'll see you at the Fourth of July party."

Slipping into the passenger seat, she nodded and smiled in his direction. "Fourth of July."

Gavin watched them disappear into the heavy Manhattan traffic while the shock of discovering who Emily really was washed over him.

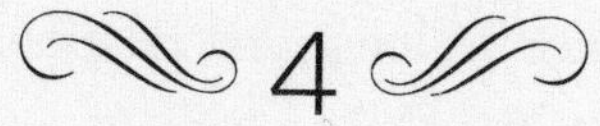

4

Unexpected Details

"MR. BLAKE, THE board is pleased with this quarter's earnings. We're also anticipating further growth next quarter for Blake Industries, considering the new Armstrong account you've acquired."

Gavin stroked his fingers rhythmically across the sleek mahogany conference table. "That's wonderful news, Barry. Have we heard anything on the Kinsman account?"

Ten pairs of eyes swung to the man nervously riffling through some files.

Another executive chimed in all too eagerly. "Yes, Mr. Blake. They've accepted the offer and should be ready to move forward by the end of July, sir. I gave all of the necessary paperwork to your brother."

Gavin rose from his chair, gave a satisfactory nod, and called the meeting to an end.

As the last board member exited, Gavin sauntered over to a floor-to-ceiling window in his office. Peering down at the streets of Manhattan, he watched the chaotic lives of others rumble on below him. At the age of twenty-eight, he knew he had the world by the balls. Blake Industries was one of New York's largest advertising agencies. Nevertheless, he lacked the most vital necessity—love. He knew it; hell, he knew it better than he knew his own facial features. Though he'd played the dating game since his long-term relationship ended, few—if any—contestants had evoked feelings within him. Finding someone who truly wanted him for who he was had become . . . interesting since the breakup.

As he watched the tiny figures below scurry along the sidewalks, his thoughts raced back to Emily. It had been less than twenty-four hours since he was hit with the fact of who she really belonged to. Gavin seethed at Dillon using him as a pawn with Monica. But despite his attraction to Emily, Gavin knew he had to cover for his friend.

Still, his emotions volleyed back and forth between the lie he had been forced to tell and the upsurge of want for her snaking its way through his mind. Sure, some of it was sexual attraction. Emily was beyond beautiful, and he couldn't deny that. However, that wasn't what fueled his desire for her. He couldn't quite define exactly what it was, but it was unlike any other attraction he'd ever had. He felt a connection to her, a deep pull within his gut that she was supposed to be with him.

Their chemistry was undeniable, an explosive current of attraction Gavin was sure she had also experienced. He'd felt it the first time he'd laid eyes on her, that drawing energy radiating from her eyes as she stared into his. Standing among the empire he had built while the sun cast its rays against the steel giants lining the streets, he fought back the overwhelming urge to pay her another unexpected visit. Shaking his head at the insane thought, Gavin moved across his office. He sat down at his desk, went through some quarterly reports, and tried to rid the woman who could never be his from his mind.

It was then that Gavin's older brother, Colton, walked into the office.

Crossing his arms in annoyance, Gavin glared at him. "Where were you? Did you not receive the message I left with Natalie regarding the meeting?"

Colton gave Gavin a wry smile. "I must say you play the role very well, little man." He strode across the office as a muffled laugh left his lips.

"Stop being a wiseass. Really, what the fuck happened?"

"Jesus, Gavin, I got hung up on the home front with Melanie and the kids. Teresa and Timothy had a preschool musical."

"Why didn't you tell me?" He frowned, rocking back in his black leather chair. He had a soft spot for his niece and nephew. "I would've gone to see it."

Colton waved a dismissive hand, his green eyes shimmering. "Don't worry about it; they did just fine without Uncle Gavin." He laughed and patted Gavin's shoulder. "And I'm sure you did just fine without me during the meeting."

Gavin snorted and muttered, "They're fucking sharks if the numbers aren't appealing to them."

"That's the business." Colton shrugged and sat on the black leather couch. "We have people who invest in our company, and we need to produce the revenue they're looking for in return."

Standing, Gavin ignored his brother's words and walked back over to the window.

"So, are you ever going to secure an evening out with Alicia?" Colton probed.

Without turning around, Gavin crossed his arms and chuckled. "I can't deny I admire the way you're able to seamlessly transition from one topic to the next, Colton."

"There's a true compliment somewhere in that statement. But seriously, man, Melanie's been bothering me about hooking you two up for a while. Just come out with us one night and decide if she'd be someone who would interest you."

"I see you two are on the finding-Gavin-a-secure-relationship mission again."

"Mission? Not quite. But I think it's about time you get over her."

Snapping his head in Colton's direction, Gavin's eyes lit up with raw amusement. "Do you think I'm honestly *not* over her?" He almost laughed. "It's been two years."

"Well, she definitely caused you to draw back from forming other attachments—*long-term* attachments, that is." Colton rose from the couch. "They're not all the same, little man. She was just in it for all the wrong reasons."

Gavin's jaw tensed almost imperceptibly. "I really have no desire at all to talk about this," he said, his voice holding a warning.

"Fair enough. Are you coming to dinner tonight at Mom and Dad's?"

He shrugged into his suit jacket, the barest suggestion of a smile playing on his lips. "Yes, I'll be there—unless you and my wonderful sister-in-law are hiding a secret date for me under the table." Colton dug his keys from his pocket, gave an impish smirk, and walked out of the office.

By the time Gavin left, Manhattan was gridlocked. Sighing, he rubbed a palm over his face as he gripped the steering wheel of his black BMW. While waiting for a herd of pedestrians to cross the street, he realized he was at the corner beside the restaurant where Emily worked. The blood drained from his face when he saw her opening the door to leave. He pinched the bridge of his nose and contemplated pulling over to say hello, but as soon as the idea entered his mind, a horn cut through his thoughts. Flipping the bird to the impatient driver, Gavin slid into first gear and navigated through traffic. He looked in the rearview mirror, trying to catch one last glimpse of her. It was then that his father's far-fetched story about love at first sight slammed into his mind.

"She's out there, son, and when you find her, you'll know it the very second you see her. She'll pull at your every instinct. Without any regard to the natural order of things, she'll just . . . appear."

"This is utterly fucking hilarious." He laughed, tapping his finger on the steering wheel. "I've got to be out of my mind thinking about this girl." With so many conflicting emotions, over the next hour, Gavin analyzed his beliefs. As Manhattan's skyline disappeared from view and the sprawling trees layering upstate replaced it, he swore he would try to rid Emily from his mind—though he wasn't quite sure if that was possible.

Applying the last bit of mascara to her lashes, Emily tore her attention away from the mirror. The slamming door signaled Olivia's arrival. She hurried into the living room. "I've been calling and texting you all day," Emily said breathlessly as she slipped on a pair of red heels. "Why didn't you call me back?"

Olivia tossed her purse on the couch. "I left the damn thing here." She walked into the kitchen and yanked her phone off the counter. Looking at Emily, she beamed a smile. "You're looking hot. What's the special occasion?"

"Mine and Dillon's nine-month anniversary. He'll be here soon," Emily hastily replied, walking over to her. "You were sleeping when I got home last night. You have no idea who I met."

"Yeah, I was wondering why you were gone." Olivia stabbed her pass code into her phone. "Okay, let me guess. Uh, Brad Pitt?"

"I'm being serious, Liv. You'll never guess, so don't even try."

"No! I want one more shot." Olivia paused. "Hmm, President Obama?"

"This is going nowhere real fast." Emily laughed and sank into a chair at the table. "I met the one and only . . . wait for it . . . wait for it . . . Gavin Blake."

"Totally hot, right?" Olivia asked, bringing her phone up to her ear.

Emily smiled. "Yes, completely."

"Now admit my description of the walking god was on point, since if I recall correctly"—Olivia tapped her finger on her chin—"when I gave you the walking god's description, you begged to differ that any man could be that delicious looking."

"Yes, you pretty much hit the nail on the head." Emily laughed. "But I'm more than sure you want to hear the details of our *prior* meetings."

Olivia quickly slid her phone shut. "Prior?" She crossed the room in two strides and lounged into a seat. "You have my attention. Spill it!"

Leaning her elbows on the table, Emily tented her fingers under her chin. "Let me see . . . Oh, yes . . . *He's* the man I had the encounter with at the Chrysler Building while delivering food that one day."

Olivia's brown eyes widened, but she remained silent, shock oozing from her face.

Emily dropped her tone huskily. "Yes, and *he's* the little stalker who came to my job, leaving me his name and number—oh, and a pretty decent tip, too."

"Shut the front door, woman! Mr. Tall, Dark, and Fuckable Handsome is Gavin?" Olivia squealed.

Emily nodded and laughed.

"Are you messing with me, Em? 'Cause if so, that's seriously fucked up."

Leaning back in her chair, Emily crossed her arms, a smirk tipping her lips. "I swear."

"You should just go out with him." Olivia shrugged. "Obviously he's made an impression on you, and you've made one on him."

Her casual words threw Emily off. "What do you mean?"

"You have this dopey, dreamy look on your face. I know you're imagining jumping his bones."

"You're joking, right?"

Olivia stood and made her way to her bedroom. "Are you asking if I'm joking about the dopey look on your face, going out with him, or jumping his bones?"

"Olivia, you know what I'm talking about."

"You're acting surprised that I would say any of those things, Em."

Shocked, Emily followed her. She leaned against Olivia's door and placed her hands on her hips. "Are you really serious about what you just said?"

Olivia peeled off her clothes, strolled to the bathroom, and stepped into the shower. "It's no secret how I feel about Douchebag."

"Ah, that's right. Because how *you* feel about my boyfriend is what matters here," Emily said sardonically as she walked into the bathroom.

"Why not give Gavin a try?" Olivia asked coolly.

Emily ticked the reasons off on her fingers. "One, I love Dillon. Two, I love Dillon. And three, guess what? I love Dillon."

Olivia mocked Tina Turner and crooned, in her finest, sultry singing voice, "What's love got to do with it?" She laughed.

"You've completely lost it, Liv. And even if I weren't with Dillon, you've already killed the ever-wanting-to-entertain-Gavin-Blake option."

Olivia poked her head out from behind the shower curtain. "How did I kill your opinion of him?"

"Let me see . . . *He's a ladies' man* is the first thing that enters my memory." Drawing in a deep breath, Emily paused. "Oh, and you don't think he's capable of staying with any woman longer than a week is another. Shall I go on?"

Olivia shut the water off and stepped out of the shower. Emily handed her a towel. "Right, he started acting like that *after* his fiancée, Gina, broke up with him. Before the infamous split, he was the total package." Olivia wrapped the towel around her body.

"He was engaged?"

"Yeppers," Olivia piped back before sliding into a pair of black shorts and a white tank top. "They dated for almost five years. One day he came home, and she was gone. Packed her shit and moved out while he was at work."

Confusion creased Emily's brows. "Why?"

"To tell you the truth, he never told my brother exactly what happened. And when I've asked him about it, he didn't want to discuss it, so I have no idea." Olivia pulled her makeup bag out of the drawer. "But you saw him. That man's been blessed by the proverbial fucking-hot-as-sin gene. He's worth millions and—really, I'm not kidding—he's a decent guy."

"So why have you never dated him?"

"Oh Lord, I've known him way too long. Even though I have the utmost respect for the glorious gene pool that fine piece of fuckable ass has been bathed in, I sort of look at him like an older brother. It'd be way too weird." Olivia crinkled her nose in distaste.

"How long has he been friends with Trevor?"

"You sure have a ton of questions for a girl who's not considering playing naughty," Olivia quipped.

Emily dismissively waved her hand as she turned to the mirror. "I'm trying to get in the loop here. Dillon tells me nothing about his friends or coworkers."

"Well, if the answer you're really seeking is if Dillon and Gavin have been friends as long as my brother and Gavin have been, the answer is no."

"Oh, for some reason, I thought they all went to high school together."

Olivia reached under the sink for the dryer, plugged it in, and turned it on high. Her voice rose as she dried her golden hair. "No, Trevor and Gavin went to high school together. Trevor works under Dillon at the firm; this you know."

Emily nodded.

"When my brother started working at Morgan and Buckingham, Dillon was already a stockbroker there. That's how my brother met your totally awesome dickhead boyfriend." Olivia laughed, and Emily rolled her eyes. "When Trevor was prepping to take his Series Seven exam to become a broker, Dillon asked him if he knew anyone with a decent bank account. Trying to impress a higher-up, my brother introduced Dillon to Gavin, and the rest is history. They've been friends for the last three years."

"Very cool." *Or not,* Emily thought.

"And supposedly, Blake Industries is the largest account Dillon handles."

Emily shrugged. "So? Big deal."

"So . . . you could thank Gavin for some of the money your boyfriend has."

Emily thought about the countless nights Dillon spent at the office landing clients to earn a living. Even though Gavin played some part in Dillon's wealth, her boyfriend worked above and beyond Blake Industries to make that money. She simply bowed her appreciation. "Well, thank you for that very educational background of the three men's histories together. You're too kind." The two women laughed.

Emily went to walk out of the bathroom, but Olivia spoke up. "Want to know something really funny, chick?" Emily stopped in the threshold and waited. "It was Gavin who was supposed to come out and visit that weekend with my brother when we were in school—not Dillon. Crazy to think that right now you probably would've been dating him instead."

A faint smile tugged at Emily's mouth as she stared into her friend's eyes. Emily's phone ringing broke through the few seconds of silence. She moved to the kitchen to retrieve the call. It was Dillon, announcing he was waiting for her downstairs.

Grabbing her purse, Emily strode to the door as Olivia blew her a kiss good-bye.

"You look amazing," Dillon breathed into Emily's hair as they made their way into a quaint little restaurant nestled on the lapping shore of Liberty State Park. Placing his hand on the small of her back, he leaned closer and nipped at her ear. "And I have to admit that pretty red dress *will* come off by the end of the evening."

Giggling at his obvious gesture, Emily pushed up on her tiptoes to kiss him. "And I have no problem with it coming off."

She took a quick moment to catalog Dillon's features, sighing with warmth at his boyish good looks. His dirty blond hair was naturally mussed as if she had just run her fingers through it, and his light brown eyes reminded her of a perfect blend of caramel and chocolate.

He had made reservations for their special evening, even making sure they had a table overlooking the water. The restaurant offered some of the best views of the Statue of Liberty in the distance. The waiter led them onto a lavish patio lined with trees and subtle landscaping. The view of the harbor under the stars swept Emily's breath away. Although it was the beginning of July, the air held a crisp, cooling breeze on this particular night.

After placing their order and enjoying two glasses of red wine each, Emily looked at Dillon. His gaze was fixed on her as she tucked a piece of hair behind her ear. She felt a blush dance across her cheeks, and she smiled. "What?" she asked.

Sliding his arm across the linen tablecloth, he reached for her hand, smoothing the pad of his thumb along her knuckles. "You really have no idea how beautiful you are." He inclined his body ever so subtly over the table.

"Oh, you're really trying your hardest to get some tonight."

Chuckling, he held her hand tighter. "Touché. I already know that I'm getting some."

Emily shook her head, a giggle escaping her lips. "You're in a very frisky mood right now."

He shrugged and casually leaned back. "Yes, I am. But how could I not be?" He gestured to her slightly exposed cleavage with his head. "Although I must say, I wish you would wear something that covered you up a little more."

Emily adjusted the straps of her dress, pulling it up higher. "Is it that bad?"

"Well, I like to keep what's mine to myself." He cleared his throat and took a sip of wine. "Okay, let's talk about something else before I take you right here on this table. How was your day?"

Not meeting his eyes, Emily traced the rim of her glass with two fingers. "It was okay."

"What's wrong?"

"I feel self-conscious now, Dillon," she replied, glancing around the patio.

"Emily, I didn't mean it like that." He reached across the table and lifted her chin with one finger. Her eyes came to rest on his. "I just don't like when other men stare. You look stunning, but like I said, you're mine."

"Okay, I'll pay more attention to what I wear from now on." A faint smile tugged at her lips. "But to be honest, I actually like when other women stare at you."

"Oh, do you?"

"Yes, I do. I know you're with me, and that's all that matters."

"Well, you're a woman, that's why. Men have other things in mind when they stare like that."

Interrupting the conversation, the waiter arrived with another bottle of wine and two plates of beef Wellington. The rest of their talk focused on Dillon taking Emily to do some sightseeing around the city. It was something that she had looked forward to, but she had yet to do it—at least not with him.

When he came to pick up their empty plates, the waiter handed Emily a dessert menu. His thick French accent slid from his tongue. "The chef recommends the crème brûlée medley, consisting of chocolate, vanilla, and banana."

"That sounds good to me," Emily replied, handing the menu back.

The faint sound of an infant crying caught Dillon's attention. He glanced at Emily. "That baby is driving me nuts. Do you really have to get dessert?"

Emily sheepishly smiled, flicking her eyes in the direction of the couple trying to soothe the baby. "It's just a baby, Dillon. And no, I don't have to get dessert, but I want to."

Dillon's head snapped up as he glared at the waiter. "Fine,

bring her the medley. But can you remove the people with the screaming child?"

Emily's smile fell, surprised by his curtness.

"I apologize, sir, but I'm not able to do that," the waiter answered, noticeably uncomfortable with the request.

Dillon's eyes hardened. "Surely there's a manager I could speak with, then."

Stupefied, Emily interjected immediately. She looked up at the waiter. "Please, there's no need to do that. You can just place it in a to-go box for me. Thank you."

"It may make for a mess in a to-go box, miss. May I recommend our cheesecake if this will not be enjoyed here?"

"Yes, that's fine. And thank you again." The waiter nodded and whisked off to the kitchen. Emily yanked the napkin from her lap and tossed it on the table. "Jesus, Dillon, what the hell was that about?"

He shifted in his chair, trying to drag his attention away from the couple and the screaming baby. He rubbed his fingers against his temples. "I'm sorry. It was a long day at work."

"Still, that was completely mortifying." She huffed, leaning back.

"I said I'm sorry, Em. I'm just exhausted from working all of these late nights."

A wave of guilt coursed through her and she reached across the table for his hand. "I know you've been working hard lately. But, honestly, what are you going to do when we have children?"

The waiter returned with both the dessert and the bill. Dillon retrieved his credit card and handed it to the man. A small smile crept over Dillon's face. "I wouldn't want you messing up that gorgeous body by having children."

"Well, I do want children eventually, so I guess you'll have to endure my messed-up body one day."

Rising from his seat, he buttoned his suit jacket and offered his hand to Emily. She stood up as well. "We have time later for children, babe," he whispered against her cheek. He signed his name on the receipt when the waiter returned. "Come on, I have something special for you."

Emily followed him out to the docks lining the restaurant, her eyes feasting on the skyscrapers. The sparkling of lights from their windows, indicating the presence of others so high in the sky, amazed her. A cool breeze swept across her skin as she slipped off her heels so they wouldn't get caught between the boards.

Walking hand in hand with her, Dillon held her shoes and led her to the end of the docks. He circled his arms around her waist. "Happy anniversary. I love you very much, Em." He handed her a black velvet box.

Emily's heart quickened with anxiety as her body trembled. She licked her lips slowly. "Dillon . . . I . . . we . . ." She stammered, unable to finish her sentence.

As he cocked his head to the side, a low laugh whipped past his lips. "You were just talking about having children with me, Em." He tenderly brushed the hair from her face. "But it's not what you think."

Letting out an audible breath, Emily stared at him. His familiar brown eyes gazed back. She opened the box, revealing a pair of stunning one-carat diamond earrings. Emily gasped at their beauty. Dillon took them from the box, removed the earrings she was wearing, and secured them on her lobes. Looking down, Emily lightly fingered one of the diamonds.

Dillon brushed her cheek with the back of his hand. "They look beautiful on you." He dipped his head, forcing her to stare into his eyes. "Though, I have to say, you looked like you were about to pass out when I gave you the box."

She raised her hand and traced his jaw. "They're beautiful. Thank you so much. I just got a little . . . nervous, you know? I'm not sure if I'd be ready for marriage just yet."

A slow smile curled his lips as his warm fingers splayed across her lower back. He pulled her to him. "Be ready soon enough, babe. Because I'm marrying you one day." With his breath in her ear, he ran his tongue along the curved edge, gently sucking her lobe into his mouth.

The hair on her nape stood on end from his rapt attention to the spot he knew would send her over the edge. Thrusting her fingers into his hair, she pressed her lips against his. He swept his tongue through her mouth, smoothed his hands down her waist and pulled her closer, his kiss growing hungrier by the second.

With her inner senses becoming too hot for the public onslaught of affection, Emily pulled back and slowly grabbed his hand. "Let's go," she breathed out, trying to contain the spiked level of need running through her. "Okay, let's talk before I take *you* right here on the docks."

"All right, but the talking ends once we get back to my place." He eyed her seductively as his grip on her hand tightened. "Okay, something to talk about . . . something to talk about . . . Oh, you took off work for this Wednesday, Thursday, and Friday right?"

Emily came to a stop, her brow drawn up in confusion. "For what?"

"Gavin's Fourth of July party. We told you about it last night."

"Right, but that's Wednesday. Why do I need off all three days?"

Dillon snaked his arm around her waist and continued to lead her to his Mercedes. "Because Gavin Blake doesn't throw what you would consider a *normal* Fourth of July party." He opened the car door for her. "We party all three days. We'll sleep there Wednesday and Thursday and head back here Friday morning."

Emily settled herself into his car, and he closed the door. Once again, she felt her pulse jump but for something completely different now. Her stomach roiled at the thought of spending two nights at Gavin's home in the Hamptons. She had prepared herself to see him again—she had to because he was Dillon's friend, and they would undoubtedly run into each other from time to time—but that . . . that was different.

Dillon lounged into his seat, and the engine purred to life. Biting her lip, Emily looked at him. "It's already Monday night, Dillon. I can't get off all three days. I told Antonio about Wednesday, and he was fine with that, but I'm pretty sure he won't be fine with me taking off so many days in a row."

"Then I'll go in and say something to him," he stated with a tone of superiority.

"Dillon, you will do no such thing," she replied in aggravation. "I'll ask him when I get to work tomorrow. Don't you dare go there and say anything."

"Whoa, whoa." He laughed, taking his hands off the steering wheel momentarily and holding them up in surrender. "Damn, Emily, it was just a gesture."

Rolling her eyes, she leaned her head against the window. She wondered two things: one, if she could actually get off work all three days, which seemed nearly impossible; and two, if she could get off, how on earth would she make it through two consecutive days and nights around Gavin without absolutely losing her mind?

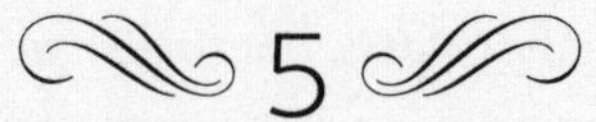

5

The Many Layers

"DAMN, EMILY, HOW much did you pack?" Olivia asked, eyeing her friend's suitcase as she slid a backpack over her shoulder. "It's only two nights, chick."

Emily's head snapped up as she tucked the last of her makeup into a bag. "You're not staying both nights like I am. It's really not *that* much."

"It looks like you've stowed a small city away in there," Olivia teased, walking over. Tossing her blonde hair to the side, she wiggled her brows. "But that's right—you'll be around Gavin for over forty-eight hours, so I'm sure you'll need enough clothing to change into. I've heard he likes black lingerie."

"You're such a drama queen, Liv. Just stop with your assumptions, okay?" Emily walked into the kitchen with her bag and Olivia followed, tickling her rib cage. Emily jumped and laughed and pushed her away. "Oh, and by the way, a whopping thank-you for the warning about this being a two-night hiatus. I'm lucky Fallon was able to cover my shifts."

Olivia held her hands up and shrugged. "Hey, I just assumed you knew."

A quick knock came at the front door, and Dillon peeked his head in. "Is everyone decent in here?"

Emily made a slicing motion across her neck and mouthed Gavin's name.

Olivia nodded and piped, "Actually, we're not. You know I'm into women now, so I have your girlfriend spread-eagled across the kitchen table."

Emily shook her head and laughed.

"That's right. I forgot about that, Ollie . . . I mean, Olivia." Dillon made his way over to Emily. "The entire male species has banned you."

"Fuck off, Douchepickle . . . I mean, Dillon. It's the other way around. I banned *them,*" Olivia hissed, grabbing her backpack from the floor. "And my girlfriend's meeting me out there, so you better not say a fucking word, asshole." Dillon laughed and shot her a wicked smile. He dropped a kiss on Emily's lips. Olivia rolled her eyes. "Is the limo here yet?"

Emily looked confused. "Limo?"

"Like I said, babe, it's a crazy party from beginning to end." Dillon yanked up Emily's suitcase, its heaviness apparent in the straining of his bicep. "Gavin sends one for us every year. And it just so happens that, yes, it's outside, ready and waiting. Let's go. It's almost three, so rush hour will be a bitch." Dillon led the way out the door and into the elevator.

Emily grabbed Olivia's elbow and whispered, "Is *he* in the limo?"

With two sharp shakes of her head, Olivia whispered back, "No, he would've slept there last night to get the place ready."

Emily took in the sight of the gray-and-black Hummer limousine as they stepped out of the apartment building. The chauffeur held the door open with a huge smile. He retrieved everyone's bags and placed them in the trunk. Emily climbed in behind Olivia, and they settled on the long, black leather seat. Dillon didn't waste any time, reaching toward the illuminated bar and making himself a drink.

"Always hitting the booze, Dickhead . . . uh, Dillon," Olivia remarked, studying her face in a small compact mirror.

He shot her a blank, frosty smile. "What are you now, my mother?"

Emily let out a deep sigh. "Would you two stop already?"

"She started it."

Reverting to a second grader's level, Olivia crinkled her nose and stuck out her tongue at Dillon.

Shaking her head, Emily sighed again. "Okay, so how far is his place?"

"It's in East Hampton, so about three hours because of traffic." Olivia got comfortable and tossed her legs across the leather seat. "But so worth the drive, Em. It's a fucking paradise right on the beach."

"Are we stopping to pick up Trevor?" Emily asked.

Olivia shook her head. "No, he's helping my parents with some bullshit at their house right now. He'll meet us out there tonight."

"How many people will be there?"

Dillon pulled Emily across his lap and smiled. "Not that many tonight. It's just his preparty with a few friends." He took a sip of his whiskey on the rocks. "But tomorrow's a totally different game. There will be over a hundred guests, and each and every single one of them is flowing with money."

Olivia laughed as she looked at Dillon. "Only you would know that. Every year you try to gain a new account by snaking your way into some rich bastard's portfolio. I have to admit you work the party like a pro."

His eyes hardened, but Emily quickly placed her hand over his mouth. "You two are done talking for the remainder of the ride."

Over the next few hours, while her anxiety steadily built to unbearable heights, Emily watched a suburban landscape replace the concrete and steel of the city. Mature trees, grass, and single-family homes flew past, reminding her of where she had grown up. She'd missed that since living in the city.

Eventually, the middle-class palette melted away. The view shifted to sprawling mansions lining the Atlantic coast. They were the types of homes Emily had seen in magazines. Her eyes widened at the absolute beauty. Rolling down the window, she deeply inhaled the salty ocean air. The chauffeur pulled up to a winding, gated driveway. He spoke with someone over an intercom before the ornate metal gates slowly swung open, allowing the limousine onto the property. Beyond the gates, a sweeping lawn holding lush trees lined the flagstone drive. A garden highlighted the front of the home with flowers of every color imaginable. Large pillars on both sides of the mammoth mahogany door caught Emily's gaze. Off to the side were sunken tennis and basketball courts. In the distance, the twinkling sun shimmering off the ocean brought Emily a sense of peace—if only for the barest second.

Olivia chucked a piece of ice at Dillon's face, stirring him from his alcohol-induced nap. She and Emily laughed, watching him blink his eyes open. He glared at Olivia with a look that promised retaliation one way or another. The chauffeur opened the door, and they each stepped out into the sunlight. Dillon stretched his neck from side to side, yawning. He reached in his pocket, patted the driver on his back, and handed him a tip.

Emily shielded her eyes from the sun as she took in the massive stone home, awestruck by its size. Though it was astonishing in every way possible, she wondered why one person needed a place of such magnitude. With that fleeting thought, the reason for her newfound anxiety—and rapid breathing—stepped out of the front door.

Shirtless.

Emily's heart nearly stopped. As Gavin made his way over to the group, she couldn't help but admire his barely there attire. Transiently, her eyes scanned his well-defined abs, segmented with definitions of hard muscle from his shoulders to his hips. A deep V that disappeared below white swimming trunks made her heart rate jump back to life.

He wasn't bulky by any means; he had a body like a runner—long and lean—with just enough muscle to make any girl's tongue dance behind her lips. It was then that she noticed he stood a good six inches over her smaller frame. His golden tan had her unconsciously biting the side of her mouth, nearly drawing blood. To add icing to the cake, he had an intricate black dragon tattoo snaking its way up from those white swimming trunks and curling around his left rib cage.

The only thought running through Emily's mind at that very second was: *Where exactly does that tattoo begin?*

Heat rose to her cheeks as she felt tension in her legs—coils of lust she knew she shouldn't have, making themselves acutely present throughout her entire body. She swallowed nervously, trying to get moisture back into her suddenly dry mouth, and immediately chided herself for having any reaction at all. He was sexy, forbidden, dangerous, completely fuckable—and she knew it.

A contagious smile washed over Gavin's face as he stepped down from the porch. He shook Dillon's hand and gestured with his head to the limo leaving the property. "How was the ride? I hope my driver treated you all well."

"He always treats us good." Dillon grabbed his and Emily's bags from where the chauffeur had set them.

Olivia tossed her arms around Gavin's neck and hugged him. "What's up, my man?" She whispered something into his ear and giggled.

Emily had a good idea what Olivia had said when Gavin's eyes flicked in her direction, a boyish smile tipping the corners of his mouth. Cupping his chin, he laughed as he looked down, shaking his head. His blue eyes swung back to Emily. "I'm happy to see you could make it. Dillon said that you might not be able to stay both nights."

"I know people." Emily laughed, not from her attempted joke, but rather from her soaring nervousness.

"Mmm, it's very good knowing people," he noted, staring into her eyes an extra few seconds. Drawing in a deep breath, he tossed his hand through his hair. "Okay, let's go party the next few days away."

As the two women followed the men, Emily shot Olivia a look, knowing she'd said something to Gavin about their prior meetings. Olivia laughed and batted her eyes like a true Southern belle as they made their way into the house.

The two-story foyer with a cascade of staircases on either side was surprisingly warm and inviting, and Emily found herself glancing down the long hall toward the breathtaking view of the ocean. Sunlight spilled in effortlessly through floor-to-ceiling windows surrounding the back end of the home. A double-sided stone fireplace was the center of attention in the living room. Gleaming, dark cherry hardwood floors led into a gourmet, eat-in kitchen dripping with black granite. Deep earthy tones were scattered throughout a library, billiard room, and dining room. Emily's amazement was evident. Olivia squeezed Emily's arm, her smile wide. "I told you it's spectacular. And you haven't seen the media room, the second level, or the backyard fucking oasis, chick."

Feeling almost breathless, Emily nodded and followed Dillon up to the room they would share. Olivia was right. The upstairs was no less amazing. The same flow of furnishings with warm accents and hues was sprinkled throughout the upper level. Emily felt as though she were in a spa when she walked into their en suite bathroom. European fixtures and a marble shower encased in floor-to-ceiling glass made her want to skip the pool altogether and opt for the hot steam instead.

Dillon prepared himself a drink at the small wet bar in their room and told Emily he would meet her out back. She nodded as she rummaged through her belongings. After applying a good bit of suntan lotion, she threw on her black bikini, slipped a sarong around her waist, and made her way into the hall.

Gavin halted midstride, grabbing his sunglasses on the kitchen island. He spotted Emily coming down the stairs and felt a dizzying force plummet through him. Something inside him twisted, burning in his stomach to the very core of his being.

So much for trying to rid her from his mind.

Just looking at her made it hard for him to breathe. He couldn't concentrate on any one particular thing about her. His eyes passed over her slowly, pausing to regard her beautiful figure. He was sure the sight of her auburn hair draping over her bikini top could send him to his deathbed a happy man. He squeezed his eyes shut, willing himself to think of something else. When they snapped back open, his eyes found hers, but the moment they connected, she looked away. Undeterred, he smiled and moved to the edge of the stairs.

Emily stopped on the second step and stared down at

Gavin. His eyes alone swallowed her whole. They were vivid, mesmerizing, and surrounded by thick, dark lashes. A timid smile crept across her face. "Hey." She sounded more breathless than she had intended.

The energy flowing between them was palpable. Gavin felt it, and he was pretty sure she could, too. He wet his lips and stared at her for a moment. "Hey."

The overt intensity of his gaze rendered her speechless. Her eyes flew to the ocean beyond the windows as she waited for him to move.

Gavin could tell he made her nervous and that wasn't his intention. He sucked his bottom lip between his teeth and tentatively placed his hand on the banister. "I know this whole thing's a little crazy." He paused for a second and smiled. "Well, more than a little, but I just wanted you to know that I'm just as freaked out about it as you are." His face softened into concern as his gaze became more intent. "But more important, I don't want you to feel uncomfortable while you're here. I want you relaxed."

Emily drew in a deep breath as she held steady eye contact with him, knowing that would be nearly impossible. She needed something to distract herself from the blazing blue of his eyes.

She moved down the last two stairs, trying with every bit of her voice and body to appear nonchalant about the whole matter. "I appreciate your concern, but honestly, I'm good."

Gavin placed his hands at the back of his neck and smiled at her. "Are you sure?"

"One hundred percent," she replied, glancing around for an exit to the pool.

"Oh, it's over here." Gavin gestured. "I'll actually follow you out. Some friends of mine that I'd like to introduce you to are out back." After retrieving his sunglasses, he and Emily strolled outside.

Inhaling as much as her lungs could hold, Emily let the salty smell of the ocean tickle her nose. An inground pool and hot tub overlooked the shores of the Atlantic. The view was spectacular from the hill where the home stood. An outdoor fireplace, a cabana with a built-in bar, and a guesthouse were part of the open-air paradise. Emily followed Gavin over to where Olivia and Dillon chatted with two men.

The moment Dillon noticed her, Emily watched him excuse himself from the group. His telling eyes let her know he wanted to talk with her. Emily cocked her head to the side in confusion and opened her mouth to speak, but she stopped when she saw his expression.

He appeared angry.

Olivia rolled her eyes and shook her head, probably finding Dillon's behavior irritating. Emily smiled at the two men, whom she had yet to meet, and followed Dillon across the yard.

"Are you kidding me, Em?" Dillon asked, eyeing her up and down when they were far enough away from everyone. "What the fuck are you wearing?"

Her brows knitted together as she tried to keep her voice under control. "Are *you* kidding *me*, Dillon?"

"Fuck no, I'm not kidding. We just talked about this the other night. Don't you have a one-piece?"

"No, I don't have a one-piece. I have a bikini that's covered by a sarong."

Puffing out an exasperated breath, he scrubbed his face with his hands. "At least go the fuck back upstairs and put on a pair of shorts, then."

"I'll do no such thing," she scoffed, placing her hands on her hips. "You're overreacting. It's blazing hot, there's a pool I plan on going in, and I want to tan."

"I'm not fucking joking, Emily. You're going to put me in a bad spot if I catch any of these guys looking at you."

She tilted her head to the side, studying his demeanor. His voice left no room for argument, and the last thing she wanted was for him to get drunk and start a fight. She walked away without a backward glance and headed upstairs to do as he asked. Beyond pissed, she made sure she slipped on the shortest pair of booty jean shorts she owned. To top it off, she left her bikini top on—uncovered.

By the time she made her way back outside, Olivia was lying on a plush beach chair, talking on the phone. Emily walked over to the four men, shot Dillon a wry smile, and politely asked him to make her a Captain and Diet Coke. He didn't look too happy with her new ensemble, but it was obvious he saw the look in her eyes this time telling him to deal with it. He honored her request and went to make her drink.

Gavin glared at Dillon as he walked away and flicked his eyes down to Emily's shorts. He knew Dillon had made her change. He gritted his teeth, not understanding why his friend couldn't be proud of what he had. Nevertheless, a charming smile ran across his mouth as he gazed into Emily's eyes. "I'd like to introduce you to my buddies Chris and Joe. Guys, this is Dillon's girlfriend, Emily."

She smiled and shook their hands. Seeing that they could pass for brothers—their eyes, hair, and features were strikingly similar—she asked, "Are you two related?"

Chris spoke up first, his hazel eyes wide. "Very good observation; we're actually cousins." He tossed a hand through his almond-colored hair.

Joe smirked and patted Chris's back. "Yes, unfortunately, our mothers are sisters."

Emily laughed with them. She learned that both men had gone to high school with Gavin and Trevor. They'd relocated to Florida and opened a landscaping business together after graduating from college. When Dillon brought her drink over, she excused herself from the group of men and got comfortable on one of the poolside beach chairs with Olivia.

"Em, he's really starting to become—"

Emily held up a silencing finger. "Please. Just let it go for now, Liv."

Olivia propped herself up on her elbow and flashed a frown. "Let it go?"

"Yes, please. I don't want to talk about it, okay?"

"I'll let it go, friend, but I have to say Douchebucket is officially a total asshole now," she remarked, securing her hair into a messy bun. She reached for the suntan lotion and smeared more over her milky-white skin. "And you need to grow a backbone with him sooner or later."

Ignoring Olivia's statement, Emily watched the waves tumble in the distance. While soaking in the warm sun, she concentrated on Bob Marley in the background, singing about how he shot the sheriff.

Over the next few hours, Gavin's gaze traveled to Emily and back to Dillon, battling an internal war. He positioned himself perfectly at the table to maintain an unobstructed view of her face while trying to focus on a conversation with his friends. However, his mind continually strayed back to the thought of her soft hand against his lips when he had kissed it a few days before. His eyes burned with adoration when she laughed with Olivia. Her smile was like an addictive drug, and her voice sounded celestial. Although they stole furtive glances at each other throughout the day, Gavin admired her from afar, not wanting to make the situation any more awkward.

As night fell, the small crowd jumped from a sudden booming sound coming from the front of the home. Lighting off a few fireworks before making his way to the backyard was Trevor's way of announcing his arrival. Beaming a smile, he strolled in and barked out his signature line, "I'm here. Let the party begin!"

Olivia's girlfriend, Tina, showed up shortly after. Olivia hopped up, squealing, and gave her a kiss, letting the men know she was hers. Chris ignored Olivia as he eyed the beautiful redhead. Olivia smacked his arm as she walked away. Strolling over to Emily, Olivia announced, "Tina, this is my best friend, Emily."

"Hey, it's good to meet you." Tina smiled. "I've heard a lot about you. It's nice to put a face with the name."

Emily stood and shook the hand Tina extended. "You, too. You made your way out here without getting lost, I see. Olivia was afraid you wouldn't be able to find the place."

Tina leaned in and kissed Olivia's cheek. "Sweetie, you were worried about me?"

Olivia blushed. "Of course I was."

Dillon made his way over to Emily when Tina and Olivia wandered off. He sighed and gently pulled her against him. "Babe, I'm sorry about earlier. I was an asshole. Can you forgive me?"

She searched his eyes, trying to understand his sudden change. "You have me so confused. You never acted like this when I was in Colorado, Dillon."

"I know, Em," he whispered, reaching for her hand. He drew it to his mouth and held it against his lips. "I just love you so fucking much. I'm afraid of losing you, that's all."

"I'm not going anywhere. I love you more than you realize, Dillon. I trusted in us enough to come out here to be with you. That by itself should say enough."

Placing his hand on the nape of her neck, he drew her face closer. "You're right." He leaned in to kiss her lips, and she accepted without a second thought as they stole a few extra moments to reconcile. Dillon pulled back slowly and stroked his fingers through her hair. "I'll ease up, I promise."

Emily smiled faintly, hoping what he said would prove to be true. Dillon playfully smacked her on the ass, gave her another kiss, and let her know he was going to play a game of pool with Chris and Joe. She watched him disappear into the house.

Emily strolled over to join Olivia and Tina where they were snuggling on a lounge chair, overly excited to be together. It was then that Gavin tossed a deck of cards onto the table in front of Emily.

Gavin smiled wickedly. "So, Trevor tells me you enjoy playing poker."

Emily looked at Trevor as he pulled up a seat. Her eyes flicked back to Gavin. "I play a pretty good game, I must admit."

"I see . . . and your game of choice would be what exactly?" Gavin questioned, placing a mahogany box filled with poker chips on the table.

"My game of choice would be Texas Hold'em."

"Mmm, very good. That's my favorite." He sat across from her. "Shall we?" He opened the deck of cards.

"We shall."

"We'll just watch," Olivia piped up. She shot Emily a teasing grin, and Emily shook her head.

"Well, you two may think you're expert players, but I'm pretty damn sure I'm going to clean you both out." Trevor laughed as he peered at them over his glasses. He threw a hundred-dollar bill on the table. "I'm a certified pro. But don't say I didn't warn you both."

Gavin huffed at his statement.

"We're playing for real money?" Emily asked.

"We sure are." Gavin tossed two one-hundred-dollar bills on the table. "I just put in for you."

"You don't have to do that," Emily replied, standing up. "I'll just get some money from Dillon."

"Don't worry about it. I'll get it back from him after I wipe you and Trevor out," Gavin remarked, flashing her one of his dimpled smiles. Trevor was too busy shuffling to acknowledge Gavin's statement, but Emily wasn't too busy to notice Gavin's heart-stopping smile.

She hesitantly sat back down and threw him a smile of her own. "You think you're going to wipe me out?"

A lopsided smirk split his face. "Oh, I'm absolutely positive I will."

Grinning, Emily leaned back. "We shall see, Mr. Blake."

The way his last name slid from her tongue had Gavin trying to contain the emotions threatening to pour from his body. He licked his lips as he stared at her and dealt out the cards.

With cards in hand, drinks flowing, and Olivia and Tina as spectators, the game began. Over the next hour, both Gavin and Emily depleted Trevor of all his chips. They continuously made fun of his earlier statement about beating them both.

"Okay, okay. But just for the record, I'm pretty drunk right now; that's why my game was off tonight," Trevor defended himself and retreated into a lounge chair next to Olivia and Tina. Olivia laughed and consoled her brother by doing a shot of tequila with him.

"The proverbial drank-too-much-and-played-like-an-ass excuse. Classic." Gavin laughed.

Trevor shook his head with a defeated look molding his face. "I'm reaching far with that one, right?"

Gavin finished the last of his beer before answering. "I'd say so. But I've experienced the same drunken play many nights before," he admitted, dealing another hand to himself and Emily.

After a few minutes of studying each other's faces for who might have the better hand, Emily cleared her throat. "I'm all in." She pushed her growing stack of chips into the middle of the table as a wide I-dare-you smile crept over her lips.

Gavin regarded her carefully as he drummed his fingers slowly against his empty beer bottle. Trying to drag his gaze from hers, Gavin looked down at his cards. He held two kings and one was already on the table. Leaning forward, he tilted his head and smiled. "You might not want to do that, Miss Cooper."

Emily leaned herself forward, mimicking his cockiness. It was harder than she thought as she stared into his unblinking blue eyes. "Afraid to call?"

Olivia, Tina, and Trevor watched closely, curious expressions tight on each of their faces. Gavin smirked and pushed his stack of chips against hers. "I hold fear at bay for a miniscule amount of things in life, but calling your bluff isn't one of them." He laughed and flipped over his cards. "I'd like to introduce you to my friends—Larry, Moe, and Curly."

Olivia belted out a gasp. "Oh shit, you're in trouble now, Em. He just pulled the Three Stooges move on you."

Emily widened her eyes in mock horror. "Hmm, I might be." She tapped the edge of her cards. "But considering I have three aces, I think I'm pretty good for now." She fanned her cards along the table as her face brightened with a huge, satisfied smile.

The small group—including Gavin—hooted out in hysterical laughter. With her smile beaming ear to ear, Emily yanked the three hundred-dollar bills off the table and tucked them into her shorts. In that moment, the tension in both Gavin and Emily's shoulders—from the way their worlds had collided—deflated and vanished like a ghost.

Eventually, Chris, Joe, and Dillon made their way back outside. Gavin took a few minutes to fill Dillon in on his devastating loss. Dillon shot Emily a proud smile. The group helped Gavin clean up, and everyone decided it was best to call it a night. Before the droves of guests arrived, the guys usually indulged in a very early morning fishing trip on Gavin's boat, so sleep was definitely needed. Everyone said good night before heading into their designated rooms.

It was well after one in the morning when Emily crawled out of bed. Dillon's liquor-enhanced snoring kept her awake. Attempting to go back to sleep, she nudged him, flipped on the television, and even placed a pillow over his face in hopes of stifling the noise. None of it worked. Deciding a good dose of fresh air might help bring on sleep, she quietly opened the French doors that led out to the balcony.

Immediately, it was as if the ocean called to her. She walked over to the edge of the balcony and peered out at the distant waves tumbling onto the sand dunes. As her senses started to absorb the sounds, smells, and sights engulfing her, Gavin's "hello" made her jump.

She whirled around, a curl of hair catching on her lips, and found him sitting in an Adirondack chair. "Jesus!" she let out louder than anticipated.

"No, it's Gavin. Gavin Blake," he deadpanned, reaching for a beer from a six-pack. "Although, in certain private, one-on-one situations, I've been referred to as God." He laughed.

With an unladylike snort, Emily laughed with him. "You're too much."

"Aren't I, though?"

"Yes, very," she replied and then turned back to the door. "I didn't realize this was a connecting balcony. I'll let you have your privacy."

"By all means, stay and have a beer with me."

With the mildest trepidation, she made her way over to him. He popped a beer open for her. "Thank you," she replied, accepting it and sinking into a chair beside him.

"You're very welcome. So what brings you out on the balcony in the wee hours of the night?"

"You can't hear that?"

Gavin's brows knitted in confusion as he looked around. "Uh, I hear the waves."

"Then you're lucky," she sighed. "Because I can still hear Dillon snoring."

"Ah, I see." He snickered, propping his feet on a small outdoor ottoman. "Us men do know how to knock it out of the ballpark when it comes to that."

Emily shook her head and took a sip of her beer. "I've tried everything short of smothering him to death to get him to stop."

Gavin nodded and winked at her. "Hmm, not a bad idea. You'd be available then."

"Be nice," she playfully chided.

"Yes, ma'am," he clipped, and Emily shook her head.

A few minutes went by as they listened to the waves rolling in the distance. The sky was clear with a magnificent view of the stars and a cool, summer breeze skirted its way across the balcony.

"So, I didn't see you go down to the water today," Gavin remarked, reaching for another beer. He popped the top off and tossed it into a terra-cotta pot that held quite a few bottle caps. "Don't you like the beach?"

"Actually, I love the beach." She drew in a deep breath as her gaze slid from his out to the water. "Some of my best memories of my mom come from endless days spent on the beach with her."

Heaviness settled in Gavin's chest. He knew her mother had passed away. When they were at the club, he'd wanted to say something to her but felt it was inappropriate to do so unless she brought it up. He continued to stare at her, struggling to find the right words. He shifted his body to face hers. "I'm very sorry about what you had to go through, losing her," he finally stated softly.

She drew her knees up under her chin and glanced over at him. "Thank you."

"If you don't mind, I'd love to hear about the memories you have of her on the beach." His voice was low and cautious as he gazed into her eyes.

A faint smile tugged at her lips. "Really?"

He nodded and smiled back. "I'd be honored."

She took a minute to compose her thoughts. "Well, when I was a kid, she'd save all year long so we could visit Santa Cruz. She'd rent a little condo right on the beach, and we'd literally spend the entire day outside. We'd fly kites for hours on end and ride our bikes on the boardwalk." She paused and smiled. "She used to love making sand angels, like the ones you make in the snow." She let out a light laugh at the memory and wiped away a tear.

"Emily, I . . ." Gavin whispered. She looked at him. "My intentions weren't meant to upset you. Please . . . I apologize."

"They're . . . good tears, Gavin. I haven't talked about her in a while. Really, you didn't upset me."

Her words left Gavin awestruck. He searched her eyes and found traces of happiness mixed with incalculable loss. It melted his heart. He longed to run his fingers through her hair and console her; he wanted to hold her and rid her of the pain. "They sound like wonderful memories."

"Yeah, they are," she replied, staring straight ahead. "It was hard seeing her sick for so many months, but to tell you the truth, when she took her last breath, a wave of relief washed over me. She was finally at peace." Wiping another tear away, Emily looked at him and then averted her gaze out to the ocean. "There was a point I actually hoped I would wake up and find out she was gone and not in pain. It still makes me feel guilty that I felt that way, but I couldn't bear watching her suffer anymore."

Gavin's emotions soared to a place he hadn't dared to revisit in a while. Again, he found himself struggling for the right thing to say. His voice was but a whisper. "I know we may seem worlds apart, but we share something in common." He hesitated, not knowing if he should bring it up. Emily looked confused. "My family almost lost my mother to breast cancer when I was twelve."

Emily breathed out, not having a clue what to say. His statement shook her from her own self-pity.

Gavin then did something impetuous. He simply felt the need to touch her, so he leaned over and wiped the tears from her cheek. Emily didn't move. "I remember what it felt like seeing her sick and in pain. The fear of not knowing what life would be like without her is something I'll never forget, but I know one day I'll have to face it. I also remember feeling exactly the way you did. I wanted it to end—for her to either just die so she could be at peace or get better. I couldn't see her like that anymore. I used to crucify myself for feeling like that. Emily, just know that what you felt—what *we* felt—is a very real, normal human reaction."

Sniffling, she glanced at him, noticing the sensual perfection of his face now touched with grief. Behind those blue eyes was the soul of a man who had gone through his own share of pain, and Emily couldn't decide what was worse: losing her mother to cancer or him living in fear that his mother's cancer could come back.

With concern edging his eyes, Gavin leaned forward and studied her face. A weak smile crept over his lips. "Now that I've managed to fuck up a pretty decent evening by making you cry, why don't we play a game to lighten the mood?"

Emily let out a gut-belly laugh due to the wide range of emotions flying through her. "You didn't fuck up the evening." She stood, wiped the last few tears from her eyes, and stretched her arms over her head. "I needed that, believe me."

He stood up with her and smiled. "Okay, good. So you'll play a game with me, then?"

She smirked, eyeing him suspiciously. "What type of game would Gavin Blake suggest we play? And no wisecracks either."

"Mmm, that's a tough request." He flashed an impish grin, and without another word, he slid the bottle-cap-filled terracotta pot to the middle of the balcony. He playfully commanded her to sit cross-legged on the floor ten feet away from it. With her expression showing her curiosity, she did as he instructed. He opened the doors to his bedroom and disappeared briefly. Emily sat for a few moments, wondering what he was doing. When he reappeared, he had a sweatshirt in his hand and a freezer bag holding additional bottle caps. Walking over, he tossed the sweatshirt on top of her head and chuckled. "You look cold. Put that on." He sat cross-legged on the floor next to her with their knees barely touching.

Smiling, she yanked the sweatshirt over her head and slipped it on. For a brief second, she tried to burn the smell of it into her memory. It reminded her of when they were in the elevator. She couldn't quite pin what the smell was—a mixture of cologne, body wash, and aftershave came to mind.

"So what's the name of this game we're about to play?"

Gavin looked into her green eyes. Under the light of the moon, they looked angelic. "It's kind of hard to pronounce," he slowly replied, staring at her lips as he tried to shake his fascination with her from his body.

"Try me."

He dropped his voice to a whisper and purposely hesitated between each word. "It's . . . called . . . 'Toss . . . the . . . Bottle . . . Cap . . . into . . . the . . . Pot' . . . right . . . there." He pointed to the pot.

Trying to ignore how sexy his voice sounded when he whispered, Emily playfully nudged his arm. "Wow, you're truly a wiseass, huh?"

"Yes, in every possible way." He handed her a couple of caps. "You go first."

Barely able to see, Emily crinkled her nose as she focused on the pot. She tossed the first one and missed by at least five feet. They both laughed. When it was Gavin's turn, he closed his eyes and sank it right in.

"I'm just assuming here, so I apologize if I'm wrong, but I'm thinking you've played this game more than once," she remarked.

"Why, I've only played it twice, of course."

Emily threw another and missed by only a foot. "Twice, my ass. There have to be at least five hundred bottle caps in that thing."

Gavin shot her a wry smile. "Close but no cigar. It's actually over a thousand."

"Drink much?"

He chuckled. "Many summers, many parties, many friends equals a huge bottle-cap collection."

She shook her head. "Speaking of collections, I noticed the many vehicles parked in your driveway. A motorcycle, a BMW, a Bentley, and I don't know the name of the other."

He smiled. "It's a Nissan GT-R."

"Yes, a Nissan GT-R," she laughed. "Boys and their many toys."

Rubbing at his chin, he gazed deep into her eyes for a second. "Don't we all have to fill voids in our lives with something?"

Taken aback, Emily searched his face, unsure how to answer. He flashed a smile and casually tossed another cap into the pot. She could tell there was more behind his question than she could possibly understand. The first thing that popped into her mind was an onion. Gavin Blake had many layers that needed to be peeled. Some were true to their form, but others were simply a cast-iron veneer she felt he wore around himself.

After several hit and missed thrown caps and much-needed laughter, Gavin looked at his watch and noticed it was past three in the morning. Standing up, he offered Emily his hand, and she accepted.

His voice slid through the air like the finest cashmere. "Even though our evening started off a little . . . sad, I had a great time with you, Emily," he stated softly, focusing his intense eyes on hers.

She felt the stroke of his heated gaze on her, warming her inside and out. She slowly pulled her hand from his and cupped the back of her neck as she stared up into his eyes. "I did, too, Gavin."

He smiled, walked away, and opened the French doors that led to his bedroom, but not before he turned to look at her one last time.

Nervously biting her lip, she made her way into the room where Dillon lay sleeping.

Still snoring.

As she closed the doors behind her, Emily leaned against them, panicky and once again breathless. Sliding her fingers down her neck, she tried to rationalize the visceral pull Gavin had over her, but she was too tired at that point to even begin to understand it.

Fireworks

A knock against the door and a low groan from Dillon registered somewhere in the back of Emily's sleeping brain. Forcing one eye open, she made out Trevor's head poking into the room.

"Fuck," Dillon shouted gruffly. "What the hell time is it?"

"It's time to get our fishing on," Trevor answered a little too cheerfully.

Dillon ran a palm over his face, shot Trevor a hard look, and lifted his head gingerly in Emily's direction. "Are you getting up?"

Peering at the clock through hooded lids, Emily saw it was only seven, so she curled the duvet tightly around her body. "No, I'm not," she moaned out and rolled over. "Just get in the shower, and I'll get up in a while."

Cursing about the early morning wake-up, Dillon slid out of bed and reluctantly padded to the bathroom.

Emily heard the door snap shut with Trevor's departure.

Sunlight filtering into the room threatened to wake her further as she nuzzled cozily into the crook of her arm. With a deep breath, her nose inhaled the heavenly, intoxicating, mind-numbing smell that was Gavin as she tried to fall back to sleep.

Gavin? What the . . . ?

Realizing she was still wearing his sweatshirt, she sat straight up. In half a heartbeat, she yanked it off, jumped from the bed, and haphazardly shoved it into a nightstand drawer.

With trembling fingers, she rubbed her eyes and tried to rid her mind of what Dillon's reaction would've been had he caught her packaged neatly in his friend's sweatshirt. After a few minutes, the unexpected anxiety ebbed, and with a sigh, she settled into the bed, but she couldn't fall back asleep.

Still groaning in agonized distress, Dillon came out of the bathroom. Emily saw he looked tired, pale, and haggard. After she tried to soothe him with a massage, she dropped a kiss on his cheek and jumped in the shower, too. When she reemerged, she found him sprawled out on the bed in a T-shirt and cargo shorts with the crease of his elbow shading his eyes.

"What are your plans while I'm fishing?" he asked, his voice low and garbled.

"I'm going to hang with Liv and Tina until they leave," she replied, plugging her hair dryer in. "They're heading back to the city later to spend the day at Tina's family's house."

Grumbling, he stood on shaky legs and sauntered out of the room. By the time Emily treaded downstairs, it was a quarter past eight. Dillon sat at the kitchen island with his head hidden between his folded arms as he mumbled to himself.

Gavin smiled at Emily over his newspaper. As it did every time she walked into a room, his whole body went on alert. He felt his blood begin to pump faster as she made her way to the kitchen island. The silky white material of her sundress gliding along her thighs and contrasting against her perfectly olive-toned skin made him nearly speechless.

Gavin cleared his throat. "He's making promises of never allowing whiskey into his system again if the drinking gods help him get through the day." He laughed and sipped his coffee. "He was never one to handle his liquor that well."

Although muffled from his arms, the words were clear and to the point. "Fuck off, Gavin," Dillon hissed.

Gavin chuckled and looked over to Emily. "Want some coffee?"

"Yeah, that sounds awesome. Thank you." She sat next to Dillon.

"You're very welcome." Gavin stood up, pulled a mug from a cabinet, poured some coffee in it, and made his way to the refrigerator. Peering at Emily over his shoulder, his smile was soft and curled with knowledge. "Just a guess, of course, but you look like a girl who takes cream and sugar in your coffee."

Her mouth fell open and then snapped shut. Shaking her head, she smiled at him. Gavin quirked a mischievous brow and walked back over with the mug. As she reached for it, he slipped something into her hand. Her eyes flicked over to where Dillon was still hiding from the light of day. Gavin set the coffee in front of her and took his seat.

Opening her hand, Emily glanced at what she held—a bottle cap. Her gaze slid over to Gavin casually sipping his coffee, newspaper in hand, with a faint smile on his lips. She shook her head and smiled back.

Dillon straightened and quickly turned around at the sound of the doorbell. He groaned as Gavin made his way over to answer it. When he opened the door, Emily watched him greet two men who appeared to be his relatives. The younger of the two was good looking with the same sharp-chiseled features and hair color but had a body slightly heavier than Gavin's. The senior, however, was Gavin's twin—fast-forward twenty years—with a hint of silver sprinkled throughout his hair. His wide grin flashed with practiced ease as they all walked into the kitchen.

Chuckling, the older man's brows arched over his blue eyes as he patted Dillon's back. "You're looking a little rough around the edges, son."

"Good morning, Mr. Blake." Dillon stood up to shake his hand. "Yeah, I drank a little too much last night."

"Well, prepare to drink a little more today, youngling," he quipped, holding up a bottle of Grand Marnier and a couple of fishing poles.

Shaking his head with a smile, Dillon looked at Gavin. "Your old man's going to kill me today with the drinking, isn't he?"

"I'm pretty sure that isn't his intention." Gavin settled back into his seat. "Right, Pop?"

"Absolutely!" He glanced in Emily's direction, a charming grin touching his lips. "So who do we have here?"

Dillon curled his arm around her waist. "This is my girlfriend, Emily. Emily, this is Gavin's brother, Colton, and his father, Chad."

"It's very nice to meet you both." She smiled and shook their hands.

"Emily, do you have any sisters for my brother?" Colton motioned with his thumb in Gavin's direction. Gavin rolled his eyes and downed the last of his coffee. "My mother wants him married off soon."

"Unfortunately, the only one I have is married," Emily laughed.

Colton tossed his arm around Gavin's neck. "Oh well, little man, the search shall continue." With his arms crossed, Gavin sighed and once again rolled his eyes at his brother's nonmission of finding him a woman.

Eventually, Trevor, Joe, and Chris made their way downstairs to join the group. "What the hell do you have on?" Gavin questioned, eyeing Trevor's attire.

Wearing his finest fishing hat and vest scattered with hooks and little plastic worms, Trevor sniffed haughtily. "Whatever, dude." He poured some coffee into a Styrofoam cup and turned back to Gavin. "At least I get on the damn boat." Each of the men—except Gavin—broke out into a riot of laughter. Gavin just shook his head with an amused grin and let the partial insult slide. Trevor slapped his back. "Is *the* Gavin Blake speechless?"

Standing up to refill his coffee, Gavin smiled. "Go ahead, lay it on me, assholes. But in my defense, it comes from my mother's side of the family."

Emily drew up a confused brow. "You don't go on boats?"

Gavin's smile was slow, making his blue eyes sparkle. "Technically, I can, but not when the water's choppy like this morning." He took a sip of his coffee. "I get slightly seasick."

Dillon stood up, walked over to him, and slapped him on his shoulder. "Slightly? You wind up praying to the sea gods to get you through the trip without puking."

Shaking his head, Gavin tossed his boat keys to his father. "Okay, each and every single one of you needs to get the hell out of my house now. And that's including you, too, Pop," he quickly added.

Chuckling, Chad patted his son on his back. The conversation and laughter flowed while the men took a few more minutes preparing for a day out on the water. After making sure they had enough ice, food, liquor, and night crawlers to last until the afternoon, they were good to go. Emily followed Dillon to the door to kiss him good-bye and let him know to take it easy on the drinking. She watched the group make their way into the dewy morning air and down to the boat.

After closing the door, Emily turned and found Gavin sitting at the island, coffee in one hand and his eyes intent on his morning paper. She went to walk upstairs, figuring it was a good time to wake Olivia and Tina, but before she could, Gavin called out and asked her to sit with him.

As she moved toward him, she gave herself a fierce mental talk. She'd enjoyed hanging out with him a little too much last night, and because of that, she had developed more than just a physical attraction. Tingles of something she had never experienced raced through her, and a strange anxiety caused by his close proximity permeated her bones—more so than before.

And that . . . that wasn't good. As she sat next to him, Emily tried to ignore the way his just-fucked-looking black hair went in every direction. It made him look . . . well . . . even hotter.

Tossing a hand through that just-fucked-looking hair, he placed the newspaper down and smiled. "I wanted to give you fair warning that within a few hours, the house will become a little . . . chaotic."

"Oh, how so?" she asked, fidgeting with the hem of her dress. "I thought your guests wouldn't be here until after three."

Gavin's eyes flicked down to her thighs and then back to her face. He tried to swallow. "Well, the caterers and the company that sets up the tents will be here soon. If you like, we can go down by the beach or get in the pool together." Emily shifted nervously, her gaze holding steady on his. "I mean, *you* . . . you can go down by the beach or in the pool," he corrected quickly. *Jesus Christ.* He slowly dragged his teeth over his bottom lip.

She watched his lips a little too intently and pushed her seat away from the counter to stand up. "Yeah, I'll see." She walked over to the stairs. "I'm just going to . . . uh . . . go wake up Olivia and Tina now."

He nodded, and she trotted up the stairs.

Emily gave a quick knock at the door, and Olivia yelled for her to come in. When she entered, both women were already getting ready to leave.

"Why are you packing now?" Emily asked. "I thought you two weren't leaving until after three."

Olivia tossed the last of her items into her backpack. "Tina's mom is sick, so she called asking if we could get out there earlier to help cook." She stretched. "Ugh, I'm really not looking forward to this drive back either."

Emily pressed her lips into a tight line and sank down onto the bed. Sighing, she leaned against a pillow, noticeably flustered.

Olivia looked at her. "Why do you look so freaked out about us leaving? You knew I wasn't staying the entire time."

"Because Gavin didn't go fishing with everyone else, and I'll be stuck here alone—with him."

"That's right—the whole seasick thing. I forgot." A slow grin slid across Olivia's mouth. "Why would you be upset about being here alone with him? I say it's the perfect opportunity to get a little taste of something . . . yummy."

"Damn it, Olivia!" Emily spat. "I'm not kidding anymore! Stop with your bullshit!"

Olivia stood aghast, like a deer in headlights, as Emily pushed to her feet and tore past her. Stalking down the hallway, Emily entered her room, tossed her suitcase on the bed, and started packing. Olivia cautiously entered the room. "What the hell are you doing, Em?"

"I'm leaving with you guys," she hastily answered. "I'm not staying here alone with him."

Olivia walked over and grabbed her by the shoulders.

"Friend, calm the fuck down, okay?" Emily pulled away and continued to pack. "Em, his mother, sister-in-law, niece, and nephew should be here soon. It's not just going to be the two of you."

Emily abruptly stopped packing. She flopped onto the bed and placed her fingers on her temples in an attempt to relax her racing thoughts.

Olivia sat next to her. "What's going through your mind?"

Emily shook her head, her voice barely a whisper. "I hate that I actually like the way he stares at me, Liv. I hate the way I can't stop myself from staring back. I hate that he's Dillon's friend and that we're all here together." She looked into Olivia's eyes and paused a moment. "And I hate that I have any of these thoughts to begin with. I owe so much to Dillon. I shouldn't be thinking anything about his friend."

Placing her hand on Emily's shoulder, Olivia's face softened. "First, you need to stop feeling like you're completely indebted to Dumbass. He did what any good boyfriend would've done. Nothing special." Emily closed her eyes and swallowed, feeling that Dillon had gone beyond her expectations. However, she wouldn't argue the issue. "But really, Gavin's family will be here soon. Also, how would you explain to Dick that you just left out of nowhere?"

Emily contemplated her question. She was right. If she used the playing-sick card, Dillon would miss a great day because he'd drive back to the city to be with her. Emily nodded. Drawing in a much-needed deep breath, she rose to her feet and pulled a book from her belongings. "Well, I'm just going to stay in here and read until I hear them arrive."

Olivia smiled and stood. "Okay, you do what you have to do, then." She walked over to the door after hugging Emily. "I love you."

Emily curled up on the bed, flipped open the book, and tried to relax. "I love you, too, Liv." And that's exactly what Emily did. She read that book. Hell, she finished it and started reading it again, but eventually dozed off during her second attempt to keep her mind off the threat behind the door. It was just past noon when she heard car doors closing. Through a corner window, she peered down and saw two women walking toward the home with two young children following them.

Recovering from her earlier panic, Emily made her way downstairs. Gavin was correct. The house was buzzing with caterers dressed in black and white, preparing a smorgasbord of food. When she couldn't find him inside among the frenzied scene, she strolled out to the backyard. Under a dozen large, white tents, workers draped red, white, and blue linens onto tables while hollering song requests to a DJ setting up in the corner. Huge, festive centerpieces consisting of silver stars anchored a patriotic array of balloons at each table.

Emily scanned the crowd and locked eyes with Gavin from across the yard. He immediately smiled and motioned for her to join him. As she approached, he looked concerned and leaned into her ear. "Are you all right?" he whispered. "Olivia said you didn't feel well when she left."

"Yeah, I felt a little ill earlier, but I'm better now."

He cocked a disbelieving brow. "Are you sure?" With an answering smile, she nodded. "Well, let me know if you need anything, okay?"

"I will, thank you."

"Not a problem." He smiled and turned toward one of the women Emily saw pull up to the house. "Mom, I'd like to introduce you to Dillon's girlfriend, Emily. Emily, this is my mother, Lillian."

"It's very nice to meet you, Mrs. Blake." Emily offered to

shake her hand but felt pleasantly surprised when the woman leaned in to hug her.

"Call me Lillian," she exclaimed, her large green eyes twinkling when she released her hold on Emily. "'Mrs. Blake' makes me feel old, and I'm far from it."

Emily felt the vibrant warmth pouring from her demeanor. "All right, it's very nice to meet you, Lillian."

"Atta girl."

Emily smiled and studied her striking features. She would've never guessed Lillian had two older children or that she was ever sick, with cancer no less. Her chestnut hair, twisted up in a flattering style, glistened against the sun. Her sweeping cheekbones and flawlessly golden skin looked ageless.

"My sister-in-law, Melanie, is around here somewhere," Gavin stated as his gaze roamed the backyard. Before he could ask his mother where she was, from out of nowhere, his niece and nephew jumped on his back. Playfully rolling to the ground with them, Gavin looked up to Emily and laughed. "Well, here's her offspring."

"Uncle Gaffin! Stop tickling me!" the little girl squealed, her golden locks spilling over her face as she thrashed her head from side to side under his comical assault.

"I help you, Teesa!" the little boy cried out. Like a certified hero saving a damsel in distress, he began his own tickling attack on Gavin.

Emily and Lillian laughed and watched the three of them roll around. Ultimately, the two children won the tickling battle by ganging up on their uncle. Gavin succumbed to the fact that he was outnumbered and pleaded for help as he laughed.

Standing up, Gavin wiped tiny blades of grass from his swimming trunks and looked at Emily. "These two little nuts are my niece and nephew, Teresa and Timothy." He quickly lunged at them as though he would restart the tickling match. They both jumped back, giggling. Gavin hunched over and slung an arm around their shoulders. "This is Molly . . . I mean, Emily." Emily shook her head, feeling a small flush spread across her cheeks. "You two better be nice to her. I don't think she feels like getting attacked today by either one of you."

The little girl looked up at Emily and tugged on her sundress. "I like your dress, Emm-mi-me."

Emily kneeled down and smiled at the little freckle-faced beauty. "Well, I really like your dress, too, Teresa."

"Did you haf a dress like dis when you was three?"

"Not as pretty as the one you're wearing." Teresa threw her arms around Emily's neck, almost knocking her off balance. Emily laughed and hugged the child back.

Like a mini-gentleman, Timothy offered his hand. "Are you Uncle Gaffin's girfend?"

Emily smiled up to Gavin and then looked at the little boy as she shook his hand. "No, but I'm his friend's girlfriend."

"We're twins," Timothy said with a proud smile.

"I thought you were." Emily smiled. "Well, you two are the cutest little twins I've ever met."

"Will you come swimmy with us, Emm-mi-me?" Timothy asked, his hazel eyes sparkling as he wiped a sweaty strand of blond hair away from his forehead.

"Hmm." The little boy smiled and eagerly awaited her answer. She gave his nose a quick, gentle pinch. "I think I will. Just let me go inside to put on my bathing suit, and I'll be right back." Both children jumped up and down, clapping in obvious delight.

Emily made her way through the throng of workers and headed upstairs to slip into her bathing suit. Taking careful measures not to piss off Dillon, she threw on a scarlet-and-gray

Ohio State University T-shirt over her bikini. After removing her makeup, she breezed back outside.

The two children—already in the pool with Gavin—gleefully splashed at him as he made a fine attempt at acting like a shark. Submerging, he tented his hands over his head and plunged toward them.

"Emm-mi-me is here!" Teresa hooted out.

Gavin looked at Emily and slicked his soaked hair away from his face. "Like my *Jaws* impersonation?"

"It was decent," she replied flatly as she got into the water. "But I'm pretty sure I could do a better one."

He smirked and cocked an incredulous brow. "Oh, you think so?"

"No," she smiled. "Just kidding."

He laughed and reached for a large, multicolored beach ball. "Okay, so how's about a friendly game of pool volleyball?" He flashed a crooked grin. "Girls against boys, of course."

Emily raised her chin in playful defiance. "Bring it, Blake."

With both teams positioned on either side of the net, the game began. The kids screeched into a loud burst of laughter when Emily jumped up, spiked the ball onto Gavin's head, and knocked his sunglasses clear off his face. After Gavin resurfaced from retrieving the sunken shades, his eyes trained on Emily. He smiled a promise of retaliation. She gave a quick high five to Teresa and shot Gavin a smirk, quite pleased with herself and the point gained for the girls.

Tossing his arm around Timothy's shoulder, Gavin whispered something. He chucked his sunglasses onto a beach chair and eyed Emily with a devious smile. She knew he was up to no good. She shook her head and laughed. Before she could warn Teresa of her uncle's mischievous intentions, a huge wave splashed into her face—courtesy of Gavin.

Emily gasped and spit water. She shot Gavin a smirk and splashed him back. With all his little might, Timothy tossed the beach ball over the net, scoring a wicked point for the boys. Startled by the sudden attack, Teresa began to cry out in hysterics. Without hesitation, Gavin swam over and scooped her up.

Perched on the pool stairs, Gavin cradled her. "Teresa, Uncle Gavin's sorry, honey. I didn't mean to scare you."

"Uncle Gaffin, you hurt Emm-mi-me," she sniffed.

"No, Teresa, he didn't hurt me." Emily held out her arms, coaxing her to sit by her. Teresa sat in Emily's lap. "He just splashed me, that's all."

Teresa sniffed again. "Uncle Gaffin is a meanie; you should hit him."

Gavin playfully frowned as his eyes widened. "You think she should hit me?" Teresa giggled and nodded. Gavin looked at Emily and shrugged, pointing to his arm. "I guess Colton and Melanie are raising some hostile children. Take your best shot, doll." Smiling, Emily acted as though she hit him, and Gavin howled out in his best wounded voice. Teresa giggled again, quite satisfied by the blow.

"Mom said you made my daughter cry, Gavin?"

Gavin turned around and smiled. "Hey, Mel. Yeah, I scared her a little, but she's okay now. Aren't ya, squirt?" He tickled Teresa's toes.

She squeaked and kicked her feet away from him. "Uncle Gaffin's girfend hit him for me."

With a sweep of her arm, Melanie motioned to Timothy to get out of the pool. She tossed her long blonde hair over her shoulder, quirked a curious brow, and smiled in Gavin's direction.

"She's not my girlfriend," Gavin noted, standing up. "She's

Dillon's girlfriend. Emily, this is my wonderful sister-in-law, Melanie."

Holding Teresa's hand, Emily rose to her feet and smiled. "It's nice to meet you."

"The pleasure's all mine," she said, returning the smile.

"Your children are adorable."

"Thank you, but I bet you'd beg to differ when they're screaming and fighting with each other over a box or something crazy like that." Emily laughed. Melanie turned to Gavin, an impish grin touching her mouth. The threat in his eyes told her not to go there—but she would. She turned back to Emily. "Emily, do you have any available sisters or friends Gavin might be interested in dating?"

Emily looked at Gavin. "Ongoing family thing?"

Crossing his arms, Gavin nodded. "Bingo."

Smiling, Emily looked at Melanie. "I do have a sister, but she's married already. I can call a few friends, though."

"Perfect," Melanie replied, placing her hand on Gavin's arm. Teresa tugged at Melanie's leg as she rubbed her sleepy eyes. Melanie picked her up. "Emily, make sure to call them soon. My brother-in-law's getting too old to still be single." She took off in a pretty fast pace toward the back door.

Sighing, Gavin smiled and handed Emily a towel. "She's a . . . difficult one, my sister-in-law."

"She seems nice, though." Emily accepted the towel as she tried to drag her gaze away from his tattoo, wet and glistening in the sunlight. Blowing out a breath, she swallowed hard and refocused her eyes on his face. "I find it funny that everyone's trying to get you hooked up with someone."

"Yeah, tell me about it. They have this odd thing about me being single right now."

As Emily was about to ask him if he really wanted her to

call some friends for him, Dillon snaked his arms around her waist from behind and kissed her neck. Surprised, she jumped and squealed. The rest of the anglers strolled into the backyard looking sunburned, tired, and just a tad intoxicated. After some light conversation regarding the amount of fish each man caught and a little more teasing of Gavin for not being able to attend, the group dispersed to take showers.

"So you went swimming, I see," Dillon remarked, peeling the shirt from his body as he and Emily entered their room. Closing the door, he shed the rest of his clothing and tossed it into a pile.

"Very good observation," Emily replied, exhausted from the heat.

Dillon walked into the bathroom, turned on the shower, and got in. "I hope you kept the body that belongs to me covered up around my friend."

Emily rolled her eyes and searched her bag for a particular red gauzy sundress she'd brought along. Her mother had purchased it for her on their last trip to see her sister in California. She smiled when she found it and held it up against her body as she looked into the mirror.

"You're not answering me, Emily. Did you cover yourself up?"

Walking into the bathroom, she let out a frustrated sigh. "Dillon, what do you see right now?" She motioned her hand over her body, her voice a touch irritated. She clearly wasn't baring too much skin.

"What do I see right now? I see my hot girlfriend's ass hanging out from beneath her college T-shirt. So why don't you get in the shower and give your man what he needs?"

"You think I'm having sex with you right now?" she asked, her eyes bulging. "There's a shitload of people downstairs."

"Get in the shower, Emily," he commanded.

"What the hell's wrong with you, Dillon? I said no."

"Come on, Em. It's just hard for me to see you looking like that and not want to fuck around," he calmly replied as he got out of the shower. He walked over to where she leaned against the vanity. "I couldn't stop thinking about you while I was gone."

Pressing his body against hers, he quickly dipped his hand into her bikini bottom, making sure to slide his fingers inside her. A faint moan escaped her lips as she tried to push him away.

"See, you like that." His voice notched down huskily as he grazed his lips over hers. Sliding his fingers in and out, he used his other hand to glide her bikini bottom down past her thighs. "This pussy's mine. No one else's, Emily. Mine," he groaned against her cheek.

As she pushed him away again, a knock came at the bedroom door. Shooting Emily a hard glare, Dillon yanked a towel from the rack, tossed it around his waist, and leisurely strolled over to answer it. It was Trevor, letting him know a potential client who was eager to speak with him regarding a commodities plan was downstairs. Within five minutes, Dillon was dressed and out the door to go talk business. Emily was left alone, wondering what the man—whom she desperately loved—was really morphing into.

By the time Emily calmed her nerves, showered, and got ready, it was a quarter past seven, and the party was in full swing. True to Dillon's words, there had to be at least 150 people scattered throughout the property. She wove through the crowd of unrecognizable faces as she searched for him. When she couldn't find him, she sat at one of the bars set up on the patio.

After downing a shot of tequila, a slight pang of guilt for not giving Dillon the little he had asked for hit the pit of her stomach. He'd emotionally taken care of her through the most difficult time in her life, constantly complimented her—whether about her physical or educational attributes—and made her want for nothing financially. Sex in someone's home—crowded or not—shouldn't have been an issue in her mind.

Before her shortcomings in their relationship cut deeper into her heart, Emily caught a glimpse of Gavin from across the pool, talking with a group of women. She noticed as he made conversation with them, he used his hands in intimate ways—a slight touch on the nape of the neck to get their attention, a casual brush on the arm as they spoke, or a light press against the small of the back when he laughed—and the women fell all over themselves when he did. Emily swallowed hard when he glanced in her direction, essentially catching her staring. She watched him excuse himself from the eager wannabe-future-Mrs.-Gavin-Blake group, and make his way toward her.

Casually dressed in a white linen shirt and khaki shorts, he approached her with a smile and leaned against the bar. "I find it impossible that a woman as beautiful as you is sitting here alone."

Without missing a beat, Emily shook her head. "You're truly an expert at knowing what to say and do to women."

He cocked a smug brow and smiled. "I don't know about that. However, I *am* an expert at making the world's most delectable . . . ham sandwiches." He laughed and so did Emily. Holding her gaze, he took a long pull from his beer. "But, really, where's the man who should be sitting by your side at this very moment?"

She surveyed the crowd again. "He's around here somewhere."

As Gavin's eyes roamed his guests in an attempt to locate Dillon, he spotted Monica Lemay. She was making her way over to him and Emily, a malicious grin smearing across her face. He hastily excused himself, letting Emily know he'd be right back.

Monica rolled her eyes as Gavin approached. "Have you come to give me a warning as well?" She pushed up on her tiptoes and nipped on his earlobe. He recoiled, pulling away from her. "Because there's no need. I've already been *thoroughly* warned by Dillon to act as if I don't know him and to stay away from his little girlfriend over there, too."

Gavin glared at her, angling his head to the side, his eyes hard. "Oh, have you? Then why did it just appear as though you were going to say something to her?"

"Can a girl not get a drink from the bar?" she asked, affecting a venomous sneer.

"Go to one of the other bars, Monica." He leaned down to her ear, lowering his voice to an icy whisper. "You're a fucking snake. Don't think I can't see through you." He stepped back. "You stay the fuck away from her. Do you understand me?" She tossed her blonde hair over her shoulder and crossed her arms as she looked away. "Monica, look me in the eyes and tell me if you see a man who's easily deterred from ripping your whole world to shreds."

She drew up a brow, her hazel eyes wide. "What the fuck is that supposed to mean, Gavin?"

"It means that Blake Industries holds more than seventy-five percent of your father's company's stocks. I can sell off every single one of them tomorrow with a quick phone call." He leaned in closer, and she stepped back. "Wall Street will have a field day, and by tomorrow night, you and your family will be scrounging for scraps in the alleys of Harlem."

She sucked in an indignant breath. "You wouldn't!"

"Fucking try me." He turned away and ran smack into Colton.

"Whoa, little man, you look furious."

Gavin glanced over to where Emily remained seated at the bar. "I'm fine. What's up?"

"Mom needs you in the kitchen," he said, raking his hand through his hair. "I don't know—something about someone who isn't on the authorized list down by the gates trying to get onto the property."

Emily nodded in Gavin's direction when she caught his gaze from across the pool. He held up a finger to her as though letting her know he would be right back. She watched him quickly vanish through the crowd, making his way into the house. She recognized the woman he was speaking with from the bar a few days before. She wondered why he'd invited his ex to the party and why she'd showed up. They obviously still had ongoing issues.

As Emily ordered a drink, a tall muscular man around her age approached, the smell of booze seeping clear out of his pores.

Smoothing a piece of his brown hair away from his forehead, he gave her a crooked smile. "Pretty cool party, right?"

Emily glanced at him as she accepted her beer from the bartender. "Yes, it is."

"So, are you here with anyone, or am I just the fucking luckiest guy at this party to have stumbled upon a hot-looking single girl?"

That's a killer pick-up line, asshole, she thought. "Sorry, I'm here with someone."

He let out a superior huff. "Who? I know everyone here. I just may have to give him a beat down."

This is getting better by the minute. "Dillon Parker."

The man furrowed his brows. "You're not with Dillon Parker. He's still with Monica Lemay." He took a large swallow of his drink. "At least I thought he was."

Now you have my attention, jerkoff. "Who's Monica Lemay?"

"Do you know Gavin?" Emily quickly nodded. "She's the piece of blonde prime meat he was just talking with by the pool."

This moron is definitely drunk. "No, you must be confused. The woman Gavin was just speaking with is *his* ex-girlfriend—not Dillon's."

The man adamantly shook his head. "Gavin's never dated Monica. We grew up together; he can't stand her." He downed another shot before continuing. "I've spent many Fourth of July parties at this house." He pointed across the yard. "And I've witnessed Dillon and Monica stumble out of that very guesthouse many mornings after, barely dressed. They definitely fucked."

As she stood up, dazed by what he had just revealed, Emily tried to swallow. Her throat felt as if razor-sharp blades were sliding into her esophagus.

"Hey, so, you wanna give me your number or what?"

Without a backward glance, Emily pushed through the crowd. Their screeching voices, laughter, and jovial faces were a distant blur, a complete fuzz in her mind. A thin sheen of sweat beaded over her flesh as panic set in. She made her way toward the beckoning glow of the house. Walking past the kitchen, she spotted Gavin talking with his mother. He looked in her direction as she stormed into the living room.

When Emily rounded the corner to the hall, air whooshed from her lungs and her heart imploded upon seeing Dillon with

Monica. The organ suffered another devastating blow when she saw Monica snake her arms around Dillon's neck, drawing him into her, and then it happened—the kiss. Unable to fully comprehend what was going on, Emily cupped her hand over her mouth as tears welled in her eyes. Incapable of witnessing their exchange any further, she spun around and collided with Gavin's chest. He caught her by the arms, flicking his eyes down to her face and then over her shoulder. They narrowed on Dillon and Monica.

"I . . . I . . . have to leave," Emily breathed, her voice bleeding with pain. "Please. Call me a cab." She rushed to the front of the house and out the door.

Digging in his pocket for his keys, Gavin followed her. When he emerged, he found her trying to catch her breath, sitting on the stoop with her head cradled between her legs. He walked over and knelt beside her. Placing his hand under her chin, he brought her face up to meet his. "Let me take you," he whispered.

She shook her head vehemently. "No, your . . . your party . . ." She wiped the flowing tears from her eyes. "You can't just leave. Please call me a cab or have your driver take me back."

With his hand still under her chin, he gazed into her eyes. "My driver isn't here right now, and I'm not sending you back to the city in a cab. I'm not worried about the party; just let me take you back."

Without saying a word, Emily swallowed, stood up, and walked toward his driveway. He directed her over to his BMW and opened the door for her. She settled into the seat and watched as he made his way around the car, her nerves still reeling.

The two-and-a-half-hour drive back to Manhattan was quiet without a word spoken. As the sky melted into hues of orange, purple, and pink with the setting sun, Gavin searched his mind for something to say, knowing he'd played a role in Emily believing Monica was his girlfriend. Her grief was so tangible it nauseated him. Glancing at her, he knew he had to explain. When he pulled into a parking spot in front of her building, he closed his eyes for a beat and took a breath. "I'm sorry I lied to you," he whispered.

Emily slowly pulled her gaze from the passenger window. "You think I'm mad at *you*?" Her tone was as low as his, but the shock of his apology hung in her voice.

"How can you not be? I lied to cover for him. Although I didn't know he was still . . ." He drew in a deep breath and paused. Emily knew what he didn't want to say. "I knew who she was; that's why I pulled her outside. I didn't want her to . . . hurt you, Emily. I'm so sorry."

She stared into his unblinking blue eyes. "You don't know me from a hole in the wall, Gavin." She swiped tears away from her cheeks. "It wasn't your responsibility to tell me the truth; it was his. So please don't feel the need to apologize." Climbing out of the car, Emily stopped as her gaze slid up to the bloodred and vibrant blue colors exploding like shooting stars in the sky. Pedestrians on the sidewalks hooted out, clapping at the displays of fireworks going off throughout the city. Gavin shut off the engine, flipped on his hazard lights, and followed her to the entrance of her building.

She abruptly came to a halt, tossing her hands through her hair as she cried again. "I don't even have my keys. My purse and my bag are still at your house."

Noticing Emily's distress, the door attendant walked over to her with concern. Gavin explained the situation. Within ten minutes, management—knowing she was indeed a resident—gave her a new set of keys.

Wanting to make sure she got in okay, Gavin walked her to her door. He watched her tremble, trying to slide the key into the lock. He placed his hand on hers in an effort to calm her down. He took the key and unlocked the door. Standing in the threshold, he watched her nervously pace back and forth across her apartment. When Emily walked back over to him, Gavin moved toward her. The loud snap of the door closing echoed throughout the apartment.

"Thank you for taking me home," she said, her voice soft.

Staring at her, his voice filled with concern. "Are you sure you're going to be all right?" Emily averted her glassy gaze to the floor. Gavin dipped his head, forcing her to look at him. His blue eyes flicked down to her lips, and Emily could see the thoughts moving behind them. She knew. As her breath hitched in her throat, her heart rate kicked up, fluttering to soaring heights, he tenderly cupped her cheek. She gently placed her hand over his, leaning into it and soaking in its warmth.

"Emily," he whispered, laying his forehead against hers as he closed his eyes. When he opened his eyes, she was gazing into them. Their quickened breaths mingled, heated, warm, and so close now. The energy flowing soundlessly around them was suffocating. He moved closer, his arm coming around the small of her back, pulling her into the heat of his body. Gavin leaned down to kiss her—his own heart slamming in his chest—but neither his body nor his mind allowed another minute to pass without fulfilling his need. Emily parted her lips to protest, but it was a moan that filtered through them as his mouth covered hers, his tongue beginning its gentle onslaught against her lips. Her mouth moved beneath his, drawing in his delicious taste. She felt herself sinking into the pleasure of the kiss as his touch destroyed her resolve and shattered her last bit of self-control.

Despite the confusion weaving through her mind, her body was making the decision for her.

No. Questions. Asked.

As Gavin kissed her, he tasted the cherry sweetness of her lips, and he drank it in as if it was the finest of red wines. Her hands moved up his arms to the back of his neck, leaving a trail of fire against his skin. A thick shiver of pleasure rebounded around him, racing through his blood from her fingers twining in his hair. A groan rumbled in his throat at the feel of her soft breasts against his chest. The scent of her skin and the feel of her curved body fitting perfectly in his arms sent him to a place he'd never known existed. His fingers explored her wavy hair as their kiss deepened; it felt exactly how he figured it would, like pure fucking silk. Emily grabbed handfuls of his shirt as he walked her backward, pressed her against the wall, and swept his tongue through her mouth. Gavin kissed her as if he'd done it a thousand times, as if she belonged to him. He kissed her the way he'd imagined he would from the moment he saw her—from the moment he knew he needed her.

"You're so beautiful," he groaned. His lips moved over her jaw as his hands smoothed down her waist. "I want you more than I've ever wanted anything before in my fucking life."

Emily nearly melted at his words. Her body pressed against his, straining for more, wanting more. Her head fell back as his mouth slid to her neck, tracing the slope of her collarbone and pressing kisses against her flesh. When he slipped his hand under the hem of her dress and caressed her hip, Emily's heart nearly stopped. Goose bumps popped over her arms as she wrapped her leg around his waist, his hand cradling the back of her head and the other holding tight to her thigh. Waves of heat cascaded over her trembling body. Each touch was a destructive whisper against her skin. The languid sweeping of his tongue trailed back to her mouth. Sucking her lower lip, he swallowed her moans of pleasure as he held her closer. Her senses blanketed themselves in Gavin's smell, touch, taste, and glorious groans.

Gavin Blake . . . Dillon's friend, someone he had known and become close with. If Dillon found out—despite his wrongdoings—he would surely lose it. Suddenly, Emily was off balance, uncertain what she was doing. Shimmering images of Dillon and their life together invaded her mind. This was bad, and she knew it. Two wrongs never computed to a right in her head—ever. A wave of guilt mixed with anger at Dillon and herself washed over her. Although her body fought against it—and fought against it hard—she had to stop. "We . . . I can't . . . Gavin," she finally breathed, barely forcing the words past her lips.

Pulling back, his blue eyes dark and wavering with lust, Gavin searched her face. Her lips were swollen from their kiss, and her breathing was as ragged as his. Tears filled her eyes, yet he saw passion as well. His heart broke a thousand times over from the look on her face. He didn't want to hurt her. He nodded slowly as his fingertips slid over her flushed cheeks before his hands dropped to his sides, taking her warmth with them.

"I'm sorry," she whispered, not meeting his eyes.

"No, Emily, I—"

"Please, Gavin, just leave. I need you to leave," she sniffed, unable to look at his face.

The air prickled uneasily between them for a long moment. Gavin desperately tried to get his tongue unglued from the roof of his mouth to say something—anything—that would fix the situation, but he couldn't. The words—the right words—didn't exist in his mind.

And this he knew.

Running a nervous hand through his hair, he turned away, reached for the door, and reluctantly made his way out.

Emily trembled as she hunched over in an attempt to catch her breath. She closed her eyes, desperately trying to block out the guilt, push it away, and purge it from her system. Her complexion was drained of all color. Her eyes were bloodshot and puffy from crying. Her stomach curled around itself in disgust—not only from what she had just done, but also because, somewhere in the back of her mind, she knew it felt right. God, it felt so right kissing him, touching him, and letting him touch her. She buried her face in her hands and cried as fresh waves of guilt crashed through every limb in her body.

Feeling mentally drained, she collapsed onto the couch, trying to regain her composure as she wiped the tears from her face. A part of her felt as though it was dying as vivid pictures of Dillon kissing Monica skirted through her head. Staring at the ceiling, Emily wondered if somehow she had deluded herself into thinking Dillon wasn't cheating on her. Her instincts had been warning her for the past several weeks, but she'd refused to listen to the sirens going off.

A sharp knock at the door roused her from the nightmare she had hoped she was awakening from. Before she could answer, the door swung open. Dillon stood in the hall with her bags. Swallowing down the rising bile in her throat, she felt the pulse in her stomach when she shot up from the couch. Closing the door behind him, his eyes met and locked with hers from across the room.

"What are you doing here?" she asked, glaring at him. "I want you to leave."

"You have to let me explain."

"Let you explain? You kissed her!" she scoffed.

"She kissed me," he corrected.

"Bullshit! I want you out!" She pointed toward the door.

"You're going to let me explain." He walked across the room, bridging the distance between them.

"You kissed her," she cried, stabbing her finger into his chest. "I saw it with my own eyes!"

He grabbed her wrist and moved closer. "What you saw was her leaning in to kiss me. You didn't see me push her away, Emily." His voice was low and steady.

"And I'm supposed to believe that?" she nearly screamed. "You lied to me about her being Gavin's girlfriend!"

She made a beeline toward the kitchen, but he grabbed her shoulders. "I didn't tell you about her that night because I didn't want you feeling uncomfortable while she was there." She immediately jerked back and gaped at him. "I'm not kidding, Emily. I didn't want you to know she was someone I used to date. I knew if you found out, you'd want to leave. I figured it was no big deal."

She moved back, almost stumbling.

"Baby, I'm not lying," he continued. "She's fucking obsessed with me. You think I would do that with her out in the open, knowing you were there?" Emily glared at him, her mouth wide open. He raked his hands through his hair. "I didn't mean it like that. I was coming out of the bathroom, and she asked if she could talk to me for a minute. I agreed, and before I knew it, she'd pulled me into her and kissed me. That's what you saw, babe. I swear to fucking God I pushed her away. You must've turned around before I did."

Shaking her head, Emily's hand rushed to her mouth as she cried. Hurt ricocheted through her heart—the pain literally slammed through her body. Could she have made an assumption too soon from the few seconds of their kiss that she saw? She had never felt so confused.

"I even warned her when she got to the party to stay away from me and you," he whispered, cautiously stepping closer and bringing his hand up to caress her cheek. Continuing to cry, she averted her gaze to the floor, not knowing what to do or what to say. "I just gave Gavin hell for bringing you back here without my permission."

Emily's head snapped up. "You . . . saw him?"

"Yes, I saw him leaving," he replied, burying his face in her neck. "You shouldn't have left with him, Emily."

She pulled back again, her green eyes wide. "You don't think you would've left if you had seen me doing the same thing?"

"I'm not sure." He paused, nibbling his bottom lip as if deliberating what to say. "I just know that I don't like that he brought you home without telling me and that you actually left with him."

Her features morphed at the shock of his words. "You're mad at *me* for leaving, Dillon?"

"Jesus, baby, I'm not mad at you." He stepped closer and brushed his hand across her neck. "I just want you to believe me. She means nothing to me." Stepping closer, he breathed against her cheek as his hands smoothed down to her waist. "I pulled away, Emily. I swear I did. You just didn't see it." He gently moved his mouth over her lips, his voice pleading as he kissed her. "I love you more than anything in this world. I would never hurt you, babe. Please, you have to believe me. I fucking love you." He tilted her head back, angled her body to his, and slid his mouth down her neck.

"Dillon, please." She moaned, grabbing onto his shirt. "God, please, Dillon, don't lie to me," she begged as tears ran down her face.

"Baby, I'm not lying." He trailed his hands under her dress and slipped it over her head. "I fucking love you, Emily. You're my world. I can't lose you," he whispered into her mouth, his breath ragged against hers. "I'm sorry you had to see that."

Her own indiscretion with Gavin tore through her as she looked into Dillon's brown eyes. Oxygen seemed to evaporate from her lungs. Guilt thrust like an ice-covered spear through her heart.

"Tell me you believe me," he breathed heavily, slowly kneeling as he swirled his tongue in hypnotizing circles down her stomach. He slid her panties past her thighs. "Tell me you believe me, baby."

She felt so torn over what she wanted to believe and what she had done with Gavin. "Yes, I believe you," she cried. "I'm so sorry, Dillon. I'm so sorry."

Before she knew it, he'd ripped the panties from her body, picked her up off the ground, and carried her to her bed. He spread her legs and held her in place as his tongue laved against her painfully pleasurable spot. Her body writhed against his mouth while he gripped her hips, sucking, licking, and tasting her essence. Her muscles convulsed with both ecstasy and guilt as his fingers slid in and out of her hot warmth. Needing to rid herself of the shame she felt and wanting him inside her at that very moment, she strained up. "Dillon, I want you now," she moaned, sliding against the pillows.

He shed the rest of his clothing, climbed into the bed, and sank inside her. She gripped his caging biceps, throwing her head back at the sensation of him pulsing into her hot flesh. He slammed his mouth over hers and stifled her moans as she closed her eyes. And then it happened. Visions of Gavin kissing her, the feel of his velvet tongue, and the warm touch of his fingertips all over her body—her every thought was consumed by him. Dillon was on top of her, but all she could feel, smell, and taste was Gavin.

Emily stopped moving; her entire body froze.

"What's wrong?" he breathed into her ear, continuing to move above her.

"I feel like I'm going to be sick." She slid out from beneath him and rushed to the bathroom.

He sighed and flipped onto his back. "What the fuck, Em?"

Shutting the door, she fell to her knees in front of the toilet as hot tears welled in her eyes and nausea threatened to spill over. Placing her elbow on the seat, she buried her hands in her hair, trying to catch her breath. She sat there for a few seconds, a few minutes, maybe a few hours. She didn't know how much time had passed when she finally stood up.

She walked over to the mirror and stared at her reflection. After throwing some water on her face, she made her way out into her room where Dillon had already fallen asleep. Quietly getting into bed, she curled the blankets over her body, hoping to find sleep and praying she wasn't heading into something she couldn't control.

7

Friendly Intentions

"MISS, YOU NEVER brought our appetizer."

Without saying a word, Emily stared blankly at the woman. Her scattered thoughts were obviously not where they should be. The woman glared at Emily. "Hello? Our dinners have arrived, and you never brought out our appetizer."

"I'm . . . I'm so sorry," Emily stammered. "I'll be right back with it."

Rushing into the kitchen, she let the cooks know she needed an order of mozzarella sticks on the fly. She made her way back to the table, apologized again, and let them know it would be another few minutes. Trying to recover any possible chance of a tip, Emily offered to pay for their dessert. With that, the missing appetizer became a thing of the past as the woman smiled and accepted.

Sighing with relief, Emily sat at the bar, thankful they hadn't complained . . . or so she thought.

"Country," Antonio said, "what just happened? Table sixteen told me you forgot their appetizer?"

"Yes, I'm sorry. Roberto is taking care of it right now."

"Did you offer them dessert?"

"I did."

"Are you okay?" he asked, placing a caring hand on her shoulder. "You seem out of it tonight."

"I just have a lot going on right now, Antonio. I'm sorry. It won't happen again."

"If you're not feeling good, I can let you off early," he replied. Concern filled his face.

"Thanks, but I'm all right."

He nodded and headed into his office.

Emily trudged through work over the next few hours. The evening passed in a blur as she found herself still trying to grasp everything that had happened. By the time her shift was over, she felt physically and mentally drained.

Peering into her purse to search for her wallet, Emily opened the door to leave and ran smack into what felt like a brick wall. An audible "oof" broke through her lips. She snapped her head up to apologize, and her emerald-green eyes locked on to beautiful baby blues.

"Jesus, are you all right?" Gavin asked, reaching out to steady her.

Emily struggled not to gasp at the subtle contact of his warm, strong fingers wrapped around her arms. Her senses were momentarily rewarded by his cologne wafting through the air. A flush crept over her cheeks from the spike in temperature, making her feel as if she might burst into flames. As Gavin looked down at her, he held her gaze—a dangerous thing to do because a girl could seriously lose herself in those eyes, especially after what had happened between them. That kiss had been devastating, painful, euphoric, and everything else she had imagined it would be—all wrapped into one.

Damn that kiss.

She wondered if she could ever pull herself to the surface to breathe again. Her heart fluttered frantically, like a butterfly trying to escape the cage of her chest. With him standing right in front of her, it bared all sorts of things she didn't want to think about. "Yes, I'm all right," she answered breathlessly, still in shock. They both seemed to be in a trance, their stares never wavering from each other.

Gavin released her arms, cleared his throat, and backed out onto the sidewalk. His heart clenched at the sight of her. Looking into her eyes, he couldn't believe only a week had gone by since he'd seen her beautiful face, kissed her soft lips, and touched her warm skin. It had felt like an eternity. He hated that his subconscious had chosen that night, knowing how vulnerable she was, and he knew he needed to apologize.

"I stopped . . ." He paused, trying to collect his thoughts. "I stopped by hoping to catch you. I wanted to know if I could talk with you."

"What's there to talk about?" she asked, trying to hide the nervousness curling through her as she stepped out of the restaurant. Her gaze traveled away from his in an attempt to keep from lingering on how sexy he looked in his tailored suit and tie.

He wet his lips and stared at her a moment. "I think it's apparent, don't you?"

Hesitantly, she looked at him, her voice low. "Yes, it is. What did you have in mind?"

Pulling in a breath, he ran his hand across the back of his neck. "I was thinking we could go grab a drink. There's a coffee house right around the corner."

A flicker of uncertainty touched her face. "I don't know. I'm not sure if that's a good idea."

"I just need five minutes of your time, Molly . . . I mean, Emily." He sent a full-watted smile her way.

"Ha-ha," she said dryly.

He grinned and held his hands up in mock surrender. "Just five minutes?"

She swallowed, wanting to refuse, but her efforts were futile. "Okay, but not a minute more."

"You have my word. It's this way," he said, beckoning her to the corner of Forty-Fourth Street.

Less than half a city block later, the two entered a quaint little coffee shop. The scent of freshly baked pastries infused the air. A few customers sat on a comfortable red couch as others at chestnut-brown tables browsed the Web. Behind the bar, the fashionably bored barista took their order, and they retreated to a tiny table in the back.

With a smile, Gavin held up his wrist and set his watch. "Okay, my time begins . . . now."

Emily sheepishly looked down at her hands twisting in her lap.

Gavin leaned back against his seat and crossed his arms, the smile falling from his face. "Emily, I'm sorry for what I did," he whispered, his eyes intense. "I made an already awkward situation worse, and I feel terrible about it."

She looked deep into his eyes, unable to believe the words coming from his mouth. "You don't have to apologize. It was my wrongdoing—not yours."

"No, Emily, it was my fault," he said, emphasizing each word. "It was wrong of me to take advantage of you. I leaned in to kiss you."

"It takes two to tango."

"Right, but—"

"I kissed you back."

A slow smile curled his lips, his blue eyes shimmering. "So you wanted to kiss me?"

"Are you serious?"

"Very."

"Gavin."

"Emily."

She sighed. "Well, what do you expect me to say?"

"I want you to say it."

"Say what?"

"That you wanted to kiss me."

"You've lost your mind," she scoffed. "And why do you need to hear me say it?"

Rubbing his chin, he analyzed her face, and his expression suddenly turned serious. "Because I need to know I didn't force you into something you didn't want."

"You didn't force me."

"Then say it, Emily."

A blush rushed up her neck to her cheeks. "You're unreal."

"Say it." He dragged the words out.

"Fine." She nervously looked around. Bringing her eyes back to his, she crossed her arms. "I wanted to kiss you, Gavin. Are you happy now?"

"No. I still feel like an asshole for putting you in that position."

"I guess we're even, then, because I still feel like shit about doing it." She stood up to leave. "What exactly was this talk for again?"

"I want us to establish a friendship." He rose to his feet, hoping to stop her from walking away.

"And how do we do that, Gavin?"

"You've admitted that you wanted to kiss me. It was *more* than obvious that I wanted to kiss you. Now we can put it behind us and be friends."

"That simple, huh?"

"That simple," he replied with a smile, though he heard the lack of determination behind his words. "Now sit back down and finish your cup of coffee with your new friend."

"You're a demanding friend, I see," she quipped, grabbing her purse. "But, really, I should get going. Dillon's at my apartment waiting for me."

Gavin glanced at his watch. "You gave me five minutes. I still have another two left."

"Are you kidding me?" she laughed.

He sat back down, took a sip of his coffee, and smiled. "What's with all of these questions, friend?"

"I'll say it again like I did at your house," she replied as she settled back into her seat. "You're truly a wiseass."

"Certified. So how've you been?"

"I've been better, and I've been worse."

"Okay, so that's not necessarily a bad thing."

"That, you're correct about."

"Very good." He smiled. "So tell me something about yourself."

"What do you want to know?"

Anything. Everything. Why'd you take him back? Sliding his hand through his hair, he shrugged. "What's your favorite flavor of ice cream?"

"Vanilla. And yours?"

"I dig vanilla, too, but I'm really a chocolate type of guy," he answered, watching the way she nervously shifted in her seat.

As a long silence descended across the table—during which Gavin gave her another one of those intensely searching looks—Emily noticed he pressed his lips together as though to stop himself from asking her something he truly wanted to know.

"So, what's your favorite color?" he finally asked.

"Gavin, can I ask *you* a question?"

"Anything you want."

"What are we doing?"

"We're playing twenty questions," he laughed.

"No, we're not. What do you really want to ask me?"

Drawing up a brow, he leaned back and propped his hands behind his neck. "Mmm, you're good at reading me." He watched her for a few more seconds, studying every beautiful curve of her face. "I've been told I'm hard to figure out by people who have known me far longer than you have."

"I find you pretty easy to read." And she did. Although he kept certain aspects of his life guarded, he was an open book in her eyes. She took a sip of her coffee. "So shoot. What is it that you really want to know?"

He contemplated her for a moment. "Are you happy with Dillon, Emily?"

She bit her lip nervously. "Why do you want to know that?"

"We're friends, and friends ask questions. And besides, you're the one who asked, don't forget."

"Right, I did." She looked down to her hands and then back to Gavin. "Yes, I'm happy with him."

Placing his elbow on the table, he pressed his chin against his palm. "Why?"

Her brows knitted together. "What do you mean why?"

"Give me the specifics." He shrugged. "Why does he make you happy?"

She stared at him, her eyes intense, but her phone going off broke her focus.

As she answered the call, Gavin leaned back and watched her. He knew he might have crossed the line asking such a personal question, but he couldn't fight his instincts. He had spoken with Dillon the night he left her apartment. He'd allowed

Dillon to think he believed his story, but he didn't—not even close. He knew his friend all too well. The only question racing through Gavin's mind was why Emily had fallen for it.

Emily stood up and tucked her phone back into her purse. "That was Dillon. I really have to go."

Gavin rose to his feet and brushed his hand down her arm. "I hope you're not upset with my question. My curiosity gets the better of me sometimes."

She swallowed hard and shook her head. "I'm not mad at you, Gavin. However, to answer the only question that matters here, yes, Dillon makes me happy for many specific reasons. You'll just have to take a rain check on me listing them, okay?"

He nodded as if that answer satisfied him, but it didn't. Nonetheless, he wouldn't push the issue any further. He dug into his pants pocket. "Oh, I forgot. I have something for you." Gavin reached for her hand. He held on to it just a little longer than he should have, but her skin felt so soft it was hard to let go. Finally, when he knew he had reached his gentlemanly limit, he slipped a bottle cap into her palm.

She looked down and smiled. "So is this going to be an ongoing little thing between us—you giving me a bottle cap every time you see me?"

"That was one of the best games of 'Toss the Bottle Cap into the Pot' I've ever played," he admitted, his voice soft. "So, yes, it'll be our little thing, along with me calling you Molly occasionally."

She smiled at him. "Thank you."

They made their way outside, and Gavin hailed a taxi for her. He closed the door behind her after she got in and leaned through the window. "She's going to Columbus and West Seventy-Fourth." He handed the driver money for the ride. "This should cover the fare and your tip." He banged on the roof, alerting the driver that he could leave.

As the taxi pulled away, Emily told the man to stop. She jumped out of the cab as Gavin walked away. "Gavin, wait!" she called, wondering exactly what the hell she was doing.

Gavin turned around with his hands in his pockets. He stared at her from a few feet away.

"I just wanted to say thank you," she said, trying to catch a steady breath. "Not just for the cab fare—that was very sweet—but also for . . . for talking with me about my mother and for stopping by tonight. I know both of those things were hard for you. It was hard for me as well, but . . ." She looked down to the ground then back to him, willing herself not to sink into his eyes. "I don't know. I'm just rambling now. I have a tendency to do that. But I just wanted to thank you . . . thank you, Gavin."

Although he wanted to move toward her—God knew he did—he had to stop himself. "You're welcome." He stared for a few lingering seconds. "I'll see you around, pal?"

Emily nodded. "Yes, I'll see you around, pal."

Gavin watched her get back into the taxi. He watched until his eyes hurt. The vehicle disappeared into the frenzied flow of traffic, turning into nothing but a tiny speckle of color. His tall, hard body was somehow at odds with his emotions. He wanted Emily. He ached for her. It wasn't just lust. Because all he really wanted to do was kiss her and feel her body pressed against his again. Every part of him longed to hold her and take care of her. Emily had stirred things within him back to life—things he had shoved away for longer than he had realized. He wasn't sure how she made him feel the way he did when she was around him, but he knew the whole situation might consume him and set him ablaze, scattering his ashes from one end of the city to the next.

So friends . . . friends was what he would have to accept.

"Hello, beautiful," Dillon said when Emily opened the door to her apartment. He got up from the couch, walked over, and pulled her into his arms. "I missed you. What took you so long?"

"We had a late rush," she replied, trying to successfully pull off the lie burning a hole through her gut. "Did you get the movie?"

"I did. Go get in the shower, and I'll set us up." He scratched at his chest and sauntered into the kitchen. "Oh, there's a surprise in your bedroom."

Smiling, she cocked her head to the side. "What did you do?"

"Nothing big." He tossed a bag of popcorn into the microwave. "I was just thinking about you today."

After dropping her purse onto the table, she made her way down the hall. In her room, she took in the sight of six dozen red roses scattered throughout the space. Each dozen was in a beautiful crystal vase. He'd even scattered some petals across her queen-sized white duvet. Although she was touched by the gesture, her smile was weak. The scent of them pleasantly assaulted her nose while she tried not to fester in her guilt of just finishing her secret "coffee date" with Gavin. Once showered, she slipped back into the living room and lay down with Dillon on the couch. His body curled possessively around hers as she absently traced patterns across his bare chest.

She looked into his eyes. "Thank you for the flowers. They're beautiful."

"Well, I'm glad you like them." He kissed the top of her dampened hair. "Like I said, I thought of you all day."

"You're too sweet." She nuzzled her nose against his neck.

"Oh, I forgot to tell you. I got a call back from one of the schools I submitted my résumé to."

"Did you? That's awesome, babe. Where is it?"

"It's in Brooklyn." She thought for a second. "Bush something. I have to look at what I wrote down. I have an interview on Monday."

"Bushwick?"

"Yes, that's the name." She smiled, reaching for the popcorn on the end table.

"Em, you can't take a job out there. It's not safe."

"Dillon, I'll be fine."

"No, Emily, I'm telling you—you're not taking the job out there. Send some more résumés out and wait for something else," he replied with finality.

"Are you being for real?"

"Babe, I'm just looking out for you. It's not a good neighborhood," he answered, pressing his mouth against her forehead. "You'll wait for something else. Besides, we've already been over this—if you need money, I'll give it to you."

"It's not that, Dillon. I've waited long enough, and I want something lined up for this coming school year."

Before he could say anything further, the door swung open. Olivia walked in with her purse swinging cheerfully from her arm. She rolled her eyes in Dillon's direction while making a gagging sound.

"Ollie, tell my girlfriend how bad Bushwick is."

Emily waited for Olivia's response, but it never came. She ignored Dillon, kicked off her shoes, and sat on one of the plush recliners. "Hey, friend," Olivia said to Emily, a beaming smile working over her lips. "How was your day?"

"Uh, my day was good," Emily replied, unable to keep the slight laughter out of her voice. "But can you answer Dillon's question? I'm interested in hearing about this badass neighborhood." Still not answering, Olivia looked away as she studied the chipped pink polish on her nails. "Liv, can you answer his question?"

Olivia's brown eyes narrowed like a snake on Dillon. "Sorry, Em, I don't talk to assholes who jockey off their sperm, sowing their wild oats with any slut who'll give them a blow job behind my friend's back," she hissed, the words rolling off her tongue like a melted piece of ice.

Emily nearly choked swallowing down a piece of popcorn. She felt Dillon's body go rigid against hers right before he rose from the couch.

He shot Olivia a searing look, but his voice remained eerily calm. "Fuck off, you stupid dyke."

Olivia plastered a smile over her gritted teeth. "Oh, that was seriously original." She sounded undaunted by his insult as she clapped slowly.

"Oh my God, Dillon, how could you say that?" Emily looked at him in shock.

"Fuck her." He casually walked to the kitchen and reached into the refrigerator.

"No, honestly, fuck you, Dickhead!" Olivia spewed.

"Holy shit, would you two just stop?!"

"I'll stop when you see the fake overcoat of charm he wears in front of you, Emily! He's fucking around behind your back, and you're oblivious to it!" Olivia stood up and wagged her finger in Dillon's direction. "But for now, he's in my fucking house, so he can take it or get the fuck out!"

Dillon plucked his shirt from the couch, tossed it over his head, and dug his keys from his pocket.

"Dillon, wait!" Emily crossed the room to go after him.

"Fuck that stupid bitch! I'll call you later!" He threw the door open and slammed it closed with a thundering force.

Emily stayed rooted to her spot in his wake. Her head fogged as she tried to process everything that had just happened. She spun around and glared at Olivia. "You promised you wouldn't say anything!" Hot tears sprung to her eyes as she moved across the room.

"Well, you know what, Em? I couldn't help myself when I saw you cozying up to him like he'd done nothing!" Emily opened her mouth to speak, but Olivia cut her off. "And not for nothing, friend! If you didn't think it was true somewhere in that brain of yours, you would've never kissed Gavin," she snarled, her words cutting straight through Emily's heart.

Emily inhaled, trying to quell the sudden urge to punch her square in the face. "You're truly fucked up," she said in a surprisingly calm tone—one that even threw Olivia off guard. "How could you say that to me, knowing what I've been through all week?"

"I didn't mean it that way," Olivia replied, cautiously moving toward her. "I just think you're in denial, Em. I think that you're in denial about the way Dillon treats you, and I think you're seriously in denial that you feel something—even the littlest bit of something—for Gavin."

A wounded cry escaped her throat. "I'm not in denial, Olivia. I love Dillon, and I believe him. Why is that so hard for you to understand?" Emily walked toward her bedroom, stopping at her door. "I didn't see the whole kiss. I saw exactly what Dillon said I did. That skank pulled him into her, and I turned around before he backed away. The only reason I kissed Gavin was because I didn't see the whole thing. I was mad. My emotions got the better of me when we got back here. That's all—it's nothing more."

An uncomfortable silence descended throughout the apartment before Emily retreated into her room, sinking onto her bed. She had never felt so mentally bruised by the stinging of

Olivia's words. Pinching the bridge of her nose from the sudden headache pulsing through her skull, she tried to put her feelings in check. She couldn't lose her best friend, and she refused to lose Dillon either. She hated the phrase "caught between a rock and a hard spot," but that was exactly how she felt. Two of the people she loved most despised each other more than ever. Emily's mind whirled as the pain of the whole situation crushed her.

Twenty minutes later, with a subdued knock, Olivia peeked in the door. "Can I come in?" Emily nodded. Olivia sat on the bed. "I'm sorry, Emily. I shouldn't have said what I did." She tucked her blonde hair behind her ear, her eyes glassy. "You've been through so much. I just want to see you happy."

"I am happy, Liv. Please trust me when I say that. I can't have you act like that around him," she said, sitting up. "You two will give me a nervous breakdown."

After a very long minute of obvious deliberation, Olivia let out a heavy breath. "Okay—only for you, because I love you to absolute fucking pieces—I won't say another thing to him. You do realize how hard that will be for me, chick, right?"

"I do. And that's why I love *you* to absolute fucking pieces." They leaned in and shared a tight hug. "I'm going to make sure he apologizes to you for what he said."

Olivia let out a huffed laugh. "I don't need his apology, Em. Besides, he's wrong. I'm not a dyke. I'm a certified equal-opportunity lover. I like both male and female, darling." Shaking her head, Emily laughed. Olivia stood up and walked to the door. "I cringe saying this—God, I fucking cringe . . ." She exhaled a breath and rolled her eyes. "But Dickhead—I'm not giving up his nickname by the way—is right. Most of Bushwick isn't a good neighborhood. Something else will come along. Just hang out—you'll see."

A faint smile played across Emily's mouth. "Thank you. I'll take both of your advice and wait it out."

Olivia blew her a kiss and walked out of the room.

After calling Dillon and vehemently insisting he apologize to Olivia, Emily attempted to go to sleep. She tossed in bed as her mind strayed back to Gavin. She tried to fight her emotions, reminding herself that she loved Dillon, but Gavin was embedded into her thoughts like a sneaky little parasite. His magnetic presence thickened the air she breathed when he was near her. His idea of inaugurating a friendship between them seemed impossible the more she thought about it. There were too many dangerous variables floating around. She felt swallowed by her confusion. As her consciousness slowly drifted toward sleep, her mind tried to fight a bloody battle against what her body already knew. She wanted him, and she wanted him bad. *Throw guilt to the wind,* it screamed. For the moment at least, her mind won the war over her body's assault, deciding not to risk the possible destruction of her life.

But damn him and damn that kiss.

8

To Hell with Self-Control

OVER THE NEXT few weeks, Emily fell into her routine at the restaurant with ease and was happy Dillon found himself in a more normal schedule. He didn't get in as late in the evenings. For Emily, things started to calm down. Dillon pulled a few strings with a client of his who held a position high up in the New York City school district, landing Emily a full-time teaching position in Greenwich Village. She was excited that in less than a month, she would finally start her career and was even happier that she'd be surrounded by first graders. She had wanted to teach first grade because she felt the beginning of a child's education was the most important.

"Are you almost ready, babe?" Dillon called out impatiently while waiting on her couch.

"Just give me two more minutes." She pinned up the last few strands of her hair.

She studied her reflection and decided that even though the auburn mess was uncooperative on that particular afternoon, it would have to do. She threw on a green-and-brown boho summer dress with spaghetti straps, grabbed a pair of brown heels, and slipped into the living room.

"You look quite delicious," Dillon remarked with a smile as he moved toward her. "Are you excited?"

"I am, but you don't have to do this." She snaked her arms around his neck, her heels dangling from her fingertips. "I have enough clothing."

"Yes, but you don't have any from the boutiques on Fifth Avenue." He pulled her closer and breathed against her cheek. "And I'd love to get you some more sexy lingerie."

"I bet you would," she replied, arching her brow.

He tilted her head back, feathering kisses against her neck. "You have no idea."

Olivia cleared her throat, interrupting them. "Where are you two lovers off to today?" she asked, rolling her eyes.

With a smart-ass smile, Dillon walked over to Olivia, slinging his arm over her shoulder. "Well, if it isn't my favorite person in the world."

"Get off me, Douche," she spat, ducking her smaller frame out from beneath him.

"Dillon's taking me clothes shopping," Emily quickly interjected. She curled her arms around Dillon's stomach and pulled him away. She slipped her feet into her heels. "What are you doing today?"

"I'm finishing up my painting and taking it to the gallery for the show." She poured herself a cup of coffee. "You're still coming, right?"

"I wouldn't miss it for anything, chick."

"Do you want to come with me tomorrow to get our nails done?" Olivia asked. "I so need a pedicure, too."

Dillon slid his arm around Emily's waist, leading her toward the door. "I hate to break up this female conversation, but I have places to take my girlfriend to, Ollie."

Emily kinked her neck back to look at Olivia. "Yes, Liv, it's a mani-pedi date. I'll see you later." Olivia shook her head and watched the two of them walk out of the apartment. "You know, you really need to stop being such a jerk to her," Emily said, settling into the seat of Dillon's car. "She's been nice to you the past few weeks."

"I'm just kidding around with her, Em." He closed the door. Emily watched as he made his way around the car and slid into his seat. "She needs to learn how to take a joke." He started the engine.

"I know, but please—for my sake—just leave her alone, okay?"

Grabbing for her hand, he maneuvered into traffic. "All right, all right, I'll leave her alone."

"Thank you."

He brought her hand up to his lips and kissed it. "No problem. Do me a favor, though. There's a file in the backseat. Can you grab it for me?"

She unbuckled her seat belt and reached for the file. After buckling up again, she glanced at the file. Her heart skidded across her chest when she saw Blake Industries on the top right corner. Although not easy by any means, she had somewhat managed to keep her "new friend" from her thoughts the past several weeks, and now out of nowhere, she was essentially holding him in her hands. "Here." She attempted to hand the file to Dillon.

"Just hang on to it for now. We're stopping by his penthouse before we go shopping. I have some papers I need him to sign before the weekend's over." He ran his hand through his dirty-blond hair. "He's a pain in my ass, I have to admit. The motherfucker's always adjusting his damn stocks."

"Oh . . . well . . . I'll just wait in the car while you go up, then." She tried to appear casual as she glanced out the window.

"You're not going to wait in the car. One, it's going to take a while because I have to go over a few things with him, and two, I want you to see what we will eventually be living in one day. His place is off the hook."

Emily sighed. Nevertheless, fifteen minutes later, she found herself stepping out of the car in front of the building that housed her worst nightmare and her wettest dream.

After tossing his keys to the valet, Dillon pointed to the top of the massive structure. "You see that?"

She tilted her head, her eyes following the slender ribbon of blue sky all the way up to the top of the building. She nodded.

"That's where he lives, like a fucking king overlooking all of this." Dillon spread his arms, gesturing over the Lenox Hill area of the Upper East Side. "One day, we'll be living like him." He smiled, placing his hand on the small of her back.

With a tip of his hat, the door attendant greeted them, acknowledging Dillon by his last name like an old friend. When they walked into the Italian Renaissance–style lobby, Emily noticed a few people milling around, swathed in some of the most expensive clothing and jewelry she had ever laid eyes on. Looking down at her summer dress from Walmart and heels from Payless, she felt more than a little out of her comfort zone.

The elevator ride up to the seventy-fifth floor was torturous. When she heard the cheerful ding before the doors parted, she wanted to melt into the walls and camouflage herself into the grain of the wood. The long walk down to the end of the hall had her feeling as if she were a bloody piece of meat suddenly cast out into a sea of awaiting sharks.

One particular shark, that is.

As they approached the door, Emily wiped her hand across

her sweat-beaded forehead, her heart drumming in her chest erratically. Dillon gave a quick knock, and after what felt like forever, it opened. Behind it stood a buxom redheaded bombshell. Other than her smile, she wore nothing but pink lace panties and a matching bra hidden beneath one of Gavin's white button-down shirts. Unbuttoned, no less.

"Wow, you look great." Dillon beamed at the woman, but his smile quickly dropped when Emily shot him a look.

"Hey, Dillon," the woman rasped, pulling him in for a hug. "Like, seriously, long time no see."

Crossing her arms, Emily shifted in her heels and plastered a smile across her face. Dillon eyed Emily, cleared his throat, and returned his attention to the woman. "It has been a long time, Natasha. I'm assuming the big man's home? I never called to let him know I was stopping by."

"Yeah, he's out on the terrace with his laptop. Like, you know how he is, all work and no play," she laughed. "I just happened to be coming out of the bathroom when you knocked."

Dillon nodded. "Yeah, I know how he is with work."

"Who's this?" Natasha asked, closing the door behind them.

"This is the future Mrs. Parker." Dillon smiled and curled his arm around Emily's waist. "Emily, this is Natasha Bradford. She's Gavin's . . . friend?"

"I'm Gavin's flavor of the month," she giggled. Emily's mouth hung slightly agape. "But it's okay with me. I get things like *this*." She giggled again as she playfully fingered a diamond necklace.

"Well, you're a lucky little duck," Emily replied, trying to will herself not to throw up.

"I am, I am." Natasha smiled. She cocked her head to the side. "So, like, really, you two are engaged?"

"So, like, we're really not," Emily quickly answered.

"Oh wait . . . I thought." She looked at Dillon, confused, and smacked his arm. "You silly man, you had me thinking, like, you were engaged when you said she was the future Mrs. Parker."

"Eventually she will be." Dillon smiled, looking at Emily. She smiled back, praying she didn't have to hear the word *like* again.

"Okay, well, like, come in. I'll let him know you two are here." Natasha laughed. Emily sighed. Natasha walked away to get Gavin.

"Babe, I have to use the bathroom," Dillon said, walking down a long hallway. "I'll be right back."

Emily nodded. At first glance, she noticed the décor was a stark contrast from the warmth of his house in the Hamptons. Although extraordinary in its own way, it felt cold and impersonal. Marble floors, black leather couches, abstract stone sculptures, and colossal black-and-white photos of different cities consumed the enormous penthouse with no hint of color anywhere. Holding business superiority throughout, it was exactly the space Emily had envisioned he lived in when she first met him. It wasn't a home; it was simply what the city expected. Another one of Gavin Blake's many layers came to her mind.

As Emily chided herself for analyzing his surroundings, Gavin stepped into view, wearing a pair of blue cotton pajama pants—shirtless. He—and his dragon tattoo curling around his rib cage—warmed the space almost immediately. Emily watched breathlessly as he whispered into Natasha's ear. She giggled at whatever he said, kissed him on the cheek, and whisked down the hall into one of the rooms, closing the door behind her.

Gavin's eyes roved over Emily as he tried to mask the excitement he felt bleeding from his pores at the sight of her. He thought that the last time he went without seeing her was an eternity; this longer stretch felt as if it were his certified death sentence. Feeling his body relax from her mere presence, he approached her with a smile. "Sorry about that." He ran his hand through his hair. "She has a distaste for clothing or something."

"But she has a love for the word *like,* so it all evens out, I guess."

"Mmm, I never noticed that," he replied, scratching his stomach.

"Are you kidding?" Emily questioned, trying to keep her attention on his face and away from the lingering thought of where that tattoo began.

He moved closer and whispered in her ear, "Of course I'm kidding. It's annoying, but don't tell her I told you that."

Between the close proximity and his warm breath against her skin, she thought she would pass out for sure. "My lips are sealed."

In one swift motion, his gaze flicked down to her mouth then back to her eyes. "Do me a favor and try not to bring any attention to those pretty little lips," he whispered, his blue eyes intense.

Emily's mouth dropped open and then snapped shut.

"Would you like something to drink?" he asked casually, ducking his head to conceal his smile.

"Are you going to watch me drink whatever you give to me? Because I may be wrong about this, but I think I have to use my lips in order to do so."

He cocked a brow and smirked. "It would be my absolute pleasure."

"What would be your absolute pleasure?" Dillon asked as he returned from the bathroom.

Emily backed away from Gavin, almost stumbling. "I was just telling Emily it would be my absolute pleasure to give her a tour of my place," Gavin replied as calm, cool, and collected as could be.

"Well, before you start giving out tours, let's get this shit done." Dillon handed him the towering stack of paperwork. "I need your John Hancock on every single one of these bad boys. I also want to talk with you about a few risks I feel you are taking dropping CMEX." Dillon walked into the kitchen to get a drink.

Gavin gazed into Emily's eyes. "I'm all about taking risks. I think it makes life a little more . . . exciting. Wouldn't you agree?" Emily knew exactly what he was referring to, and her heart tripled over into a somersault as she stared back.

"I just don't think it's a good idea to drop them," Dillon replied, popping the top off of a bottle of beer. He made his way back over to them. "CMEX is your security. You have so much invested in hedge funds right now; it may not be a good move."

"You are the professional," Gavin said with a smile. "Let's take care of this in my office." He turned to Emily. "By all means, make yourself at home. Natasha should be out in a minute. I'm sure she'll keep you . . . *like*, busy." He winked and disappeared down the hall with Dillon.

Emily stood mute as a statue in the living room for a moment as she tried to catch her breath. She licked her lips slowly as the tingles Gavin evoked from within her body worked their way up from her toes to the top of her head.

So . . . fucking . . . dangerous.

Sighing, she moved out to the terrace, hoping the fresh air would soothe the chaos wreaking havoc in her mind. The penthouse was a corner unit, and the stunning wraparound views of Central Park and the East River immediately awed her. The terrace alone was larger than her and Olivia's living room and both bedrooms put together. She cautiously peered over the edge to watch the city below her. Her hair whipped around in the wind as she breathed in the hot, humid August air. Although she was afraid of heights, Emily was calmed by the stillness, the assurance of solitude, and the lack of people that high up. The serenity was short-lived when Natasha strolled out of the French doors.

"It's, like, completely breathtaking out here, isn't it?" She handed Emily a glass of ice water.

"Thank you," she said. "It truly is beautiful up here." She studied Natasha's strapless, skintight black tube dress. "So where are you from?"

"California." She giggled.

"Really?" Emily mocked in shock. "I would never have guessed."

Natasha kinked her head to the side, her long crimson hair blowing in the wind. "Like, I know, right? People tell me that all the time."

"I bet they do."

The two women sat down on a plush outdoor couch. Natasha tucked her feet underneath her legs. "So, like, how long have you been dating Dillon?"

"We'll be together a year next month."

"That's so sweet." Natasha smiled. "He's such a cutie, too."

"Thanks. So how long have you and Gavin, uh . . ." Not sure how to ask the question, Emily brought the glass of water up to her lips and took a sip.

"Been fucking?" Emily choked on her water. "Oh God, are you okay?" Natasha placed her hand on Emily's back.

"Yes, it . . ." She cleared her throat several times. "It went down the wrong pipe," she said, pointing to her throat. "I'm all right now, thanks."

"So, like, I was saying, let me see . . ." Natasha paused and tapped her finger on her chin. "I met Gavin, like, two years ago when Blake Industries was running an ad campaign for a modeling company I worked for. We're not in a serious relationship at all, but we've been fucking around off and on ever since. Like, when he calls me, I come." She giggled again. "And I mean, literally. God, do I come. That man knows what he's doing in the sack. Like, the best I've ever had—no joke. And those lips and tongue . . . They are so, like, not only good for kissing. I mean, when he goes down and—"

"It feels like it just got hotter out here, right?" Emily interrupted and quickly stood up. She fanned her face with her hand. "Yeah, it definitely feels hotter out here."

Natasha furrowed her brows. "Hmm, I don't feel it."

"I do. I'm going to go back inside to hang out in the air-conditioning."

"Oh, okay, like, I'll join you," Natasha exclaimed, hopping up a little too eagerly.

Please don't. . . .

Walking into the penthouse, Emily found Dillon sitting on the leather couch. "You all right, babe?" he asked. "You look pale."

"Yeah, I'm okay." She walked over to him. "I need to use the bathroom before we leave."

Natasha pouted and slumped into a chair next to Dillon. "Oh no. I was, like, hoping we could all go get some lunch together. There's, like, this posh little Greek restaurant that opened up, and I'm so wanting to try it out."

"That sounds good." Dillon rose to his feet and walked into the kitchen to grab another beer. "I'm actually starving."

"Dillon, we're supposed to go shopping, remember?"

"We'll go afterward. Fifth Avenue will still be there," he replied, sliding open his phone to make a call. Emily stared at him, fuming as he started a conversation with the person on the other end.

"Oh goody!" Natasha clapped.

Gavin walked into the living room, still lounging in his pajama pants. He started massaging Natasha's shoulders. "What are you clapping for?"

"She's, *like,* really excited because we're all, *like,* going out to lunch together." Emily shot him a wicked smile, her eyes narrowing. "So, *like,* I need to use your bathroom before we go. Can you, *like,* tell me which one of these halls I need to go down to get to it?"

Natasha beamed from ear to ear.

The corner of Gavin's mouth turned up. "It's, *like,* at the end of that hall, last door on your right." Pointing down the hall, he tried to stifle a laugh.

Without a backward glance, Emily headed in the direction he pointed. She shut the bathroom door behind her. "Unfucking-real," she murmured as she studied her reflection.

After taking a few minutes to grasp the fact that she was about to spend her afternoon in a very uncomfortable situation, she emerged and found Gavin leaning against the opposite wall with his arms crossed. She heard Dillon and Cali Girl laughing in the other room, but the conversation was inaudible. "You find this whole thing funny, don't you?"

Smiling, he stepped closer. "You don't?"

She stepped back. "Not as funny as I think you find it."

Undeterred, Gavin stepped closer still. "We're pals, remember?"

Not saying a word, she took another step back, only to find she was against the wall with her sweaty palms pressed against the cool surface.

He propped his hand just above her shoulder, angling his head as he ducked down to stare into her eyes. "It's just lunch," he said, his voice low, seductive even. "Friends have lunch together all the time."

Closing her eyes, Emily tried to concentrate on Dillon's voice in the other room, but Gavin's sweet breath so close to her made it difficult. Goose bumps erupted all over her skin. "You're fucked up." Her heart ricocheted in her chest so hard she swore he could see it.

"You think so?"

Swallowing hard, she opened her eyes and nodded.

He caught his bottom lip, dragging it slowly between his teeth. "Then can I make a confession, since I seem to be a pretty fucked-up guy to you?"

His husky voice made a fresh round of butterflies explode within her stomach. Another speechless nod.

Softly running his fingertips down her bare arm, he slipped a bottle cap into her hand. He leaned in, inches from her ear, his voice nothing but a whisper. "I completely forgot to give you this when you walked in." Smiling, he backed away, walked into his room, and closed the door.

Emily let out the breath she was holding and tried to restore her jumping pulse to a normal rhythm. A knot swelled in her throat. After shoving the damn bottle cap into her purse, she made her way back into the living room and sat on the couch next to Dillon. Over the next fifteen minutes, while waiting for Gavin to get ready, she endured Natasha's mind-numbingly detailed explanation of her recent plastic surgery to lift her ass higher. Natasha seemed to be a nice, slightly confused girl, but by the time Gavin walked into the living room, Emily was more than happy to get the hell out of there.

If it was possible, the elevator ride down was more torturous than the ride up. The sexual tension in the small space was so thick Emily felt it slithering across her skin. The two couples stood across from one another. Dillon and Natasha talked about stock options he felt she should look into purchasing. Gavin casually leaned against the wall, smiling and wrapping his arm around Natasha's waist, his eyes never wavering from Emily. She watched him just as intently. He was decked out in a formfitting black shirt that strained around his muscled forearms and black slacks that hugged his tapered waist. When the cheery ding of the elevator rang on the bottom floor, Emily slipped out as fast as she could, retreating to the open-aired space of the lobby—away from him.

The couples decided they would all drive in Dillon's car over to the restaurant. Natasha and Gavin sat in the backseat, and Emily lost track of the amount of times she rolled her eyes when Natasha giggled at something Gavin whispered. No doubt something sexual.

When they arrived, Dillon helped Emily out of the car as Gavin did the same with Natasha. Although the savory smell of Greek food lingering in the air appealed to Emily's senses, she didn't have much of an appetite when the host showed them to their table.

"So, Emily, you're really beautiful," Natasha remarked from across the table. "Have you ever, like, thought about modeling? You're over eighteen, right?"

"Um, yes, I'm twenty-four. But I've never thought about doing anything like that. Besides, I like food too much," she laughed, handing the menu back to the waiter.

Dillon reached for Emily's hand and looked at Natasha. "I wouldn't want her modeling anyway."

"Why? She'd, like, make totally awesome money, and I have the best agent in New York I could totally introduce her to."

"She doesn't need to worry about money." Dillon leaned back. "It's just something I'd prefer she not do, that's all."

Natasha shrugged and flipped her hair to the side.

"So, Dillon said you'll be teaching in the city this year?" Gavin asked, glancing in Emily's direction.

"Yes," she replied, placing a napkin in her lap. "Over in Greenwich Village."

"Yeah, she's teaching first graders, so I don't have to worry about any of her students developing a crush on her." Dillon laughed and leaned over to kiss her neck.

"Ah, but you may be incorrect on that, Dillon," Gavin said. "I had a thing for my first-grade teacher when I was a kid."

Dillon took a swig of his whiskey on the rocks. "Are you for real?"

"I am." Gavin leaned back in his chair. "If I recall . . ." He paused for a second and smiled. "Her name was Miss Molly. And, man, let me tell you, I had it bad for her. She drove something in me crazy that I couldn't quite understand."

Emily shot him a wry smile and rolled her eyes.

Natasha laughed, playfully smacking his arm. "Like, you were totally after women even then, huh?"

"Apparently, he was." Emily tented her hands under her chin and eyed him from across the table. Smirking, Gavin drew up a brow but remained silent.

"Holy shit, if it isn't Dillon Parker!"

Emily turned around and observed a tall man around their age beaming, his brown hair slicked back with a good amount of gel.

"No fucking way!" Dillon stood, rounded the table, and shook hands with the man. "Where the hell have you been hiding?"

The man smiled. "Down in Cancun with the luscious señoritas, but I am back and hotter than ever."

Dillon turned to Emily. "Babe, this is an old buddy of mine from college, Keith Jacobs. Keith, this is my girlfriend, Emily."

She shook his hand, and Dillon introduced him to Gavin and Natasha. Small talk was briefly exchanged, and Dillon excused himself to go chat it out with Keith at the bar for a few minutes.

Figuring she could play the game just as well—if not better—Emily smiled and turned to Natasha. "So, Natasha, have you had the chance to visit the New York Public Library yet?"

"Oh, well, not yet, but I like to read magazines. I'm sure they have some there, right?"

Gavin smiled in Emily's direction, thoroughly enjoying her wiseass remark. He knew exactly the conversation she was referring to by bringing up the library.

"Absolutely, they do." Emily widened her green eyes. "Hundreds, if not thousands, of magazines would be right at your fingertips." She took a sip of her much-needed cosmopolitan and smiled. "I bet there's a ton of *Vogue* magazines as well."

Natasha smiled. "Thanks for the suggestion. Like, I'll totally have to check it out one day. But right now, I have to powder my nose. I'll be right back." She stood up, dropped a chaste kiss on Gavin's temple, and scooted across the restaurant, her ass chucking firmly from side to side as she adjusted her tube dress.

"That was pretty funny," Gavin remarked as he slightly leaned across the table. "I've said it before and I'll say it again, you're a pretty funny girl."

"Really, Gavin? A man of your stature dates a ditz like that? I guess you weren't kidding when you said you attracted the all-beauty-and-no-brains type."

He shrugged. "I told you we all have ways of filling voids in our lives. She gives me what I need, and I give her what she needs. It seems fair to me."

"Oh, that's right, 'cause who could honestly miss the rock hanging from her neck?"

"You seem . . . upset?" he replied, his voice monotone and his face impassive.

Emily's temper flared, but she kept her tone to a whisper. "You want to know what I'm upset about?" He nodded, not once taking his eyes off her. "I'm upset that you blatantly go out of your way to make me uncomfortable. What happened to your whole wanting-to-be-friends gesture?"

"Am I making it that hard for you?" he asked mockingly.

"Yes, Gavin, you are," she quietly spat, her fingertips white-knuckled around her glass.

With his need for her trapped inside—blistering hot, sweltering, ready to explode—he leaned closer, dropping his voice. "Good, because whenever you're near me, I fucking lose every bit of self-control I have left."

Emily's throat tightened at his unexpected words. She exhaled heavily, the sound hanging in the air as tingles crashed through her entire body. And, to top it off, with every second he stared at her that way, she got hotter. The impact created an explosion between her legs, causing a chain reaction of anger mixed with more desire for him than ever before. Emily returned his hot gaze with one of her own, showing a streak of defiance as she tried to catch her breath. "What do you want from me?"

"I want you to give in to what I see behind your eyes every time I'm near you." Slowly—so slowly—he licked his lips. His brilliant blue eyes hardened with palpable lust. "I want you to give in to the way you trembled in my arms when I touched you, the way your breathing becomes faster when I look at you."

She stared at him, her heart ricocheting in her chest, but she couldn't form a sentence.

"I loved the way your lips felt against mine, and I'm pretty sure you did, too. I also enjoy the way I can almost feel you becoming wet for me right now." Leaning in closer, he dropped his voice to a hard whisper. "Are you going to pretend you don't feel anything for me, Emily?"

He wasn't even touching her, yet he was correct—her panties were damp. She hated that he was right; she hated that he noticed every physical and emotional reaction she had toward him. And she hated that she wanted him so badly she could taste it. *Damn him.* "I'm not answering your question."

"You don't like answering questions," he stated through gritted teeth, trying to fight his urge to drag her clear across the table and into his arms. He could've devoured every inch of her right there. Like a tornado ripping through anything in its path, her presence alone pulled him to her. *Damn her.*

"No, Gavin, I don't like answering *your* questions," she quickly whispered. "And it looks like I don't have to because your void filler is walking this way."

Gavin's pupils lost her gaze and dilated with awareness of what she'd said. Casually leaning back, he plastered on a fake smile as Natasha approached. Before sitting, she leaned down and pulled him in for a kiss. Emily was foolish not to peel her eyes away from their open-mouth exchange. She felt a nauseated pang deep in the pit of her stomach at the sight of Gavin sliding his hot tongue over Natasha's mouth. She didn't know why she had such feelings, but watching them, she felt pissed, and she knew she had no right to. When the kissing skit finally ended, Gavin's blue eyes flitted over to Emily. His gaze was unsteady with a strong hint of something akin to an apology shimmering behind them.

One corner of Natasha's mouth tipped in a satisfied smile before she sat next to him. "Sorry I took so long. Like, I had to totally empty out my purse to find my lipstick."

Emily drew in a long breath and almost jumped up when she felt a large hand squeezing her shoulder gently. She turned around and met Dillon's gaze. She tried to get her heart to slow from its frantic shock of the conversation that had just ended.

The waiter eventually brought their food. Heated glances exchanged between her and Gavin for the remainder of the meal kept Emily's hands nervously dancing with her silverware.

After being forced to endure an hour of mind-fucking conversation regarding Dillon's concern over Gavin's stock portfolio choices, Emily was elated when the couples finally retreated to Dillon's car, putting an end to an afternoon that had left her stomach in knots. She was practically silent during their drive across the city to drop off Gavin and Natasha, but if Dillon noticed her sudden change in demeanor, he didn't comment. When they arrived at Gavin's high-rise, Emily claimed she wasn't feeling well, grasping for any excuse to stay in the car while Dillon walked them to the entrance. He politely kissed Natasha's cheek and bade farewell to Gavin with a firm handshake. While Dillon headed back to the car, Emily's eyes were magnetically drawn to Gavin, who held the door open for Natasha as she sauntered into the lobby, flipping her hair. Before he followed Natasha, Gavin turned around, both of his hands buried in his front pockets, and threw Emily one last longing, piercing stare that would stay burned into her memory for the rest of the afternoon.

Dillon lounged into his seat and smiled. "Ready for some Fifth Avenue shopping?"

Although feeling as if she had just escaped from a psychiatric ward, Emily plastered on her own fake smile and nodded. "Yes, let's get out of here."

9

Home Run

THE MIDMORNING AIR in Central Park was mild but cooler than usual for the second week of August. Emily spread a small sheet under one of the maple trees that provided shade from the vibrant sun. Placing her backpack beside her, she took out two sandwiches, a couple of bottles of water, and her favorite novel, *Wuthering Heights*. All she needed now was Dillon. When she glanced at her watch, she noticed he was already twenty minutes late. As the city hummed its daily incessant chatter—even in the serene peace of the park—she decided to give him a call to find out what was taking him so long.

He answered on the first ring, his voice traveling through the phone with a hint of remorse. "Please don't be mad at me." Taken aback by his greeting, she didn't speak. "Em, are you there?"

"Yeah, I'm here, but you're not. Where are you?"

"I'm in New Jersey, but—"

"You're in New Jersey?" she interrupted. "Dillon, what the heck? I'm sitting in Central Park."

"Emily, would you just let me explain?"

"Fine, Dillon, explain."

"Remember the Japanese tycoon I told you was interested in investing with Morgan and Buckingham?" He paused, awaiting her reply, but none came. "Takatsuki Yamamoto?"

"Get to the point."

"Shit, Emily, I'm trying to." She sighed, and he continued. "He flew in from Japan last night and is only out here for the next two days. He asked to meet with me personally. I got the call early this morning from my boss, telling me to come out here." He answered a question directed at him from someone in the background while Emily waited. "Babe, I have to go. I'm sorry, but this account is huge."

Again, Emily said nothing.

"Come on," he breathed. "We'll do it another day."

"I know; it's just that I took off from work, and I was really looking forward to—"

"Emily, stop trying to make me feel bad," he said, his tone clearly annoyed. "This is important to me. I'll be at your place by six." With that, the line went dead.

After the shock of him hanging up on her wore off, Emily rose to her feet and reluctantly started packing up what was supposed to be their little romantic getaway. As she tucked the sheet into her backpack, she straightened at the sound of her name being called out from a distance. Before she even turned to see the face, a familiar tingle traveled up her spine. She knew who it was. When she finally spun around, Gavin was jogging across the park, smiling, with his niece and nephew at his side. The backpack slipped through her fingertips as she took in his casual attire—a white V-neck T-shirt, cream-colored cargo shorts, and a blue New York Yankees cap. Emily tried to gather her racing thoughts as he approached.

It wasn't just that his presence pulsed through her. It wasn't that his masculine scent lingered on her senses, burning in her mind and plaguing her every dream. It wasn't even that damn kiss. It was his unwavering charm, bold confidence, insane sexiness, and the undeniable dominance he exuded. Every bit of it seeped from his pores. All of those things—a truly lethal cocktail—scared and fascinated her. It was as if a twisted paradox occurred whenever she was around him. As much as she felt the need to flee from him, she also felt unmistakably drawn to him. Suddenly, she became aware of the heightened charge in the air. A tense kind of feeling seemed to press in on her lungs, making her feel breathless. To top it all off with a heavy dose of whipped cream, seeing him flooded her mind with their last encounter two weeks ago.

Breathe, Emily . . .

"Emm-mi-me!" Teresa squealed, running toward her.

Kneeling down to hug her, Emily looked up at Gavin. "What are you guys doing here?" she asked as nonchalantly as humanly possible, considering the circumstances.

Gavin hunched over and propped his hands on his thighs, trying to catch a decent breath. He stood straight up and smiled. "I'm babysitting and decided to take these two squirts here to play some soccer."

Timothy wrapped his arms around Emily's leg. "Uncle Gaffin took us to feed the duckies, too."

Gavin swished his hand through Timothy's hair. "Yep, we had a certified feeding fest with Donald and Daisy."

"Very cool," Emily replied with a smile. "A business mogul and a nanny all in one."

"Add it to my résumé." He laughed.

"I can't believe you spotted me here."

"Well, I actually didn't see you; these two did."

"Uncle Gaffin told us to say we saw you first, Emm-mi-me," Teresa confessed, curling her finger through Emily's hair. "But he did saw you first and said to come wif him to say hi to you."

Drawing up a brow, Emily watched Gavin's face turn a light shade of crimson. "Using children to tell a fib, huh?"

He shook his head and smiled. "Damn, you caught me. Add that to my résumé as well." Emily laughed. "What are you doing here?"

"Dillon was supposed to meet me, but he got called into New Jersey." She lifted her backpack from the ground. "I was actually getting ready to go home."

Teresa pouted. "Can you stay and play soccer wif us, Emm-mi-me?"

"Umm," she replied, her eyes flicking up to Gavin, "I'm not sure. Maybe another time?"

Teresa frowned.

"You won't have to endure the torture of being around me too long." A smart-ass smile molded his face. "Colton and Melanie should be here in ten minutes to come get them."

Emily smiled coyly, almost challenging him. "Okay, fine. I think I can handle fifteen minutes of grief." She placed her backpack down. "Can you handle it?"

"Mmm, I can handle it, and handle it *very* well. Can you play soccer?"

"I'm a quick learner."

"And I'm an excellent teacher."

He dropped the ball, giving it a quick kick. Teresa and Timothy ran after it.

"And being around you is not torture, Gavin," Emily said, jogging after the kids.

He caught up to her. "Right, you made it clear that it's only grief. But no worries, I really do take that as a compliment." Emily simply shook her head and laughed.

Over the next fifteen minutes, although he did play a little, Gavin mostly hung back a bit and watched Emily play with the kids. Sitting on top of a picnic table, his senses reeled at everything about her. His eyes swept over her body, ultimately settling on her face as he admired her smile. He listened to her laugh while his mind tried to wrap itself around the way his niece and nephew clung to her. Children had a keen sense of the auras that surrounded people, so their behavior only confirmed what his heart already knew—her presence was magnetic. It consumed others, swallowing them whole, and left no room for regret.

As she ran around with them, he watched Emily's wavy hair bounce, the summer sun creating a fiery halo of rich auburn. His need for her snaked through his bones, cutting straight down to the marrow. From the moment he'd laid eyes on her, she made something strange happen in his chest when she looked at him. Something tightened in his stomach, and he realized he could find himself in deeper than he already was if she looked at him like that too often.

His mind hawked at the description of his feelings, knowing he couldn't do anything to satisfy his hunger. The only thing he knew for sure was that his emotions were caught in a clusterfuck of epic proportions. Being around her was self-inflicted pain at its finest, but he was willing to endure it if for one reason only—to be close to her. Colton calling his name dragged him from his thoughts.

After he and Emily hugged the children and bid Colton and Melanie good-bye, Gavin walked with her to gather her belongings.

"Mr. Blake, it's always a pleasure," Emily said with a smile, extending her hand.

Gavin didn't shake it because he knew if he touched her, he wouldn't be able to resist the urge of pulling her into his mouth. Running his hand through his hair, he backed away slightly. Emily smiled awkwardly and slung the backpack over her shoulder. Gavin found his words stuck in his throat like verbal gridlock. "Wait, that's it? You're going to just leave me here all by myself?"

"You're a big boy. I think you can find something to occupy your afternoon."

He laughed for a moment and then suddenly his face became serious. "I just thought this could be an opportunity to redeem myself."

"Redeem yourself? What for?"

"For my behavior the last time I saw you. I'm sorry I made you uncomfortable, but . . ." He lowered his voice and stared into her eyes. "I'm not sorry about the way I feel about you, Emily. They're my feelings, and I can't deny them. But I really just need to be friends with you."

She swallowed nervously, her voice as low as his. "Gavin, we've talked about this before, and—"

Cutting her off, he stepped closer. "I promise you this time. I swear to God I won't say or do anything to make you uncomfortable. I just wanted to get it out there—about the way I feel about you—but now I'm done." He shifted and stepped back, not letting his eyes stray from her face. "You've got me twisted for some reason I can't understand, and I don't know if I ever will. I find you to be the most remarkable . . ." He drew in a deep breath. "I don't know. There's something about you that just . . . sets you apart from any other woman I've ever met. And because of all of it, I'm willing to put my feelings aside just to be your friend." *Just to be near you . . .*

Not only did her heart pause at his words, but her stomach curled in a disturbingly pleasant way as she gauged his face. True emotions swirled behind his eyes, and something deep down told her he was sincere. "Okay, we'll try this again. So you want me to hang out with you here for a little while?"

Gavin took in a deep lungful of air, the knot in his chest releasing as he realized he had been holding his breath awaiting her answer. "You like baseball, don't you?"

"How did you know that?"

"The night I found out you were really Emily and not Molly?" He grinned. "Before you came into the club, Dillon told me his girlfriend was a huge baseball fan."

"You want me to play baseball with you?" she asked, furrowing her brows.

"You can take in all of the spectacular sights New York has to offer, but you haven't experienced New York to its fullest until you've been to a Yankees game." He smiled. "Trevor was supposed to come to the one o'clock game today, but he canceled on me at the last minute." He pulled tickets from his back pocket and held them up. "I have season tickets, but it would be a shame to let these go to waste."

A confused smile touched her mouth as she contemplated him for a moment. "You want me to go to a Yankees game with you?"

"I do."

"I don't know," she replied, looking at the ground and then back to him. "That might be a little too much."

His smile was slow, making his blue eyes sparkle mischievously. "Surely, in a stadium filled with fifty thousand people, I should be able to keep myself from attacking you."

Emily screwed her mouth to one side. "True. But I'm not even a Yankees fan. I'll be rooting for the underdog. Is that something else you can handle?"

With widened eyes, he placed a hand over his chest, mocking a wounded heart. "Mmm, keep talking like that, and you may find a way to get me to *not* admire you as much as I do. I'm a diehard Yankees fan, Miss Cooper. But, yes, I'm sure I could handle sitting next to a non–Yankees fan that I've brought with me."

She shook her head and laughed. "Okay, I'll consider this friendly outing under one condition."

"Anything. Let's go," he said, reaching for her backpack.

"Wait, you don't even know what it is."

He placed his hand on the small of her back and started leading her out of the park. "No problem. Whatever it is, I can most definitely handle it."

She came to an abrupt halt and giggled. "You *will* listen to me, or I go nowhere with you, Gavin Blake. Do you understand?"

A delicious grin slid across his mouth. "I'm all ears."

"Like that." She motioned to his hand resting on her back. He smiled and pulled it away. "No touching me, no undressing me with your eyes, and no doing that . . . that damn stupid thing with your mouth when you pull it between your teeth."

He smiled. "Does me sucking on my lip bother you that much?"

Only 'cause it's so insanely hot . . . "Yes. It's annoying."

He slowly dragged his bottom lip between his teeth, ending it with a luscious popping sound. "Well, the same goes for you, then."

She kinked her head to the side and sighed. "Such a smartass. You've already warned me about not bringing any attention to my lips." She covered her mouth with her hand, muffling the rest of her words. "Is this better?" He nodded and laughed. "But I don't look at you like I want to rip your clothes off, and surely, I don't touch you."

He shrugged. "Since we're being honest, you have no idea how much I would love it if you did touch me."

She dropped her hand from her mouth and let it hang open for a second. "See, this is exactly what I'm talking about." She turned on her heel to walk away.

Letting out a full, throaty chuckle, he jogged over and gently grabbed her elbow. She eyed his hand. He quickly let go and smiled. "Emily, I'm just kidding. Come on, it's just jokes. . . . It's who I am, really."

She cocked a brow, unable to keep the smile off her face as he stood there with an innocent boyish grin. She knew he was anything but. "If you want me to go with you today, you keep your hands to yourself, Blake. Got it? If not, I *will* make you pay severely for it."

"Sounds kinky." He smirked. She sighed. "However, I'm nothing but a peasant to your request of being a gentleman." He playfully bowed. "Now let's go. We need to catch the number four."

"Wait, we're taking the bus?"

"Uh, no," he stated, a questioning look appearing on his face. "The number four's the subway."

"Oh, I thought we would drive?"

"Hell no." He took the backpack from her and tossed it over his shoulder. "We're doing this certified New York, doll."

Despite her surprise that she was actually spending the day with him, Emily followed. A couple of city blocks later, they hopped onto the subway. Between a teenage couple making out as if they were at a house party, a guy in a flowered sundress talking to himself while eating Chinese food with his hands, and the mass of overly aggressive Yankees fans chanting, "Let's go, Yankees," Emily was more than thrilled when they finally arrived at the stadium.

Once there, they both got something to eat. Emily ordered a hot dog and a bottle of water, and Gavin chose a bag of peanuts and a beer. He showed Emily to their seats right behind home plate. Gavin looked like a kid in a candy store, and Emily thought a man of such power getting so excited over being at a baseball game was cute.

Gavin glanced at his watch as the stadium started to fill. "We have some time. The game will start in thirty minutes."

Emily nodded and looked down at her phone, noticing she had a missed call from Dillon. She shifted in her seat and rethought what she had actually gotten herself into. She debated whether or not to tell Dillon where she was, but before she could delve too far into her dilemma, Gavin spoke up.

"Let's play twenty questions while we're waiting for the game to start." He popped a peanut into his mouth. "I get to go first."

"Bullshit, you went first the last time. I get to go first."

"You don't miss a beat, do you?"

"Not usually."

"Okay, seems fair. Ask me something."

Emily's mind roved over what she wanted to ask him but was unsure if she should. Nonetheless, it was her turn to let curiosity get the better of her. "I want to know why you and your ex-fiancée broke up."

His expression became guarded as he stared off into the stands. Emily saw the bright blue of his eyes change as though a cloud had passed overhead—and in that moment, she regretted bringing it up.

He leaned forward, placed his beer on the ground, and looked back to Emily. "Hmm, my first question addressed to you the last time we played was about your favorite ice-cream flavor. You're going straight for the kill, I see."

"I'm sorry. I shouldn't have asked," she whispered, looking down.

"No, it's okay. I just wasn't expecting that right out of the gate. But I feel comfortable talking to you about it."

Emily's head snapped up. "You do?"

"Yeah, for some reason, I do." Pulling in a breath, he leaned back and hesitated for a few seconds. "She left me because Blake Industries was going under at one point. My father offered Colton and me the funds to keep it afloat. But us Blake boys tend to be a little stubborn, and we refused his help, knowing we would get it back on track on our own." He ran his hand through his hair. "I explained everything to her, let her know we needed to cut back on some of our spending until I could resurrect the company. She argued that I should accept my father's money and called me crazy for thinking we could get back on our feet without his help. Along with Colton, I was firm on my decision not to take the money. She was living with me in my penthouse after we got engaged. I came home one day after work to a letter—in beautiful handwriting, I have to add—saying she couldn't take the risk of not living the life I had afforded her." He reached down for his beer, took a sip, and exhaled. "Five years together and her good-bye to me . . . was a letter."

Emily searched his eyes and saw the pain swirling behind them. "You loved her," she whispered.

He gave a quick shrug. "Yeah, she broke my heart. I thought she loved me for the man I was without the glitz and money. I mean, when we first met, I was in my senior year of college, so I wasn't as successful as I eventually became. She betrayed the faith I had in love when she left." He pressed his lips into a hard line. "Don't get me wrong; looking back on it now, I know we weren't made for each other. One, she was too concerned about the way we appeared in public—anything from what cars we drove to what parties we attended." He rubbed at his chin absently and continued. "She wasn't like that when we first met; the change was gradual. Our biggest difference was that she made it clear she never wanted children. I loved her enough to consider a life without having any, but like I said, looking back, she wouldn't have been worth giving up the chance to have a family."

A faint smile touched Emily's mouth. "You want kids?"

"I want bucketloads tucked neatly into a minivan," he admitted, his lips curling upward into their faint smile.

"Gavin Blake in a minivan?"

"Absolutely," he replied, reaching for his beer. "A funky forest-green one, too."

Out of the corner of her eye, Emily watched him adjust his baseball cap, feeling a little shocked by everything he just told her. She started to understand his need for filling voids. "So you haven't seen her since?"

"I have, actually. I saw her recently, to tell you the truth."

"So how did that go?" she asked reluctantly.

"It was . . . interesting. I ran into her while out with a couple of my buddies. She talked a bunch of shit, saying she was happy to see the company doing well. She admitted she missed me and still loved me, and then she confessed that leaving me was the biggest mistake of her life." He popped another peanut in his mouth and smiled. "You can see where I'm going with this, right?"

"Yes. Now that you're financially secure again, she wants you back."

"Bingo, doll. I knew you were quick." He took a swig of his beer. "Besides, her name is Gina, and mine, of course, is Gavin—two Gs. I think it was an omen or something—destined to not work out."

Although he laughed, Emily saw the leftover pain in his eyes and decided at that point to drop the subject altogether. "I got the invitation you sent me and Dillon."

"I was going to ask you about that," he replied, motioning to one of the workers selling beers. He ordered another and turned to Emily. "I figured it would interest you, considering . . . well, you know."

"Yes, and thank you for the invite, but what is it that your mother does exactly?"

"Since she knows she's blessed to be a survivor herself, she started an organization to raise money for those in the New York area affected by breast cancer—women who are either in the midst of battling it or are in remission, and the families of women who died from the disease. The donations collected at the benefit are spread out to help pay for ongoing treatment, follow-up care, or—God forbid—funeral expenses."

Emily breathed out. "It's beautiful that she does that."

"Yeah, this will be the tenth year since she founded it. She throws it every October during Breast Cancer Awareness Month. It's pretty spectacular, too. Black-tie, champagne, and all of New York's well-to-do gathering for one evening to spend their money on something other than a fucking cruise to Fiji or a new car."

Emily laughed. "Well, we'll definitely be there."

"And I'm happy that you will."

With not a cloud in the sky, the opening ceremony began, and soon after, the game was in full swing. A hard crack of the bat, plunging the ball into the outfield, started the Yankees off on a high note. Throughout the game, Gavin repeatedly brought unwanted attention to Emily, letting every Yankees fan within earshot know she was rooting for the underdogs, the Baltimore Orioles. Fans surrounding them booed her every time the Orioles scored. She playfully nudged Gavin, promising retaliation in whatever form she could conjure up. Still hungry and more relaxed with the overall situation, Emily ordered a pretzel and decided to have a beer with Gavin. By the bottom of the seventh inning, the game was tied four–four, bases loaded, with the Yankees up to bat.

Gavin smirked in Emily's direction and rubbed his hands together. "Your birds are about to go down."

"You seem pretty confident about that," she pointed out with a smile. "I wouldn't be too sure, though."

Gavin's eyes flicked down to the corner of her beautiful mouth where the smallest amount of mustard waited for him to wipe it off. Without even thinking, he brought his hand up to her lip and, with the pad of his thumb, he whisked it away. Startled by his sudden movement, Emily flinched. "There was . . . mustard on your lip," he slowly replied. Quelling the urge to lick it off his finger, he grabbed a napkin.

"You broke the no-touching-me rule," she breathed, ignoring what her body was fighting so hard to deny. Even as fleeting as it was, his touch felt insanely good in an insanely bad way.

He flicked his gaze down to her lips and then back up to her eyes. "I could've let it stay there."

"And you could've told me about it, too, wiseass." A smile twisted his mouth, one so contagious she couldn't help but respond with a smile of her own. "Looks like I have to follow through on my promise and make you pay severely for not playing fair."

He cocked an incredulous brow. "Not that I'm against public affection, especially with you, but how do you plan on accomplishing that in a stadium filled with people?"

Emily shot him an evil grin and leaned forward, tapping the shoulder of a woman in the row in front of them. The woman and her friend sitting next to her turned around. "I'm very sorry to bother you," Emily said to the blonde. "My friend here is interested in giving you his number. He finds you very attractive and didn't have the nerve to say anything to you himself. Do you have a boyfriend?"

Gavin smiled, shook his head, and all but buried his face in his hands with embarrassment.

The woman and her friend laughed. "I do, but I could break up with him for *him*."

"Well, not that it matters that you do, because it won't deter my friend here," Emily replied coolly. "Do you have a pen and a paper?"

The woman dug in her purse, retrieved a pen, and ripped out a piece of her checkbook. She handed them to Emily, and in turn, Emily handed them to Gavin.

"There ya go, pal. Jot down those digits for the pretty lady." Emily nudged him with her elbow. "And stop being so damn shy about picking up women."

With his dimpled smile, Gavin quickly scribbled on the piece of paper and handed it back to the woman. She took a quick look at it and smiled at him. "Gavin, huh? Cute name to go with that cute face. You'll definitely be hearing from me."

Gavin gave a quick nod and turned back to Emily. "You're ruthless," he whispered, throwing a peanut shell at Emily's head.

Giggling, she plucked it out of her hair. "I warned you."

Many chucked peanut shells into Emily's hair later, the game ended with the Yankees winning by three. During the entire subway ride back to Manhattan, Gavin took great pride in reminding her of the score every few minutes. He also confessed that the number he had jotted down for the woman was a fake. His defense was that he was no longer into blondes. Shaking her head, Emily sassed him about his little lie. He made sure to see her home, catching a taxi with her back to her apartment. After asking the driver to run the meter, he walked her up to the entrance.

Once again, Emily offered him her hand. "It was a pleasure hanging out with you today, Gavin."

"I can shake your hand?" He smiled. "I don't want to break any more rules."

"Yes, it's fine."

He obliged and took her hand, experiencing the same rush of heat he felt every other time he had the chance to touch her. Feeling like a malicious entity—selfish and wanting—he eventually let go. "The pleasure was all mine."

Drawing in a deep breath, Emily watched him walk back to the taxi and drive away. Riding the elevator up to her apartment, her head grew pleasantly fuzzy thinking of the wonderful day. She tried to settle her nerves because she knew she shouldn't have been with him at all. The balance was hell, but the release was sweet in a disturbing way. She'd learned things about him she had never thought possible. Something nudged in her chest, a heightened longing for him mixed with hurt over what he had gone through.

In an effort to take her mind off him, she concentrated on the fact that Dillon was most likely awaiting her arrival. To her relief, he was comfortably splayed out across her couch when she walked in. Over the next hour, he thoroughly filled her in on his achievement of landing one of the largest accounts his firm had acquired in more than ten years.

Although she debated whether or not to tell him about her day with Gavin, she decided against it, not wanting to dismantle Dillon's happiness. Now all she had to do was convince herself that Dillon's happiness was actually the reason she would hide such a thing. She settled the argument firing up in her head as simply as she could. He didn't ask how her day went, so she didn't tell.

Just a Lil Bit

"GOD, EM, COULD you hog the mirror anymore?" Olivia nudged her hip against Emily's in an attempt to see her own reflection. "You look banging. Now let me see myself."

Emily teased her fingers through her hair, trying to give it a little more bounce without unnecessary hairspray. "You're in my bathroom, friend. Go use yours."

Sighing, Olivia frowned. "But I like yours better; now scoot." She jerked her hip against Emily's with more force. "Besides, your friend's waiting in the other room, so don't be rude. I'll be done in a second, and then we can go party until we drop!"

Laughing, Emily shot one last look in the mirror and strolled out of the bathroom. She plucked her outfit off the bed. After slipping into a short black twill skirt and a red short-sleeved button-up blouse, she threw on a pair of black heels and called out to Olivia for approval. Emily playfully spun around, modeling her attire.

"You look like a sex kitten," Olivia trilled. Emily smiled and made her way into the living room.

Fallon jumped up from the couch, her gray eyes wide. "Damn, Emily, you clean up well."

Placing her hands on her hips, Emily smirked. "I'll take that as a compliment."

"Yeah, Country, it's a compliment." She tossed her red-and-stark-white-streaked hair over her shoulder. "The only clothing I've seen you in is that horrid black-and-white uniform they make us wear."

"Well, thank you, Fallon," Emily laughed. "For another horrid black-and-white-uniform-wearing waitress, you don't look too bad yourself. I could never pull off fishnet stockings like you can."

Fallon's mouth curled wickedly as she propped her leg onto the coffee table. "These old things? Damn, if I could live in a fishnet bodysuit, I would. Though I usually don't care what people think, society wouldn't consider that very proper, would they?"

Emily shook her head and laughed. "I'm thinking you might be right."

Olivia emerged from the bedroom sporting a red dress and matching heels. Her hair was pulled up off her shoulders, and the dress hugged her hourglass physique like a glove. After twirling around for Emily and Fallon, she made her way into the kitchen, pulled out three shot glasses from the cabinet, and topped each one off with a heavy dose of tequila. "Come on, ladies," Olivia squealed. "Let's do a couple of mind-fuckers before we hit the club."

The three women indulged in a shot, excited for a much-needed night out on the town. After they downed a second "mind-fucker," a quick knock came at the door. Dillon walked in.

"Why even bother knocking, Douche?" Olivia asked, rolling her brown eyes. Emily elbowed her in the gut. "I mean, Dillon, of course," she huffed out from the impact.

Dillon pinned Olivia with an icy grin, and then his eyes flicked over Fallon. He looked back to Emily with a quizzical expression. "What are you doing? I thought you were hanging out with me tonight?"

Smiling, Emily moved across the room and tossed her arms around his neck. "No, I told you the other day I was doing a girls' night out with Fallon and Olivia."

Dillon lightly gripped her hips and leaned into her ear, his voice low. "Can I talk to you in the other room for a second?"

Emily nodded, and he swiftly grabbed her by the hand, leading her into her bedroom. He snapped the door shut and crossed his arms. "What the fuck is that out there?" he whispered.

"What are you talking about?"

"That fucking space-cadet, Goth-looking freak in the black leather shirt and skirt," he answered, stepping closer. "Jesus Christ, she's wearing a fucking spiked collar, Emily. She has piercings on her lip, nose, eyebrow, and who fucking knows where else?"

Emily groaned as she moved toward the door, but he blocked her and grabbed her arm. She looked at him. "Are you really going to start with me about her? She's a nice girl, Dillon. Who cares what she looks like?"

"If my girlfriend's going out with it, I care what it looks like." He tilted his head to the side, his eyes narrowed. "What kind of attention do you think she's going to bring, looking like that?"

Emily yanked her arm away. "I'm not worried about what kind of attention she's going to bring," she whispered in a heated tone.

He plowed his hands through his hair. "Well, what kind of attention do you think *you're* going to bring, wearing that?"

"I'm not doing this with you tonight, Dillon. I swear I'm not," she answered in a low and hostile voice, attempting again to move past him.

He grabbed her by the waist. "Okay, okay. I'm sorry. You look beautiful." He nuzzled his nose against her cheek as he lifted her arms over his shoulders. "Which club are you going to?"

Emily sighed. "Cielo."

"On West Twelfth?"

"Yes."

"All right, I'll call a few of the guys from my office and go do something with them tonight." He pulled her closer and pressed his lips to hers. "You owe me one for this."

She spoke against his mouth. "I told you about tonight, Dillon."

He let out a low groan as he sucked in her bottom lip. "I must've forgotten. I've been working late again with this new account—you know that." He smoothed his hands down her waist. "What time are you going to be back?"

"I'm not sure," she said, wiggling out of his embrace. "But I have to go. They're waiting for me."

He pulled her in for another kiss and walked back to the kitchen with her. Emily quickly introduced him to Fallon. With her eyes, she warned him not to say anything to embarrass either of them. He simply smiled, but Emily could tell he was still displeased. After the women gathered their belongings for the evening, he followed them outside, hailed a taxi, and paid the driver for their ride.

He ducked his head through the back window. "Not too late, okay? We're having lunch with my parents tomorrow."

Emily nodded and leaned up to kiss him. With that, the driver pulled away.

"Your boyfriend's . . . nice?" Fallon said while her fingers moved over the keyboard of her phone like a well-oiled machine. Olivia laughed but tried to hide it by covering her mouth.

"Thank you, Fallon," Emily drawled as her eyes traveled to Olivia. "He can be a little overprotective sometimes, but he's a good man."

As Olivia laughed again—this time without trying to conceal it—Fallon gasped. "Oh shit! A friend of mine's having a house party in Staten Island tonight." She continued to frantically text. "His pad is incredible, and he throws killer parties. Let's go there instead."

"I'm down for whatever," Olivia replied, rummaging through her purse. She glanced in Emily's direction. "Is that cool with you?"

"Aren't we all a little overdressed for a house party?"

Fallon pulled a flask from her bag, unscrewed the top, and took a sip. She shook her head. "No, believe me, it's an anything-goes party." She handed Emily the flask. "Here, it's my specialty."

Emily took it and smelled its contents. "What is it?"

"Just take a sip, Em," Olivia piped up. "You're always worried about how much you drink."

"I'm already a little buzzed from those tequila shots, and I had some wine while I was getting ready." They both shot her a look, waiting for her to drink it. "Okay, fine." She took one last whiff of the liquid and chugged some. She started to cough and tried to blink back the stinging tears in her eyes. "What the hell is that?"

Fallon's eyes brightened with silent laughter. "Moonshine, baby."

"Oh hell yeah," Olivia chirped and reached for the flask. "I had this once when I was in high school." She tossed some back, her face crinkling from its taste as she wiggled her head back and forth.

"Okay, so are we going to my friend's party?" Fallon laughed.

Emily shrugged. "Let's do it."

After redirecting the driver to their new destination, they pulled up to a swanky three-story townhouse in the Todt Hill area of Staten Island thirty minutes later. Olivia paid the driver the difference, and the women slipped out of the taxi, each a little wobbly from the moonshine. The music hammered out of the closed windows, vibrating the ground beneath Emily. With a hiccup, she laughed, and they made their way up the stairs and into the house.

Multiple high-end speakers towered in every corner of the downstairs level, magnifying the racket to the point where Emily could barely hear her own thoughts. She scanned the party, and she realized Fallon wasn't kidding. It definitely was an "anything-goes" gathering. From people sporting casual attire to others dressed as if they were headed to prom to girls wearing close to nothing the crowd was a mixed array of every type of partygoer.

Linking hands, Emily, Olivia, and Fallon snaked through the throng of a hundred or so people, ultimately finding the owner, Fallon's friend Jacob.

After hugging him hello, Fallon yelled over the music. "Jakey, this is Emily and Olivia."

Without saying a word, he smiled widely and picked each of them up off their feet, hugging them as if he had known them for years. Once he placed them down, Emily and Olivia burst out laughing hysterically.

"Welcome to *mi casa*, ladies!" He flashed a smile, his voice booming. "Alcohol's in the kitchen; free lap dances from some of the hottest strippers in New York are located in the downstairs den; pool table's to the rear of the house; bathrooms are strategically placed on each level; and if you decide to get a little out of control with someone, bedrooms with king-sized beds in each are plentiful on the second and third floors." He said it all in one breath.

"Fuckin' A, cool!" Olivia smirked. "You have strippers here?"

Running a hand through his carrot-colored hair, he smiled devilishly. "They come in droves to my parties."

Olivia grabbed for Emily and Fallon's hands. "Shots are needed in my system right about now, chicks." She turned back to Jake and gave him a wink. "Thanks, bud."

He nodded and disappeared into the crowd. The women skirted multiple dancing bodies, a guy running around with underwear on his head while a topless girl chased after him, and several couples making out. Eventually, they made their way into the kitchen, where a fully stocked bar awaited them.

After consuming two more shots of tequila each, they headed out to the backyard to partake in an hour-long game of "Flip Cup." Emily was using Captain Morgan as her preferred liquid, so her head was becoming pleasantly fuzzy to say the least. Walking back into the house with Olivia at her side, she leaned up against a wall. "Olivia," she slurred. "I'm pretty . . ."

"I know you're pretty, Em," Olivia chirped, her own words slurring. "But stop bragging about it."

Slowly shaking her head, Emily laughed. "No . . . you didn't let me finish, bitch." Her head lolled to the side. "I'm trying to"—she hiccupped—"tell you that I'm pretty"—hiccup—"drunk right now."

"So am I, chick." She laughed and snorted like a pig.

Emily shook her head again. "No, but I"—hiccup—"am

pretty sure that I'm seeing things, too." She pointed toward the front door as she squinted in its direction. "Look. Those two guys"—hiccup—"that just walked in look like Gavin and Trevor."

Olivia let out a laugh. "You silly girl, you're not seeing things. It *is* Gavin and Trevor."

Emily looked adorably confused as she peered at the two blurry images headed straight for them. "You're joking with"—hiccup—"me, right? How would they know"—hiccup—"that we're at this house?"

Olivia bit her lip and swayed from side to side. "Since I know that you're digging Gavin—as a friend, of course—I decided to call my brother. He was hanging out with Gavin tonight." She gave Emily an innocent frown. "I told Trevor an itsy-bitsy, teeny-weeny lie to get them to come out here."

Before Emily could inquire about the little lie, Gavin and Trevor approached them, both of their faces filled with concern. Gavin placed his hands on Emily's shoulders. "Are you all right?" His eyes roved over her body as if assessing if she were hurt. She stared at him with a blank expression.

"Well, where the fuck is he?" Trevor asked Olivia, clenching his hands into fists.

"Calm down, brother," Olivia squeaked. "He was tossed out already."

Trevor's eyes traveled to Emily. He lifted her chin and moved her head back and forth. "How bad did the guy hurt you?"

Now she had Gavin's hands on her shoulders and Trevor's fingers under her chin. Speechlessly glaring at Olivia with a confused what-the-hell-did-you-tell-them stare, Emily . . . hiccupped.

Olivia grabbed Trevor's arm. "He didn't hurt her. She was just getting her dance on with the dude, and he got a little frisky. Like I said, the owner got rid of him."

Gavin stepped back and dropped his hands from Emily's shoulders. "Liv, you said the guy smacked her."

Olivia buried her face in her cup. "Did I say that?" she laughed.

"Yes, Olivia. You made it sound like she got bitch-slapped and tossed to the ground," Trevor barked.

Fallon stumbled over and interrupted what was about to become a public sibling argument. She studied Gavin for a second. "Hey, you're the guy from the restaurant that I asked Emily to give my number to."

He smiled. "Yeah, that would be me, I guess."

Fallon returned the smile and flicked her eyes in Trevor's direction. If it were possible, her smile widened even more. "And who might you be?"

"I'm this overexaggerator's older brother." He pointed to Olivia and returned his attention to Fallon. "And who might *you* be?"

"I'm a girl who's really into cute guys with blond hair and glasses."

"Nice . . . I fit that description." Trevor beamed. "And I'm a guy who's into a pretty girl who speaks her mind. Wanna dance?"

Fallon grabbed his hand, threading his fingers with hers, and led him into the living room. Trevor turned back to Gavin, giving him a thumbs-up.

"Soooo," Olivia drawled, a smirk spreading across her face. "I'm just gonna go get a lap dance. I'll see you two later." She disappeared into the crowd, her giggles echoing over the music.

Gavin smiled at Emily. He noticed the telltale glazed sheen in her eyes. "Well, you look like you're feeling pretty good right about now."

She stepped closer and tilted her head up to look at him. "Has anyone ever told you that you're very shmexy?"

"*Shmexy?*" He laughed, having expected an answer and not a question. He certainly hadn't expected that question. "Don't you mean sexy?"

"Nope, there's shmexy, and there's sexy. And you, my friend, are *shmexy*."

He cocked a brow, her throaty phone-sex voice arousing him instantly. "Mmm, which is better?"

"Shmexy."

"Well, thank you. You're pretty shmexy, if I must say so myself."

She grabbed his hand and walked toward the kitchen. "Come do a shot with me, Gavin."

"You haven't had enough to drink already?"

As she came to an abrupt stop, Gavin's chest collided against her back. She spun around and stumbled into him as he grabbed her waist to steady her. "Has anyone ever told you that you have the most amazing, gorgeous, and shmexy blue eyes?"

"What's with all of these questions, pal?" he asked, quite amused.

"We're friends, and friends ask questions."

He cautiously moved her hair behind her shoulders and smiled. "Yes, I've been told that I have nice eyes."

"No, they're not just nice," she hiccupped. "They're . . ." She paused, wetting her lips. "They're bedroom eyes."

"So I'm shmexy, and I have bedroom eyes, huh?"

Nodding, she laced her hand with his again and dragged him into the kitchen. Standing in front of the spectacular array of alcohol, she plucked a red plastic cup from the towering stack and handed it to him. "What's your poison, shmexy bedroom-eyes man?"

Crossing his arms, Gavin studied her for a moment. "I think I'm going to hold off on drinking for right now."

Her eyes widened as she swayed back and forth. "What? No, you're doing a shot with me." She brushed her fingertips across his cheek. "Come on, pretty please?"

Never mind the cute, girlish way she asked, her soft fingers lingering on his face had him second-guessing his original gut feeling not to drink with her, considering she was pretty drunk. He swallowed. "Just one."

She beamed. "Okay, back to my question. What's your poison?"

"I'll take that bourbon." He gestured to a bottle of George T. Stagg with his head.

"This one?" she asked, holding it up. He nodded and handed her his cup. She started filling it—and kept on filling it.

"Whoa, wait a minute, killer," he chuckled and took the cup. Walking over to the sink, he poured three-quarters of it out. "This should be enough for now."

She mouthed the word *boring* and once again clasped his hand, tugging him into the frenzied living room. "Dance with me," she rasped, looking into his eyes with a seductive smile curling her lips.

"Nah, I'm just going to chill right here." He motioned toward a couch filled with people equally as out of it as she was. He smiled. "You go ahead. I'll just sit back and watch with blatant male appreciation."

She lifted her chin in defiance. "Pfft, your loss, buddy."

He laughed and watched her wiggle through the crowd. She eventually found Trevor and Fallon still going at it. Gavin saw her gazing at him. Her waves of auburn hair, hanging wildly, swayed as her body moved provocatively to the music. It took everything he had not to stand up and pull her into his arms. But he knew that dancing with her in the state she was in, along with his increasingly aroused frame of mind, would be dangerous. She was definitely putting on a show for him. She backed against Fallon's chest and caressed her hands down her waist. Trevor's eyes widened at the display, but nonetheless, he positioned himself behind Fallon, grinding his hips against her ass.

Emily's eyes caught Gavin's again and she gestured with her fingers for him to join her. He narrowed his eyes and cocked his head to the side, pretending to be confused as he pointed to himself. Smiling, she nodded. He mouthed the word *no* and pointed to some girl passed out next to him. Although he couldn't hear her, Emily giggled, beaming ear to ear as she continued to grind her backside against Fallon.

Gavin's attention broke from Emily's for a second when the incoherent girl beside him abruptly sat up and decided that the pillow she was lying on was the perfect spot to throw up. One of her friends witnessed the disgusting scene, dragged the girl from the couch, and helped her to the bathroom. Standing, Gavin moved across the living room, skillfully dodging several drunken people clinging to one another in order to remain upright.

He leaned against the wall and scanned the crowd for Emily. When he spotted her, Trevor and Fallon weren't with her. Their replacement was some guy with his hands moving down her waist, his eyes undressing her, his mouth in her ear—wait—now it was on her neck. Gavin evaluated her with the stroke of his eyes, and she seemed to be content with what was happening, but Gavin wasn't. A surge of jealousy slithered through his body, and in a few strides, he was next to Emily. With the rigid set of his shoulders, a muscle working in his jaw, and his blue eyes filled with lethal calmness, Gavin pinned the other man with a glare. Gavin didn't say a word, but he didn't have to because the drunk got the point and backed away slowly.

"You've come to dance with me," Emily breathed, her skin glittering with sweat. Without warning, she slid her hands across Gavin's taut, muscular chest and then wrapped them around his neck. She drew his face down to hers. "I like dancing with shmexy guys."

With their faces inches apart, a rush of adrenaline-spiked heat coursed through Gavin's veins. His lips tingled in anticipation as he gazed at Emily's plump lips, remembering how they felt plastered against his. He tried—God knows he tried—to keep his hands off her, but he couldn't. He found them gliding slowly down her waist, lingering as he hooked his thumbs in the waistband of her skirt. He pulled her closer, reveling in the way her sweat felt against his skin.

It was Emily's turn to drag her lip through her teeth as her eyes bore into his with pure, unadulterated lust. The pulsing music and his hard arousal pressed against her stomach fueled her further. She didn't know if he heard it, but a soft moan wisped past her lips. She turned around, arched her back against his chest, and tilted her head up. Her head barely reached his shoulder. Slowly—so slowly—he pulled her arms around his neck. As her fingers tangled in his hair, he smoothed his hands down the curve of her elbows, skimmed the sides of her breasts, and ultimately settled back on her waist. With their bodies moving in sync to 50 Cent talking about "Just A Lil Bit," Emily felt her heart trip over itself when Gavin's lips grazed the shell of her ear.

Now she wanted to turn back around and face him, to see his beautiful eyes and soak in every inch of his delectable body, but when she attempted to, he held her in place. He was teasing her, and she knew it. His touch left searing heat with every inch that made contact with her sensitive flesh. It left her wanting—no, craving—more. His attention was fast becoming an addiction she didn't think she could ever get enough of. If Mother Nature weren't calling her name, she would've stayed in that position the entire night.

Quickly turning to face him, she stared into his eyes. "I have to use the bathroom." The words came out as breathless as she anticipated they would.

"I'll take a walk with you," he replied, wiping a thin sheen of sweat from his brow.

"You don't have to."

He smiled at her almost questioningly. "I'm not letting you wander through this mayhem alone."

She playfully flexed her bicep. "Really, I'm a tough girl."

"Well, you're a *beautiful* tough girl, so I would feel better making sure you don't get mauled on your way to relieve some of that alcohol from your system."

She shrugged. "I guess you have a point."

He led her gently by the elbow to one of the bathrooms on the first floor. The long line wrapped around the kitchen, so they decided to try one of the others available on the second level. Emily peered at the mountain of stairs with a look of grief. Gavin smiled at her reaction and helped her climb to the top. To her dismay, the line for that bathroom was longer. Gavin let out a full, throaty laugh at the look on her face. She shook her head and explained there was a third level with more bathrooms. As before, he helped her up the stairs. The top level was essentially empty and had no line at all, so Emily was in and out in two minutes. When Emily emerged, she found Gavin leaning against the wall, his eyes locking on hers as she walked over. Mocking his position, she stood next to him, their shoulders barely brushing. She turned her head to look up at him. "Thank you for making sure I didn't get attacked on my way up here."

Pushing off the wall, Gavin stepped directly in front of her—so close he felt the heat emanating from her body. "Not a problem. Are you ready to go back downstairs?"

Tempting her own destruction, she shook her head. The sounds from the music and party below faded away. Other than her own quick breathing, Emily could hear only his voice, see only his eyes, and feel only his hot breath feathering her cheeks.

Gavin felt the emotions filtering through her eyes. Lust. Desire. Want. Need. All of which mirrored his own. He stepped closer, their eyes never unlocking. "Tell me what you want," he whispered.

Not answering and acting on pure impulse, she pressed against him, melting into the solidness of his defined, hardened muscles. She slowly brought her arms up around his neck, stared into his eyes, and pulled in the smooth, woodsy scent of his cologne through her nose. She anchored him with a salacious gaze, their lips inches apart, with her sweet, alcohol-infused breath dancing across his face.

"Say it, Emily." The words came out in a low growl as he grasped the curve of her hips. "I need to hear you say it."

Even in her alcohol-induced daze, she knew what he meant. With her chest rising and falling from her labored breathing, she barely got the words past her lips. "I . . . I want you."

With the weight of his body, he pressed her against the wall and licked the soft spot below her earlobe. "Tell me how much you fucking want me," he breathed.

Heat pulsed in her stomach, tingling through her entire being, as his tongue traced a wet, torrid line up her neck. "Oh God, Gavin," she moaned, her body trembling. "You're in my dreams, in my thoughts, in my skin."

Before she could catch her breath, he claimed her mouth.

His lips were a shock to her system, breaking the rhythm and certainty of her beating heart. He tasted of mint, a little bit of booze, and something inherently Gavin. Delicious heat curled through every muscle, fiber, and cell in her body. With one hand splayed across the small of her back, he buried the other in her tangled curls. Emily moaned softly as the heat of his mouth moved easily over her lips. The assault on her nerves was close to overwhelming, not allowing a single coherent thought to pass through her mind. He might have stolen her breath the first time they kissed, but there and then he was trying to steal her heart.

With alcohol, lust, and desire reeling through her veins, Emily was dimly aware of them haphazardly stumbling into an empty bedroom. With the back of his foot, Gavin kicked the door closed. They embraced each other like a boa constrictor wrapped around its prey. Gavin groaned as their lips briefly tore apart, allowing enough time for Emily to pull his shirt up over his head. Gavin's fingers fumbled to unbutton her blouse, eventually tossing it to the floor. With both of their chests heaving for air—Emily in her bra, skirt, and heels and Gavin left only in his pants—they stood face-to-face, staring at each other for a beat.

The connection caught and ricocheted through them. Never breaking his gaze, Gavin bent his head and crushed his mouth to hers again, her lips tasting better than he remembered. His hands roamed over her soft skin as he studied every inch, reading her flesh like a novel written in braille. Everything about her was pure deliciousness. He kissed her as though the brief time they had been apart had starved him of all basic human necessities. Emily released a soft whimper as his tongue laved over her ear, down to her neck, and across the curve of her collarbone. That whimper—that lusty little whimper—

sent Gavin's body and mind into overdrive. They fell back onto the bed.

Dillon's familiar face vaguely surfaced in Emily's mind, along with guilt over what she was about to do, but the thought of him swiftly faded when Gavin pulled down the scalloped edge of her white lace bra. Pushing his knee between her legs, coaxing them open, he leaned down and licked the soft swell of her breast. Circling his lips around one taut peak, he sucked it softly. Emily flushed and grew hot as she pressed against his mouth, her body writhing with burning pleasure under his attack. His tongue skillfully made the burning heat in her stomach unfurl while each slow, glorious circle and gentle stroke unraveled her by the second.

Gavin pulled her skirt above her waist, his kiss growing frantic as his hands skimmed the smooth flesh between her legs. Emily moaned as he yanked her panties down. Her breath caught again as his smoldering blue eyes watched her reaction when he slid two fingers—and then a third—inside her wet folds. Her back arched against the sensation. Her eyes never left his as she gasped. She brought her arms up, threading her fingers through his hair, and pulled him back down to her lips. As the kiss grew deeper, Gavin's response was a long, drawn-out groan, only increasing the fervor running through her.

His mouth was hot and hungry over hers—tongue sliding in and out, tasting her sweetness until he strained for more. His body pulsed with pleasure as her nails bit into his shoulders, clawing and digging as she circled her hips against his hand. Pulling back, his mouth abandoned her lips as he continued to thrust his fingers inside, her breath mounting faster while his gaze raked over her beautiful face.

As Gavin stared into her green-and-gold-flecked eyes, a knot suddenly formed in his chest, nearly blocking his ability to breathe. She was forbidden fruit, and God knew he wanted a taste. He was ready to do anything to have her. He craved her. He needed her. But he realized as much as he ached for this moment, he couldn't take her drunk. He wouldn't allow himself to have her like this—in some stranger's home. He wanted her when she was in the right state of mind—and in *his* bed. He wanted to wake up with her beside him, and he needed to know that the alcohol wasn't making the decision for her. He withdrew his fingers from inside her in an attempt to stop, but as soon as he did, she reached for his wrist and pulled his dampened fingers into her mouth—sucking on each one like a lollipop.

The simple act was so deliciously hot, he felt his blood rush through his body even faster. Once again, his lips slammed into hers, stifling her moans while he plunged his fingers back inside her warmth. He kissed her harder, groaning when her legs lifted to frame his waist. When Emily released her hold on his hair and ran her fingers down his stomach to unbutton his pants, he knew he had to stop again. With tortured, brutal, agonizing restraint, Gavin shot up from the bed, his chest heaving. He walked clear across the room, dragging his hands through his hair.

Lying on the bed in utter shock and trying to catch her breath, Emily looked at him with the flush of desire still blooming on her cheeks. "What's wrong?" she breathed, her voice a ragged mess.

"I can't do this, Emily." He plucked his shirt from the floor and pulled it over his head. Grabbing hers, he tossed it onto the bed, making sure he didn't get too close to her again. If he did, he knew there was no turning back. "Get up and get dressed."

Sitting up, humiliation tore through her and she shrugged into her blouse. She was panting and confused beyond any rational thought. "But I thought this is what you wanted."

At a loss for words, staring at her beautiful face and still trying to talk his own raging hormones down, Gavin swallowed and simply shook his head.

"Oh my God, I knew this would happen," Emily whispered, stumbling to her feet, her head still dizzy. "You don't want me. You never wanted me. I'm just one of your sick, twisted void fillers for the night—another pawn in the let's-fuck-with-women's-heads game."

In two quick strides, Gavin was across the room. Taking her chin in his hand, he rubbed his thumb across her bottom lip. "No, Emily, just listen to me."

She swatted his hand off her face as tears sprung in her eyes. "I can't believe this. I feel like such a fool."

"Emily," he whispered. Seeing that she was clearly drunk made him feel less of the man he thought himself to be. "Please don't think that I don't want you. What just happened . . . What just occurred . . ." he said, pointing to the bed. "That little bit I had of you makes me want so much more—just that little bit puts anyone I've ever been with to shame. I want you more than anything. I just can't have it happen like this."

Seemingly unaffected by his declaration, Emily attempted to button her shirt. "You don't want me. I need to leave." She sniffled, trying to make her way toward the door.

Gavin caught her by her elbow and spun her around, placing his hands on her hips. She tried to pull away, but between his ironclad grip and the amount of alcohol running through her system, her effort was worthless. He leaned down and looked her in the eyes. "Do you think it was easy for me to stop, Emily? You have no idea how much I want to do this with you . . . to touch you again," he whispered, brushing his hand across her cheek. "To taste you again." He licked his lips, savoring her lingering juices. "To finally feel you beneath me." His fingers slowly teased into her hair. "I told you . . . I want you more than anything, but not here in this house and not while you're drunk."

A frown marred the space between her brows as she wiped a tear from her face. "Oh, the epiphany comes now, huh?" She yanked out of his hold, wobbling toward the door again. "Go to hell, Gavin."

Still trying to assist her, Gavin scooped her up in one graceful movement, like a groom carrying his bride over the threshold. Having no choice but to cling to his neck, Emily breathed heavily. "Put me down."

"You can barely walk."

"I can walk just fine. Now put me down!"

Gavin ignored her request and pulled the door open. Upon emerging from the room, the once-empty hallway looked like a certified brothel, with couples making out in every direction Gavin turned. Knowing he had had Emily pent up inside that room in a scene like this only sickened his stomach further. He bolted down the stairs with her. Although she tried to squirm out of his embrace, her efforts were futile. Her head lolled back and her eyes closed with every step he took. Not even the deafening music pulled her from her drunken stupor.

Scanning the maddening mess of intoxicated bodies, Gavin made eye contact with Trevor, who had Fallon curled up in his lap on a recliner. Trevor's forehead creased when he saw Gavin with Emily. Seeming out of it herself, Fallon stayed rooted to the chair when Trevor stood and walked over to Gavin. "What's wrong with her?"

"She doesn't feel good," Gavin answered. "Go find your sister and meet me in my car."

Emily gingerly lifted her head from Gavin's shoulder. She smiled in Trevor's direction. "I feel fine, Trevor," she slurred.

"But Gavin's an asshole." She closed her eyes, her head plummeting back against Gavin's shoulder with her arms dangling to the side. Trevor cocked a brow.

"Don't even ask right now," Gavin remarked. "Just do what I said."

"Well, I'm pretty sure I'm going back to Fallon's place tonight." Trevor beamed. "Go ahead, get Emily into your car, and I'll find Liv and send her out."

Gavin gave a quick nod and wove through the party. A few guys whistled and cheered, yelling that he was going home with "a nice piece of drunken ass." Fighting back the urge to set Emily down and knock them all out, Gavin continued to snake through the throng of partiers and eventually got out the door.

Emily's eyes fluttered open as Gavin attempted to place her on her feet while he opened the passenger-side door. "I'm not sitting up front with you, Gavin," she slurred.

Stumbling away, she grabbed for the rear door and slid across the backseat. Within a split second, she was out cold.

Shaking his head, Gavin moved around the car, got in, started the engine, and pulled to the front of the house. A few minutes later, with her brother's aid, Olivia got into the front seat.

After closing the door, Trevor poked his head into the car. "Make sure you get my two girls home safe. I'll call you tomorrow, man."

Gavin nodded.

"Love you, bro." Olivia blew him a kiss as they drove away. She glanced back at Emily, slipped her heels off and propped her feet on the dashboard. "She's fucking down for the count, huh?"

Gavin didn't answer as he stared straight ahead.

Olivia looked back at Emily and flicked her eyes over to Gavin. "Oh shit. Did something happen between you two?"

Shaking his head, he clenched the steering wheel tighter. "Just do me a favor, Olivia. You let her know when she wakes up that I stopped for all the right reasons and nothing more."

Having known him long enough, Olivia didn't prod further and remained silent for the rest of the ride. The only time Emily woke was when Gavin stopped to pay a toll going back over the Verrazano-Narrows Bridge. She mumbled something inaudible and quickly fell back asleep. By the time they arrived at the apartment building, Olivia had also dozed off, and Gavin had to wake her up.

The sound of car doors closing awoke Emily, and she sat straight up, swaying. With her vision blurred, she was slightly able to make out Gavin standing next to the car, talking with Olivia. Sliding across the backseat, Emily threw the car door open and all but fell to the ground in an attempt to exit the vehicle. Gavin caught her by her arm before her knees kissed the concrete.

Emily shot him an icy look and yanked her arm from him. "Don't touch me!"

Grabbing her by the waist, Gavin pressed her body to his and pinned her against the car, his breathing heavy and his expression granite. Olivia's eyes widened at their exchange. "Go inside, Liv," he said without turning to look at her, his eyes locked on Emily's. "I'll bring her up in a minute."

"Gavin, I'm sorry. This whole thing was my fault. I shouldn't—"

"Olivia, it's not your fault. Just go inside," he replied, his voice harder. Olivia cupped her hand over her mouth and walked away.

Emily looked at him, a wry smile tipping her lips. "You sure do love breaking girls' hearts, don't you?"

With his calculating eyes searing into hers, Gavin's large

hand came around the back of her neck and pulled her into his mouth. Emily didn't resist. As a matter of fact, she gripped his hair, yanking him harder against her body. Moaning into her mouth, Gavin easily dominated the kiss. He didn't care about the passing onlookers—hell, he didn't even care if Dillon walked up to them. All he cared about was Emily knowing how badly he wanted her.

And as quickly as Gavin started that kiss, he ended it. Again playing the role of a groom carrying his bride, he scooped Emily up and carried her through the lobby and into the elevator. As he placed her on her feet, their eyes locked. It was only a matter of seconds before they were at it again, both slamming hard into each other's mouths. A power struggle of the fiercest kind followed—hands sliding up and down, Emily's back pressed against the wall, Gavin's hair being pulled, her legs wrapped around his waist, his growls, and her moans. Gavin was fast becoming desperate to rip off her clothes and plant himself firmly inside her right there in that elevator.

When the doors parted, the battle stopped. Gavin raked his hands through his hair, mussing it further, and Emily adjusted her skirt. Walking her into her apartment, they found Olivia sleeping on the couch. He followed Emily into her bedroom and watched as she climbed into her bed. Without a second look in his direction, she rolled over, sighed, and passed out.

Crossing his arms, Gavin leaned against the doorway. His eyes took in her chest rising and falling with sleep. If not for the front door snapping shut, pulling his attention away from Emily's slumberous body, he would've watched her all night. Gavin walked down the hall and into the kitchen, where he found Dillon tossing his keys onto the counter.

Dillon leveled him with a suspicious stare. "What the hell are you doing here?"

"The girls went to a house party in Staten Island, and Emily had a problem with some asshole. Olivia called Trevor, and we went out there to make sure everything was all right."

Dillon's forehead creased. "Wait, they were at a house party? She fucking lied to me. They were supposed to be at Cielo." Gavin started to answer, but Dillon spoke up again. "And why the fuck didn't anyone call me?"

Not liking Dillon's tone, Gavin angled his head to the side and narrowed his eyes. "I guess they decided to go to the party instead. Last time I checked, women had the right to change their minds." Gavin stepped closer. "If every once in a while you checked your fucking phone while you were out, you would've seen Trevor did call you. Why don't you try clearing out your voice mail so someone can actually leave you a fucking message?"

Crossing his arms, Dillon cupped his chin, the look in his eyes glacial.

Gavin stared at him for a second, trying to quell his adrenaline, his voice eerily calm. "Like I said, we went out there, made sure everything was okay, and I brought them back here." He dug his keys from his pocket, his eyes never leaving Dillon's. "Be a good boyfriend and have some aspirin and water at her disposal when she wakes up. She's gonna need it." Without another word, Gavin walked out the door.

11

Sea of Uncertainty

THE NEXT MORNING, Gavin brewed a pot of coffee, hoping the caffeine buzz would jolt his thoughts away from Emily. Walking over to a window, he found the sky besieged by threatening gray clouds hovering over the city. It fit his mood perfectly. Agitation over his lack of self-control crawled through his system as stealthy recollections of Emily's sweet lips weaved through his mind. The smell of her perfume permeated his pores . . . and by God, it intoxicated him by the minute. Though his body still hummed with pleasure from their encounter, his mind was caught in a tangled web of emotions. A knock at the door broke through the heated events rolling around in his head. Opening it, he found Trevor wearing a wide smile. He was in a far better frame of mind than Gavin.

"Damn, dude, you look like shit," Trevor said, settling on the couch with his long legs sprawled out in front of him.

Gavin poured a cup of coffee and perched on a bar stool in the kitchen. "I couldn't sleep."

"Sorry about that, bro. I, however, slept like a baby wrapped in Fallon's arms."

A weak smile tipped Gavin's mouth. "Sounds like it went well."

"Beyond well," he replied, victory heavy in his expression. "I actually dig her. She has this funky, cool personality, and to top it all off, she's a little freak. I mean, she goes both ways."

With the cock of his brow, Gavin smirked. "Your sister goes both ways, too."

Trevor cringed. "Did you really have to kill my buzz, bringing that up?" Gavin shrugged. Trevor stared at him for several seconds, seeming to read something in his eyes. "So are you going to tell me what's going on with you and Emily?"

"Nothing's going on with me and Emily," he clipped, his tone harsh.

"Dude, we've known each other for fourteen years. I had a feeling something was up with you two, and last night only confirmed it."

Gavin got up and sauntered over to the window as he contemplated what to say. His answer was slow and apprehensive. "I'm in deep."

"Bro, please don't tell me you fucked her."

He turned and pinned him with a hard glare. "No, I didn't fuck her, Trevor."

"Well, what the hell's going on?"

Nibbling at his lip, Gavin paced the room like a caged animal. He didn't know how to explain what he felt for Emily. He didn't know how Trevor would perceive him after he confessed everything either. The only thing he knew was that he couldn't make sense of his emotions, and in that moment, he didn't care. He felt what he felt.

End. Of. Story.

"Dude, just come out and say it."

Gavin plowed his hands through his hair and regarded him from across the room. "I think I'm falling for her."

With disapproving eyes, Trevor's mouth hung agape. He stood up and walked over. "You do know Dillon's our friend, right?"

A frown marred Gavin's features. "What kind of question is that?"

"Come on, Gavin. How did you fall for our friend's girl?"

"I met her before I knew she was with Dillon," he replied through gritted teeth. He padded over to the counter and downed the rest of his coffee.

"Wait, I thought the first time you met her was that night at the club."

Gavin sighed deeply, placing his hands on the back of his neck. "No, it's complicated. She delivered food to my office. I tried to get her number. . . ." He paused, his stomach twisting as he remembered the first time he saw Emily. Even now, the thought of her nearly evaporated the oxygen from his lungs. "Or maybe I tried giving her my number. I can't fucking remember; it was back in June. I went to her job the next day to see her, and we were introduced a few days later."

Trevor walked back over to the couch, sinking into it. "Look, dude, I'm going to be brutally honest here." Gavin eyed him from across the room. "He's planning on marrying her—soon."

Again, oxygen nearly depleted, Gavin swallowed and leaned against the counter. "He told you that?"

"Surely he's mentioned it to you?"

"Yeah, but I didn't think he was serious." A gut-wrenching ache ran through his stomach as his chest constricted at the thought. "Besides, he doesn't love her. Do you honestly believe he stopped fucking around with Monica? I sure as shit don't."

"Knowing him, you're probably right. But to tell you the truth, bro, I don't think about it. What he does is his business. Emily's with him for her own reasons, and as far as I'm concerned, she chooses to see what she wants. It's as simple as that."

"Well, it's not that simple for me," he replied, his tone rising.

"It has to be. You need to kill whatever the fuck is going on between you two."

"I don't think I can." Hesitating, he drew in a lungful of air, his voice dropping a notch. "She's supposed to be with me."

"Dude, this can only end in disaster. Gavin—seriously—you need to really think about what you're doing. Just think about it. She loves him, too."

"She doesn't love him," he scoffed. "She's just confused. He may be my friend, but just like all the rest, he fucks with her head and drags her into his morphed sense of need."

"No. You're fucking with your own head by thinking she doesn't love him. Listen to yourself, bro. Take a step back and honestly listen to what you're saying here." Although Gavin didn't speak, his eyes hardened like shards of glass. "Look, man, I'm just being honest. It's a bad situation. You know it, and I know it."

"I'm not denying it's a bad situation!" Gavin tossed his hands up, the words cracking like thunder. "Do I look like some kind of asshole? A snake is a snake, no matter how many times it sheds its skin! He's no fucking good for her!"

Blowing out a breath, Trevor walked to the door. He turned around and looked back at Gavin. "You're like a brother to me, dude, but I think you're trying to vilify Dillon for your own personal needs. And to tell you the truth, you're putting me in a bad spot. I can already see this shit's gonna get crazy, and I don't want any part of it."

Oh, damn it all to hell. The last thing Gavin wanted to do was put Trevor in the middle. Sitting back down, Gavin looked at him from across the room, defeat weighing heavy like lead in his eyes. "What the fuck am I supposed to do?"

"You need to forget about her. The whole fucking thing's a mistake. And, more important, you have to remember that Dillon's your friend." Trevor exhaled heavily and shook his head before walking out the door. "I'll call you later, bro."

The advice was so simple. Just forget her. The words couldn't be closer to the truth. This might have been a huge mistake, but the man at the receiving end couldn't see that. He outright refused to. Emily would never be a mistake to him, no matter how many people he hurt in the process—including himself. Everything he and Emily could be was real for Gavin. When he said he felt she was supposed to be with him, it wasn't just a heated statement. It wasn't just an inclination. From the first time their eyes met, he felt it down to the lowest depths of his soul, right down to the bottom of his core. She had been made for him in every possible way. Even though she was the very definition of off-limits, his mind and heart screamed to throw it all to the wind and let the whole fucking thing burn to the ground. Therefore, into the sea of uncertainty he would plunge—trying to make her his—and he feared neither friend nor foe could stop him. He just prayed the woman who saturated his thoughts felt the same.

Emily awoke feeling as if she had swallowed a handful of nails. Her throat was burning raw as reckless images of the night before played through her mind. The thoughts, scattering around like marbles, only made her temples blossom into a full-blown headache. Guilt for what she had done to Dillon and their relationship burned almost as hot as her insatiable arousal for Gavin.

With thin and shaky breathing, she lifted her head and peered around the room. Dillon wasn't in the bed. She sighed with relief when her eyes glanced over to the nightstand. Along with a note explaining that he would be back soon, he had also left two aspirin and a glass of water she couldn't consume quickly enough. The cool liquid and the magic little pills slid into her stomach, eventually offering up some relief, but not nearly as much as she needed.

Groaning, she stared miserably at the drab light filtering through the window shades. She whipped the blankets back over her head. She wanted the image of Gavin on top of her, kissing, touching, and tasting her, to blur, melt, and recede, banished to a place she could never find again.

However, the more she rehashed the undeniable pleasure he'd produced in their all-too-short exchange, the more she craved him. His dominant yet soft kiss, his hard but gentle caresses, the way his fingers—oh God, the way his fingers had tunneled deep inside her—had merely teased her senses with the sweet taste of what he was truly capable of. Not even the worst of hangovers could keep her body from yearning for more. The smell of his cologne in her hair did nothing to help ebb any of the thoughts that had her loins teetering on the edge of orgasm right there.

Despite all of this, her head was under attack, barraged by her mother's voice. *"Dillon's a good man, Emily. Make sure you hold on to him and never let go."*

Clear visualizations played out of all the times Dillon had helped while her mother was ill. Emily had all but fallen to her knees before she died. Frozen with fear and unable to aid in her mom's last few days, it wasn't her who kept watch over her mother—it wasn't even her sister, Lisa, because she had been in a near-fatal accident a few days before—it was Dillon. There was no limit to the amount of times he helped her mother. He held her hair as she retched into a bedpan while Emily sat sedated in a chair across the room in utter shock at what was unfolding around her. Beyond paying for hospital bills and taking care of the funeral expenses on his own, he even allowed Emily and Lisa to keep what little the life insurance policy provided.

And this is how I repay him?

The thoughts forced out hot, helpless tears as she slid from her bed and grudgingly padded into the bathroom. Lingering liquor sloshed around in her empty belly. It was then that she realized she was still draped in last night's clothing. She cringed as she tore it from her body, wanting to burn it in a blazing fire, along with the memory of what'd happened.

To rid her flesh of caked-on makeup and the scent of Gavin from her lips, she splashed warm, soapy water onto her face, once again finding her stomach wretched with guilt. She looked in the mirror with disgust, anger, and hate—but in that moment, she decided she wouldn't wallow under her own scrutiny of what she did. She'd been drunk; that was her story, and she was sticking to it. If sober, surely, none of it would have ever happened. Her body might want Gavin, but in no way, shape, or form did her mind. In all his pleasure, he was simply a serpent companion to the sexual demon hidden beneath the surface of her skin. At least that's what she tried to convince her short-circuited brain on this particular Sunday morning.

Hovering over the sink to allow more water to flow into her cupped hands, she nearly jumped out of her skin when she felt a soft touch against her shoulder. "Jesus, Dillon, you scared me," she said, her voice timid and riddled with an acute underlying panic she was trying desperately to suppress.

Can he tell? Do I look different? Oh God, do I still smell like him?

He gave a soft smile, his tone low, calming even. "You're shaking, babe." He brushed the matted hair away from her face. "Let's get in the shower, okay?"

Swallowing back the acid steadily building in her throat, she nodded as he slid her panties down, her body quivering in the process. She stepped out of them and unhooked her bra, her eyes latched on his. Grabbing her hand, he led her to the shower and turned it on. He gestured for her to get in. With unsteady breathing from mounting nerves, she watched him undress. Grabbing for the soap, she hastily ran it across her body in an attempt to get rid of Gavin's lingering saliva from her pores. Stepping into the shower, Dillon pressed her back against his chest as he began to massage her shoulders. Drawing in the deepest of breaths, she let her head fall back, trying to savor the heat from the water.

"Is Olivia awake yet?" she asked, attempting to stir up conversation.

"I don't think so. Her bedroom door's still closed." He continued to massage her shoulders. "She must've gotten up from the couch because that's where she was passed out when I came in last night."

"What time are we meeting your parents?" she reluctantly asked.

"We need to start getting ready as soon as we're done in here." Emily nodded. "So, you were pretty hammered last night."

She reached down for the shampoo and bit her lip. "Yeah, I was."

"What did you do last night, Emily?" His voice hardened just enough to send a shiver up her spine.

Attempting to catch her breath, she turned to face him. "Wha . . . What do you mean?"

With his eyes intent on hers, he slowly lifted a hand and brushed his thumb across her chin. "You lied to me."

Heart ricocheting in her chest, Emily shook her head, struggling against her tears. "I . . . I didn't lie to you about anything."

He took the shampoo, poured some into his hands, and lathered it up. Eyes still locked on hers, he gathered her hair and started washing it. "I ran into Gavin last night when I walked in."

Trying to hide the panic she knew crossed her features and wanting to drown, choke, gasp, or maybe even die right there in that shower, Emily stared back, unable to form a sentence. A knot formed in her throat, threatening to cut off all oxygen.

"He told me you girls didn't go to Cielo."

Swallowing down said knot, oxygen silently whooshed back into her lungs. "Oh," she said breathlessly. "Umm, yeah, we decided to go to a party at someone's house that Fallon knows."

"Right, you lied."

"I didn't lie, Dillon," she whispered, rinsing the shampoo from her hair, knowing she was harboring a far greater lie. "It was a last-minute change in plans. That's all."

Pulling her body against his, he ghosted his mouth down the curve of her jaw. "Okay, last-minute change of plans that I wasn't made aware of." He circled his arms around her waist. "What if I'd gone to Cielo, Emily? I would've thought something happened to you."

"You're right," she conceded. It was the least she could do, considering . . . well, considering everything. She knew he could've easily made a quick phone call to check on her, but she wasn't about to push her luck. "I should've called you. I had too much to drink, and honestly, I didn't think about it. I'm sorry; next time I'll call."

Appearing satisfied, he handed her the soap and turned around, placing his hands on the tile. "Can you wash my back?" Lathering up the soap, she did as he asked. "I'm not sure there will be a next time—you hanging out with that freak again."

"But, Dillon, she . . ."

"Look, I'm not in the mood to argue with you, Emily. I've never seen you so out of it. I tried to wake you up, but you wouldn't budge." He tilted his head from side to side and rolled his shoulders. "At one point, I honestly thought you had alcohol poisoning until you finally mumbled something. She's obviously not a good influence on you. End of story. You're not hanging out with her again."

At a loss for words, she stilled her hands. Turning around, Dillon gently pulled her head back by her hair and branded his lips against hers. He couldn't see them, but silent tears trickled down her cheeks amid the water flowing over her face. Today—in these moments and seconds—she wouldn't protest his ridiculous words. She couldn't. It wasn't in her. She barely had any fight left—not after the self-destructive stunt she'd pulled less than twelve hours ago with his friend. When Dillon began to make love to her, it wasn't just his hands present on her flesh. The guilt slid over her skin, manifesting inside her like a disease. Now she would use the last remaining fight she had left to avoid the overwhelming sense of shame threatening to swallow her whole instead.

Sitting in an Italian restaurant on the Upper East Side, Emily picked up her silverware and regarded Joan Parker, Dillon's mother, from across the table. "Yes, I actually start next week."

"That's fantastic," Joan went on, lacing her fingers together. "I'm just happy that my Dillon got you the job in Greenwich Village. The schools there are wonderful." Suddenly, Joan's face morphed with displeasure. "But I have to say, it horrifies me to think you were actually considering a job in Bushwick of all places. It's filth, just absolute filth."

Although the statement didn't shock her, Emily inwardly cringed, biting back a crude reply. Joan had been known to strictly surround herself with people who sported cars that cost a small fortune. With her overpriced, dyed-blonde hair, monthly Botox injections, and acrylic nails, Emily wasn't sure if the woman had one original body part left—even her breasts were questionable. The only thing about the "mannequin" Emily knew to be real was that she was a certified uppity, gold-digging snob.

"Now, Joan, I'm sure Emily had no knowledge of the city's demographics when she submitted her résumé," Dillon's father, Henry, replied. Slicking a hand through his brown hair, he leaned back in his seat and gave her a warm smile. "Am I correct or what?"

Emily nodded. "You're correct, Mr. Parker. I just visited New York State's Department of Education Web site and applied to anything available."

Grabbing for Emily's hand, Dillon shot his mother a searing look. "I take full responsibility for not warning her about certain areas. She had no idea where to look."

Emily smiled in his direction, squeezing his hand a little tighter.

"Oh, Dillon, honey, it's just like you to defend her obvious lack of proper research before moving to a new state." She sweetly patted her son's back right about the same time Emily's smile fell. "That's all it would've taken, just a little bit of research to avoid—"

Cutting in, Emily schooled her voice carefully, trying to keep the edge of hostility to a minimum. "In case you've forgotten, I had a lot going on. It must've slipped my mind in the middle of—I don't know—my mother's death." Emily topped the reply off with a cute little head tilt.

"Well, of course I didn't forget that," she quickly twittered, flipping her hair behind her shoulder. "I was just simply saying—"

"*Mother*," Dillon said with heavy emphasis. "Drop it." He put his silverware down and rested his elbows on the table, the look in his eyes firmly stating for her to zip her lips.

With a gasp, Joan shifted in her seat and adjusted the collar of her tweed Chanel suit, which Emily guessed had probably cost the same as two months of her and Olivia's rent.

Sliding his arm around the back of her chair, Henry looked at his wife. "Yes, let's drop it for now, shall we?"

Joan gave a curt nod and reached for her glass of red wine. "Fine."

Over the next half hour, Emily sat mute, trying to stir up some plan to get out of there. Sudden blindness, acute respiratory distress, hell, even cardiac arrest topped her list of imaginary ailments to claim as an excuse to leave. The tension in the air hovered as thick as fog. The actual mind-numbing, hangover-induced migraine forging its way through her skull only intensified her need to leave. She was grateful when Dillon's father broke the silence, buffering out one of his infamous jokes involving a hooker and a chicken.

Dillon looked at Emily after the waiter cleared their plates. "Babe, you're having dessert, right?"

She shook her head. On second thought, stuffing another piece of food into her mouth had her seriously thinking she might get out of the nightmare by heaving all over the table. The idea held a certain amount of appeal. "Actually, I will."

While waiting for her tiramisu, Emily glanced at Dillon and noticed he was starting to sweat, nearly all color draining from his face. If she wasn't mistaken, he looked as bad as she felt. And that was bad. Placing her hand on his cheek, she asked, "Are you all right?"

He nodded, and with a shaky hand, he plucked a napkin off the table, wiping the perspiration from his brow. Emily handed him her water, and in a few gulps, he drained the entire glass. She looked over at his parents to gauge their reaction to his freakish demeanor and found both of them smiling like the Cheshire Cat.

Huh?

When her eyes traveled back to Dillon, he was rising from his seat, one hand gliding not so smoothly into the pocket of his pants. For the next few seconds, the sights and sounds played out in slow motion for Emily.

Her heart began to race like a frightened little mouse fleeing its predator.

Dillon pulled his chair away from the table.

Thump . . .

Dillon slowly got down on one knee.

Thump . . . thump . . .

Dillon produced a small black velvet box.

Thump . . .

Thump . . .

Flat line . . .

Beeeeeeeeeeep . . .

Somewhere in the midst of what Emily was witnessing, her fogged brain registered the distant sound of other patrons letting out gleeful gasps as they watched her boyfriend. A thick dryness—one that could easily mock the Sahara Desert—plagued her tongue. With blurred vision, she scanned the crowd—most of them holding wide smiles, some pointing in her direction. One man even yelled, "Go for it, buddy," ending his hoot with a whistle through his fingers.

Staring down at him kneeling in front of her, interminable anxiety had Emily stuttering most of her words. "Dillon . . . Wha . . . What are you doing?" she whispered.

Pulling in a hurried breath, he lifted Emily's hand to his mouth and planted a soft kiss on it, his voice quivering low. "I love you, Emily." He cracked open the box, highlighting a princess-cut engagement ring well over three carats in size. His eyes twinkled with what appeared to be tears. "You make me whole in every way imaginable. Would you please do me the honor of becoming my wife?"

Still trying to process his proposal and desperately seeking a normal pace of breathing, Emily cupped his cheek, her voice lower than a whisper. "Dillon, can we go talk in private, please?"

Almost immediately, the smile he was wearing fell from his face, but before he could answer, his mother spoke up. Her face contorted as if she were offended. "Surely, you're going to say yes to my son?" She fretted.

Henry sent his wife a lethal, silencing stare.

With no response, Emily bit her lip and looked down at her hands twisting in her lap.

Dillon slowly rose, offering his mother a scrutinizing glare. He reached down and gently took Emily's hand. "Umm . . . okay, babe." His voice was low and cracked slightly. "There's a banquet room we could use."

Emily let out the air her lungs were holding hostage. With her head downcast in embarrassment, she followed him to the back of the restaurant. Out of the corner of her eye, she saw onlookers straightening in their chairs and quietly resuming their meals. Low whispers descending throughout the restaurant rang loudly in her ears like a high school marching band.

Dillon closed the door to the vacant room, his unspoken question heavy in the air. The dejected look in his eyes said everything as he crossed his arms and slowly sauntered over to a window.

Emily's voice was barely above a whisper, but it still carried across the room to where he stood, unmoving. "I just need some time, Dillon. That's all."

Without turning in her direction, he exhaled a weighty breath, his voice as low as hers. "I don't understand, Emily. We've talked about this quite a few times. I thought you loved me."

Emily sobbed, despite all of her resolutions to keep it together. "God, Dillon, of course I love you. I love you more than you could ever imagine." The words tasted foul in her mouth as haunting thoughts of the night before soured her stomach. The last thing she needed was to think of Gavin, but it was no use. He was there lingering in her thoughts. His smile . . . his eyes . . . his laugh . . . Everything about him added to her confusion. Her theory about her mind not wanting him was blown to shreds. Just like that, her heart sank a little more. "We don't even live together yet. I thought that would be our first step before marriage."

Dillon faced her. "I wanted you to move in with me when you came to New York, Emily. You're the one who didn't want to commit to that." As Emily tried to compose herself, he moved across the room. With a trembling hand, he stroked her cheek. "I love you. This *is* our next step, baby. Please tell me if this has something to do with what your father did to your family. I would never do that to you, Emily. I swear to God I wouldn't."

Emily's vision tunneled back to a memory nearly twenty years old. As much as she denied having any recollection of the man . . . she did. One in particular: the morning he walked out of the house and her life for good. Flashes of her confused five-year-old face looking up to a tall figure—whom even at that young age, Emily knew she loved to pieces—cascaded her mind. Her tiny arms gripping his leg in an attempt to make him stay invaded her thoughts like an unwelcomed guest. Though she tried—and Lord knows she tried—she couldn't hold on tight enough. He was too strong for her little body. She could still hear the torturous sound of her mother and sister's cries as he drunkenly cursed each of them with words her fragile ears shouldn't have heard.

Clinging to a teddy bear, Emily followed, crying out for him, as he stumbled to the front door. It was a sunny day—that's another thing she remembered. The sun shone upon him, silhouetting his body like the angel she believed him to be, as he walked away and got into his car. She recalled thinking he would come back. He didn't, though. No matter how many times she sat with pretend tea and her dolls, awaiting his arrival, he never showed up. That's all she did—waited for someone who would never return. Gone. Vanished like a ghost. The sickening memory brought a fresh set of tears to her already soaked eyes.

However, those disturbing memories had nothing to do with her not wanting to rush into marriage. She was scared. Actually, terrified was more like it. She needed to live with Dillon before making any decisions. At least right now, that's the way she felt. Looking back, maybe she should have moved in with him from the beginning, but she couldn't change the past. Nevertheless, today it came knocking on her door in many wicked forms. Though she wouldn't allow her guilt for what she had engaged in last night to cloud her into accepting Dillon's proposal, surely, it had her questioning her moral judgment—drunk or not. "It doesn't have anything to do with my father," she whispered, staring up into his brown eyes. "I just need a few days to think this through."

Pressing his lips into a hard line, Dillon nodded tightly. "All right, I'll give you the time you need."

"Are you mad at me?" she asked, more tears spilling down her cheeks.

He shook his head and gently wiped the tears from her face. "I'm not mad at you, Emily. Shocked and confused, yes, but not mad." Dillon pulled her into his arms and kissed the top of her head. Her body shook against his as she sobbed a little more. She didn't want to face his parents—particularly his mother—nor did she want to walk back through the restaurant. Her embarrassment was simply too overwhelming. Somehow feeling her anxiety, Dillon handed her a ticket for the valet and walked her to an exit on the side of the building.

Stepping out into a small alley, she reluctantly turned back to face him. Holding her gaze, Dillon hesitated a moment before heading back to retrieve her purse. His eyes held a sadness Emily knew she had caused, and his once-confident shoulders hung low. The man she had come to know as a self-assured soul lost something on this particular Sunday afternoon in late August. Her heart sank further than she could've ever imagined. The pain-stricken look in his eyes would forever be embedded in her memory. As he closed the door, Emily's palms felt slick with sweat, her eyes were rimmed pink from crying, and her body ached with a deep sadness of its own.

A few days . . . I just need a few days, and then I'll let him know. . . .

12

Out of My System

THE WORDS WERE simple, the design elegantly understated. Gavin's office was completely silent, except for the steady, rhythmic rapping that echoed from him tapping the letter-pressed card on his desk again and again. He had lost count of the amount of times he'd glanced at it throughout the day.

Before us lies the open road . . . a future filled with timeless love . . .
Please join us as we
EMILY M. COOPER & DILLON R. PARKER
Celebrate Our Engagement
Saturday, the Twenty-Third of September
Two thousand and twelve
Six o'clock in the evening
The Diamond Room
30 West Fifty-Ninth Street
Hosted by Joan and Henry Parker
RSVP 212-981-1275 by September Fifteenth

The sound of the invitation tapping restlessly against Gavin's desk wasn't the only sound in the room. However, unless someone was standing close to him, they wouldn't have heard the others. Those sounds were the annihilation of his heart and his shallow breathing. Gavin wasn't surprised, but it was proof that she was going through with it.

Gavin had heard the news a few days earlier. Dillon had been thrilled when he'd announced his engagement, his words sucking the hope, along with the air, straight out of Gavin's lungs. During his brief conversation with Dillon, Gavin had felt like Jekyll and Hyde, considering he had to act happy for them. Knowing his tone had to hold some semblance of excitement, he'd played it off better than he'd expected as he congratulated Dillon. After hanging up, not throwing his phone against the wall had taken every atom of his self-control. It didn't matter, though. The blade was already shoved deep into his heart, mutilating it.

Gavin was so focused on the invitation that he almost didn't notice Colton shuffle into his office. Lifting his gaze from the torturous announcement, Gavin peered at him. Colton was aware of what was going on and wore an expression of concern. Gavin knew what he would say, and for fuck's sake, he didn't want to hear it.

"It is what it is, little man. You need to get her—"

"Shut the fuck up, Colton," he hissed. "You have no idea what's going on in my head right now."

The shock on Colton's face was palpable as his brows dipped low over his green eyes. "Then go after her, Gavin. When you want something this badly, you don't just give up. You fight and fight until you absolutely can't fight anymore. It's in the Blake bloodline, so it should be easy enough for you. Besides, I've never known a more stubborn little bastard in my entire life."

Gavin almost choked on a bitter laugh, but he briefly pondered his brother's suggestion. He knew he could barge into Emily's life and try to break down her defenses. The thought of holding her captive in his apartment, in his arms, in his bed until she cracked and swore to be his became more appealing with each passing second. He could tell she was hiding feelings for him, and he understood her fear of unleashing them. The risk was huge on both their parts. After they confessed their need to be together, the scrutiny they would suffer from others would be hard for them, but they could endure it together.

But what was the use of going after her? The thought that he might bide his time with her and possibly—no, definitely—fall in love with her only to have her decide she didn't want to be with him seared his heart. He'd be shit-all stupid to consider it. But, God, he couldn't do anything but close his eyes and think of her. The surge of helplessness to do something consumed him.

"Have you lost your fucking mind? Fight for her? She's marrying him."

"You're asking *me* if I've lost my mind?" Colton questioned incredulously. Taking a seat across from Gavin, he tilted his head to the side. "Brother, not only have you decided on attending this engagement party, you've also accepted Dillon's request to be one of his groomsmen. Who's the one who's lost his mind here?"

"How the fuck am I supposed to decline?" Gavin groaned. "Remember, I need to act somewhat normal around him."

He shrugged. "Tell them you're sick."

Gavin emitted a humorless laugh. "Believe me, I just might book a trip out of the country at this point." Rising from his chair, he grabbed his suit jacket and shrugged into it. "I need a fucking drink."

"I'm inclined to agree."

"Are you coming or not?"

"Sure, if I get to pick the place."

"Pick away."

Twenty minutes later, they pulled up to a cocktail lounge in the East Village. Gavin was impressed with the neighborhood and Colton's choice. A true mecca for artists, musicians, students, and writers, St. Mark's Place was definitely hopping during happy hour. Gavin's goal was simple: become hammered enough to remove the haunting images of Emily from his thoughts. He was pretty damn sure a decent amount of bourbon would aid in the exorcism of her from his mind.

Numb.

He wanted to feel absolutely, one hundred percent fucking numb.

As they exited Gavin's vehicle, Colton came to an abrupt stop. "Now, *there's* something that might drag Emily from your head." He motioned to a woman having car trouble.

Gavin studied her demeanor as she ducked out from under the hood of her vehicle. Holding her cell to her ear, she looked stressed and her frantic, caramel-colored eyes locked on Gavin. Beautiful long hair—the same color as those eyes—whipped around in the wind, along with her knee-length skirt. Unsteady in her heels, she tossed her purse strap over her shoulder as she slammed the hood down.

Colton nudged Gavin's arm. "Go give her a hand."

"She's already on the phone. I'm sure she has someone coming to help her."

No sooner did Gavin finish his sentence than she approached them with tears streaming down her face. "I'm sorry to bother you, but do either of you gentlemen have a cell I could use? Mine just went dead."

"Yeah, no problem," Gavin replied, digging in his pocket. He handed her his phone.

"Thank you," she sniffled as she accepted it. She hastily dialed some numbers and sauntered a few feet away.

Gavin looked at his brother. "Go get her a tissue or something. I'll wait here with her."

Colton sent him a smirk that had him rolling his eyes. As Colton strolled toward the lounge and opened the door, the sounds of a live jazz band spilled out into the busy city streets.

The woman eventually made her way back to Gavin. "Thank you, I appreciate it. My brother owns a tow company, and he'll be on his way soon."

"Not a problem," he said, tucking his cell in his pocket. "Looks like your head gasket's blown."

Once again, she sniffled. She glanced at her car and back to him. "You can tell without checking it?"

"There's white smoke coming from the tailpipe. That's usually a pretty good sign."

"Oh, are you a mechanic?"

Gavin smiled. "No, I just have a thing for cars." She sheepishly smiled back. "I sent my brother to get you a tissue."

"Thank you. I feel so foolish crying like this. It's just been a tough few weeks."

While he felt bad for her, he really didn't have any idea what to say. So Gavin found himself slightly relieved when Colton reemerged.

Handing her the tissue, Colton asked, "Were you able to get ahold of someone?" She nodded and let Colton know she was waiting on her ride. "While you're waiting, why don't you come inside with me and my kid brother?" Colton asked with a smirk aimed in Gavin's direction. "Our treat, of course."

Gavin quelled the sudden urge to knock him clear across the street.

With mild trepidation crossing her features, the woman smiled. "That actually sounds good. I could definitely use a drink, that's for sure."

Opening the door, Colton sent Gavin another wicked smile. "I know quite a few people who need a drink today."

Gavin shook his head and followed them into the lounge. The melodious notes of a saxophone player belting out "La Vie en Rose" hummed through the air. Jazz was something Gavin couldn't help but come to love over the years. It was a constant entity throughout his childhood since his father was a huge fan. The barest smile crept over Gavin's mouth when the memory of his parents swaying on their back porch to the exact same song flooded his mind. With the words fitting what he felt for Emily, this particular song was one he'd imagined dancing with her—pressed close against her body nestled tightly in his arms. The illusion he had created of them possibly being together couldn't have been further from reality now if he tried. Like a slow fire burning, the ache for her—and the need for more than a few shots of bourbon—curled through his thoughts.

After finding a table next to the dance floor, the woman, who had introduced herself as Stephanie, retreated to the restroom to fix her appearance. Promptly ordering three shots of bourbon and a beer, Gavin descended into what he hoped would turn into the numbness he so desperately sought. Within seconds of the waiter delivering the liquid comas, Gavin downed two of those shots and glared at his brother. "Don't even go there tonight."

Smiling, Colton casually leaned back in his seat. "I didn't say a word."

"Right, you don't have to," he replied, his voice holding a

heavy warning. "Your face is reeking of it, and I'm seriously in no fucking mood right now."

With a proper arch of his brow, Colton chuckled. "So, let me see, you're choosing the road that will inevitably leave you wallowing in your own self-pity?"

"You really have no fucking clue, do you?"

"No, brother, I do. Like I told you earlier, either fight for her or just let her go."

Shaking his head, Gavin downed the third shot. "I don't need you schooling me, Colton."

"I know you don't, little man. However, you can try to drink Emily away all you want," he noted, giving a leisurely shrug, "or you can take advantage of the beautiful damsel in distress wiping mascara from her pretty eyes right about now inside the restroom."

"So now you want me to take advantage of women, huh?" he huffed as he cracked open his beer. "Not only are you annoying the fuck out of me, but you're a walking contradiction."

Colton laughed. "You know what I meant. Take a chance on something more solid than what you're running after right now."

The nonchalant remark hit its target dead-on, but Stephanie approaching the table saved Colton from being told off. She sat across from Gavin and smiled. "I apologize for taking so long."

"No need," Gavin replied. "What can I get you to drink?"

"I'll take an Absolut and cranberry with a twist of lime."

Gavin motioned for the waiter and gave him her drink order. Upon closer inspection, Gavin found her to be as beautiful as Colton said. Her rich chestnut hair was glossy despite being slightly mussed, and her light, almond-shaped eyes edged with thick lashes would've normally had him pulling out a line or two—but not tonight. Unfazed and unaffected, Gavin kept the conversation with her to a minimum and focused on his internal battle over Emily instead. Colton made sure to keep her entertained, though, occasionally throwing a jab of humor directed at Gavin.

As the evening wore on, Gavin noticed Stephanie staring in his direction more intently. Wanting to crucify himself for paying her no mind, he ordered another few drinks and tried to focus on her a little. He learned she was in school for journalism and would graduate the following May. Along with an older and younger brother, she'd grown up in Lindenhurst, a moderately sized town on Long Island. She enjoyed fine arts, music, traveling, good food, family, friends, and lazy summer days.

Still, with all of the fine attributes she clearly possessed, Gavin couldn't stop comparing her to what he wanted the most, craved the most, and what he unequivocally needed the most.

Emily . . .

No chill ran down his spine when Stephanie spoke. Nothing lit up inside of him when she laughed. Even the slight touch she grazed on his arm every so often while she talked did absolutely nothing for him.

Nothing.

For this, he felt like a total asshole for even carrying on a conversation with her because it was clear to him that she was interested.

And more clear to him that he wasn't.

Nonetheless—whether the alcohol had accomplished its purpose or because he'd finally convinced himself that having Emily in his life was a bad idea—by the end of the evening, Gavin found himself exchanging numbers with Stephanie.

"Did she really have to come with us?" Olivia asked, her face coiled in disgust.

"Do you think I want her here?" Emily whispered, poking her head out of the bridal changing room. Dillon's mother was fanning through endless wedding dresses with one of the consultants. "She wanted to come, and I wasn't about to argue with her. Besides, she has some kind of dinner benefit at seven o'clock, so she won't be here much longer."

Snapping her gum, Olivia rolled her eyes. "The woman's like a fucking plague, devouring anything in her sight. I've never been able to stand her."

Emily drew in a breath and turned her back to Olivia. She studied the Reem Acra wedding dress she was wearing. Turning from side to side, she asked, "How does this one look?"

Olivia twirled a lock of her blonde hair around her finger. "Want honesty or flattery?"

"Come on, Liv," she said, placing her hands on her hips.

"You look like a damn mermaid." Emily shook her head. "Well, you asked for it, chick, and I chose the honesty route," Olivia chirped. As if a lightbulb had gone off in her head, she added, "Oh, and I have an idea. How's about *you* actually pick out your wedding dress, since it's your wedding? I swear if Plague Bitch comes in here with another fucking dress that she insists you try on, I'm dropping her right here in this boutique and beating her ass down."

"Can you please calm down?"

"No, Emily, I will not calm down. You have my head so fucked right now with this whole wedding thing that I don't even know what to think."

Pressing her fingers against her temples, Emily closed her eyes. "What do you want me to say?"

"I want you to tell me again why you're rushing into this. It's still not registering quite right in my brain. I'll be honest though—I give Dingleberry props for hounding you for a decision when he said he'd give you time. But, really, Emily . . . November? It's the first damn week of September already."

"I told you, Liv, Dillon's the last grandchild to get married, and they don't think his grandmother's going to make it past six months. She's pretty sick right now," she replied, motioning for Olivia to help unbutton her. "His family wants her to see him get married."

Olivia stood up and padded over. "Right, because you should base your future on his ancient fossil grandmother who might croak an hour after the wedding."

"That's not the only reason, and you know it. Do you know how long the wait is to have a reception at the Waldorf Astoria? Three years, Olivia. Dillon's parents have connections, and there was a cancellation. That was the available date, so we took it."

Olivia helped her slide out of the dress. "I'm gonna say two more things whether you like it or not."

"As I expected you would," she sighed, reaching for an airy chiffon A-line gown she'd chosen.

"One, there would've been nothing wrong with waiting three years to get into the Waldorf if that's the time you needed to really think this through." Emily went to speak but was silenced by Olivia smashing her finger against her lips. She placed her hands on Emily's shoulders and stared deeply into her unblinking green eyes. "And two, you failed to mention *loving* Dillon as one of your reasons, friend."

Emily held her stare for a moment, turned around, and quietly stepped into the non-mermaid-looking dress, pulling it up over her body. "You know I love him."

Olivia came up behind her and zipped the dress closed. They looked at each other in the mirror. "I also know what happened between you and—"

"Don't," Emily quickly cut her off, feeling that all-too-familiar pang deep in her stomach.

Still standing behind her, Olivia leaned into her ear and whispered, "He's miserable, Emily. Trevor told me he's never seen him so out of it."

Emily's heart wrenched at the thought of Gavin hurting, but she couldn't fall like this—not now, not with him. It wasn't right. No matter how much she sugarcoated it, it was wrong. "I don't want to talk about this, Olivia," she whispered, stepping down from the pedestal.

"And you're miserable, too, Emily. I can see it. Ever since that night, you haven't been the same."

"I'm not miserable," she breathed, trying to unzip the dress. "I was drunk, and it was a bad choice. The whole thing was a bad choice."

"Do you need help with that?" Olivia asked softly.

Noticeably flustered, she sighed. "Yes, please."

Olivia helped unzip the dress, her voice low. "Sometimes bad choices bring us to the right people, Emily."

As her nails bit into her palms, those words sent a shiver from the tips of Emily's toes to the roots of her hair. Gavin generated a steady tidal wave of emotions within her that were bigger and far more dangerous than anything she'd ever known. Confusion, hurt, pain, and feeling scared to death of him and herself just skimmed the surface of the storm brewing in her head.

It all ran through her mind in those seconds, but before the torment sank her right there in that room, another entered. This particular torment was swathed in a Valentino pantsuit, her silk Hermès scarf swinging with every step she took in her stiletto heels. "Donna," Joan said to the bridal consultant, "I can take it from here."

The middle-aged woman looked at Emily. "I'm fine, Donna." Emily smiled. "Thank you for your help."

"You're welcome, Miss Cooper. Just let me know if you need anything," she replied and exited the room.

"Oh, Emily, you're really not considering that A-line, are you?" Joan asked with a sigh. "It's so bland. Besides, you have a petite, hourglass frame fit more for this Elie Saab." She held up a gown Emily believed she would lose her lunch all over.

Olivia let out a melodramatic laugh. "Is this a joke? I wouldn't allow her to be caught dead in that thing—let alone walk down the aisle in it. She'll look like a damn cockatoo."

Joan sent her a venomous glare. "You've never been one to hold your tongue very well, have you, Olivia?"

Olivia smiled, but no hint of humor was evident in her voice. "Shocker."

"Joan . . ." Emily reached for the dress. Joan tore her glare from Olivia. "I love Elie Saab, just not this particular style." Emily hung the mass of feathers back up and reached for a Monique Lhuillier gown she had tried on earlier. "I think this is the one I'm going with. I love the appliqué lacing and the scoop neck. The long sleeves are perfect for a winter wedding, too."

Joan exhaled. "That's the one that made your hips look triple their size." With wide eyes, Emily's mouth hung open and snapped shut.

"Holy shit," Olivia blurted out, her brows snapping down. "Emily, one, you're too tiny to have hips that could ever look wide." She shot Joan a murderous look and turned back to Emily. "Two, I'm about to drop it like it's hot." She unclipped her earrings and rolled up her sleeves.

Joan's eyes hardened.

"No," Emily quickly interjected, rushing over to Olivia. "Just take a seat, Liv." Her eyes pleaded with her friend. Crossing her arms, Olivia sank into a chair with a scowl in Joan's direction. "All right, I'll try it on, but don't you have to leave soon?"

Joan's eyes flicked down to her watch as she inhaled sharply. "Jesus, I do," she clipped as she grabbed her purse. "Okay, so you'll try on the Elie Saab. I also showed Donna a trumpet style that would look just fabulous on you. Make sure you have her bring that one in." Nodding, Emily plastered a smile on her face. "Excellent. I'll call you later, then." Joan set off at a brisk pace after she and Olivia traded vicious stares.

Olivia shot up from the chair. "You're seriously not—"

"Trying that horrible thing on?" Emily interrupted with a laugh. Olivia started to laugh right along with her. "Forget about you not allowing me to be caught dead in it. I wouldn't allow *myself* to be caught dead in it."

Emily changed back into her jeans, off-the-shoulder red sweater, and black Converse sneakers. She plucked her purse from the chair and made her way to the front desk. She notified Donna that the Monique Lhuillier gown was the one she was going with and handed the receptionist Dillon's credit card to satisfy the down payment. After discussing and scheduling appointments for a few fittings, they also arranged for the boutique to take care of the maid of honor dress fitting for Emily's sister, since she lived out of state. Feeling overwhelmed by the enormity of it all, Emily was more than happy to get out of there.

"I'm starved," Olivia said as they rocked out of the boutique and into the cool city air. "There's a funky sushi bar not too far from here that serves up some pretty decent rolls. Wanna check it out?"

"I'm game."

A few city blocks later, they approached the sushi restaurant. Before entering, Emily stopped and started digging in her purse.

With her hand on the door, Olivia asked, "What are you doing?" Ignoring her, Emily continued her endeavor. "Hello, Emily, what are you doing?"

"I have a killer headache. I'm looking for a bottle of Advil I know I have in here," she replied, her hands working frantically through the mess of credit card receipts, sunglasses, and an overstuffed makeup bag. With a smile, Emily found it and sighed with relief. She headed toward the entrance and watched Olivia's face morph into noticeable shock.

Emily cocked her head to the side. "What's wrong?" She placed her hand on Olivia's shoulder.

"Umm, turn around, Em."

With furrowed brows, she gave Olivia a questioning look and whipped around.

Oh God . . .

After the air left her lungs, she took in Gavin's BMW double-parked in front of the restaurant. Colton was in the driver's seat shaking his head as Gavin not-so-gracefully stumbled out from the passenger side.

"I'll go get us a table," Olivia said.

"No, wait," Emily whispered, sweat beading on her forehead even in the crisp air. "Don't you dare leave me here."

Olivia narrowed her brown eyes but kept her tone even. "You have to talk to him." Without a backward glance, she opened the door and disappeared into the restaurant.

With her heart racing, Emily tried to compose herself as he approached. "You're drunk," she breathed, noticing the way he was swaying side to side.

As he tossed his hand through his unruly black hair, a grin tipped the corner of his lips. "And you're simply exquisite."

The drowsy cadence of his liquored voice nearly left her in ashes in the middle of Manhattan. Still trying to regain her bearings, she stared at him, her breath hitching in the back of her throat. As disheveled as he looked standing in front of her—his suit jacket off, tie loosened, and sleeves rolled up haphazardly—she had never known a man as breathtaking in every possible way. Not just physically either—because Lord knew she found him to be the sexiest man on the planet—it was beyond that. His very presence manifested itself in a thrum beneath her skin.

Slow and unsteady, he inched toward her. "You're exquisite . . . and engaged now," he said softly, reaching for her left hand. He lifted it and studied her ring. Although she wanted to, she didn't pull away. Essentially frozen by his touch, she couldn't move. "Mmm, with as much money as I have, I don't think I would've gotten you something so gaudy looking—not for a beautiful hand like this. It deserves much better. I would've aimed for something more elegant."

Streams of pedestrians dodged them on the sidewalk as they stood with her hand in his, but neither of them noticed. The blaring mixture of car horns, laughter, and music from a nearby club thrashed and echoed around them, but neither of them heard the noise. They were simply lost in each other in that moment, and nothing else existed. Emily tore her gaze from his, and as quickly as she did, Gavin caught her by her chin and lifted it so she was staring directly into his blue eyes. A soft gasp was the only sound that made its way past her lips.

"After the brief encounter we shared, I never thought Dillon would be the lucky man slipping a ring onto that pretty finger."

Breathing heavily, Emily swallowed and continued to stare at him. His raw, unrelenting, sexy determination hit her with a force strong enough to rock the earth beneath her. "I was drunk," she whispered, not taking her eyes off his. "I . . . I just needed to get you out of my system."

Still cupping her chin, he slid his thumb slowly across her lips, his tone as low as hers. "Doll, you're going to get me out of your system as much as I'm going to get you out of mine. It's impossible."

Before she could process his words, he bent his head and grazed his mouth against hers, catching her bottom lip between his teeth and sucking on it gently. She pulled back slightly, but her fight would go down in history as mild at best. Sliding his tongue against her lip, he tightened his hold on her chin just enough that she couldn't move. Gavin let out a long groan and gave her lip one last mind-blowing tug between his teeth. Emily might have seen it if her eyes weren't closed, but a reverent smile broke out across his face. He turned, pivoting gracefully, and walked away, leaving Emily fighting for air. Reaching for the restaurant door, she watched breathlessly as Gavin slipped into the passenger side of his car, and before she knew it, he disappeared into traffic.

After the fog of euphoria and the shock pulsing through her system lifted, Emily found herself hazily walking into the restaurant with dampened panties, added confusion, and a heightened need for quite a few shots of sake.

13

Confessions of Every Kind

EMILY CONVINCED HERSELF she was mentally prepared, but she couldn't have been more wrong. As she and Dillon greeted their guests the night of their engagement party, she found her head becoming dizzy with fear. Looking at her watch, a frantic string of emotions raced through her mind, knowing she would soon face Gavin. The heavy weight of it had her feeling as though her nerves were fraying like a rope, one fiber at a time. Her spinning thoughts slowed when she felt Dillon's gentle touch brush against her arm. For tonight, she needed to focus on him—and him only—no matter how difficult it would be.

"Are you all right?" he asked, scooping her into a hug. He planted a kiss on her lips and moved her hair away from her shoulders.

"Yes, I'm fine," she answered, sliding her hands down the lapels of his black suit.

"Well, you look beautiful tonight," he crooned. "I just may have *you* for dessert when this whole thing's over."

"I heard that, Dillon," Lisa's voice broke through the air, one brow drawn up above her hazel eyes. "Please refrain from referring to my baby sister as dessert."

Dillon smirked and pulled Emily closer. "But she's so . . . delectable, Lisa. I mean, honestly, I can't get enough." Emily shook her head and laughed.

"Okay, I seriously don't need to hear how delectable she is." She gave Emily's arm a light tug, releasing her from his hold. "I'd like to speak to my sister in private for a second, if that's okay with you."

"She's all yours," he replied, branding one last kiss on Emily's lips.

Reaching for her hand, Lisa led her through the knot of guests trickling into the banquet room. Emily smiled and returned their greetings along the way.

As the two sisters made their way through the party, Emily noticed Dillon's parents had spared no expense. The restaurant was truly beautiful. A mahogany bar was located in the corner of the room beside a massive window overlooking New York Harbor. Deep red leather couches and matching upholstered wingback chairs were scattered throughout. Ornate sconces hung on the walls, while an exquisite, dimly lit chandelier anchored the room. Adjacent to a baby grand piano—echoing music through the air—was a crackling fireplace that set the romantic mood for the evening.

After turning a corner to an empty hall, they ducked into a vacant room, and Lisa closed the door. Lisa placed her hands on Emily's shoulders, her eyes softening with concern. "I can tell you're a nervous wreck."

Emily slanted a hand through her hair, the weakest of smiles taking over her lips. "Is it that obvious?"

"Not to others, but I know you better than anyone else," she said softly, reaching for Emily's hand. "Is he here yet?"

"No. Believe me, when he's here, you'll know it," she replied with a nervous laugh. Biting her lip, she paused, her features smoothing. "I wish Mom were here, Lisa."

"Oh, sweetie, I do, too," she whispered, leaning in for a hug. Emily squeezed her tight, her warmth reminding her of the woman they were still mourning. Grief swelled in Emily's chest like a fresh bruise. "But even if she were here, Emily, she'd tell you to go with what your heart wants. She couldn't make your decision any easier. I just need to know—just like Mom would—that this is what you want."

With the slightest hesitation, she answered, "Yes, I do want this."

"Okay, then let's go enjoy your party." Lisa grabbed Emily's hand and started heading back into the main dining room.

The amount of guests had doubled—the majority consisting of Dillon's family, coworkers, and friends. Sure, Emily had met a few of them over the last year, but most were a distant blur of Dillon's aunts, uncles, and cousins she had encountered briefly at family gatherings. Essentially, the amount of people Emily knew in attendance could fit at one table.

In a room filled with people, in that moment, she felt oddly alone—until her eyes locked onto Gavin's. For Emily, the world seemed to stop. The music whispered in the background while voices became muted. Again, the undeniable connection between them was apparent from across the space, even if not witnessed by anyone else. It was there—unwavering and unrelenting. She found it hard to breathe as the overwhelming tidal wave of emotions took hold and pulled her into the current, pounding and roaring with a power greater than hers.

Her eyes swept over him. He was wearing a charcoal-colored suit that covered his built yet graceful frame. Beneath, he wore a white-collared shirt and pinstriped black-and-gray tie. His lustrous dark hair was sexily mussed as if he hadn't bothered fixing it after showering. His impressive presence was that of polished power, economical grace, and unyielding demand. He simply was a force she couldn't help but notice. Although he had his arm snaked around what Emily believed was one of the most beautiful women she had ever seen, his eyes were steady and focused on Emily's. He sent her a smile that still managed to disarm her, leaving her in a sea of desire, want, and need, struggling to resurface.

Clenching Emily's sweaty hand, hazel eyes bright with curiosity, Lisa asked, "Is that him?"

Emily nodded and a lump wedged itself between the walls of her throat as she watched Dillon approach Gavin, motioning her over. Licking her dry lips, she squeezed Lisa's hand, and with trepidation, she started making her way across the room.

God, she's so beautiful, Gavin thought to himself as he watched Emily close the space between them. Her body swayed with elegant poise beneath an emerald silk evening gown. His eyes followed her sleek legs down to a pair of silver strappy stilettos adorning her feet. He tried to keep his eyes from traveling back up to her subtle curves and long, auburn locks of hair. He fought to push the familiar ache away, but his body continued to respond as she drew nearer. He felt his pupils dilate as she swept her tongue across her lips, causing his blood to pump with brutal force toward necessary extremities.

He had a desire for every inch of her—the smell of her sweet breath on his hungry lips, the taste of her tongue, the soft feel of her skin, and the sound of her husky voice whispering in his ears. She was an assault on his senses, a constant thirst needing to be quenched. He'd had a taste, but he feared the only thing he would have left was his instinct of wanting her more and needing to feel her again and again. With all of this, what captivated him the most were her eyes—those deep pools of alluring green felt as if they were boring into his very soul. His grip may have tightened around Stephanie's waist, but in his mind, his hands were on Emily.

When Emily and Lisa approached, Dillon reached for her, positioning her back against his chest. "Babe, this is Gavin's date, Stephanie."

With a smile, Emily pulled in a slow and shaky breath. "It's very nice to meet you, Stephanie."

"You, too," she replied, tucking a few errant strands of caramel-hued hair behind her ear. Her porcelainlike features emphasized her large, whiskey-colored eyes. "Congratulations on your engagement."

"Thank you," Emily said.

Gavin's gaze captured Emily's, a smile on his face. "Yes . . . congratulations."

With his voice so calm, cool, and collected, Emily couldn't help but wonder if she was the only ball of nerves standing there. Smiling, she simply nodded her thanks. As soon as she did, her stomach recoiled when she swore she saw a sparkle of amusement in his eyes at her reaction.

"Just an assumption," Gavin continued, turning in Lisa's direction, "but there must be some sort of relation between you and Emily. Your features are strikingly similar."

"Yes," she replied, "I'm her sister."

"Mmm, younger or older?" he asked casually with his dimpled smile.

"Oh, he's quite the charmer." Lisa laughed, looking at Emily. She brought her attention back to Gavin. "I'm older by ten years, but thank you for the compliment."

"He certainly is," Emily deadpanned, shifting nervously

against Dillon. A smirk curled the brim of Gavin's mouth, but he remained silent.

"I'll keep my thoughts to myself about that one," Dillon clipped with a smirk of his own. Gavin shook his head. "But, for now, I need another drink. Babe, do you want another glass of wine?"

There was only one way she was going to survive the rest of the night. Emily smiled. "I'll take a shot of something strong." Dillon nodded and walked away.

Gavin flicked Emily another stroke of amusement with his eyes. She could tell he felt her sinking, and all it was doing was pissing her off. Before she could dwell too long on her desire to knock him clear across the head, Trevor and Fallon approached. Emily smiled at them, happy they were working out as a couple. They genuinely enjoyed being together and seemed to be a perfect match of fire and ice. She guessed Dillon would beg to differ, since he'd laughed at the whole courtship when he'd found out about it. Nonetheless, Emily was thrilled, knowing he would have no choice but to accept Fallon as her friend. To seal the deal, she'd made Fallon one of her bridesmaids.

Formal introductions were made between Stephanie and Fallon before Trevor asked if he could steal Emily away for a dance. She obliged, placing her hand in the crook of his arm as he guided her out onto the floor. With the pianists playing "Summer Wind" by Frank Sinatra, they began dancing.

Looking up at him, she said, "I didn't know you liked slow dancing."

He chuckled. "I don't, to tell you the truth. I actually hate it." Emily gave him a questioning look. "I just wanted to talk to you about what I said the last time we spoke."

Emily knew he was referring to the mess between her and

Gavin. It had come as a surprise when Trevor called to let her know his feelings on the situation. He wasn't harsh about the whole matter, but one would consider his approach a little less than understanding to say the least.

"Oh." She nodded. "Well, you've explained that it puts you in a bad position. I understand that, but to be honest, nothing more's happening between us."

His face softened as he lowered his voice. "I consider you my adopted sister, and I wanted to apologize for the things I said—well, mostly, the way I said them. I just wanted you to know that, whether or not you and Gavin decide to carry on anything, it's none of my business. You're two grown adults, and it's your lives. Would it be an odd situation for me because I'm friends with Dillon? Absolutely. But I would have to learn to deal with it."

Widening her eyes, she tilted her head to the side. "Trevor, I'm engaged now, and like I said, nothing more's happening." His devil-may-care sneer lit up his features, showing his amusement at her remark. "Why do you have that look on your face?"

"I may wear glasses, Emily, but I'm not blind."

"What's that supposed to mean?" she asked, pulling back slightly.

He gently pulled her closer. "One, I've known Gavin since I was a kid, and perseverance going after something he wants has never been an issue for him. And two, even though I haven't known you as long as I have him, I can see it all over your face when you look at him."

She stopped swaying to the music, but Trevor kept them moving. "I don't want to talk about this," she said with a smile, trying to appear unfazed in the crowded room.

"That's cool with me. I just wanted to put it out there."

"Well, I thank you for your blessings, which are not needed

in this case, *Dad*." He laughed. "Now let's move on to the next subject, okay?"

"Absolutely." He smiled. "So, how do you feel about Dillon being gone for a few days in October?"

"He's going away? He never told me that."

"Yeah, we both are. The firm's sending us to Florida to score an account from some Japanese mogul, Takatsuki Yamamoto." He struggled to pronounce the name correctly.

A frown creased her brows. "Wait, Dillon told me he'd already landed that account."

"No, not yet." He shook his head. "You must have it confused with another one. We're trying to get it now."

Skimming through her memory, she was almost positive that had been Dillon's reason for bailing on their date in Central Park. She remembered he'd said he was in New Jersey. However, with everything that had happened since, she started questioning herself.

The sound of Dillon clearing his throat broke through her thoughts. "May I cut in?" he asked, looking at Trevor.

Bowing gracefully, Trevor chuckled. "Go for it. I'll catch up with you two in a bit."

Trevor made his way back over to Fallon, Stephanie, and Gavin. Olivia and Tina had also joined the group.

Smiling, Dillon curled one hand around Emily's waist. "Are you having a good time?" he whispered into her hair, his free hand stroking her arm.

"It's a little overwhelming right now, but yes." He pulled her closer. "Can I ask you something, Dillon?"

"As long as it's about what positions I plan on putting you in after I slip you out of this dress tonight, sure."

She sighed. "I'm being serious, Dillon."

Sincerity flashed across his face. "Okay, okay. What's up?"

"Why'd you tell me you were in New Jersey the morning we were supposed to meet in Central Park?"

He cocked his head to the side, his hold on her waist tightening. "Because I *was* in New Jersey. That was weeks ago. Why are you asking me about this now?"

"Why are you going to Florida in October?"

He stopped moving, his eyes narrowing. "Why are you answering my question with another question?"

"Because you're not answering mine," she replied without hesitation.

He dropped his hands to his side. "Emily, just get to your fucking point."

Taken aback, she studied his demeanor. "You told me you were in New Jersey that morning because some guy from Japan flew out and wanted to meet with you personally, correct?"

"Yeah, Emily, he wanted to meet with me. I met with him and gained his account for the firm. Like I said, get to the fucking point already."

Still shocked at the way he was acting under her scrutiny, she drew in a deep breath. "My point, Dillon, is that Trevor just said you two are going away on business in a couple of weeks to meet with the exact same Japanese gentleman you claimed to have already landed an account with."

Emily watched his eyes scan the room as if debating what to say. Waiting for his response, she impatiently crossed her arms.

Pinching the bridge of his nose, his eyes traveled back to hers. "Okay, I lied."

"What?" she asked breathlessly, feeling bile quickly making its way up her throat. "Where were you?"

Although she pulled away, he circled his arms around her and drew her near. "That was the morning . . ." He hesitated a second. "I was picking up the engagement ring." She parted her lips to speak, but he continued. "They thought there was a problem with the set, and I got held up there. I almost fucking lost it, thinking I would have to go somewhere else to get one."

Before she could question him, his mother floated over, her blonde hair twisted into a tight bun. "Dillon, Uncle Bruce and Aunt Mary just arrived. They're not feeling well with their emphysema. Damn smokers. Anyway, they want to say hello to you and Emily. Do me a favor and go over and greet them." With a flick of her wrist, she motioned toward the couple sitting comfortably at a table across the room. Each had their own breathing machine anchored next to them.

Dillon reached for Emily's hand. "Sure, we'll be there in a second."

"Actually, I need to use the restroom," Emily replied, walking away. "Go ahead without me, and I'll meet you over there in a few minutes."

Tossing his hand through his hair, Dillon looked at her and nodded. As he crossed the room with his mother, Emily sighed. She didn't need to use the restroom. She needed to clear her racing thoughts. Confusion spun through her mind. She didn't understand why, even though she had explained that she knew about the upcoming trip, he had continued to lie to her. She understood he couldn't have actually told her where he was on that particular morning—especially if he was indeed purchasing her ring—but here, right now, why not just confess? When one of the waiters approached her with much-needed bubbling champagne, she earnestly plucked two glasses off the tray, downed one, and thanked him. With that, she turned in the direction of the terrace only to discover Gavin watching her every move. Ignoring him, she made her way outside.

Gavin shifted uncomfortably in his chair, trying to drag his eyes away from Emily as she exited the restaurant. She looked like a princess—so beautiful she made his chest ache with the need to touch her. Even though laughter and conversation between Stephanie, Fallon, and Tina hummed around him, he couldn't resist the urge of somehow finding a way to follow her outside. His chance came when Trevor approached the group.

"Anyone need a drink?" Trevor asked. "I'm going over to the bar."

"Get me and Tina an Alabama Slammer each," Olivia piped up, adjusting the straps of her silver dress. "Actually, get us two each." Trevor nodded at her request.

Rising to his feet, Gavin smiled. "I need another, and I'll take a walk with you." He turned to Stephanie. "Did you want something?"

"No, I'm okay, but thank you."

Feeling like the slithering snake he knew he was for leaving Stephanie, Gavin surveyed the crowd in an attempt to locate Dillon. He found him consumed in a conversation with a few men around his age. Gavin figured they were his friends from high school or college. As he and Trevor approached the bar, it was apparent to Gavin—based on the look in Trevor's eyes—that his friend knew something was up.

Trevor placed the order with the bartender and turned to Gavin. "You don't need a drink, do you?"

"No, I don't," Gavin stated, his gaze moving over the room. "I want to talk to Emily for a few minutes. Keep an eye on Dillon for me."

The bartender slid the glasses across to Trevor. "What about Stephanie?"

"Tell Olivia to keep her busy; she'll be fine."

Shaking his head, Trevor lifted his drink and sipped from it. "You're playing with fire, man."

"Just do what I asked."

Without another word, Gavin navigated the crowd, dashing and darting through the maze of evening gowns and tailored suits. When he emerged on the terrace, he found Emily with her back to him, her auburn hair whipping around in the cool, late-September air. Unaware of him watching, it was as if her body beckoned him. He tried—God knew he tried—to stay away. The past few weeks had been hell, and he had attempted to save them both by not going to her job and not showing up at her apartment when he knew Dillon wouldn't be there. However, seeing her, being here with her, sucking in her presence had him feeling as though his mind was possessed. Every neuron fired into a tempest of sparks, and he couldn't believe his body was able to contain it. He was amazed his flesh wasn't cracking into a million glittering pieces. No matter the situation, right there and then, he needed to go to her.

He stepped forward, and as if she sensed him, she whipped around, a piece of her silken hair catching in her mouth. "What are you doing out here?" she asked, her voice low, shaky even.

He moved toward her, allowing only a few feet to separate them. "I need to speak with you."

"There's nothing to talk about," she said, turning her back to him again.

"There's a lot we need to talk about, and you're going to turn around and face me, Emily." The rough whisper was breathed out with classic male dominance as he stepped closer.

His tone caught her attention, her heart slamming to a stop before jump-starting again. She twirled around and stared straight into his eyes. He was looking at her as if he was trying to read her mind, and she felt naked under his gaze. He was so sexy, dangerous, and completely confident, it almost sickened her. As arrogant as his demand was, it still managed to suck her into a vortex of spiraling desire. Like a defiant teenager pissed at a parent, she crossed her arms and waited for him to speak.

"Do you feel me when I'm not with you, Emily?"

With shock shimmering in her eyes, she laughed nervously. "What kind of question is that?"

"One that I'm asking you," he growled, "because I can feel you when you're not with me. Now answer my question."

"We're back to this again, huh?"

"Yes. Now get those pretty lips to answer the question," he demanded as he stepped closer.

The glass woman beneath her skin smashed under her passion, lust, and want. The splinters of herself scattered and recomposed themselves into the man who consumed her every thought—the man who was standing right in front of her. This was it—her breaking point. She wasn't going to deny him or herself what she felt anymore. Gavin brought her to the edge, and there was no looking back. Her stomach knotted over knowing what she was about to confess, but more so because of how much she was about to confess. "You want to hear me say it?" she hissed.

Oh, he felt her now.

With blatant intention, he did the one thing he knew would get her riled up: He slowly dragged his bottom lip between his teeth as his eyes bore right through her. "Yes, I want to hear you say it."

"Fine! I want to fuck you just like you want to fuck me, Gavin," she blurted out in a hard whisper. "I've wanted to fuck you since the first moment I laid eyes on you. I've dreamt of you. I feel you when you're not with me. I've even masturbated with a clear picture of you in my thoughts. Are you happy now?"

Hell, he couldn't count the amount of times he'd gotten himself off thinking about her, but that wasn't what was driving him. His expression creased with a mix of shock, anger, and hurt from her accusation. "No, I'm not happy. You think this is about me wanting to *fuck* you?"

At that, she laughed again. "Oh, give me a break. What else would it be about? I know I'm naïve when it comes to certain things, but I'm not a dumbass, Gavin."

Something in her eyes and the set of her body filled him with heat. The edge of vulnerability in her voice sliced at his chest, and hell, it tore him apart. But combined with her explosion of defiance and anger, it made the need for her eat into him like a painful disease. He stepped forward, bringing his arm around her waist, pinning her close to his hip, as he quickly guided her out of view. They'd gotten lucky thus far, but he knew it was only a matter of time before that ended.

"What are you doing?" she huffed, struggling against him, her heels clicking frantically against the concrete.

Anger of his own surged hot and deep inside him as he backed her against a wall on the side of the terrace. He stared at her, his blue eyes brooding in the dimly lit space with an expression so hard it was granite. "This has nothing to do with me wanting to fuck you."

"Oh, it doesn't?" she breathed, wiping her windblown hair away from her face.

"No, 'cause let's not forget that I could've fucked you." Positioning his hand on the wall above her, he pressed his entire body against hers. She brought her hands up against his chest and tried to push him away, but his strength overpowered hers. Grazing his lips against her ear, he drew his words out in a slow, hot whisper. "I could've fucked you over . . . and over . . . and over again, and I could've fucked you *very* well, but I stopped because that's not the way I want you."

With her chest heaving, heart racing, and panties saturated

in desire, she looked away. "Then what do you want from me, Gavin?" she asked, her voice an aggravated whisper.

He caught her by the chin and made her look at him. His eyes—that light, wild blue—blazed into hers. "Damn it, Emily, I want us! You belong with me, not him." He half snarled the declaration. "Every part of you was made for me. Your lips were made to kiss mine, your eyes were made to wake up to me looking at you in *my* bed every morning, and your fucking tongue was made to roll my name off of it. I am more certain of us than I'm certain I require oxygen to breathe."

Like a thief in the night, his words nearly stole her breath. She looked practically on the verge of tears and went to speak, but Gavin suddenly brought his hand up and covered her mouth. He gave a quick shake of his head. At first, she didn't realize what he was doing, and then Dillon and Trevor's voices cut through their frantic breathing. With widened eyes, Emily's heart quickened as she stared at Gavin.

"Well, where is she?" Dillon asked, his tone filled with anger and concern. "And where the fuck is Gavin?"

A few seconds went by before Trevor answered, and as fast as Emily's heart was pounding, she was sure Dillon could hear it. All Dillon had to do was round the corner to find her and Gavin in the shadows.

"The room was too loud, and Gavin had to take a business call. He went upstairs to find somewhere quiet." Trevor cleared his throat a few times. "Let's go back in, and I'll have Olivia check the restrooms again."

Emily heard Dillon let out a heavy breath, and then their footsteps receded.

As oxygen refilled her depleted lungs, Gavin slowly dragged his hand away from her mouth. Other than the distant sound of laughter and conversations, deafening silence descended as they stared at each other. Emily pushed from the wall and started to walk away, but as soon as she did, Gavin called out to her. She came to an abrupt stop but didn't turn to face him.

He came up behind her, brushing his hands down her arms, his words muffled into the crook of her neck. "I'd never hurt you, Emily. Stop fighting me. Stop fighting what you already know."

With his touch heady and intoxicating and her heart slamming in her chest, she didn't turn around. She couldn't. On shaky legs, she made her way back into the party, the sudden need for absolute numbness overriding her thoughts. She gave the room a once-over to make sure Dillon wasn't in sight. As soon as she knew it was clear, she weaved through the guests, her mind racing a mile a minute with the fear that Dillon could've caught them. Her body jerked with a surge of adrenaline when she felt a hand grab her elbow, but the tension in her shoulders deflated when she turned to find Olivia.

"Come with me," Olivia quickly said, leading her to the front of the restaurant. They stepped outside, and Olivia handed her a bottle of aspirin. "Tell Dillon you had a headache, and you sent the valet to bring the car around because you needed to get these from the glove compartment."

"Dillon has the valet ticket," Emily hastily whispered.

Olivia flashed a smile. "Don't worry about it. I used to fuck around with him." She motioned toward a lanky valet attendant watching them.

With a half smirk, Emily flicked her eyes in his direction and then back to Olivia.

"What?" Olivia chirped. "It was my prewomen days, and he owed me a favor. I already talked to him, and he said he would back up the story if need be."

Emily nodded. "Okay. This will work, right?"

"Oh, your fiancé," she replied, crinkling her nose, "is definitely pissed, but yeah, the excuse should work."

With that, they walked back into the party, and as soon as they did, Emily's gaze locked on to Gavin's. He was coming back in from the terrace, watching her as intently as she watched him. He strolled over to Stephanie, reached for her hand, and spoke to her for a few minutes. With Stephanie on his arm, he made his way through the crowd, heading straight in Emily's direction.

Olivia nudged her arm. "Well, you have to find the humor in all of this, chick."

Emily shot her a look. It was far from humorous. It was painful, confusing, and draining, but before she could tell Olivia any of those things, Gavin and Stephanie approached them.

He wore a smile, but Emily could see the pain evident in his eyes. "It's getting late, so we're gonna get going," he said as he looked at Emily. "Just tell Dillon I'll talk to him during the week."

Emily nodded, wanting to somehow comfort him. After tonight, she felt they both might be going to bed licking their wounds—at least she knew she would. "I'll tell him," she answered, her voice just above a whisper.

"It was nice to meet you." Stephanie smiled. "Again, congratulations to you and your fiancé."

"Thank you," Emily replied.

Olivia leaned in to give Gavin a hug. When she released him, he cast one last weary look toward Emily, and without another word, he and Stephanie walked out of the restaurant.

Although it came without alcohol, Emily felt numb after he left. Pain and confusion continued to crush in around her for the remainder of the evening. Olivia was correct. Dillon bought her story of needing a dose of aspirin for a headache, but that didn't make Emily feel any better. As she carried on conversations with guests, Gavin's words echoed through her head, burning a hole in her heart and taking the last piece of something away from her. Just a few months before, Emily had believed she could see through and peel away some of his many layers.

However, tonight, Gavin had peeled away hers.

14

Broken

ANOTHER BARKING COUGH tore through Emily's throat. Her eyes followed Dillon as he rounded the taxi after closing her door. Forget the fact that Gavin would be there tonight; she felt like shit, and her body ached from head to toe. Gavin would only bring on a different kind of pain for her at this point. She couldn't believe she had allowed Dillon to talk her into going, but something in his unrelenting persistence and intolerant tone brooked no argument. Already intoxicated, he haphazardly slid into the backseat and let the driver know their destination.

After digging in his pants for his wallet, he looked at Emily. "Oh, come on, babe. You've got to be feeling better by now."

Between the smell of alcohol on his breath and the nausea from medication pumping through her system, she was sure she was going to throw up right there and then. "No, Dillon, I don't feel better." She sighed and leaned her head against the window. A crowded bar was the last place she wanted to be. "I don't see what the big deal is if I didn't come."

Shaking his head, he scooted over and draped his arm around her shoulder. "It's Trevor's birthday—that's the big deal."

"I already spoke with him earlier. I told him I'm sick and couldn't go." After another coughing fit, she added, "He was perfectly fine with it."

"Well, don't forget, I leave for Florida tomorrow morning for a few days." He pulled her closer, positioning her legs across his lap. "You don't want to hang out with me before I go, do you?"

"You know that has nothing to do with it," she replied, coughing. "We could've stayed home and hung out. Plus, why the hell you want to go out tonight when your flight leaves so early is beyond me."

He leaned into her ear and smoothed his hand under her skirt, his fingers making small circles against the lace of her panties. "I can handle an early flight, babe. Let's just hope you can handle me once we get back to my place."

As she attempted to push his hand away, shock crossed her features. "You don't really think you're getting laid tonight, do you?" She slid away, amazed he could possibly be thinking about that. She was sick, and he knew it.

In one sweeping move, he pulled her arm, yanking her toward him. He anchored one of his legs over hers. "I *know* I'm getting laid tonight, Em." He slid his tongue across her neck as he dipped his hand back under her skirt. "I'll be gone for a few days. I need a little bit to hold me over."

"Get off me, Dillon. You're drunk already!" She backed away, trying to ignore the driver staring at them through the rearview mirror. To make sure Dillon wouldn't come at her again, she let loose a gurgling cough in his direction, hoping the microscopic germs made their way straight into his nostrils.

Unfortunately, it didn't stop him from trying again. Fortunately, her reprieve from his drunken attempt at taking her right there in the taxi came when his phone started ringing. Pinning her with a cold look, Dillon pulled it from his pocket. Emily slid across the seat, making sure to stuff her coat and purse between them.

Sighing, she tried to ignore his conversation. However, she couldn't ignore the growing anxiety steadily filtering through her veins, knowing she was about to spend the evening in Gavin's presence. After their last encounter, the past several weeks had been nothing short of . . . difficult. Though she had plunged headfirst into her new teaching job, apartment hunting with Dillon, and planning for the wedding, Gavin was in the back of her thoughts like a lingering beautiful shadow—never leaving, never letting go, just there.

She was hurt and confused, and reminders of him were abundant. Certain songs she knew he liked stopped her dead in her tracks when she heard them. Thoughts of him constantly distracted her from what she was doing. She'd found herself becoming unproductive in a heartbeat when he clouded her mind. He stimulated her emotions, her nerves, and all her senses. She may want Gavin, but she knew she shouldn't have such reckless feelings for him, especially since her wedding was less than a month away. She hated that she felt powerless around Gavin. That he'd resurrected feelings that needed to stay buried deep inside. He made her want to take risks on him—on them. He made her question things like her upcoming marriage to the only love she'd ever known—the only man who had ever been there for her. Gavin did this to her. She did this to her. Fate did this to her. She didn't know who or what to blame, but the one thing she did know was the whole situation was tearing her apart.

Pulling up to a sports bar in Tribeca, she drew in a deep breath and stepped out into the crisp, late October air. It would be an understatement to say she wasn't looking forward to tonight.

Gavin saw Emily the moment she walked in. It was impossible for him not to. Even among the frenzied crowd, she shone bright, like a blazing star illuminating a dark sky. His dark sky.

The invisible wire tightened around his throat, rendering him nearly breathless. She looked incredible—clad in a black skirt, sexy knee-high boots, and a tight green sweater that enhanced every curve God himself had graced upon her. Gavin had never known a woman so beautiful. He'd sunk himself into work the past several weeks, trying not to think of her. His intention was to obliterate her completely from his thoughts, but the more he had tried, the more she took root in his mind.

She wasn't supposed to be there tonight—at least, that's what Trevor had told him. Now, as he watched her weave through the ocean of bodies, he suddenly felt as though his heart was slamming out of his chest. His body pulsed with energy, colliding with his desire, want, and need for her. The connection and pull she extracted from him—even from the first time he'd laid eyes on her—still amazed him. In the seconds before she and Dillon approached, Gavin's voice of reason piped up, telling him to let it go and be done with her. As much as he wanted to listen, his head was already in overdrive. She was the recipient of all his pent-up emotions—for she alone stoked all his fires. She was nothing short of agonizingly addictive. Gavin's eyes found hers, but she looked away, essentially ignoring his very existence. After shaking hands with Dillon, Gavin watched as she walked over to Trevor.

"You made it," Trevor hooted, leaning in to hug Emily. "Feeling better, I assume?"

Backing away with a weak smile on her face and a cough, she answered, "No, I don't feel better, so you might not want to hug me." Trevor smiled and pulled her into his chest despite her warning. She looked up to him. "Trevor, I'm serious. I'm as contagious as they come right now."

He squeezed her tighter and laughed. "Em, I have enough alcohol running through me right now to kill off any fucking germs you might spread."

Managing a laugh, she returned his hug. "All right, then, but you asked for it." He smiled at her. "Happy birthday, big man. What's the number tonight, the big three-zero?"

"Not quite. The ripe young age of twenty-nine," he answered, snaking his arm around Fallon's waist. He flicked his eyes down to her. "And what a year it's gonna be."

Fallon leaned up to kiss him and looked at Emily. "I'm a lucky girl."

"You *are* a lucky girl, and he's a lucky guy, too. Don't forget that." Emily smiled. "I love the new color."

Fallon fluffed her crimson hair to the side. "Do you? I'm not used to one color at a time."

"I do. It's becoming on you." Emily looked around. "Where are Olivia and Tina?"

"Apparently, you're not the only one sick in Manhattan tonight," Trevor answered. "Tina didn't feel good, so Olivia took her home."

Emily nodded and settled in a seat next to Dillon. He was ordering a few shots and steadily on his way into deeper alcohol oblivion.

"If you'll excuse me," Trevor continued, "I'm gonna go get my sweat on with my hot lady here."

Emily watched Trevor and Fallon disappear onto the dance floor. Over the next half hour, Emily and Gavin exchanged nothing more than the occasional apprehensive glance. She listened to him and Dillon talk about baseball. The Yankees had made it into the playoffs, and game three was currently being displayed across several large flat-screen televisions throughout the bar. Their rival—go figure—was the Baltimore Orioles. Emily had to smile at that.

Unable to numb her anxiety with alcohol because of the medication she was on, she endured the situation as best as she could—paying no attention to either man. As she accepted a glass of ice water from the bartender, her cell phone lit up in her purse and caught her attention.

Pulling it out, she noticed a text from a number she didn't know: *I must admit . . . you play the game very well. . . .*

With furrowed brows, having no idea who it was, she texted back: *Who is this?*

After a few seconds, the reply: *However . . . your birds have no clue how to play the game . . . so it all evens out. . . .*

Snapping her head up in Gavin's direction, her heart skipped a beat. Though he was perched on the opposite side of Dillon, he was in Emily's line of sight. He was staring at her, his smile wide and uninhibited. She flicked her eyes in Dillon's direction. He was paying no mind to her or Gavin and was clearly more intoxicated than when they first arrived. He was in the midst of a conversation regarding the game with another patron as they laughed and shared a few shots.

Another incoming text vibrated her phone: *Take a look at the score. . . .*

Nervous, she looked over at Gavin again.

Smiling, he leaned his chin in the palm of his hand and gestured to one of the televisions with his bottle of beer.

Averting her eyes to the screen highlighting a Yankees lead by five, she let out the breath she was holding. She looked back to him and yet another smile broke out across his face.

Emily texted back: *How did you get my number?*

His reply: *Admit that your birds don't have a chance against my Yankees . . . and perhaps I will release that information. . . .*

Coughing, she lifted a brow and looked at him. He smiled and casually shrugged. "The nerve," she mumbled under her breath as she texted him back: *I will do no such thing. . . .*

Her eyes shifted to his again. With a perplexed look on his face, he smiled, and she watched him swiftly run his fingers across his screen.

Then you're left with your original assumption of my personality. . . . I'm a stalker, and you're my beautiful prey. Boo.

Shaking her head at the true wiseass he really was, curiosity got the better of her: *Fine, my birds aren't playing their best tonight. . . .*

Sighing, she heard Gavin let out a full throaty chuckle.

He replied: *I'll make it simple. . . . Your team S-U-C-K-S. And since you wouldn't admit that your birds have no chance against my beloved Yankees, I have the sudden urge to make you . . . beg. Kinky, right? I'll be waiting for your response. . . .*

Taking a sip of her water, she scoffed. "He's seriously lost his mind." She watched a superior smile wash over his face.

She began to text him back, letting him know she wouldn't beg for an answer, but he sent another before she could push send: *I decided I'm in a generous mood tonight since my team is whipping some serious ass. Forget about you begging me . . . which I know you would've. . . . Text back the magic word, and I will relinquish the information you so desire. Clue . . . It starts with pretty. . . .*

She rolled her eyes and texted him back: *Please . . .*

His answering text was quick: *I knew I could get you to beg . . . Molly.*

Now she couldn't help but laugh. Her text was a little more demanding this time: *Emily to you, "stalker boy." You didn't get me to beg for anything. I want the information.*

Oh, his smile was teetering between lewd and mischievous when she looked in his direction. He responded: *You begged, doll, and I'm pretty sure . . . no, I'm positive . . . I could get you to beg for plenty of things if given the proper chance to do so. Plenty. But, to answer your question, Olivia gave me your number. I would assume my source doesn't come as a shock. . . .*

She sighed. *I disagree with the begging part. I call it being courteous. Not sure how to answer your second statement except to say that you're an arrogant bastard. No, I'm not shocked about Olivia being your partner in crime. . . . The both of you are certifiably nuts. . . .*

Between becoming consumed in her text session with Gavin and the roaring Yankees fans, Emily didn't notice Dillon had disappeared. However, she couldn't help but notice Gavin staring directly at her with only a bar stool separating them now. Her breath hitched in her throat as he closed that distance by sliding over into the seat next to her. He propped his elbow on the bar, his smile no less cocky than before.

"So, says the 'arrogant bastard,'" he began, shifting to face her, "are you still going to deny that I made you beg?"

The familiarity of his humor-filled voice sent chills down her back. With a smirk, she let out an exasperated breath. "You're relentless."

"Always," he answered evenly. He took a long pull from his beer, his gaze never leaving hers. "I figured it was a good way to break the tension."

"You have a funny way of breaking tension, Gavin."

"And why do you say that?"

"Let's see . . . Trying to get me to admit I was begging." She crossed her legs and then quickly added, "Which I wasn't."

"You begged, doll, but I'll let it go."

Laughing, she shook her head. "I give up; you win."

He smiled, and for a minute, he let himself drown in her, getting lost in the memory of her touch. "In all seriousness, I figured my little texting skit might go over well." His eyes shimmered with something akin to an apology behind them. "I'm *hoping* it did, at least."

He was right; the tension that had built up inside her had seemed to dissipate. Drawing in a deep breath, she nodded. "It did."

Slowly, he slid a bottle cap over to her and smiled. "Truce?"

Looking down at the smooth-lacquered bar, she picked up the cap and rolled it in her fingers with a weak smile on her lips. In whatever way she could take it, she needed it to be right with him—needed it to be right with them. Emily knew fate wasn't playing fair with either one of their hearts. Fate had broken all the rules in their case, creating a no-holds-barred wicked game that was demolishing both of their inner beings. Tugging at their deepest thoughts with strength unlike any other, it was bringing the strongest of men down to his knees and had her questioning her decisions—but she wouldn't let it destroy either of their lives any further. Drawing in another deep breath, she met his gaze and nodded. "Yes, Gavin . . . truce."

As relief soaked through his veins, Gavin analyzed her face, hoping to burn the vision of her into his memory. It'd felt like forever since he'd seen her. "So, how've you been?"

"I've been doing okay. You?"

"Yeah, I've been all right," he lied, praying she couldn't tell. She gave him a weak smile that had him second-guessing his acting abilities. "So, Olivia told me that, since Dillon's leaving on business tomorrow, she's your official date to my mother's fund-raiser this weekend."

"Yes, she is. Tina's going away to her grandparents' home in Texas, so we figured we'd make it a certified ladies' night."

"Very cool." He smiled and leaned back in his chair. "I'm sure you'll have a great time."

Nodding, she let out a cough. "Well, I'm looking forward to it."

"You don't sound good," he said, placing the back of his hand against her forehead. She flinched away slightly but smiled. "You actually feel feverish."

"You can tell by feeling my forehead, huh?" She brought her hand up to her forehead and started rummaging through her purse, looking for Tylenol. "Now your résumé consists of business mogul, nanny, and doctor, too."

He shrugged. "The nanny part coincides with the doctor part. I've watched Timothy and Teresa a few times while they were sick." He took a swig of his beer. "You shouldn't be out, feeling the way you do."

She sighed. "Yeah, I know I shouldn't be." He looked at her questioningly. Popping the medicine into her mouth, she downed some water. "Long story."

Though he had a pretty good idea who'd made her come out, Gavin didn't probe.

Staring at him, curiosity got the better of Emily as she wondered why he was there alone. "So, uh, what happened to that girl you brought with you to the engagement party?"

She wasn't you. . . . "She moved to the West Coast to be closer to her family," he replied, the lie tumbling from his mouth effortlessly.

"Oh, I'm sorry about that."

"Nah, it's no biggie."

Trevor and Fallon approached the two of them, both sweat-riddled from their dancing.

"Country," Fallon breathed heavily, wiping the back of her

neck, "take a walk with me to the restroom. I need to fix my makeup. I'm pretty damn sure it's all over the place right about now."

"Sure," Emily said, rising from the bar stool. She looked at Gavin. "Could you keep an eye on my purse for me?"

He nodded, but Trevor yanked it from the bar and slung it across his body. "I'll keep an eye on it. Blake might steal some freakish keepsake of you for himself."

They all laughed, and the two women headed toward the restrooms. As Emily weaved through the endless fans celebrating the Yankees' win, she spotted Dillon playing a game of pool. He was hanging out with a cluster of men and women across the bar. She could tell it was taking all of his efforts to remain upright as his body swayed while lining up a shot. A ripple of laughter washed over the crowd when he sank the eight ball.

"So much for spending time with me," she mumbled.

Fallon pulled the restroom door open, and they walked in. "I know I don't know Dillon that well, Country, but I'm assuming he forced you to come out tonight."

"Well, I could've said no," she replied as she observed her appearance in the mirror.

Ripping a piece of paper towel from the dispenser, Fallon doused it with some water and started wiping her face and arms. The corner of her mouth turned up a smirk. "Right, but you didn't."

Emily shrugged. "I felt bad about not coming. I love Trevor."

Fallon tossed the paper towel into the trash and looked at Emily, her gray eyes twinkling with concern. "And Trevor loves you, but you need to find your voice with your man. Put him in his place when need be."

Emily studied her for a second, feeling slightly confused. "I think I do put him in his place, Fallon."

Cocking her head to the side, Fallon placed her hand on her shoulder. "I'm not trying to start anything with you, Country. I just think you could be a little tougher with him, that's all."

A faint smile tugged at Emily's lips, but she didn't answer. Fallon grabbed her hand and led them out. Upon their emerging, a large group had gathered just outside the door, making it difficult for them to maneuver through the crowd.

"Shit," Fallon said. "I think I just got my damn period. Go ahead back to the bar with the guys. I'll be right out." Emily nodded and tried to make her way through the crowd.

"Looks like you're stuck here," a man standing next to her yelled over the blaring music. Emily's eyes shifted to his smile, his height intimidating her as he brushed his hand over his buzzed head. "I could lift you up and carry you to where you have to go."

"Umm, no thanks. I'll make it through." Emily sighed as she continued her attempt to squeeze her way through the other patrons.

"Eric," he said, extending his hand while trying to also dodge the masses.

She shook it. "Emily. It's nice to meet you."

"Well, Emily, I'm here with a few friends if you want to come to our table and have a drink with us. They're right over there," he said, gesturing to a booth a few feet away. "If we make it over there. It doesn't look like we'll be moving too far in all of this."

"Thanks for the offer, but I'm here with my fiancé."

"Getting married? Very nice. When's the big day? Not a Halloween wedding, right?"

"No, but that would've been a cool idea." She stood on her tiptoes in an attempt to see over the still-lingering crowd. "It's November twenty-fourth."

"Awesome," he replied. "Can I see your ring?"

Emily thought his request was odd, but nonetheless, she figured she might be able to use it to her advantage. "How's about we do a little bartering here, Eric?" She smiled. "I'll let you take a look at my ring if you part this group like the Red Sea so I can get back to my friends."

"It's better than nothing," he quipped, grinning broadly. Emily lifted her hand, and he held it. With widened eyes, his mouth hung ajar. "That's a fucking rock if I've ever seen one. Well, congratulations to you and your fiancé. I wish you both—"

"Emily," Dillon interrupted, his voice filled with anger. He pinned her with a hard look, and she shivered. Pulling her hand away from Eric, she started to speak, but Dillon directed his attention to the other man. "Why the fuck are you grabbing my fiancée's hand?"

"Dillon," Emily nervously blurted out, "he was going to—"

"Shut the fuck up, Emily," he growled. "Answer my fucking question, man. Why the fuck were you touching her?"

Eric narrowed his eyes. "Chill out, buddy. I asked if I could see her engagement ring."

Without another word, Eric's head flew back when Dillon punched him square in the nose. His blood spewed on Emily's sweater. With a gasp, Emily's heart tripled over in her chest as she watched Eric's body slump against the wall. Stumbling to his feet, Eric rubbed his nose for a second and started swinging wildly at Dillon.

Fallon walked out from the bathroom, her eyes wide with shock. "Holy shit!"

"Dillon!" Emily cried out as he lunged toward Eric, tackling his body against the wall with brutal force.

"I'm going to get Trevor and Gavin!" Fallon yelled, pushing her way through the crowd forming a circle around the two men.

Emily wept as she screamed out Dillon's name, shock tearing through her system while the two men continued their venomous onslaught. As the bloodthirsty patrons watched the fight, roaring like caged animals, Emily's body was pushed and pulled in every direction during the hysteria. Within a few seconds, two monster-sized bouncers pushed through the growing crowd, looking as though they were undoubtedly ready to brawl. With little effort, one bouncer had Dillon strung up by his arm, pulling him off Eric, while the other yanked Eric away from Dillon. They yelled for everyone to clear the area or else they, too, would be thrown out. With their warning, the crowd receded back into the bar, still riled up from the madness.

As the crowd thinned, Fallon, Trevor, and Gavin came into view, both men wearing heated looks, with Fallon appearing just as shocked.

"Oh God, Dillon, you're bleeding," Emily cried out.

Gavin looked at Dillon, his tone harsh. "What the fuck happened?"

"She fucking happened! Get your fucking shit, Emily!"

Something flared in Dillon's eyes—something Emily didn't dare to question in that moment. She'd never seen him look so dark and full of vengeance. With her body shaking, she watched one of the bouncers feverishly escort him out of the bar by his elbow. Still crying, Emily came to a stop, her hand rushing to her mouth as she frantically looked around. "My purse. Who has my purse?"

"I do," Fallon said, quickly handing it to her.

When they emerged from the bar, Emily found Dillon pacing back and forth in the parking lot, both of his hands gripping his hair.

"Dillon," Gavin yelled out, approaching him. "What the fuck happened in there?"

Not answering, Dillon stalked over to Emily and pulled her by the arm. She tried backing away, but his ironclad grip was too tight. He grabbed her chin, forcefully yanking it up. "You just let some random guy touch you! What are you—a fucking whore?"

All. Gavin. Saw. Was. Blood. Red.

The hair on his arms stood on end. With a muscle working in his jaw, hostility bleeding from his shoulders, and the light blue of his eyes blazing like hot coals, Gavin delivered and connected a sharp, brutal jab to Dillon's jaw, snapping his head back. Dillon hit the asphalt with a sickening *thud,* his body unmoving—completely down for the count.

Emily stumbled back from the impact and landed on the ground. Sliding against tiny pieces of gravel, she felt the bottoms of her palms and wrists rip open.

Paying no mind to his unconscious friend, Gavin's eyes immediately flew to Emily. His heart clenched in his chest. In one gentle, sweeping motion, he lifted her from the ground and searched her face worriedly. "Jesus, Emily, tell me I didn't accidentally hit you." He ran his fingers across her cheeks, eventually caressing them through her hair. With his body shaking, he stared into her eyes, his voice a low whisper. "God, please tell me I didn't."

She swallowed tightly, shock settling through every limb in her body. "No, you didn't hit me," she choked out, tears streaming down her face.

For the second time tonight, relief washed through Gavin. "I'm taking you back to your apartment," he whispered, his hands sliding down her arms.

"I . . . I can't ju-just leave him here, Gavin," she stammered, wiping her eyes.

"You can, and you will," he answered softly. He looked at Trevor. "You'll bring him to your place tonight."

Crouching next to Dillon with his hand on his pulse, Trevor looked up and nodded. "Yeah, but you're helping me get him in my car."

Although it took every ounce of his self-control not to throw Dillon into Trevor's trunk and sink him somewhere in the Atlantic, Gavin reluctantly agreed. After a very drunk and very knocked-out Dillon was tossed into Trevor's car, Gavin took Emily home. The entire ride over, his stomach twisted with pain, listening to her cry as she explained what had happened. Her expression was vulnerable, and the need for answers swirled in her eyes.

After they entered her apartment, Gavin had her sit down on the couch as he retrieved a washcloth and bandages from the bathroom. He filled a bowl with cool water. When he emerged from the kitchen, he found her rocking back and forth, cradling her face in her hands. Heaviness settled in his chest like a brick. The urge to take her into his arms and shield her from the pain she was feeling was almost impossible for him to resist.

Sitting on the floor in front of her, Gavin dipped the washcloth into the water and reached for one of her wrists. She flinched back in noticeable pain as he laid the washcloth across her skin. Now he felt anger surge within him, knowing Dillon had caused all of it. Gavin gritted his teeth as he squeezed the excess water from the cloth, noticing its white was tinged pink from her blood. The blood from this beautiful woman was brought on by an asshole—an asshole who didn't deserve her smile, her touch, her warmth, or her love.

None of it.

Wanting to tell her how much better he could treat her, see to her every need, and take care of her in every way possible, Gavin found his voice trapped in yearning, not wanting to upset her further.

"I'm sorry I caused this, Gavin. I'm so sorry," she whispered as tears trickled down her cheeks.

With his brows creased and head tilted, Gavin applied the last bandage. He looked up and tried to understand why she would say that. "You think this was your fault?"

"Yes. Dillon was right. If I hadn't let that guy touch me, none of this would've happened."

"Emily . . ." He paused, bringing his hand up to cup the curve of her jaw. "You're not responsible for what happened. Do you understand me?"

Sniffling, she adamantly shook her head and stared into his eyes. "No, Gavin, I'm responsible. I had no right talking to that guy to begin with." She sobbed uncontrollably. "You and Dillon were friends, and now you won't be after this. I can't believe what I've caused."

He could see the mixture of confusion and pain on her face, and it only heightened his confusion. *Damn Dillon.* He had her under a tighter hold than Gavin could've ever imagined. "He makes you think it's your fault, Emily." His words were spoken low but unwavering. "And I'm not worried about his friendship right now. I don't think I ever was. I'm worried about you—you, Emily—not him."

Shaking her head, she continued to cry, barely managing a breath in between. Gavin rose to his feet and settled on the couch next to her. Placing a pillow on his lap, he gently pulled her down and rested her head against it. He wasn't surprised she didn't resist. The woman he'd come to know was broken—torn to pieces by a man who saw through her weaknesses. Weaknesses he used against her every chance he got. It could've been seconds, minutes, or possibly hours—Gavin didn't know—but he stroked Emily's hair until she fell asleep. With bloodshot eyes, Gavin watched her chest rise and fall peacefully. As each one of those seconds, minutes, or possible hours passed, Gavin knew—and not for the sake of what he wanted for him and Emily, but for the sake of Emily alone—he needed to get her away from Dillon.

15

Letting It All Go

THE COLD, INFINITE October sky held an unobstructed view of a full harvest moon as Emily and Olivia stepped from their building. Pulling in a deep breath, Emily stared at the twinkling stars spreading across the backdrop of towering buildings. She'd longed for this season. The air, although crisp, managed to warm her, reminding her of Colorado.

Home.

If there was ever a time in her life she felt she needed her mother, it was right now.

"We look amazing, chick," Olivia trilled, waving a taxi over. "My mother always says the best money spent is money spent on hair, makeup, and nails for an evening like this."

Before Emily could agree, a sleek black limousine pulled up. The chauffeur stepped out, and Emily recalled he'd driven them out to Gavin's home in the Hamptons.

"Good evening, Miss Martin," the gray-haired, plump gentleman said to Olivia. "Please forgive my tardiness this evening.

The city has quite a few blocks closed down for repairs that I was unaware of."

"Hey, Marcus," Olivia replied with a smile. "Did that sneaky bastard send you?"

"Yes, Miss Martin. Mr. Blake told me to arrive at six o'clock sharp for you and Miss Cooper. Again, I apologize for being late."

"Hell, I love surprises. I figured we were hailing a taxi over to the party." Olivia turned to Emily, her brow drawn up. "Apparently, Mr. Blake showers people he desperately wants in only the best . . . because he's never sent one *before*." Emily shook her head and slipped into the limousine. After getting themselves comfortable, Olivia popped the top off of a bottle of champagne, pouring them each a glass. "Has Dinkerbell called you again today?"

"Dinkerbell?"

"Yeah, like Tinkerbell. Did he call you again?"

"That's a new one." Emily sighed. "What do you think?"

"Well, I figured he might've gotten the point already since you haven't taken his calls." She shrugged. "And no flowers came to the apartment today, so I assumed he'd finally given up."

Emily knew it wasn't in Dillon to just give up that easily. "Right, maybe not to the apartment, but he sent them to Bella Lucina while I was working."

"Shut up," Olivia let out, her eyes wide. "How many this time?"

Emily considered her over the rim of her glass. "Let's just say there were enough for Antonio to decorate each table and the entire bar area, and he had an extra dozen left over to bring home to his girlfriend."

Draining her drink, Olivia leaned back, her expression soft. "Well, I'm proud of you for not giving in. In all honesty, I hope you stick to your guns when he finally gets back from Florida. When I spoke to Trevor earlier, he said all the idiot's been talking about while they've been down there is how he's determined to get you back."

Emily looked out the window, her eyes taking in the glittering lights of the city. As she watched them go by, she thought about how much she felt like a victim of a violent crash—so battered and bruised. Although she had no broken bones, her heart bled from the wounds Dillon inflicted. His words kept running through her head, stinging just as much now as when he first said them.

She couldn't deny she felt guilty for causing the whole situation. She knew she could've prevented what had happened. Regardless, she wouldn't cave. She couldn't. She made sure to send his every call straight to voice mail. He even went as far as calling the elementary school where she worked. She ignored those messages as well. However, her biggest surprise was when his mother showed up at her apartment unexpected, unannounced, and quite pissed. Emily cut the visit short by slamming the door in her face.

"I have to speak with him when he gets back," Emily sighed. "I can't just end it with him without closure."

"Why not? He doesn't deserve any kind of closure, Em."

"I'm not talking about his closure, Olivia. I need closure of my own." Emily tossed back the rest of her champagne and promptly refilled her glass. "No matter how you slice and dice it, he did a lot for me and my family. I know he was wrong for what he did, but he was drunk, and that's something I need to take into consideration."

Olivia glared at her from across the limousine. "You're falling right back into his trap."

"How am I falling into his trap, Olivia? He's not even here."

She started tapping her temple. "Right, he's in that brain of yours like a little fungus. My brother gets hammered and doesn't freak out on Fallon." Olivia leaned over and poured herself a second glass of champagne. "I've dated plenty of guys who got smashed, and they didn't pull the shit he pulled with you. I'm sure you've had ex-boyfriends who didn't do that either."

"I didn't really date much before Dillon." Emily shrugged. "I really have nothing to compare it to."

Olivia's face creased with confusion. "Why would you need something to compare it to, Em? End of fucking story—drunk or sober, low or high, mad or happy—a guy's not supposed to place a hand on a woman. Ever." Taking a sip of her champagne, Emily looked away. "I'm not kidding, Emily. You may think that what your father did to your mom is the norm, but it's not, friend. It's far from it." Swallowing hard at the tainted memories, Emily brought her attention back to Olivia. "I suggest you rid yourself of needing closure from that asshole because he's just like your dad. Box up the shit he has at our apartment, and I'll have my brother get your stuff from Douche's place." Crossing her legs under her red silk gown, she added, "Thank God you hadn't signed a lease on that apartment you two found."

"I don't want to talk about this any more tonight," Emily said, her voice teetering between frustration and pleading. "I want to enjoy one evening without thinking about this whole mess with Dillon. Please, Olivia?"

"Okay, but I'm back on your ass come tomorrow, then."

Emily sighed and nodded. "That's fine."

Five minutes later, the limousine pulled up to the St. Regis hotel. Marcus opened the door for them, and each slipped out onto the sidewalk, thanking him for the ride. Pulling her shawl over her shoulders, Emily locked arms with Olivia, and they made their way into the lobby.

After Olivia checked her coat, they floated into the expansive ballroom. The fund-raiser was in full swing. Music from a live band hummed through the air while white-gloved waiters traveled the room with caviar and flutes of champagne. The whimsical space held vaulted, cloud-dappled ceilings highlighting gilt chandeliers. Soft, pale pink lights, honoring the color of breast cancer awareness, made the white silk material draping the tables look like cascading waterfalls. Beautiful pink roses and carnations sprayed up from glittering mounds of hydrangeas in the center of each table.

The second Emily made her way into the ballroom, her eyes found Gavin's. She also found she had to remind herself how to breathe. A smile broke out across his face as she watched him excuse himself from a group of men. Not only did Emily focus on him as he strolled across the space, but she noticed the eyes of every other woman in the room gravitated to him. Young, old, tall, short, black, or white—women couldn't help but stare. He looked amazing, wearing an Armani tux tailored to perfection. Sliding his hand through his hair, he crossed the room with a stride that was sexy, powerful, and strong.

Olivia leaned in to hug him when he approached. "Thank you for sending the limo for us." She paused, a knowing smile teetering her lips. "Well, not for *us,* but either way, it was a nice gesture."

Shaking her head, Emily bit her lip to hide the rush of embarrassment that dipped in her belly.

"Of course I sent it for you both." He chuckled, lifting a guilty brow. "I just never thought to send one before."

"Sure, whatever you say, Blake," Olivia replied, her voice holding playful skepticism. Gavin laughed again. He knew she was on to him. "Where are your parents? I wanna say hello."

"They're over there," he answered, gesturing to a table in the center of the room.

"Cool, I'll catch up with you two in a bit." With that, Olivia skirted through the party toward Chad and Lillian.

Gavin turned to face Emily, his eyes slowly languishing over every inch of her body. God, she looked exquisite—a princess among peasants. It was all he could do to catch a decent breath. A black strapless velvet gown, accentuating her cleavage, flowed to the ground, hugging her subtle curves like a fitted glove. His gaze swept past a diamond choker, ignoring its sparkle, and fixated instead on the startling fullness of her glistening ruby-red lips. Tiny diamond pins held up her hair, with a few tendrils framing her heart-shaped face. Smoky hues of gray shimmered over her eyelids as her beautiful emerald eyes locked on to his icy blues.

Trying to compose himself, Gavin reached for her hand and regally lifted it to his lips, placing a soft kiss on it. "Words fail to describe the way you look this evening."

"Thank you," she breathed nervously, grasping her clutch. "You look great, too."

"Why, thank you." An affectionate smile lifted his mouth. "Shall we?"

With mild trepidation, she nodded, and he tucked her hand in the crook of his arm. He led her across the room, pausing briefly to engage in conversation with some of the guests who stopped him. Along the way, he introduced Emily to a few of the families his mother's foundation had helped over the years. Their smiling faces showed their gratitude. Among the guests were some of New York's leading breast cancer researchers, organizations, and a few politicians whose families had been affected by the disease. With the subject hitting so close to home, Emily felt awestruck at the generosity Gavin and his family had extended to those in need.

Gavin pulled out a chair for her. "Emily, you remember my brother, Colton, and his wife, Melanie."

Nodding, Emily reached across the table and shook their hands. "I do. It's nice seeing you both again."

"You, too," Melanie replied. "My children have actually asked for you quite a few times."

"They have?" Emily questioned, shock dancing in her eyes.

Draping his arm over the back of Melanie's chair, Colton answered, "They sure have. They said you're the best soccer player in the world."

"That's too funny," Emily pointed out through her smile. "Well, tell them I said hello. I'll have to muster up another soccer game with them."

Gavin smirked and took a seat next to Emily. "Don't let her fool you. If I recall, I'm the one who taught you how to play soccer." Looking at her, he pitched her a wink. Emily boasted another smile and shook her head.

"Ah yes, brother-in-law, take all the credit." Melanie swept her blonde hair over her shoulder, her eyes holding years of knowledge behind them. "Emily, be forewarned that all the males in the Blake family try to take credit for anything they can." Emily quirked a brow in Gavin's direction, and he laughed. "But for right now, this Blake *woman* is about to take credit for teaching her husband how to dance." Melanie rose and reached for Colton's hand. "Aren't I right, sweetie?"

Standing, Colton curled his arm around her waist and planted a kiss on her head. "I have two left feet, so yes, I'll give you credit for trying to teach me how to dance."

"Don't fall flat on your ass, brother," Gavin yelled out as the couple moved to the dance floor. Colton turned around and flipped the bird in Gavin's direction.

"Hmm, do I sense sibling rivalry?" Emily asked.

"All-out sibling rivalry," he answered, motioning one of the waiters over. "I revel in any chance I get to make him look like a clown."

"You're too much," she laughed.

Gavin smiled mischievously. "I know, but he deserves it."

The waiter approached the table with a bottle of expensive bubbly and a towel draped over one arm.

"What would you like to drink?" Gavin asked.

Knowing she and Gavin didn't mix well with liquor, Emily figured she would keep it light. "Actually, I'll just take an ice water."

He creased his brows. "Are you sure?" With an answering smile, she nodded. After ordering himself bourbon on the rocks, Gavin leaned back in his chair and looked at her. "I'm happy to see you're no longer sick."

"Thank you. That was a rough few days."

"I'm sure it was," he replied, knowing they were hard enough for her without being sick. "I stopped by the restaurant to check in on you, and Fallon said you'd already left."

"I know. I meant to call you, but it completely slipped my mind. I'm sorry about that."

"No need to apologize. I just wanted to make sure you were doing all right."

"Well, thank you for checking on me." She smiled and placed a napkin over her lap. "I truly appreciate it. But I'm okay, honestly."

She may have smiled, but Gavin couldn't see a trace of happiness in her eyes. Throughout the evening, he kept their conversation on lighter topics, staying far away from anything to do with Dillon. Gavin learned that, although her teaching position was supposed to be full-time, it had fallen through, and she was only working part-time as a substitute. Either way, she seemed happy about it. He ribbed her a little more regarding his Yankees making it into the World Series, promising her that by the end of her lifetime, he'd turn her into a certified fan. She begged to differ, but nonetheless, it made her laugh, and that's all that mattered to him.

After everyone enjoyed dinner, Gavin's parents approached the table. The stately couple's arms were locked together, their faces flushed from dancing and champagne.

"Olivia," Chad said with a roguish grin, "my beautiful wife's given me permission to dance with you."

She lifted an incredulous brow. "Oh, has she?"

"Indeed, she has," he noted, reaching for her hand.

"Are you sure, Lillian?" Olivia stood up. "I just may steal him from you."

"He's a very debonair man." Lillian smiled, her green eyes shimmering with delight. "He just might sweep you off your feet, kiddo, so I'd be careful."

"Can't say I'd disagree with you on that." Olivia strolled over to him. "Come on, old man. I'll show you how we younglings do it." Chuckling, Chad placed a kiss upon his wife's cheek and led Olivia onto the dance floor.

"You look beautiful this evening, Emily," Lillian said, sitting next to her. "I hope you're enjoying yourself."

"Thank you, Mrs. Blake, so do you. I am enjoying myself. Everything's spectacular."

"Tsk-tsk." She thoughtfully patted Emily's hand. "Remember, 'Mrs. Blake' makes me feel old. But I'm happy you're having a good time."

An affected smile hinted at Emily's mouth. "Thank you, Lillian."

"You do look beautiful tonight, Mom." Gavin rose from

his seat and placed his hand on her shoulder. "I may have to keep an eye on you to make sure no men steal you away from Dad."

Looking up at him, she cupped her hand over his. "You've always been my biggest fan, Gavin," she trilled, her joy evident. "But, really, sweetheart, after thirty-five years of marriage, I'm not going anywhere. It's pretty safe to say your father doesn't have to worry about that."

"Doesn't have to worry about what?" Colton asked, approaching the table with a drink in hand.

"Oh, it's nothing. Your brother's just being overprotective," she laughed, rising to her feet. "Where's Melanie?"

Colton pointed over his shoulder. "She's in the lobby, calling the babysitter to check on the kids."

"Perfect timing, then," Lillian replied as she locked arms with Colton. "Care to dance with the woman who brought you into this world?"

"Certainly." He tossed back the rest of his drink. "I'll try my hardest not to step on your toes."

As son and mother whisked off to the dance floor, Gavin looked at Emily. "Would you like to dance?"

Biting her lip, Emily glanced around the ballroom and back up to him. "Dance, huh?"

"Yes, dance," he clipped, feigning innocence. "I promise I'll be good."

"That, I highly doubt, but I'll trust you this one last time." He let out a warm chuckle as she removed the napkin from her lap. Standing, she smiled. "But I must warn you, I'm probably no better than your brother."

"That's impossible," he said, the grin splitting his face as hearty as ever. "Just wait here a second. I'll be right back." She nodded and watched as he strolled over to the band. He spoke with the lead singer for a few moments and then made his way back to her, a mischievous smile running across his face.

"Why do you look like you're up to something?" she asked, curiosity crossing her features.

His dimpled smile widened as he reached for her hand, tucking it in the crook of his arm. "That would be because I *am* up to something."

"And what would you be up to?" Leading her out to the dance floor, he remained silent, but the smile on his face never faltered. "Gavin," she said with a laugh.

"Emily."

"What are you up to?"

He waited until the band struck up the chords to his request. "Do you listen to jazz?" He placed a hand on the small of her back. Lacing his other hand with hers, he tucked it against his chest and drew her into him.

Taken aback by their very close proximity, it took her a second to gather her thoughts. "Umm, yes, I have. My grandmother used to listen to it while she cooked."

"Mmm, are you familiar with this song?"

"I don't know the name of it or the singer," she answered, fighting to ignore how enticing he smelled. "But I do recall remembering how beautiful it was the first time I heard it."

Looking down at her, Gavin couldn't help but notice the nervousness in the way she held onto him as he rocked them in a slow sway. His heart swelled. "It's called 'La Vie en Rose,' and the original singer was a French woman named Édith Piaf, but I favor Louis Armstrong's version."

"It's beautiful."

"It is. And *this* is what I was up to," he whispered into her ear.

Trying to catch her breath, she bit her lip as a shiver traveled her length. "What do you mean?"

"Well, I've pictured us dancing together to this very song."

"You have?" she asked, attempting to hide any hint of shock at his confession. She inwardly laughed at herself, considering the confessions she'd made to him.

"Yes, I have." Voice soft, affection poured from his words. "So thank you very much for this dance."

"You're welcome." She saw the look in his eyes—the same one that nearly drowned her every time he stared at her like that. She averted her gaze over to where his parents were dancing. "It's amazing that they've been together so long. It's almost impossible to believe a love that strong exists."

Gavin studied her face as she watched his parents. Something in her weary tone and distant eyes ached to have something deeper than what she had with Dillon. It was then that Gavin knew he needed to wake up with her lying next to him. He longed to see what shade of green her eyes were when they were still lazy with sleep. He wanted her hair tangled in a mess and draped over his strong arms when he woke up to her smiling at him. In the coldest of winters when blankets didn't provide her body enough warmth, he wanted to be that warmth. Most of all, he wanted Emily to fall in love with him. It was more than a desire for her body; it was his need for her heart and soul. If he could have one night with her, Gavin was sure he could convince her they were made for each other. His warm fingers lazily traveled up her spine, coming to rest on the nape of her neck. "You deserve to be loved like that," he whispered against her hair.

When he pulled back, their lips were close. With the slightest movement from either, they would connect. With his whisper bracing soft and sexual, Emily pulled in a ragged breath and tried to ignore the electricity tingling over her skin. The combination of his touch and his seductive voice had her body aching with need. Now she was breathing harshly. She felt her breasts rising and falling and noticed his gaze flick over them as she looked away, not saying a word.

Gavin stopped moving, and Emily brought her attention back up to his face. His touch was almost unbearable, whispering over her jaw as his gaze penetrated into her. "I can still taste you on my lips."

Heart ricocheting through her chest, Emily lost all ability to think and simply drowned in the feeling of his hands tenderly floating down her waist. Unable to speak, she simply looked up into his blue eyes.

"I miss the way your body feels against mine." Wetting his lips, he clenched her waist tighter. "I miss feeling the way your pulse accelerates when I touch you." He swallowed, closed his eyes, and inhaled her scent, the sweet smell of jasmine intoxicating him. When he opened his eyes, his voice notched lower, softer even, as his hands framed her face. "I want to take my time with you, brushing my fingers over the spots that he's neglected. He's never loved you the way you need to be loved," he whispered into her ear, pulling her closer. "Let me love every part of you. Your mind . . ." He trailed his fingers down her neck. "Your body . . . your heart . . . your scars . . ." His hands ghosted down her waist. "Your quirks . . . your habits . . . your thoughts . . . all of you. Give me all of it, Emily."

Swallowing hard, Emily's body shook. She backed away, not meeting his eyes, her voice low. "I can't do this with you, Gavin. We . . . We can't do this." He moved toward her, but she stepped away. "Tell Olivia I'll meet her back at the apartment. I have to leave." She spun on her heel and headed for the table to grab her clutch and shawl.

With shock on his face, Gavin watched her scurry through the ballroom, making her way through the crowd. However, he wasn't about to let her go. He wasn't about to let her walk out of his life.

Not now. Not ever.

In a few quick strides, he made his way through the throng and caught her elbow in the lobby. Eyes filled with confusion, he looked at her, his heart pounding. "Why are you running from me, Emily?"

"I'm not running from you," she whispered, her eyes brimming with tears.

Sighing, he plowed his hand through his hair. "You *are* running from me, and I want to know why."

She looked away. She refused to see the pain in his eyes—and refused to feel the pain in her heart. "It'll never work out. You and Dillon were friends, and he'd never allow this to happen."

"*What?*" he asked in disbelief. "How do you think he'd be able to control anything between you and me?"

"He will," she said as tears slipped down her cheeks.

"The hell he will," he breathed, stepping closer. Before she could back away, he gripped her waist and wiped the tears from her face. "You're supposed to be with me, and you know it. You said it yourself that you feel me when I'm not near you." Dipping his head, he looked straight into her eyes, his voice low. "God, Emily, please . . . You have to give us a chance. Let me take care of you. Let me love you."

She waited for the words—the right words—to come to her, but they didn't. Cupping her hand over her mouth, she stumbled back, feeling Gavin's fingertips fall from her waist. A steady stream of tears dripped from her eyes. She looked at him for a moment while her heart grated to shreds, and without another word, she fled the lobby.

Watching her slip into a taxi, Gavin stayed rooted in her wake, his heart sinking as he tried to process what had just happened. He knew Dillon had a hold on her, but Emily believing he could come between them fucked with Gavin's head—and fucked with it bad. Before he knew it, he was digging in his pocket for his keys and heading out to his car. After texting his brother to let him know he had left the party, Gavin found himself driving all over the city. Part of him wanted to drive over to her apartment and push the issue further, but logic told him he had pushed far enough. He couldn't say anything more to her, so all he wound up doing was going home.

Upon entering his penthouse, Gavin shrugged out of his tuxedo jacket, grabbed a bottle of bourbon, and promptly poured himself a shot. After tossing it back, he ripped the bow tie from his neck, kicked off his shoes, and sat at his kitchen island. He couldn't help but laugh, although inside, he wasn't laughing. He was sinking—sinking further into what he needed. Pounding his fists on the counter, he damned himself for not going to her apartment. Remembering his brother's words, Gavin knew right then and there that he hadn't fought hard enough. Standing up, he paced, staring at his phone while debating what to do. He went to dial Emily's number but stopped himself. Their situation didn't merit a phone call. He needed to go to her—and he refused to stop himself this time. "Fuck it." He dug into his pocket for his keys.

Swinging the door open, he all but forgot about his shoes, but it didn't matter—because he was met by the most beautiful green eyes staring back at him. They didn't say hello. Words were unnecessary. They both knew right then that they would speak volumes through their actions before dawn broke. Spontaneous combustion ignited within both their bodies as they lunged at the same time—colliding—their mouths sliding over each other. Somewhere in between, the door snapped closed, and Gavin's shirt was ripped off.

Cradling the back of her head, Gavin's kiss exploded like tracer bullets against Emily's lips. Before she knew it, he had her lifted off the ground and pressed against the wall. Placing her arms above her head, he shackled her wrists in his hand as she wrapped her legs around his waist. With the hard, rigid set of his body pushing against hers during their heated kiss, Gavin's free hand fell to her thigh, sliding her dress up over her waist. The air hissed with the sound of her panties being torn from her body. In anticipation, her wet, slick center ground hard against the refined material of his pants. As a deep yearning desire began to blaze through Emily, she pulled her wrists from his hold and feverishly unbuckled his belt.

"I couldn't get out of the taxi, Gavin. God, I couldn't get out," she moaned against his mouth. The feeling of want, the feeling of need, and the feeling that they belonged together was something she couldn't ignore anymore. She didn't want to ignore it anymore. He was all she craved, and the only thing she feared was that she wouldn't be able to get enough of him.

"I was coming to get you," he growled, sliding his tongue across her jaw. "I wasn't letting you go this time."

Reaching down, Emily slipped her hand below his boxer briefs, skimming over his thick, hard length. She started stroking him, reveling in the feel of his pearly fluid against her thumb circling his tip. A deep, ragged groan tore from Gavin's throat as she stroked up again, releasing his shaft from its confinements. His lips moved from her mouth to her ear and down her throat, biting and sucking, as she pumped her hand around him.

"I need to feel you inside of me right now, Gavin, please."

"I have to get a condom," he groaned against her mouth.

"I'm on the pill," she breathed, sweat glistening on her neck.

That was all he needed to hear before he hoisted her

higher—only to pull her down onto him. As he pushed up inside her hot, wet warmth, Emily's head snapped back against the wall, unable to believe how incredible he felt. She let out a forceful breath as she wrapped her arms around his neck. She arched her back, and he thrust inside her again, completely burying himself. Tongue sweeping in and out, Gavin groaned when she tightened her legs around his waist, her hands knotting in his hair. Although her back chafed against the wall with each thrust, the pleasurable burning of his girth overrode any pain.

Gavin pulled back, and they gazed into each other's eyes, drinking up the emotions in the air. Their chests rose and fell together with every shallow breath they took. As ripples of pleasure shook through Emily's body, Gavin slammed his mouth over hers, continuing his exploration of her tongue as he carried her into his bedroom.

A small groan escaped her lips when he placed her on her feet. Emily stood before him, her body trembling from head to toe as she tried to catch her breath. Without hesitation, he rid himself of his boxer briefs and socks, his predatory gaze hot and focused on her quivering lips.

Emily's eyes traveled from his beautiful face and moved lower to take in the delicious sight of his taut abdomen, the V leading her straight to the long-awaited answer of where his tattoo ended. It was magnificently beautiful. It snaked its way down his left rib cage, curving over his hip before dipping lower still. As Emily's eyes followed its progression, she admired the elaborate black ink circling his thigh, the dragon's tail wrapping around and around. She imagined her fingers or even her tongue following the same path.

"There's not a man on Earth who doesn't wish he was me right now," he said, cupping her face while brushing his thumb over her lips. Like a wild animal stalking its prey, he slowly moved around her, ghosting his lips over her shoulder and sliding his tongue up her neck. "Your mind and your body will never forget the things I'm going to do to you tonight. Every . . . single . . . inch of your body is going to feel me."

Forget about his teasing touch, his words alone had Emily feeling as though she were about to combust. "Oh my God," she breathed.

"Yes," Gavin said with a cocky smile.

He continued to circle and tantalize Emily's body with soft kisses, ultimately stopping behind her. With his breath heated and warm, he kissed her ear. Lashes fluttering closed, she felt pleasure streak through her body with each soft brush of his lips. Gavin slowly unzipped her velvet dress and watched it slip to the ground and pool around her heels. "Step out," he whispered into her neck, unclipping the diamond pins holding up her hair.

Her hair cascaded down her shoulders and tumbled over her breasts. Trying to breathe, she stepped away from her dress as a heightened level of sexual desire slicked over her skin. Still standing behind her, Gavin unhooked her strapless bra with one hand while the other floated around to the front of her stomach. She froze. Burying his face in the curve of her neck, Gavin gently gripped the back of her thigh and drew her leg up onto the bed. A moan escaped Emily's lips as he slipped his fingers deep inside her. Fiery pleasure shot through every nerve ending in her body. Lifting her arms up behind her, she dug her fingers into his hair, clawing and grasping as tight as she could. Cupping her chin, Gavin angled her face to the side just enough to crush his mouth over hers, groaning while his tongue flicked in and out. As one hand worked deeper inside her wetness, the other smoothed along the globe of her breast, rolling her hardened nipple between his fingers. A hot shiver rippled in Emily's stomach, tingling through her entire system. Panting, Emily pulled his dampened fingers up to her mouth, sucking and swirling her tongue along them. Before she took another breath, Gavin spun her around and slammed his lips against hers.

"You fucking unravel me when you do that," he groaned, his voice harsh, hoarser.

Heart racing, she delved her fingers into his hair. "Good, now unravel *me*," she moaned, her body hot, riveting with need.

"Oh, I'm going to." He skimmed his lips over her collarbone. "Now lay that beautiful body down on the bed but keep your thigh highs and heels on," he commanded.

His words sent shivers straight down the length of her spine. She couldn't do anything but simply comply with what he had asked. Cool silk sheets slid against her heated body as she scooted along the massive California king–sized bed. In a few strides, he was standing before her, so close she felt the heat and desire emanating from his pores. Emily's heart sped up when she felt his hot gaze slide over her naked body, his eyes devouring every exposed inch.

With his blue eyes penetrating hers, Gavin slowly dropped to his knees and pulled her body to the edge of the bed. He spread her thighs, opened her wide, and arranged her legs over his shoulders until nothing was hidden. He reveled in the sound of her moaning before making contact with her flesh. Stroking one hand along her stomach, he lifted her foot and kissed her ankle through her stocking.

"Tell me how much you want me to taste you," he whispered, slowly licking up her calf as his finger lightly circled her wet opening. She was soaked in her desire for him, and it was all he could do to control himself.

"Oh my God, Gavin, please," she begged, raising her hips and squeezing her breasts.

Spreading her legs farther, he breathed out one last hot breath against her pussy before his tongue laved slowly along her clit. Sliding his fingers inside, he licked through the sweet juices easing from her body. And by God, they were the sweetest juices to ever slide over his tongue. He licked deeper and tunneled his tongue inside her, pulling in her moisture in fear he would never get to experience it again. Honey . . . She was pure fucking honey. Gavin would give up everything he had acquired to taste her—to smell, feel, and explore every inch of her—so intimately every day for the rest of his life. "You taste so fucking good," he breathed, pushing his fingers deeper inside her.

Emily's breath rasped through the air, her body arching and trembling against his mouth, and it only made Gavin hungrier. His dick was hot and hard, every inch of him straining to be inside her. Every time she cried out his name and tugged his hair, he felt his own body tremble with an anticipation he had never known. It was all he could do not to explode without even being inside her. When he felt her growing close to the edge, he slowed his tongue, brought her back down and began the whole thing again—again and again—until he knew she couldn't take any more. When her thighs quaked and shook from waves of climax, he gripped the sides of her hips, yanking her harder against his greedy mouth. As she cried out his name, he nipped, sucked, and pulled her swollen, velvet-soft flesh between his teeth.

Before she could come back down from the superior heights of ecstasy he brought her to, he licked languorous circles back up her body. Pausing over her stomach, he looked into her eyes, her face flushed and her breathing labored. "God, you're so beautiful," he groaned, sliding up her body. He buried his face against one of her breasts, and his tongue swirled and sucked its taut peak. He grabbed the back of her knee, hitching her leg around his waist.

Emily's breath caught while he hovered over her, continuing to tease his tongue across the swell of her nipple. Every touch was deliberate, each flick intended to evoke a reaction. And she reacted. Her moans echoed through the room, her heavy breathing piercing even her own ears. His tongue—swirling around her breast, gently nipping here and there—caused her body to lurch toward his devilish mouth.

Emily couldn't take in enough air when he finally sank himself inside her. Ribbons of flames licked and thrummed their way through her core. Every thick, long, and hard ridge of him felt magical. For no man—not even Dillon—made her body feel the way Gavin did.

For a beat, they drowned themselves in the moment as they gazed into each other's eyes, unnamed emotions swirling in the air. It was then that Emily felt Gavin's claim on her—unspoken and silent. She had lost her body; now it was defined solely by his.

Groaning, Gavin pushed himself deeper, and Emily breathed out hard, pulling his mouth down to hers. He slid his tongue in and out, burying his hands in her hair as their breathing quickened from the sensations spilling through them.

"You like the way you taste on my tongue, don't you?" he asked, his breathing rough and ragged.

She panted, her nails biting into his back as she kissed him harder. "Yes."

"Your body was made for mine." He slid his tongue down her jaw, his hands cradling the back of her head. "Every fucking inch of you was made for me, Emily."

Kissing her, Gavin stroked his hands though her hair as Emily dug her head into the pillow, raising her hips to meet his thrusts. Their bodies moved together as if they were ideal components made for each other, both writhing under their suffused heat and need. Even though every inch of him was clad with muscle, his embrace was soft and gentle. He did nothing fast or hard. His patient, measured movements showed control while he took his time soaking in the moment, worshipping every inch of Emily's body. As their breaths mingled and danced, their mouths played over each other, their hands whispering across each other's bodies. Quickening his pace, Gavin cupped her breast, filling his hands with her softness, while his ears cherished every moan that left her lips.

Gavin dipped his lips to the hollow base of her neck. "You're my weakness, Emily," he groaned, sliding his tongue against her neck. "Such a sweet weakness."

Thrusting her fingers into his hair, Emily pulled him to her mouth as he buried himself deeper inside her warmth. Gavin felt her climax coming as she gripped his biceps, digging her nails into his flesh while her slick pussy tightened around him like a vise.

Bringing his arm under her back, he pulled her up against his chest as his fingers knotted in her hair. "Come for me, Emily," he groaned, sweeping his tongue through her mouth. His muscles quivered from holding off on his own. As soon as he felt her body start to fall apart under his, he let himself go with her. Their bodies entwined in sheer orgasmic delight as they shook, jerked, and trembled in each other's arms. Sweat against sweat and soul against soul, they soared and fell together, each wondering if they'd ever be able to come down.

When their breathing and bodies slowed, Gavin stared into her eyes. He gently moved her hair away from her face, still awed she was there beneath him. He took his time passionately kissing her, his tongue giving thanks to her mouth, her neck, and her shoulders.

As she looked up to him, Emily's hands slowly worshipped him back, her fingers smoothing through his hair, caressing down his chiseled face, and ultimately tracing his mouth.

Gavin had never felt so connected to someone in his life. Holding her completed him, feeling her made him whole, and he needed to let her know that. "I love you, Emily," he whispered over her lips. "I think I've loved you from the second I laid my eyes on you." He pulled his head back slightly, and Emily went to speak, but he placed a finger over her lips. "I don't expect you to say it back. I just need you to know this wasn't just sex for me." He placed another soft kiss along her jaw. "I want it all, Emily. I want to spend my nights holding hands with you," he breathed the words into her ear. "I want the all-day texting." He kissed her temple and caressed her cheek. "I want the laughing and the forehead kisses." He softly ran his lips over her forehead. "I want the date nights, the movie watching, and the breakfast making." He dragged his hands through her hair, his teeth tugging gently at her bottom lip. "I want the late-night drives, the sunset watching, the screaming, the yelling, and the crying." Still kissing her, he smiled against her mouth. "I know I'll *definitely* want the makeup sex that comes after all of the screaming and crying. I want the good, the bad, and the in between. All of it is what's going to make us amazing together."

Although she found it hard to swallow, she didn't take long to reply because there was no second-guessing in her mind. Emily knew clear to the depths of her soul—through every fiber of her being—that she loved him, too. His touch, the emotions bleeding from his words, and the sincerity in his eyes cast any fear of him—of them—away.

Staring at his beautiful face, she wound her hands around his neck, tears spilling from her eyes. "I love you, too, Gavin." Leaning up, she softly kissed his lips, and she could feel the shock moving through him. She kissed him deeper in an attempt to alleviate that shock. It worked because she felt his body relaxing. "I want all of those same things . . . and I need them with you. I want to make you happy."

Leaning his forehead against hers, he took her chin in his hand and brushed the pad of his thumb across her lips. "There's no way you couldn't make me happy. It's impossible."

Gavin rolled to the side, taking Emily with him. With that, they made love—unrelenting and sweet—into the early morning hours.

16

The Opening of Floodgates

THE LUSTROUS SUNLIGHT spilling through the window shades stirred Emily from one of the best nights of sleep she had experienced in months. With a long, lazy stretch and a smile, she pulled the mountain of tangled blankets tight around her chest, sat up, and leaned against the headboard. Her eyes scanned the expansive room for Gavin. The sound of the shower running echoed through her ears as she soaked in just how incredibly awesome her body felt.

Normally, she never worried about the way she looked upon rising; however, this morning was different—very different. Knowing her hair must've looked like a rat's nest and her face was most definitely sporting last night's smudged makeup, she promptly slid from the bed, dragging the blankets along with her, in an attempt to study her reflection. When her bare feet hit the cold marble floor, so did something else. Looking down, she found a large box with a red bow tied around it. Picking it up, she sat back down on the bed. It was addressed to her—well, not her, but Molly. She laughed. "Such a wiseass."

Shaking her head, she started to open it and saw movement in her peripheral vision. Lifting her gaze, she was rewarded by the sight of Gavin coming out of the bathroom—a white cotton towel wrapped around his waist. Swallowing hard, Emily clutched the blankets around her chest and slid back against the headboard. Running his hand over his dampened hair, Gavin smiled at her from across the bedroom, his muscles rippling in his abdomen as he stretched. Sheepishly smiling back, Emily took in the sight before her. He was magnificent to say the least. She couldn't help but let her eyes roam over him; it was impossible not to. He was beauteous, not just his amazing stature but also his face. That strong angular jaw that complemented his high cheekbones, and the light stubble on his chin only added to his masculinity—and further added to her quickened breath.

And. God. Bless. That. Tattoo.

"You found your gift," he said, smiling.

Emily lifted a slow brow. "Well, I found a gift for Molly. But, yes, I found a gift."

Chuckling, he padded over to the bed and sat next to her. "If I recall correctly, you're the one who said I'd never let you live that one down, so I'm just holding up my end of the bargain." Shaking her head, she playfully smacked his arm. He chuckled and slowly tucked her hair behind her ear. "Mmm, I knew you'd wake up pretty."

Biting her lip, noticeably embarrassed, she averted her gaze away from his.

Mesmerized by the look in her eyes, Gavin felt captivated by the fact that she clearly didn't realize how beautiful she was. Her lips, the hue of a deep, ruddy wine, alluring green eyes, and the subtle curves of her body all tantalized his senses. Staring at her, his heart beat as her devotee while his eyes mapped out every inch of her face. It wasn't just her physical beauty. It was everything about her, right down to the smell of her flesh—the things he would do just to obtain her scent. She brought him warmth the entire night like a sweater on an autumn day, and he was willing to sacrifice anything in order to keep her for himself. His long, drawn-out thoughts and daydreams of this very moment—when he would share with her his cravings and she would do the same, trusting as only lovers could—unfolded with such vibrancy as she brought her gaze back to his.

High.

Gavin felt completely fucking high. No amount of money could buy this feeling, and he knew it. Placing his hand under her chin, he stared into her eyes. "You look beautiful," he whispered, gently coaxing her face toward his. Slowly, he brushed his lips over hers—gentle, passionate, and soft. Emily's fingers instantly delved into his hair, tugging just hard enough to make him groan. They sat there making out like two teenagers on a date—both content in just that . . . nothing more . . . just kissing.

After a few minutes of reveling in the minty taste of his lips, Emily pulled back. Gavin looked at her, his eyes essentially making love to her in the process. "What's wrong?" he asked, a boyish grin tipping the corners of his mouth.

"I, uh . . . need to brush my teeth," she said, tightening the blankets to her chest.

Letting out a light laugh, he reached for the unopened gift and handed it to her. He placed another luscious kiss on her lips. "You taste delicious to me, but here. Open it."

She smirked. "That's a pretty big box for a toothbrush."

He stroked his knuckles along her jaw. "It is, isn't it?" With furrowed brows and a smile that trumped all the rest, she stared at him suspiciously. "What?"

"When did you have time to go out and get me anything?"

"Well, sleepy head, it's not that early," he said, motioning to a clock highlighting that it was nearly eleven in the morning. "But to answer your question, I had my assistant run out to pick up a few things for you from a list I gave her."

"Ah, your assistant."

"Yes, my assistant." Playfulness danced across his features. "But I'd be willing to replace her for this stunning woman sitting in my bed right now."

"Oh, you'd hire me as your assistant, huh?"

"Without hesitation," he whispered, the words spoken into the crease of her neck as he grazed his teeth down her shoulder. Emily's body nearly went lax under his touch. "Though I'm not quite sure we'd get much work done." Pulling back, he smiled. "Now open your gift."

With one hand holding the blankets against her chest, Emily attempted to open the box with the other. Gavin chuckled, realizing she was trying to keep her naked body covered. This he found insanely cute and sexy at the same time. Without saying a word, he smiled and helped her.

Upon opening it, she found two medium-sized boxes and one thinner box inside. With a huge grin, Gavin opened one of the medium boxes for her, pulling out and holding up a hooded New York Yankees sweatshirt-and-sweatpants outfit.

"You've completely lost it." The words flew past her lips in an exasperated giggle. She plucked it from his hands and tried to give him a disapproving glare, but she was inwardly approving too much at his cute gesture of attempting to turn her into a fan. "If you think I'm going out in public wearing this, you're wrong."

His eyes slowly wandered over her face, his lips but a breath away from hers. "Who said we're leaving my place today?"

"Hmm, we're not?"

"No, we're not. I'm holding you hostage here," he replied, his voice low, as he leaned in to kiss her. "The outfit's purely for my own personal entertainment."

"Sounds interesting," she replied and kissed him back. "And what do you have planned for us today?"

Nipping at her bottom lip, he smiled. "I figured we'd order in all day."

"Uh-huh, food is a necessity," she half moaned as he continued to ghost his mouth over hers.

"Sleep a little since we were up so late."

"Yes, we do need to keep our strength up." She ran her hand across the back of his neck.

Still kissing her, he lifted her other arm around his neck, the blanket falling from her chest. "Curl up on my couch and watch scary movies."

"I like scary movies," she said, massaging her fingers into his hair while sexual heat pulsed through her system.

Catching her bottom lip between his teeth, he slowly smoothed his hands across her exposed breasts. He smiled when she moaned. He loved the way she responded to him. "In between all of the food eating and movie watching, I'd like to reenact last night's events play by play." He pulled her onto his lap, her hair cascading over his shoulders as their kiss deepened. "Over . . . and over . . . and over again."

Right about the same time Emily started peeling away the annoying barrier of the towel wrapped around his waist, his cell phone rang. Gavin showed no intentions of retrieving the call.

With quickened breathing, Emily pulled back and looked at him. "You really should answer that, Mr. Blake."

He threaded his fingers in her hair and guided her back down to his mouth. "No way," he groaned as he leaned back against the headboard, his kiss becoming harder. "Whoever it is can wait."

"Uh, uh, uh." She pulled back again with a teasing smile. Though it took massive effort, she figured she'd play a little game—one *he* thought he was the master of. "It could be your mother."

He ran his palm over his face and let out another groan. His lips curled into a sensual smile. "You're killing me, Emily—literally killing me."

She smirked, reveling in the fact that she could make such a powerful man crumble. Rolling off him, she started to laugh. "Hmm, who's begging *now*?"

Shaking his head, he swung his legs over the side of the bed. "Oh, you *will* pay for that one, I promise."

As she listened to him speak with whoever was on the other end, she smiled and ran her fingers across his back, hoping he would make good on his threat.

"Can't it wait?" he asked the caller. Emily sat up on her knees and feathered kisses along his shoulders. Loving the way she felt, Gavin rolled his neck to the side, inviting her into his mouth. She kissed him for a few seconds before he spoke again. "All right, give me a minute." Cupping his hand over his cell, he turned to face her. "It's Colton. I have a few things I need to go over with him about some bullshit at work. I might be a while." Emily nodded.

He touched her cheek with the back of his hand, stroking the curve of her chin. Settling his lips over hers, he kissed her tenderly. "Open the rest of your gifts, go take a shower, and I'll make us some breakfast when I'm done talking with him."

She nodded, her eyes following him as he made his way out

of the room. Trying to tame her heated senses, she drew in a deep breath and started going through the rest of the items. Along with a pair of pink-and-gray Nike Shox sneakers, she also found the necessities needed for her to take a shower. From shampoo to an array of body wash and razors, he seemed to have covered all the bases. There was also a bottle of Jimmy Choo perfume. Emily figured he must have spoken with Olivia, because that was her favorite kind. Opening the thinnest box, she smiled when she found a pair of black lace panties and a matching bra.

After gathering everything together, Emily slipped from the bed and padded into the bathroom where she indulged in a hot, soothing shower. Though her body felt at ease in complete bliss, her thoughts were anything but. Overwhelmed would have been an understatement. She had a lot that she knew she had to face when Dillon got back. Frankly, it terrified her right down to her bones. She ran over the things she would tell him. However, she still couldn't push away the feeling that somehow the whole scenario was about to go up in flames—torching her, Gavin, and Dillon in the process. Stepping out from the shower, she grabbed a towel and tried to push away the festering negative thoughts taking residence in her head.

Once dressed in her less-than-appealing Yankees attire, she made her way into the living room, her eyes sweeping over Gavin's collage of black-and-white photos; most were massive. Unlike her last visit, this time she actually studied them. It was then that she noticed every picture was a building or famous structure. She recognized the Pantheon in Rome. Another was a French portrait of the Palace of Versailles. Her eyes scanned over the Taj Mahal, the Eiffel Tower, and the Gateway Arch. She wondered if they were places Gavin had already visited or if they were on his list of places to see.

With that thought, she followed the voice of the man she wanted to know more about. She found him in his office, sitting at a large mahogany desk with Manhattan's skyline just beyond the floor-to-ceiling window behind him. Although the structures of the most powerful city in the world towered over his frame, he looked like a king seated on his throne.

And now that king was hers.

With his eyes downcast, staring at his laptop, still in business mode with his Bluetooth receiver in his ear, Gavin didn't notice her observing him from the door frame. To her disappointment, he'd already gotten dressed. However, as casual and relaxed as he appeared in a pair of black sweatpants, a white, V-neck T-shirt, and reading glasses, in that moment, she felt drawn to him. Quietly, she moved across the room. It wasn't until she was within arm's length of him that his head snapped up, a contagious smile washing over his face. He held his finger up, signaling her another minute—but she didn't want to wait. No. Instead, she found herself slowly sliding her sweatpants off, her gaze intent on his.

Today, she was the huntress . . . and Gavin was her prey.

She watched him swallow, his Adam's apple bobbing, as he leaned back in his leather chair, crossing his arms. His smile widened. He kept his voice cool and monotone—continuing his conversation as if unaffected by her striptease—but his physical reaction rising through his sweatpants told another story.

Positioning herself directly in front of him, she planted her foot on his chair between his legs. A salacious grin tipped the corners of his mouth as she leveraged herself, slow like a snake, slithering her body on top of his desk. With his head at even height with her stomach, he rolled forward and gripped her waist as he looked up to her. Sucking in his bottom lip, he smirked and shook his head as if warning her of the wonderful things to come.

"Colton, it's not a good move," he said. He paused a moment and listened, his eyes never leaving Emily. A wave of heat coursed through her body as his hands gripped tighter around her waist while the pads of his thumbs stroked slow circles against her sensitive stomach. She showed no mercy either as she teasingly pulled her sweatshirt off, her bare foot gently sliding against his crotch. The come-hither look in her eyes nearly sank Gavin right there.

If Emily wasn't mistaken, a light groan rumbled in the back of his throat, and she swore it was the most erotic sound she'd ever heard. Her awareness of him was quickly becoming painful as the flesh between her legs tightened viciously. She tipped her head back and seductively ran her hands over the black lace of her bra, kneading her fingers against her breasts, in hopes of shortening his conversation.

"Right, I understand, but that account is months away from going live, so it's not something I'm worried about right now," he said, his voice cracking slightly. "Look, I have to go. I'll talk to you about this later." He yanked off the earpiece and tossed it on his desk.

Bingo . . .

He went to pull off his glasses, but Emily caught his wrist, stilling his movements. "No, keep them on," she rasped, her gaze sweeping over his face. "You look sexy in them."

Wearing a boyish grin, he tilted his head to the side and studied her. "I look sexy in glasses?" he asked, his hands spreading her thighs wide open. Nodding, she let out a breath as her palms slid against the cool surface of the desk. "Mmm, I don't know about that." He eased her panties to the side and slipped one finger inside her. He pulled it out, licked her juices from it, and then gently pushed two in.

"Gavin, yes . . . please don't stop," she moaned, her back bowing under his assault as her hips circled shamelessly against his thrusting fingers. While the fingers of his one hand worked inside her, the other tore and snapped the panties away from her body.

"Fuck, you're so wet," he hissed through gritted teeth as he quickly rose from his chair. With his free hand, he swiftly shed his clothing while his other continued to push in and out of her. His rhythm was steady and unhurried as his thumb circled her sensitized clit. Emily's sex rippled eagerly around his fingers, her grip white-knuckling the sides of the desk. "I do this to you, Emily. I make your body get like this."

A moan left her lips, and she reached for his dick, sliding her hand up its length from root to tip. She helped him guide it through her saturated folds, and when he was finally snug inside her, she sucked in air as he deliciously stretched her out. After lifting his shirt off over his head, she unhooked her bra and tossed it to the side.

"Ah Christ, you're so fucking tight," he bit out, his blazing blue eyes intense as he watched her. "I love the way you feel around me."

With his hands fisting her waist, Gavin's head fell back and he let out a deep, guttural groan. His pace was fast and hard—and Emily loved it. Her face flushed, her skin misted with sweat, and her body shook as he pounded into her, driving the message home repeatedly. Holding on to his neck, she pulled him down to kiss him, but he resisted.

"What are you doing?" she asked, panting as he thrust inside her again—this time slower but with more force. "I want to kiss you, Gavin."

Pulling out a fraction, he stared at her, his mouth curving wickedly. "I know, but I'm not letting you kiss me."

With her nails digging into his shoulders, she leaned forward again in an attempt to catch his mouth, but he steadied her, his hand cupping the curve of her neck. He brushed his thumb over her lips as he pushed deeper, and she gasped, arching her back. Her body felt as if it was about to combust into flames. "Why won't you let me kiss you?" she breathed. Ripping his glasses from his face, she flung them to the side as waves of screaming pleasure tore through her.

He smirked, and with another slow, rough thrust, he groaned. "I want to see your beautiful face the entire time. See what you look like when I'm inside you—when you come for me." He jerked his hips forward, harder and deeper as his hands gripped the sides of her thighs. Her folds sheathed every stiff inch of him, her body shaking and clenching around his. "You're going to let me watch you come, Emily."

Finding his demand excruciatingly carnal, her mind went wild for him, its ferocious desire needing to give him what he wanted. Her entire body shuddered, and within seconds, her core convulsed with rippling orgasms tearing through every cell in her body. It radiated outward until she was trembling from head to toe, mindless in her ecstasy.

As soon as she did, Gavin caught her by the nape of her neck, slamming his mouth against hers. He growled and Emily's name tore past his lips as he licked his tongue across the side of her jaw. Still battering into her, Emily felt his body tip over the edge, fraying. She felt his hot liquid warmth flow within her as he groaned into her neck, his body shaking with his own climax.

As the scent of sex filled the air and a seductive mixture of love and pheromones raced through their bodies, Gavin picked her up and carried her into the living room. Dragging her down with him, they collapsed onto the couch. With ecstatic spasms still rushing through each of their muscles, Gavin reached for a blanket, tossed it over their naked skin, and pulled Emily against his chest.

"You're amazing," he whispered, kissing her forehead. She let out a satisfied sigh and smiled at him. They held each other, absorbing the aftershocks as their breathing slowed and evened out. Gavin brushed the damp tendrils of hair away from Emily's face, his fingertips gliding across her lips and down the curve of her jaw. Arms, legs, and bodies intertwined, they both drifted off into a glorious haze of sleep, neither wanting to wake from this dream.

With the sun dipping below the horizon, the only sound in the penthouse Gavin could hear was Emily's shallow breath as it whispered against his bare chest. Stroking her hair from her shoulder, he was all too aware that the minutes they had left together were fading quickly. Closing his eyes, Gavin breathed her in, trying to hold on to the moment, but his thoughts were consumed with something he wasn't used to.

Fear.

Gavin usually feared nothing, and now he felt overtaken by it. Though Dillon wouldn't be back until Tuesday, Gavin knew that when he returned, things could possibly change for him and Emily. Gavin had no reservations in his heart that she didn't love him; she'd spent the last twenty-four hours proving that she did. However, he couldn't ignore the possibility she might change her mind once Dillon returned. He knew she felt tied to him, bound to the small morsels of kindness he'd shown her every now and again. There was no doubt the Asshole would use those times against her. Staring at her sleeping form curled against him, Gavin kissed her forehead. He prayed that the woman who delivered more than she'd ever know—who filled his empty life by her mere presence—didn't crumble under Dillon's pleads to take him back.

Trying not to wake her, Gavin slid from the couch and moved to the kitchen. He pulled out a menu to order them dinner. Since he so clearly recalled their encounter in front of the sushi restaurant, he figured that was a safe bet. After the order was placed, Gavin padded into his office to retrieve their discarded clothing. He got dressed, and when he returned to the living room, he found Emily awake. She smiled at him and stretched out her long arms before she rose from the couch, dragging the blanket along with her. Gavin watched the woman who owned his heart make her way toward him, his breathing spiking instantly the closer she got. With the blanket wrapped tightly around her body, Emily shoved up on her tiptoes, draped one arm over his neck, and started kissing him. Smiling, Gavin slipped his arms around her waist, holding her close as he reciprocated, soaking her sweetness into his mouth, her scent into his nose, and her touch into his skin.

She pulled back, her eyes lazy with sleep. "It's almost dark outside. I can't believe I slept that long."

A smart-ass smirk crossed his features. "Well, you've kept us very . . . active since last night."

"And you partook in every moment of it, Mr. Blake," she said matter-of-factly. "And if I'm not mistaken, you enjoyed every second of it as well."

"Mmm, you caught me. I enjoyed every millisecond, to tell you the truth." She laughed, and he cupped her jaw, his thumb stroking her cheek. "I just woke up myself, actually," he said, flashing his dimpled smile. "You're hungry, right? I mean, considering we slept through breakfast and lunch, you must be."

"I'm starved."

"I ordered sushi. Good?"

"Perfect," she answered, placing a kiss upon his cheek. "I'll be right back. I'm gonna go clean up and get myself dressed in the wonderful Yankees attire you've forced me into wearing today." Leaning against the counter, he chuckled and watched her slip into the bathroom.

"Wiseass!" she called out before closing the door. Emily giggled when she heard him laugh at her comment, but her smile fell once she glanced in the mirror. Though her body may have been brought to extreme heights of ecstasy over the last few hours, her disheveled appearance said otherwise. With her hair matted, lips swollen from frenzied kissing, and eyes showing lack of sleep from the night before, she decided a quick shower was in order.

After finishing up, she realized she had forgotten to bring that fashionable Yankees outfit into the bathroom. Wrapping a towel around her wet body, she opened the door to find Gavin standing there with her clothing in his hands. He poked his head in, dangling the attire in front of her. Every time she tried to grab it from him, he'd yank his arm back.

"Would you stop?" she pouted, once again reaching for the clothing.

"Do you have any idea the self-control I'm exercising right now?" She cocked her head to the side and smiled. "However, you've lucked out. The food's already here, and I don't want you to starve any more than you already have." He handed her the clothing. "But I make no promises after we're done eating, though."

"Sounds like fun."

He leaned in to kiss her and walked away, but he stopped in the hall and turned around. "Emily."

"Gavin."

"Don't forget," he warned, his smirk exploding off his face, "my impatient hands ripped the panties from that pretty body of yours earlier, so it looks like you're going commando, doll."

"Gavin," she said, her expression mocking his.

"Emily."

"I enjoyed every millisecond of you ripping those panties from my body."

As Gavin tried to walk back into the bathroom, Emily closed the door and locked it. "The food will get cold," she yelled out, trying to stifle a laugh.

"It's sushi; it's supposed to be cold. And I'm giving you five minutes to come out here and eat it," he groaned. "If not, I'm beating the door down, and *you'll* be what I'm having for dinner, Miss Cooper."

Laughing, she heard him walk away and found herself trying to hold back the sudden urge of allowing him to acquire her as his main dish. Though his threat held massive appeal, she got dressed, blew her hair dry, and made her way into the living room. To her surprise—and very much to her liking—he'd dimmed the lights, turned on the gas fireplace, and set up a makeshift picnic in front of the crackling flames. Again, she found herself observing him without his knowledge. Mystified by everything about him, she watched him pour them each a glass of red wine, his body relaxed as he sat cross-legged on the blanket. Leaning against the wall, she crossed her arms and wondered what the last year of her life would've been like had he been the one to visit Olivia with Trevor instead of Dillon. However, in that moment, a sickening paradox occurred within her thoughts. No matter how badly her scenario with Dillon had ended, Emily could never forget the things he'd helped her through, and a part of her would always love him for that. Nevertheless, her heart now lay in Gavin's hands. He was her new love, a new path, and the new road she wanted to follow.

On a sigh, she walked over to Gavin and knelt astride him. He smiled as he curled his arm around her waist. She leaned in and placed a soft kiss on his lips, and when she did, the heat he resurrected in her body made itself acutely present—but at the same time, guilt filled her soul. Some of it was guilt for Dillon, but most was guilt that she was the reason Gavin was about to step into a catastrophe. They had opened up the floodgates to something that could devastate them both. The only thing she could do was pray he was strong enough to endure the turmoil they would find themselves in once Dillon returned. "I love you, Gavin," she whispered.

Pulling back, he searched her eyes. "I love you, too, Emily," he said, brushing his fingers through her hair. "I honestly do."

She gave him a weak smile and moved across the blanket, careful not to knock anything over. She started to open some of the containers and placed a few rolls of sushi on her plate.

Handing her a pair of chopsticks, Gavin studied her for a moment, picking up immediately on the shift in her demeanor. He couldn't help but feel his heart sink, if only for a second. "Are you all right?"

She took a sip of wine and nodded. "Yeah, I'm good."

"Are you sure?"

"I am." She leaned over and stroked his cheek. "Thank you for all of this. It's perfect."

Her reassuring touch settled his thoughts. Letting out a breath, he smiled. "It's me who needs to thank you."

"Don't be silly." Her forehead crinkled in question. "Thank me for what?"

"For everything, Emily," he replied, his voice and eyes soft.

She looked at him, her movements stilled by his tone. "Thank you for falling in love with me. Thank you for sharing yourself with me. God, thank you for not wanting to fucking kill me every time I pursued you during all of this. I know I put you in a bad position, but I couldn't . . ." He paused, drawing in a long breath as he looked down to his plate. When he brought his gaze back to hers, he could see tears brimming in her eyes. "I just couldn't stay away from you," he whispered. "I felt you the second you walked into my building. Hell, I think I felt you before you walked in. I've never experienced anything like that before in my life. It all flashed in front of me—marriage, kids, growing old together. You pulled me in, and I knew . . . I just knew right then we were supposed to be together."

Now she moved to him, uncaring of knocking anything over. She sat up on her knees and inched her way across the blanket, where she snuggled in his lap. Draping her arms around his neck, she pulled him down to her mouth. Any and all doubts she had that he wouldn't be able to endure what they were about to go through together evaporated from her mind.

Vanished. Poof. Gone.

"You're crying," he whispered over her lips, wiping a tear from her cheek. "I always manage to make you cry."

"These are definitely good tears this time, Gavin," she said, sniffling.

"And that's all they'll ever be." He leaned down to kiss her. "I swear to God that's all they'll ever be, Emily."

Still sitting in his lap, she reached for a pair of chopsticks and plucked a roll out of one of the tins. "Open up," she said, holding it to his lips. "I want to feed you."

He did as she asked, smiling while he chewed. "I could get used to this."

"I bet you could." A roll of giggles crawled up her throat.

"But of course." He lifted his glass and took a sip. "I'll take more," he said, opening his mouth wide.

She popped another into his mouth. "Can I ask you something, Mr. Blake?"

"Anything."

"Have you been to all of these places?" With a sweep of her hand, she motioned to the pictures on the walls.

Swallowing, he took a second to look at some of them. He nodded. "I have, actually. I went to study them."

"For school? I thought you took business management."

"I did take business management," he said, smiling. "But I originally wanted to become an architect. I'm fascinated with the way things are created—from stories in books to buildings." He traced the curve of her jaw, down to her collarbone, and then over her shoulder. He felt her shiver. "I find it amazing that a thought can turn into something so beautiful and so life-changing—just from a simple vision or idea."

"Why didn't you go to school for that, then?"

His gaze swept over the pictures again. "After my grandmother passed away, Colton and I were each left a considerable inheritance. He wanted to open Blake Industries." Reaching for another piece of sushi, he popped it into his mouth and shrugged. "He needed my half of the inheritance to start it up. Instead of becoming a silent partner, I went in as part owner. Essentially, the advertising industry creates things, so I figured why not. Besides, it was something he really wanted, and I didn't want to let him down."

Emily cupped her hand over his cheek. "You did it for him."

"Kind of." He shrugged. "But I'd never let the prick know that."

"Do you like it, though? I mean, are you actually happy doing it?"

"I'm happy with how successful we eventually became."

Quirking a brow, he smirked. "And I don't usually go into work until ten in the morning most days, so that's a plus."

"Lucky you. I wish I could go in that late," she sighed. "But you didn't answer my question, Blake." He smiled, and she adjusted herself in his lap. "Are you actually happy doing it?"

"You want honesty?"

"Yeah, I'm pretty sure that's what I'm shooting for here."

"I hate it. It bores me pretty close to death."

"You should be happy with what you do for a living," she said, leaning up to kiss him. "Have you ever thought about selling your portion off?"

Stroking the hair away from her face, he kissed her forehead. "I have, and I will eventually. Considering we just got her back on her feet again within the last few years, I want to make sure she's solid before I do."

"You're a good brother, you know that?"

"Oh, I'm as pretty fucking cool as they come." They both found amusement in his comment, and Gavin pulled her closer. "Enough about me. What made you decide on a career in teaching?"

"Well, I'm dyslexic. When I was growing up, I attended a school that either didn't recognize I had it or didn't have the staff to help me." She reached for her glass of wine and took a sip. "Other kids made fun of me because it kept me from advancing, to a point. As I struggled through high school, I decided I wanted to become a teacher because us dyslexic folk notice right away when a child has it. I figured if I could help just one kid get diagnosed early on, it would be worth it."

He stared at her for a few seconds and smiled. "You know, *you're* as pretty cool as they come."

"Oh, am I?" she questioned, beaming. "I've never been referred to as cool. Ever."

He gently pulled her up, positioned her legs around his waist, and brushed his lips against hers. "Yes. You're undoubtedly the coolest woman I know," he said, sucking on her bottom lip. "And I promise to always refer to you as being cool."

"Well, thank you for that." She giggled against his mouth. "And I promise to always refer to you as a wiseass."

"Mmm, you have my permission to call me whatever you want." She smiled and continued to indulge his overly skilled mouth. After a few minutes, Gavin pulled back, the proverbial elephant in the room resting heavy on his chest. "Could I ask you a question now?"

"Absolutely," she replied, placing a kiss on his jaw.

"How are we going about telling Dillon?" Gavin felt her body tense. He brought his hand around the back of her neck and cautiously coaxed her face within inches of his, his eyes soft. "Emily," he whispered. "We. I said we. I'm not letting you tell him alone, do you understand me?"

Swallowing hard, she nodded. "I do, but could we not talk about him right now?"

Gavin searched her eyes. He could tell she was nervous, and he knew the risk she was taking was far greater than his—but he also felt confused. "We have to talk about him, Emily."

"I know we do," she answered, lifting her hands to his cheeks. "It's just that he doesn't get back until Tuesday. It's Sunday night, and I just want right here and now to be about you and me. Not him . . . just us, Gavin." She found his perfect mouth again and kissed him ferociously, wanting nothing more than to rid Dillon from her thoughts. Gavin tightened his hold around her waist and groaned into her mouth. She slowly pulled back and looked at him. "Tomorrow night, okay? We'll go over everything tomorrow night."

"All right, but you have to swear to me that you won't say

anything to him before." He smoothed his hands through her hair. "I want to be there. Again, this is us."

"I know this is us. Thank you," she whispered, leaning her forehead against his. "But, honestly, I haven't even answered his phone calls."

"Okay, I just want to make sure—"

Emily placed a silencing finger over his mouth, and he smiled. "Stop," she said, removing her finger and replacing it with her lips. While his tongue swept through her mouth, she tried to relax her nerves down from the conversation. That didn't take too long at all.

"You're staying with me tonight again, I assume," he whispered, his mouth grazing over her jaw.

She tilted her head as his kisses moved down her collarbone. "I can't. I've been substituting, and I have papers to grade. Besides, I have to be at school by seven tomorrow morning."

"You teach first grade, don't you?" he asked as he lifted her arms, gently pulling her sweatshirt off.

"Yes, that would be the grade I teach." She unclasped her bra and tossed it aside. "Why do you ask?" Gavin focused his eyes on her luscious breasts, and a reverent smile broke out across his face. Wetting his lips, he remained silent. Emily placed a finger under his chin, bringing his gaze back to hers. "Why?"

He pulled her into his mouth and started kissing her. "Why what?" he asked, nipping at her lip.

"Gavin," she laughed. "You asked if I teach first grade."

"Oh, right," he chuckled, swiftly removing his shirt. "You said you can't stay with me because you have papers to grade, correct?"

"Yes."

"Don't they all just automatically pass at that age?" he clipped, sweeping his hand beneath her knees as he stood and carried her to his bedroom. "I mean, it's only coloring and shit like that."

"No, they don't automatically pass," she playfully asserted, nuzzling her nose against his cheek. "And they don't just color."

Placing her on the bed, he watched her slide her naked body toward the pillows. He shed the rest of his clothing and climbed under the blankets. "There's nothing I could say to you—wait, strike that. There's nothing I can *do* to you that would make you change your mind about staying with me tonight?"

She smiled and ran her hands over his shoulders. "I really can't. But I'll let you try to convince me."

"Mmm, you drive a hard bargain," he breathed, feathering his lips along the curve of her neck. "But I'll take it, Miss Cooper."

Over the next several hours, both Gavin and Emily thoroughly enjoyed . . . *dessert* multiple times. Though he hounded her a little bit more about spending the night, he couldn't get her to stay. By the time he brought her home, despite his best efforts with passionate, tender kisses and even offering to pay her a year's salary for the night, he watched her close the door to her apartment. He cursed the fact that tomorrow was a Monday, and she had to work.

With his body racing with excitement and his heart soaring with love unlike any he'd ever felt, it was all that Gavin could do to make his way home without getting into a car accident. His mind replayed the last twenty-four hours repeatedly like a vivid movie, a vivid love story. To hell with *Casablanca*. He was in love—and now he truly felt like a god.

Now he had it all.

He knew he looked like a goofy lovesick fool as he padded into his building whistling. The door attendant greeted him with the tip of his hat and a curious expression. Even he knew something had changed in Gavin. Smiling, Gavin patted his shoulder, shook his hand, and headed for the elevators.

Gavin decided to forgo a shower—wanting to hold on to Emily's scent—but it was well past eleven by the time he sat down in front of his laptop to get some work done. It was also well past eleven when his front door buzzed. Snapping his head up, he couldn't help the smile washing over his face as he made his way down the hall. Emily had promised that if anything changed, she would come back. He reached for the doorknob, and upon opening it, he was met by familiar green eyes.

Unfortunately, they weren't the eyes he had expected. As he felt the blood drain from his face, confusion clouded his head. "What the fuck are *you* doing here?"

"That's a nice way of greeting someone you spent a half a decade with," Gina replied, wiping tears from her face as the smell of booze wafted through the air around her. Gavin poked his head out and glanced from side to side down the hall. "What are you doing?" she asked, stumbling back.

"I'm looking for the fucking hidden camera crew—that's what I'm doing," he bit out. His brows furrowed like raven's wings over his darkened eyes. "Is this some kind of joke?"

"No, Gavin, it's not a joke," she choked out, slurring her words. "I know I'm the last person you want to see, but the only reason I'm here is because my father died."

Pinching the bridge of his nose, he looked down and shook his head. "Gina, what do you want?" he asked, his voice calmer.

"Jesus, Gavin, I just told you that my father's dead," she sobbed, moving closer. "My brother's in Greece right now. You know I have no one else." She cried, burying her face in her hands. She brought her bloodshot, swollen eyes back to his, her lips quivering. "Can you at least let me come in for a few minutes?"

Swallowing hard, he stared at her for a long moment as his thoughts ran over every possible scenario that might allow him to escape the situation. Watching the woman he had spent so many years with tremble and shake like a lost, brokenhearted child, he couldn't stop his thoughts from weaving over to Emily. He wondered what the woman he was in love with would think if he actually let his ex-fiancée come in.

"Please, Gavin. I just need someone to talk to right now," she whispered, staring at the floor as her body swayed slightly.

"Gina, you do understand you're only coming in to talk, right?" She wiped the tears from her face and nodded. "I want to make myself very clear. I'm giving you fifteen minutes, and then you have to leave."

"Okay," she cried, looking into his eyes. "Thank you."

Without another word, he ran a nervous hand through his hair and reluctantly stepped back to allow her into his penthouse. His mind struggled with his decision as he snapped the door shut. She stumbled into the living room, removed her jacket, and dropped it onto the floor as though it were a used tissue. "Do you have any alcohol?" she asked, sinking into the couch.

"I think you've already had enough to drink," he replied, sitting on a chair across the room. "What exactly happened?"

"He hanged himself," she sobbed, folding her hands across her stomach as if she were in physical pain. "He got himself in deep and lost everything. He dragged me down with him this time."

Gavin knew immediately what she was talking about. He'd spent the five years of their relationship digging her father out from one gambling mess to the next—everything from horse races to long weekend trips the asshole spent in Vegas. The tally was close to $300,000, if not more. With a heavy sigh, Gavin folded his hands together and leaned forward. "Do you need help with the funeral expenses or your rent? Which is it?"

Plowing her hand through her blonde hair, she sucked in an indignant breath. "How could you even say that to me right now? You think I came here for money?"

"To tell you the truth, I'm pretty fucking sure that's why you came here."

Using the back of her hand to wipe her nose, she stared at him, her mouth wide open. "I can't believe what you're saying to me, considering—"

"Considering what?" he cut her off, his tone harsh. "You walked out of my life, and now you show up at my door out of nowhere, laying all of this on me. If you're looking for a shoulder to cry on, I'm not your guy." He rose from his chair, padded into the kitchen, and flung open one of the cabinets. Yanking a bottle of bourbon from the shelf, he poured himself a shot and tossed it back. "I'm sorry to hear about your father—I honestly am—but I don't know what you want from me."

"Gavin, I came here because you're the only person in the whole world who really knows and understands me," she gasped, her tearstained eyes wounded. "You know my mother left us. I have no one. How can you be so heartless?"

"Yeah, I'm the heartless one. I learned from the best; let's not forget that. If you need money, just fucking say it already. Goddammit!" He slammed the shot glass on the counter so hard Gina jumped, startled by his anger.

Somewhere between the adrenaline coursing through his veins and her sobbing, Gavin faintly registered the sound of his cell phone ringing. For a moment, he felt as though his feet were frozen to the floor. He couldn't believe the woman who'd hurt him so badly and put him through so much heartbreak was sitting on his sofa, asking him to alleviate her pain. Shaking his head, Gavin turned away and shuffled out of the living room to answer the call. By the time he made it into his office, the phone had stopped ringing. His heart dropped when he realized it was Emily who'd called. He reclined into his leather chair, stabbed his pass code into the damn thing, and retrieved the message she had left.

"Well, hello there, wiseass. I know it's pretty late, and I was about to go to bed myself, but I just wanted to call and thank you for one of the best nights and days of my life. I know you and I have a tough ride ahead of us . . ." She paused and lowered her voice. *"But as afraid of all of this as I was, I'm not scared anymore, Gavin. I'm really not. You depleted me of any doubts I had about us. I don't know. I'm just rambling on now, but I wanted you to know that I do love you, and I'm excited to see just how amazing we're going to be together. I'll see you tomorrow night. Sweet dreams."*

Gavin lost count of the amount of times he listened to Emily's message, her voice like an angel amid the nightmare sitting in his living room. Sighing, he scrubbed his palms over his face and debated sending her a text. He decided against it, considering she said she was going to bed. Rising from his chair, he made his way back into the living room—only to find his nightmare ex sound asleep on his couch, wearing only her sweater and panties. On the floor, next to her jeans, the bottle of bourbon was tipped on its side, nearly empty.

"How can a day so fucking good end so badly?" he mumbled as he moved across the room toward the couch. "Gina," he said, leaning over her as he nudged her shoulder, "you need to leave."

She swatted her hand at him but severely missed her mark. "I'm too drunk to go anywhere, Gav," she slurred. "Don't worry; I won't steal your millions while you're asleep."

"No, Gina, you're not sleeping here," he replied, his voice insistent. "Get up."

"Pick me up if you want me out, then," she said, giggling as she reached for the blanket.

Gavin cringed because the blanket draped across her drunken body was the blanket he'd spent the day tucked underneath with Emily. He pretty much decided he would torch it after this.

"I'm not picking you up. You're not even dressed." His voice showed his patience was wearing thin. He nudged her shoulder again. "Get up, Gina. I'm not kidding."

She didn't verbally answer. However, her light snoring did all the talking, showing signs she wasn't leaving any time soon.

Picking up the bottle, Gavin walked into the kitchen and emptied the rest of its contents into the sink. Letting out a heavy sigh, he chucked it into the garbage, leaned himself against the counter, and peered at Gina from across the room. Short of removing her, couch and all, Gavin resigned himself to the fact that she was indeed staying the night. With that, he flipped the lights off and headed into his bedroom, his muscles tensing with aggravation and anger with every step he took. It was well after midnight by the time Gavin climbed into bed. It was also well after midnight when he decided his conversation with Emily tomorrow night would be about more than just Dillon. It would also consist of his unexpected houseguest.

He only prayed Emily would understand.

17

Master of Trickery

GAVIN FELT HER hands sliding down his neck, tracing his pectorals, and ultimately inching down his abdomen. He couldn't help but smile; it was utterly impossible not to. As her hand dipped below the sweatpants she was pulling off his body, he felt her silken hair drape over the flare of his naked hips. Gavin sucked in a deep lungful of air when her tongue licked over his hardened arousal, swirling languorous circles along its tip. With his eyes still closed, he fisted her hair as her head steadily bobbed up and down—her mouth taking in every hard inch of him, her tongue greedily flicking for his juices. He could hear the sound of her cheeks hollowing and unhollowing with each naughty pull, and—goddamn—it was driving him nuts. Needing to take in the beautiful sight of the woman he so desperately loved sucking him off into absolute oblivion, he leaned up on his elbows and found his worst nightmare staring back—her eyes wicked as she continued her exploration.

Gina.

Gavin flew back against his headboard only to find it was just a nightmare and nothing more. Plowing his hands through his dampened hair, he sighed with relief. His body broke out into a cold sweat as his eyes flew across his empty bedroom. With his heart slamming through his chest, he sat on the edge of his bed before making his way into the living room. "Gina, you have to get up," he called out, padding into the kitchen where he brewed some much-needed coffee.

The thought of adding alcohol to his mug became very appealing, considering the mess lying on his couch, but he decided to forgo it. Before dozing off last night, Gavin had called Gina's brother and found out her whole story was a lie—one huge, bullshit-filled lie Gavin figured was some sick ploy to either get him back or get money from him. Her brother confirmed their father was indeed in another gambling mess, but he was alive and well, hiding out in Mexico.

She mumbled something inaudible and pulled the blanket over her body as she turned her back to him, waving him off as if he were the nuisance on this fine Monday morning.

"I'm serious. You have to get the hell up. Let's not forget you have a funeral to plan. And at this point, it may not be for Daddy with the mood you have me in." He grabbed a mug and looked at his watch, noting the time to be a quarter past seven. Gina didn't move, so he figured he would up the ante. "I've never physically assaulted a woman in my entire life, but you have me second-guessing my morals. Get up. *Now.*"

That caught her attention. Sluggishly, she sat up and rubbed her eyes. "Why are you in such a rush to get me out of here?"

"You never did cease to amaze me," he huffed, shaking his head. He sipped his coffee. "Never."

She rose from the couch and walked into the kitchen, her body still lacking jeans. "Come on, Gavin." She grazed her hand against his jaw. He jerked away and stepped back. "What the heck's wrong?" she asked, her eyes bulging. "You used to love when I touched you. You're acting as though I'm contaminated."

He placed his mug on the counter, a frown marring the space between his brows. "Everything about you is contaminated," he whispered through gritted teeth. "I need to get in the shower. When I get out, if you're still here, I *will* physically remove you."

He went to walk away, but she grabbed his arm. "I still love you," she cried out. He yanked his arm away. "Leaving you was the biggest mistake of my life, Gavin. Please. We can work this out."

"Like I said, when I get out of the shower, if you're still here, I'm removing you myself." His tone said not to fuck with him. He headed toward his bedroom, but before entering, he faced her again with a smirk plastered across his face. "And by the way, I'm completely head-over-heels, please-don't-wake-me-from-this-motherfucking-dream in love with someone else. She's everything you're not and then some. So I guess I owe you thanks. Thank you, Gina, honestly. Thank you for leaving me and fucking up my life for a while. It was the absolute best thing you've ever done for me." With the smirk holding steady, he graciously bowed, laughed, and turned toward his bedroom.

"Fuck off, Gavin," she spat, her eyes wide at his final denial of her.

With that, he closed the door to his bedroom but not before letting out one last throaty laugh.

The heavenly smell of freshly baked New York everything bagels wafted through the taxi Olivia and Emily were sharing. As heavy sleet pelted against the vehicle, rumbling like coins dropping from the heavens, it was all Emily could do to not reach into the bag and start eating one.

"I can hear your stomach growling over the sleet," Olivia chirped. She handed Emily an apple. "Here, at least eat this for now before you get to his place."

"But I want to eat breakfast with him," she replied, accepting it. "That was the whole point of picking up bagels. They're his favorite."

Emily looked out the window and took in the sight of the mess New York had turned into overnight. Plows worked furiously, trying to remove the wintry mix. Considering it was the last two days of October, Emily was shocked by its assault, but nonetheless, she was also thrilled. Upon waking, she'd retrieved a message from her phone saying the school was closed for the day. Her plan was a surprise visit to Gavin's place. Knowing he didn't go into work until later in the morning, she was overly excited to grab a few hours with him.

Olivia cocked her head to the side and laughed. "Right, like you two are really going to eat. Just eat the damn apple."

Shaking her head, Emily took a bite. "We *are* going to eat. . . ." She paused, drawing up a mischievous brow. "And then I'll send him to work a happy boy . . . after I allow him to feast on other delectable items." Both women giggled. Not realizing how hungry she truly was, Emily finished the entire apple.

"Uuugh, I'm so jealous you have today off," Olivia grunted as she stretched her arms. "Maybe I'll become a teacher so when shit like this happens, I can play hooky."

"You'd be miserable. You love working at the art gallery."

"I could become an art teacher." Olivia shrugged and reached into the bag of bagels. She snatched one out and took a bite. "On second thought, you're right. I'd be miserable. I don't do kids that well." Emily shook her head. "Hey, buddy," Olivia quickly called out to the driver. "I get off at the corner here. You might wanna slow down, considering the streets are covered in potential death."

The gruff-looking driver rolled his eyes. "I got you to your destination on time," he clipped, pulling over in front of Olivia's workplace. "You're still alive, so no worries. That's $22.50. Without tip."

Olivia rolled her eyes right back. She started digging in her purse. "Yeah, yeah, I know how it works. Keep the change." She handed him $30. His smile widened. Pulling her purse strap over her shoulder, Olivia turned to Emily and kissed her cheek. "Okay, so other than eating breakfast and then fucking the shit out of your millionaire boyfriend before he goes to work, what are your plans for the day?"

Olivia's statement seemed to pique the interest of the driver, who was now smirking at them through the rearview mirror.

Emily's mouth dropped open, her eyes wide. "Jesus, Olivia."

"Well, it's the truth," she pointed out. "And you'll get in a decent amount of time with him, considering he's right around the corner from here. So fuck, fuck, fuck away, friend."

"Okay, I'm officially ending this conversation." Emily all but pushed her out of the taxi. She leaned over Olivia to open the door for her. "Get out, psycho."

Laughing, Olivia hopped out of the cab, nearly slipping on the slickened sidewalk. "Get food shopping done at least."

"Yes, I'll do the food shopping. I won't see you until later tonight. I have some errands to run, and then I'm meeting Gavin at his office at five. We're going out to dinner to try to figure out this whole Dillon mess."

Poking her head back into the taxi, Olivia cupped Emily's chin, her eyes soft. "And it's a wonderful mess to try to figure out. Don't forget that." She planted another quick kiss on Emily's forehead, ducked out of the vehicle, and closed the door.

Sighing, Emily watched her make her way into the gallery. Less than two minutes later, it was Emily's turn to dig into her purse and pay the driver for the short distance. Cautiously, she slipped out of the taxi and thanked him. The door attendant swiftly made his way over, offering his hand to help her navigate the slush-riddled sidewalk. Digging in her purse once again, she went to tip him, but he waved her off, explaining that he was more than happy to help. After thanking him, she shuffled into the lobby and headed for the elevators. On her way up, she couldn't help but recall what previous times in this very elevator felt like. This time, even though a steady flutter of butterflies tickled her stomach, she was relaxed.

After making her way down the hall to Gavin's penthouse, Emily rang the doorbell. That relaxation she had just been experiencing suddenly turned into a mixture of shock and confusion when the door swung open. With her heart pounding in her chest—its speed that of a jackhammer—her eyes swept over the woman who had opened the door wearing nothing but a sweater and panties.

Over her rapid breathing and sweat-soaked body, Emily managed to get out, "Who are you?"

With the tilt of her head, Gina eyed Emily up and down. "I'm Gina. Who the hell are you?"

Somewhere in the back of Emily's mind, Gavin's comment at the baseball game flooded her psyche. *"Besides, her name is Gina, and mine, of course, is Gavin—two Gs. I think it was an omen or something—destined to not work out."*

A writhing ball of hurt tore through Emily's stomach when she realized who she was. Gavin had made her feel as though she stood a chance with him, but she really didn't. She couldn't compete with the greatest love of his life—the woman he'd loved enough to want to marry. Without another word, Emily quickly turned and headed for the elevators. She wouldn't talk to him. She couldn't. Pride kept her feet moving and kept them moving fast.

"Hey," Gina called out, "are you going to answer my question or not? Who are you?"

"Apparently, I'm no one. I had the wrong address," she answered, badly wanting to cry.

Wanting to know that she wasn't numb.

That she was still feeling.

As it turned out, she needn't worry if she'd lost her ability to feel, because her heart was crushed like a pressed flower in a tattered book. She felt every bit of pain. Her body tried desperately not to let go of the contents of her stomach. Her spirit felt defeated, broken, beaten, and torn—the assault brought on by a man she'd been naïve enough to trust. Worse, she was naïve enough to believe he actually loved her.

By the time the elevator reached the main floor, despite her best efforts to contain it, Emily's stomach decided to fight back, releasing the small amount of food it held. Right there in the middle of the crowded lobby, she dropped the bag of bagels as she dry heaved repeatedly after throwing up. Embarrassed, her brain faintly registered a woman gasping in shock. Cupping her hand over her mouth, Emily fled from the building. The icy-cold air shocking her system offered no reprieve to her sweating flesh.

As the heart of the world hummed around her with commuters walking down the packed city streets, Emily fought to gather her senses and swallow her pain. However, her wounds rang loud, like the rushing winds screaming in the wintry storm around her. Clutching her purse, she found herself walking, her thoughts wholeheartedly derailed. She made her way into a diner around the corner and took a seat at a table, her hands trembling—and not from the frigid temperature.

Peeling off her sleet-beaded coat, she ran her fingers through her wet hair, and it was then that she completely lost it. The tears flowed steadily down her cheeks as she tried to make sense of what'd just happened. She tried to make sense of her toxic, muddied perception of who Gavin had made himself out to be in front of her. In her eyes, he was the master of trickery, delivering nothing but words tainted with lies and betrayal. The long road they were supposed to travel together was now riddled with pieces of her heart—pieces he'd strategically placed for her to trip and fall over. He was everything she wanted, and apparently, she was nothing he needed.

Nothing.

He'd shown her what she really was: just another void filler. Emily didn't know how long she sat in that diner crying, completely uncaring of patrons whispering and staring. By the time she hailed a taxi back home, she was torn, her heart feeling as if it'd been sent through a grinder. Eyes blurry from tears, she made her way into her bedroom, rid herself of her soaked clothing, and changed into a T-shirt and sweatpants.

After brushing her teeth, she moved into the living room and sank onto the couch, her body still trembling. Gavin had stabbed her in the heart. He'd carefully ripped through her chest, exposing the pulsing red tissue with his lies, and no amount of sutures could close the wound. She'd surrendered who she was for who she thought they would be together. Nevertheless, none of it was real; it was all an illusion. She'd trusted him and thought she had decoded him. But the truth was simple. She'd been Gavin's puppet for a night, and she had danced to the beautiful melodies he had played. However, she would never allow him to hurt her again.

Never.

Throughout the day, she ignored numerous texts from him, proclaiming how excited he was to see her. He called once, but she sent it straight to voice mail. Without listening to the message, she deleted it. It was obvious to her he didn't know he'd been caught, and all it did was sicken her further.

As her mind continued to wrap itself around everything, a subdued knock came at the door, temporarily pulling her from the nightmare Gavin's lies had created. With dulled reflexes, she rose from the couch. Upon opening it, her heart suffered another devastating blow as her eyes met Dillon's. He wasn't supposed to be back until tomorrow. She wanted to ask what he was doing there, but the words froze on her tongue as the stretching silence between them enveloped the room.

His words came out soft and reluctant as he stared into her tear-soaked eyes. "Please . . . talk to me."

Unable to move, she stared at him without a coherent thought able to pass through her lips. He tentatively lifted his arm, placing an unsteady hand on her cheek, and wiped away her tears. Her feet remained planted to the ground, but she broke out in hysterics as her body and mind fell apart under the pressure of two men. Dillon reached out to steady her, his hands gripping her arms tightly as he pressed his forehead against hers. She stumbled back, and the sound of the door closing echoed through the apartment.

"Em, I'm so sorry, baby." Dropping to his knees, Dillon circled his arms around her waist, pressing his face against her stomach as he, too, began to cry. Emily shook more, the ache in his voice and his crying nearly killing her. "Baby, I swear, I'm gonna get help. I'm gonna stop drinking, Emily. God, please, I can't lose you, baby. I can't."

Emily believed, without any intervention, she was losing

her mind. At one point, Dillon was the reason she was still alive, but here and now, he was one of the two reasons she felt as though she wanted to die. She didn't want to give him power through her tears, and the worst part was that the man on his knees before her actually loved her. Gavin, on the other hand, had tried, tested, and tortured her with his cruel and lying tongue, but her heart still ached for him. Her mind was firing off conflicting thoughts in every direction. There'd been a time when Dillon was picture perfect, but that had shattered, and all that was left were fractured pieces—a collage of what he'd once been in her world. As she struggled to stay afloat in the poisoned waters the day had sunk her in, she knew she couldn't deal with any of it.

Backing away cautiously, she looked down to him. "I can't . . . I can't talk about this right now," she whispered, her body trembling. "You have to go, Dillon. Please. You have to leave."

Still on his knees, he buried his face in his hands. His sobs piercing Emily's ears sent a shiver down her spine. "Emily, please. I won't make it without you. I won't. I'll fucking kill myself if you leave me." He rose to his feet, his body shaking as he stepped toward her. He lifted his hands to cup her dampened cheeks. "My God, baby, please give me another chance. Look at yourself. You're just as fucked up over us as I am. We need each other."

As she grabbed his wrists, he leaned his forehead against hers, his eyes intense. "Let me make this good. Let me make this better. I was drunk, Emily. You know I would never have touched you if I weren't. I would never have, babe."

"Plea-Please, Dillon," she stammered, shaking her head. "You have to leave. I can't do—"

"No, baby, please listen to me," he cried with his forehead still pressed against hers. "I kept thinking about the first time

I kissed you. I kept thinking about the first time we made love. Do you remember that? God, I'll never take you for granted again, Emily. Please." She went to speak, but he wouldn't let her. He crushed his lips to hers. She tried to back away, but he moved his hands to the nape of her neck, tears flowing from his eyes as he continued his pleas. "Do you remember what your mother told us before she died, Emily?"

Now she pulled away. Her eyes narrowed while her sobs became harder. She tried to catch her breath. "Don't you dare bring her into this, Dillon. Don't you dare."

He stepped forward, once again placing his shaky hands over her cheeks. "She told us to take care of each other. She told us to stick through whatever uphill battles life throws at us and to never give up on our relationship. This is my battle, and you're going to leave me like this, Emily? Let me fix it," he whispered, sniffling. "I can fix it and make us better again. I can bring us back to where we used to be."

She stared at him for a long moment. The tears streaming down her face felt like acid burning into her flesh. Before she could answer, the sound of keys jingling in the door ripped their gaze from each other.

Olivia walked into the apartment, the shock on her face palpable. "What the hell are you doing here?" she spat, her eyes hardening on Dillon.

Running his hands through his hair, he backed away from Emily, his voice heated. "Don't even fuck with me right now, Olivia."

"Let me tell you something," she answered, sauntering over to him, her body movements and tone showing she was in no way intimidated. "If you don't get the fuck out of my apartment right now, I'm calling the cops. And just to fuck with you further," she hissed, ramming her finger into his chest, "I'll make sure to sic my father's best friend—who happens to be a district attorney—on your ass."

Mentally depleted and her stomach twisting into knots, Emily ran into her bathroom, landing on her knees in front of the toilet. Her body viciously retched up bile as tears soaked her eyes.

"You're a fucking asshole!" Olivia screamed at Dillon, making her way into the bathroom. He followed closely behind her. She hovered over Emily, holding her hair away from her face. "Look what you do to her! Now get the hell out of here!"

"Dillon, please," Emily managed as her body continued its assault, the acrid taste in her mouth stinging her tongue. "I'll call you later—just leave."

He stepped into the bathroom, reaching to help hold Emily's hair, but Olivia swatted his arm away. "Jesus, did you hear what she said? Leave now, Dillon!"

He scrubbed his hands over his face, stared at Olivia for a second, and with his shoulders slumped and eyes downcast, he walked out of the apartment.

The door slamming behind him made Emily jump. Standing, she leaned against the wall and tried to catch her breath. Olivia gently took her arm and helped her to the sink. Turning it on, Olivia soaked a washcloth under cool water and ran it across Emily's face as she continued to sob uncontrollably. After brushing her teeth, Emily swung open the medicine cabinet, her hands shaking as she skimmed over several medications. She was looking for one in particular—a bottle of Valium her doctor in Colorado had prescribed after her mother died. She filled a plastic cup with water and popped a pill into her mouth, hoping it would temporarily drag her from this nightmare. She made her way back into the living room.

Falling onto the couch, she covered her eyes with her arm

and tried to compose herself. She'd remembered feeling this way only three days in her entire life: the day her mother passed away, the day of her wake, and the day of her burial. Emily's nerves were shot and sizzled beyond comprehension. All she wanted to do was fade away.

Olivia sat down next to her and lifted Emily's legs over her lap, her voice riddled with concern. "God, Em, I can't believe he actually came here. Are you all right?"

Without removing her arm from her face, she nodded.

Olivia sighed, rubbing her hand against Emily's leg. "Wait until Gavin finds out about this shit. He's going to freak out." She looked at her watch. "It's already five. Aren't you supposed to meet him at his office soon?"

"No. I'm not going there," she choked out, beginning to cry again.

Olivia's brows knitted together. "Em, what's wrong?"

"When I got to his place this morning, Gina opened the door," she sobbed, rising from the couch. She walked into the kitchen, shaking her head, still unable to process everything. "She was barely dressed. And the bastard had the nerve to call and text me all day, too."

Olivia jumped up from the couch, her eyes wide. "Holy shit! What?"

"I don't understand," she sniffled, reaching for a napkin. She blew her nose. "I feel like an asshole—like a complete fool. He used me." She tossed the napkin into the garbage and sat at the kitchen table, her hands covering her face. Olivia pulled up a chair and stroked Emily's hair away from her shoulder. "I know what it was, though, Liv. He couldn't have me from the beginning, and I became some sick, twisted game for him to conquer."

"Have you talked to him yet?"

"Hell no, I haven't talked to him, and I'm not going to."

"Well, I'm calling the dick. I can't believe this," she huffed, rising from her seat. Setting off at a brisk pace, she yanked her purse from the couch and cursed under her breath.

"No, Liv. I don't want you calling him. He'll just come here, and I can't deal with any more right now."

She pulled out her phone, essentially ignoring Emily. She glanced at it. "Looks like I don't have to call him."

Emily wiped her nose against the back of her hand. "What do you mean?"

"I have four missed calls and two texts from him." Olivia studied them, her eyes widening. "He's on his way here."

"What?" Emily hopped up and walked over. She grabbed Olivia's phone and looked over the messages.

Gavin: *I've called and left a few texts for Emily. Have you talked to her? I haven't heard back from her at all. The ever-impatient and somewhat nervous G.B.*

Gavin: *Forget it. I just talked to your brother, and he said Dillon flew back early. I'm on my way over to your apartment. Leaving my office now. G.B.*

"I guess you're talking to him tonight, Emily."

"No. I can't deal with him right now." Emily paced the room. Even with the Valium working through her system, her nerves were no less calm. "Between Dillon coming here and everything that's happened today, I just can't, Olivia."

"Well, what are you going to do?" Olivia asked, her voice soft. She walked over and placed a hand on her shoulder. "He sent that last text twenty minutes ago. Even with traffic, he'll be here any minute."

"Tell him I'm sick in bed or something."

"Friend, if I talk to him, I'm gonna lose it. I love him to absolute death, but I'm so pissed at him right now, there's no possible way I could hold back. Then he'll know everything and still come in to talk to you."

Without hesitation, Emily crossed the room, plucked her cell off the counter, and sent him a text.

Emily: *I'm fine, Gavin. I'm home sick in bed.*

His answering text came relatively quickly.

Gavin: *I wish you would've told me, sweets. I could've taken care of you all day. Be there in five. I'm right around the corner. Do you need me to pick up anything? Love you.*

Shaking her head in disgust, she tried to stifle a sob, but it was no use. As her hands trembled, she texted him back.

Emily: *Don't come here. I'll talk to you another time.*

His next text didn't come as fast. Emily started to get nervous, but nevertheless, he answered back.

Gavin: *What's going on, Emily? Is Dillon there with you? I know he's back.*

"Jesus Christ, he thinks Dillon's here," she let out, wiping tears from her face. "What do I say now?"

Olivia sighed. "Emily, you have to talk to him."

"Liv, I'm not fucking talking to him right now. What do I text him back?"

Emily didn't wait for her answer. Instead, she panicked and texted him what she hoped might work.

Emily: *I'm not home right now.*

"Well," Olivia said, "what did you tell him?"

"I told him I wasn't home." She tossed her phone onto the table; the thought of smashing it into pieces became more appealing by the second. "Now he won't come here."

"Oh my God, Emily. Now he's definitely coming here."

"Why would he show up thinking I'm not even home?" she asked defensively.

"Gavin's no fool, that's why." Olivia walked into the kitchen to grab a bottle of water. "If anything, you just drilled into his head that Dillon is here with you."

"He won't come here," she replied, sinking onto the couch.

"Friend, I'm telling you, he's coming here."

No sooner had Olivia finished her sentence than a knock came at the door—and a rather hard knock at that. Heart racing, Emily hopped up from the couch and made her way over to it. She looked through the peephole to see Gavin in the hallway.

"Fuck," she whispered.

Olivia walked over. "I told you. What the hell are you going to do now?" she asked, her voice as low as Emily's.

"Tell him I lied about not being here. That I'm really sick in bed, sleeping, and . . ." She paused, wiping away tears as she gathered her thoughts. "That I didn't want him seeing me because I look horrible or something."

"How the fuck do I keep him from coming in here?" Olivia urgently whispered.

Gavin knocked again, and Emily swore she felt as though someone were holding a gun to her head. "I have no clue, but don't say anything to him right now about what I know. I'll talk to him soon. I just can't . . ." Her voice trailed off. Cupping her hand over her mouth, Emily started to cry again.

"Em, I understand, okay? I won't say anything to him. Just go in your bedroom, turn the lights out, and get into bed. I'll try to keep him in the hall." With her heart in her throat, Emily did as Olivia said and hastily made her way into her bedroom. Olivia threw open the door, quickly stepped out into the hallway, and snapped the door closed behind her. Crossing her arms, she glared at Gavin.

Gavin stared at her for a moment, his intuition eating away at his stomach. "What the hell's going on? Is he in there with her?"

"No. He's not in there with her, Gavin. She's in bed, sick, and very alone. She just passed out from some medicine I gave her earlier."

"First of all, she just texted me less than five minutes ago. Second, why did she change her story all of a sudden?"

"Well, she has a low tolerance for any kind of meds. And like I said, I gave it to her a good half hour before she texted you." Olivia drew in a deep breath. "To address her changing her story, let's just say she's had a painstakingly tough day, and she looks like shit. She didn't want you to see her like that."

The corner of his mouth turned up in a smirk. "Do I look like some kind of fucking moron to you, Olivia?" he blurted out, garnering a surprised look from her. "Because if I do, you're sorely mistaken. If she's in there trying to work shit out with him, the least she could do is fucking tell me instead of lying."

"I just told you he's not here. You've known me long enough to know I'm not a conniving, sneaky liar, Gavin." Sighing melodramatically, she looked down at her nails. "It's a shame I can't say the same thing about *certain* people I know."

Although confused by it, Gavin could tell there was more behind Olivia's statement, but he wasn't about to get into it with her—not then. However, he was definitely going to make sure he wasn't being played. Walking right past her, he reached for the door and walked in. With his heart thumping erratically, hitting the pit of his stomach, he scanned the living room for Emily.

"I told you she's in bed sleeping," Olivia said insistently.

The word *bed* reverberated through Gavin's head like a drumroll as a wave of nausea crept over him. Without thinking—and feeling quite like the certified paranoid psychopath he was convinced he was turning into—Gavin bolted down the hall toward Emily's room.

"Holy shit! What the fuck are you doing, Blake?" Olivia let out, following right behind him. "She's sleeping."

Hoping to God Olivia wasn't lying, he slowly opened Emily's door. With only the faintest light spilling into the room from the kitchen—indeed showing Emily alone in her bed—Gavin was sure his sigh of relief that seared from his lungs and passed through his lips had awoken her. He pulled in a heavy breath, leaned against the doorway, and plowed his hands through his hair.

"See? She's sleeping, Gavin," Olivia whispered. "Now come on. She doesn't feel good."

Gavin felt like a total asshole for not believing the woman he was supposed to trust. He couldn't leave. He felt frozen as his ears soaked in the sound of her breathing—the breathing of the woman who'd repeatedly said she loved him less than twenty-four hours ago. By God, he adored and loved her, but even if only for a beat, he'd doubted what she'd told him. He didn't intend to wake her, but he needed to touch her. He needed to feel some part of his angel's body. Against Olivia's pleas, Gavin found himself moving across the room. He approached the bed, where Emily lay with her back toward him. He let a bittersweet smile form on his lips as his fingertips lightly brushed through her hair. He leaned over her, his movements careful so as not to wake her as he grazed the side of her jaw with his knuckles.

"I love you, Emily," he whispered before he softly kissed the back of her head. "I wish I were here today to take care of you, doll." That was all he needed—just that little bit—and he knew he'd be able to sleep through the night.

With her breathing increasing from his wanted and unwanted touch, Emily's head screamed, *You infuriate me; you disgust me; you've shattered me,* while her heart cried out,

Please stay; I need you in my life; we're supposed to be amazing together. A hot tear trickled down her cheek as her fingernails dug into her clenched fists. But she didn't move. She was still until she heard him leave the room. Olivia walked him out of the apartment—and out of her life. Releasing the breath she had held from the moment he'd walked in, Emily turned over. Through tear-flooded eyes, she took in Olivia's silhouette just outside her door.

Olivia went to walk in, but Emily spoke up. "I just need to be alone," she cried out. "Okay? I'm . . . I'm so sorry I put you through that, Olivia. I'm so sor-sorry," she stuttered through her cries. "Thank you so much. But I just can't . . . I ca-can't talk about it."

"Are you sure you'll be all right, Em?" Olivia whispered, her voice thick with concern. "I'm supposed to meet Tina in a little while. I could stay home if you need me to."

Sniffling, Emily shook her head. "No, you go. Go have a good time. I'll be okay."

Olivia stood there for a second, let out a heavy sigh, and then slowly closed the door.

In the pitch dark, Emily curled the blankets tightly around her trembling body, her head trying to absorb the wicked day that'd been cast upon her.

Sleep.

She needed sleep like she needed oxygen, water, and food—yet she was pretty sure she wouldn't find any tonight. No. Sleep wouldn't be her friend this evening.

Instead, loneliness, hurt, confusion, and pain would replace it.

18

Swallowed Whole

HE CALLED HER and left a few messages.

Nothing.

He texted a couple times.

No reply.

Sitting at his desk in his office at Blake Industries, Gavin picked up his phone for what seemed like the hundredth time that morning. Placing it back down, he leaned back in his chair and tented his fingers beneath his chin as he carefully assessed the disturbing feelings taking root in his head. Something was wrong. Even if Emily was still sick, he knew he should've heard from her by now. However, the calmer side of his brain told him to relax. There could be several reasons why she hadn't gotten back to him yet. Considering she had missed a day of work, it was quite possible she was busy trying to catch up on other obligations.

Yes. That's what he would go with for now.

Nevertheless, as the morning dragged on, blurring into the late afternoon, Gavin was sure he was just trying to convince himself that nothing was wrong. Though his physical body was forced into several business meetings, his mind was in no way present during any of them. His thoughts became consumed and sickening scenarios clenched around his heart with every passing minute he didn't hear back from her.

After completing a conference call with a potential client, he rose from his seat and moved across his office, wondering what the fuck was going on. Peering down at the chaotic streets as rush hour crept over Manhattan, he decided to shoot Emily another call.

Before he could, his secretary's voice traveled through the intercom, cutting clear through his troubled thoughts. "Mr. Blake, you have a Dillon Parker here to see you."

Turning around, Gavin stared at his office door. Although a steady stream of adrenaline rocked through his system, his demeanor showed nothing but calm. Before he answered her, he slowly walked over to his desk and, with unhurried movements, he peeled his suit jacket from his body and laid it across his chair. In the same breath, he loosened his tie and casually rolled up his shirtsleeves. His every male instinct screamed that his friend knew he and Emily were together, and Gavin had a feeling his unannounced visit was about to become very . . . interesting. Gavin was more than aware that a jail cell might very well be his sleeping quarters this evening. Drawing in a slow breath, he stretched his neck, squared his shoulders, and hit the button to the intercom. "Go ahead and send him in, Natalie. Thank you." With his jaw clenched, Gavin watched Dillon enter his office, both men locking eyes the second the door closed.

After a few moments of thickening tension, Dillon broke the silence, his tone low but his expression hard. "What you did is fucked up."

Crossing his arms, Gavin leaned against his desk as he stared Dillon down. "Maybe if you treated Emily the way she's supposed to be treated, I wouldn't have done it. Ever think of that?" His voice was measured, but his thoughts weren't even close. Between thinking about Dillon grabbing Emily and the fact that she had said something to Dillon without him being there, Gavin was ready to draw blood.

Dillon remained as still as stone. "I shouldn't have to think about anything, bro. You had no fucking right doing what you did."

"I might not have, but what's done is done," he stated firmly, reducing the distance between them by half. "Perhaps I need to reiterate it for you. If you'd treated her the way a real man treats his woman, maybe things would be different for you right now."

"I was drunk. I would've never touched her if I weren't," he said, his eyes still glued to Gavin's. "You fucking sucker punched me. That wasn't fucking cool, man."

Gavin rubbed his chin absently. Apparently Emily hadn't said anything. "Wow, that's original. 'I was drunk,' so that makes it okay?" He didn't let Dillon respond. "So let me get this straight . . ." He chuckled, shaking his head. "You're here to talk shit to me because I knocked you out for *manhandling* Emily the way you did?"

"Yeah. Why the fuck else would I be here?"

Gavin decided to skirt over that particular question with one of his own. "What the fuck are you really here for? Because let me make myself very clear about the way I roll, Dillon. If I saw you do that to a *dog*—let alone Emily—I still would've done the same thing. When have you ever known me to sit back and watch a man do that to a woman? Tell me, because I'm honestly fucking curious now—and quite amused by the whole fucking thing."

Dillon's granite expression softened imperceptibly. "Look, I don't want to argue with you. I'm—"

"Oh, you don't?" he interrupted. "It sure as fuck seems like you do. If you can't understand why I did what I did, then there's no reason for us to continue this conversation. If you're going to use that pussy excuse of you being drunk to dismiss what you did to her, then there's definitely no reason for us to continue." Gavin pointed across the room. "The door's right there if you're going to play that card with me."

Dillon stared at him a moment, his eyes narrowing. "Like I said, I don't want to argue with you, Gavin. I'll admit I messed up, and I told Emily I'm going to make things better." Gavin cocked his head to the side, wondering exactly when they'd spoken, since Emily had told him she wasn't answering his calls. He remained quiet and let Dillon continue. "The problem I'm having is that *you* seem to have a bigger fucking problem with what happened than my own fiancée does."

"Fiancée?" Gavin asked, trying to ignore the cracking in his voice and the sudden spike in his body temperature. "She broke up with you."

"Yeah, but I talked to her, and the wedding's back on."

Dillon continued to speak, and although Gavin was staring straight into his eyes, he didn't hear him. He couldn't. Swallowing hard, Gavin's ears stung from Dillon's announcement, its insidious whisper settling like acid in his lungs. Searing pain—deep and brutal—pumped through Gavin's veins, manifesting itself like a deadly cancer.

Lifting his arm, Gavin slowly ran a nervous hand through his hair. "The wedding's back on?" he asked, his voice low, bleeding with confusion.

"Yeah, man. I just went through the whole thing with you.

It's back on," he replied, a hint of confusion tainting his tone as well. Dillon let out a breath and shook his head. "Look, I get it, okay? You're right. I shouldn't have used drinking as an excuse. Though I remain firm that you shouldn't have hit me, I'm willing to forgive you."

"You think I need *your* fucking forgiveness?" Gavin snapped, still trying to recover from the hurt anchoring itself in his chest. "You have some balls coming to my fucking office, telling me you're willing to forgive me. You're lucky I'm not knocking the shit out of you right here."

"See, this is what I'm talking about. I'm trying to smooth things out with you, and you're acting like a fucking lunatic. What the fuck, man?"

Gavin glared at him for a long moment as flashes of Emily flooded his mind. Crossing his arms, he walked over to the window. The sun had long since made its descent below the buildings, and a full moon had taken its place. Inhaling deeply, Gavin nodded. He was in no way being benevolent, and he sure as shit wasn't forgiving Dillon. His sole purpose was to end the conversation and get to Emily in whatever way he could. Therefore, he would play the game.

He vaguely remembered her saying she was covering a dinner shift tonight at Bella Lucina. Just as he had so many months ago, he would pay her an unexpected visit. However, this time he would go to her a very broken and very confused man looking for answers. He just hoped he would find them.

"You're correct, Dillon," he said, his voice so devoid of any emotion it shocked even him. "I *am* acting like a nut." He turned and faced him, his facial features smoothing into unreadable impassivity. "If you're able to forgive me for doing what I did, then surely I can get over what you've done to Emily."

Gavin carefully watched as the guard in Dillon's eyes seemed to evaporate into thin air. "Okay, so we're good, then?" Dillon asked. Crossing his arms and without a word spoken, Gavin simply nodded. "All right, cool," he said, looking down at his watch. "I'm going out for a couple of drinks with some buddies from work. I think we both could hammer back a few after this. Why don't you come along?"

"I have some business to attend to," he replied, his voice even. "*Very* important business."

"Well, if you get done early enough, I'll be at Ainsworth Prime over in Penn Plaza."

Gavin nodded, and Dillon walked over to the door. "One more thing," Gavin said, walking across the room, his voice low. Dillon turned to face him. Gavin pinned him with a look, and in that moment, he knew his expression told all. "If you ever touch her again, I'll fucking kill you with my bare hands."

Cocking his head to the side, Dillon returned his glare and went to speak but didn't. He shook his head and walked out the door. As confusion rolled off his body in waves, Gavin took a few minutes and tried to compose himself. His body shook as he tried to breathe. Still in shock at what was happening around him, he moved across his office and sank into his chair. With Emily's words tumbling around in his head, it was no use. Composing himself was impossible. His head pounded, and his vision blurred. Emily had swallowed him whole, lied about wanting a future with him, and spit him out once Dillon came back. Incapable of waiting any longer, Gavin closed his eyes for a beat, inhaled, and dug his keys from his pocket. He rose from his chair and stalked from his office. Hurt, anger, and pain tightened his chest with every step he took. He knew it would be a few hours before Emily's shift ended, but when it did, he would be waiting for her.

"Country," Antonio said, approaching the table where Emily and Fallon were sitting. "If your side work's complete, you can get out of here."

Emily lifted her eyes to him as she screwed the top onto a saltshaker. She nodded. "Thanks, Antonio."

"What about me?" Fallon asked, tossing a wrapped set of silverware into a plastic bin.

"You're out of luck, kid," he chuckled. "You're the scheduled closer tonight."

Fallon pouted her lips. "Come on, Antonio. It's pouring outside, and I've only had two tables in the last three hours. It's already eight. It's so dead in here right now; you could handle the place on your own."

Shaking his head, he mumbled something in Italian and walked away.

Fallon smirked. "I guess I should take that as a no?"

"I'm thinking that's a safe bet," Emily quipped, rising from her seat. She stretched her neck and untied her apron. "Is Trevor picking you up tonight?"

"He sure is. We're going bowling later," she replied, beaming.

"That sounds cool. Have a good time." Emily made her way over to the coffee bar to retrieve her purse. After ducking out from under the counter, she found Fallon beside her, her face filled with concern. Emily looked at her suspiciously.

Twirling her black hair between her fingers, Fallon hesitated. "Trevor told me you took Dillon back."

"I did. We worked things out," she replied, grabbing her jacket off the coat rack. "Why are you bringing it up now?"

"Well, I didn't want to upset you during your shift."

"Why would that upset me?"

Fallon cocked an incredulous brow. "Come on, Em. I know what happened with you and Gavin."

Emily tried to ignore the pang of hurt in her chest when she heard his name, but it was no use. It ricocheted through her system. She slipped on her jacket and gave Fallon a questioning look. "How do you know what happened between us?"

Fallon blinked her gray eyes and shrugged. "Olivia told me."

"Of course." She sighed and headed toward the door. She zipped up her jacket, slung her purse over her shoulder, and sighed again. "Well, I'm fine," she said softly, lying as smoothly as she could. She wasn't fine. She was a mess, and by the look on Fallon's face, she was pretty sure Fallon could tell.

Fallon approached her and placed a hand on her shoulder. "Why are you marrying him, Emily?"

Emily's features morphed into shock. "Fallon," she let out, exasperated, "what do you mean why am I marrying him?"

"I think the question is pretty straightforward, Country." She dropped her hand. "Why are you marrying him when you're in love with Gavin?"

Bewildered by the breakneck pace of their conversation, Emily figured she would answer as truthfully as she could. "I think the *answer's* pretty straightforward, Fallon. I'm marrying the man who loves me. I'll talk to you later," she said, setting off at a brisk pace toward the door.

"Emily, wait!" Fallon called out.

Emily held up a silencing hand and reached for the door. She opened it, and her breath caught when Gavin's brilliant blue eyes locked on hers. Shock rushed through her limbs, settling like heavy steel in her chest. She stared at him leaning against his car, uncaring of the cold rain pelting down around him. With his arms crossed, Gavin's eyes raked over her from head to toe, and if Emily wasn't mistaken, they showed something akin to anger. Momentarily, confusion crossed her features, but it faded as anger of her own set in. Though she didn't want to deal with any bullshit excuse he was about to spew out of his mouth, there was no hiding this time. She needed to face this—face him. Pulling in a quick breath, she gathered her nerve, composed herself, and stepped out onto the sidewalk.

"Ah, there she is. The girl who's smashed my heart to pieces," he said, his voice loud and menacing over the rain. "Was that your sole purpose—breaking my heart? Because if so, you've thoroughly accomplished that."

"How dare you say that to me!" she yelled, her anger welling, bubbling deeper now.

"How dare I say that? I was nothing but a fucking reprieve for you while he was gone!" He stepped forward, flinging his hands aloft in complete surrender. "Is this some kind of fucking joke?" He laughed with no hint of amusement. "I took that pretty face for many things, but a sick little player wasn't one of them."

Emily's mouth hung agape. The frigid rain had nothing on the tenacity he had showing up and accusing her of being a player. That alone had her nearly frozen in disbelief. However, she decided to remain quiet. If he wanted to play games, she would allow him, but she would win at the end. Something inside her screamed to let him bury himself. She crossed her arms as defiance shimmered in her eyes, inviting him to his own funeral.

And Gavin would take the bait because the look in her eyes nearly drove him mad. Though she'd ripped his soul from within his body, not touching her wasn't an option. Not kissing her was impossible. He had to kiss her right there as the rain fell around them. Gavin moved to her with the fluency of a tiger attacking its prey. Before Emily could stumble back, he captured her by the waist and brutally crashed his lips over hers, his tongue parting them while she tried to push him away.

For a second, she could taste his anger, aggravation, and possessiveness—and, damn him, if it didn't confuse and piss her off more. As he sucked the rain clear off her bottom lip, lightning flashed, cracking to the earth in the distance.

"Are you fucking crazy, Gavin?" she hissed, jerking her head back as she tried to wiggle out of his hold.

"Am I crazy? Like a fool, I had faith in you—in us!" he growled, his voice rising, barely controlled as he gripped her waist. He looked into her eyes, watching beads of water trickle along her lashes and down her cheeks. "When did you take him back, Emily? Answer me that fucking question!"

Puddles pooled around their feet, and rain-soaked commuters dashed past them. She stared at him, her heart pounding, with mutiny bold in her eyes. "I took him back about an hour after you left my apartment!" she hissed, her voice malicious in her attempt to cut every piece of him to shreds. She tried to pull away, but he held her firmly in place. "I took him back an hour after you brazenly hovered over me and told me you loved me!"

Glaring at her, his hand came around the nape of her neck as he pulled her face within inches of his, their noses brushing. She felt his hot breath fan over her cold cheeks as her chest rose and fell. "You were awake when I was there?"

"Oh, I was awake and very well, as a matter of fact." She laughed maniacally, her words dripping with rage.

Gavin couldn't believe what he was hearing or seeing. Surely this wasn't the same woman he was with only a few nights before. He'd heard of people deemed temporarily insane, and in this very moment, he was completely ready to drive her straight to the nearest psychiatric ward.

No. Questions. Asked.

"How seriously twisted can you be?" he growled, his expression thunderous. She went to speak, but he cut her off. "Did you fuck him last night, Emily?" Her breath hitched, and her body heated as he tilted her head back, his hand fisting her hair. He grazed his lips over the corner of her mouth. He slowly slid them to her ear, the slight stubble on his face brushing against her flesh, his voice a hot whisper. "And if you did fuck him last night, did he feel as good inside that beautiful pussy as I did? Was he able to make you beg for more the way I can?" He gently nipped her earlobe, nearly melting her right there. "And one final question for you, doll. Did you come as hard with him as you came for me?"

As the fierce downpour assaulted the pavement, her eyes narrowed, her heart exploding with grief and anger all at once. He loomed over her, their drenched clothing clinging against their bodies, their breathing heavy. "He made me come harder!" At this, Gavin looked shocked—hurt, even—but it didn't stop her. "He felt just as awesome inside of me as your dick felt buried inside of Gina!"

Gavin reared back. "What are you talking about?"

"Gina," she clarified slowly, her voice venomous. "I came to surprise you yesterday morning with breakfast, and it turned out the surprise was on me. Looked like you already ate. Your sheets were still warm from the two of us, and she opened your door practically naked. Give me a fucking break!" She watched as his expression shifted to one of unease.

Gavin knew her eyes were the enemy, betraying her in so many ways, but he also knew his actions by letting Gina in had caused the battle. God help him if this was a battle he was about to lose Emily over.

Tread.

He knew he had to tread lightly. The woman before him

was broken and hurt, but his mind was frozen. He couldn't seem to formulate his words quickly enough.

His lack of a speedy reply seemed to confirm what Emily knew to be true. He knew he'd been caught, and he had no idea what to say. Before Gavin could register what was happening, Emily brought her hand up and smacked him hard across his face, the sound pitching over the pelting rain. He staggered back slightly—completely stunned.

"You bastard!" she yelled, uncaring of passersby watching their exchange. She glared daggers at him and went to smack him again, but his hand darted forward and caught her wrist.

"You have to listen to me, Emily," he breathed, his voice firm. She tried to yank her wrist away, but he pulled her into his chest. With his free hand, he smoothed the wet hair away from her face. "She was already gone by the time I got out of the shower. I had no idea you were there." Emily's eyes widened as she tried to pull away again. "No, wait! Fuck! It's not at all what you think!"

Emily was still trying to free herself from his grasp, tears spilling from her eyes. "Is that the best you could come up with?" she huffed, affecting a wicked sneer.

Trapped.

She felt trapped under the glare of those beautiful blue eyes, and she wasn't about to let him suck her back under their spell. "You're out of your mind if you think I'm falling for that one! You can't lie your way back into my heart, Gavin. I hate what you did to me, what you did to us, and most of all, I hate you!" Part of her froze when those words tumbled from her mouth because she didn't hate him. She couldn't. She loved him—loved him clear to the bottom of her soul. However, everything she knew he stood for from the second she'd met him was everything he'd proven himself to be.

Gavin recoiled as though she'd hit him again. His heart sank as shock shifted to the realization that he may have lost her—and losing her meant he would lose himself. "You don't hate me. You love me," he choked out, not trying to hide the pain ready to crush him. Lifting his arms, he held her face between his hands, stroking the pads of his thumbs over her lips. "And, Jesus Christ, Emily, I love you with everything inside of me, with everything I am, with everything I'll ever be. Please. Don't leave me like this, knowing if I just hadn't let her in, this wouldn't be happening right now. She came to my house, and I shouldn't have let her in. I know I shouldn't have, but she was drunk, and her—"

"Stop!" she blurted out, shoving viciously against his chest. It worked, because she finally freed herself from his hold. She stepped onto the curb, hot, angry tears rolling down her cheeks as she flailed her arms to hail a taxi. With curtains of rain falling from the sky, her efforts went unnoticed as drivers sped past, drenching her further.

Approaching her, Gavin felt light-headed, hollow, and empty. He took her firmly by the elbow and spun her around. Their eyes, equally dripping with hurt, bore into each other's. Bringing his arms up again, he cupped her cheeks and lowered his forehead against hers. "You have to believe me," he whispered harshly, his voice laden with pain. "She passed out on my couch. I slept in my fucking room, and nothing—nothing at all—happened." Now sobbing uncontrollably, Emily tried to back away, but Gavin moved his hands to the back of her neck and held her in place, his forehead still pressing against hers. "I told you I'd never hurt you, and I meant it. I meant every fucking word. Please don't do this to us . . . please. I'm not lying to you. I'm not him. I'm not Dillon."

Feeling trapped in the darkness of his gaze, Emily's heart

paused as she watched tiny droplets of water trickle down his face—down to those perfect lips that had worshipped every inch of her body. Those perfect lips that had also worshipped another woman's body after she'd left. Her tears came in a torrent as the thought of what he had done hit her with brutal force.

Shaking her head, she took several steps back, her eyes glacial. Turning around, she raised her hand to hail a taxi again, and to her surprise, one pulled right over. She reached for the handle and swung the door open. Gavin's hand quickly slammed against it, keeping it shut.

"Let me get in, Gavin!"

"No. I'm not letting you go," he said, his voice booming. "You don't believe me?"

"I'm not kidding! Let me in!" she commanded, the viciousness of her tone startling them both.

Running his free hand through his soaked hair, Gavin gritted his teeth. "You'll believe the fucking lies he tells you on a daily basis, but you can't believe me?"

"Oh, now you're really reaching." She scoffed, trying to remove his hand from the door. "He's not the one who's lied to me!"

"Goddammit, Emily!" he snapped. Abruptly, he caught her by the waist and hauled her tight against his chest. She sucked in an indignant breath as she stared into his eyes. "Don't mistake my pleading with you as weakness; I'm no asshole. I told you I'm not lying, but if you think for one fucking minute, he hasn't—or that he's not—then there's seriously something wrong with you."

"Hey," the impatient driver called out, "is she getting in or not?"

"Yes." "No." They quickly yelled in unison.

Gavin's angry eyes snapped to the driver. "She's not getting in. Leave. *Now.*"

With a pissy look, the man shook his head and sped off.

"I can't believe you," Emily cried out, tears streaming down her face. Each one of her tears crashed around Gavin's heart. She pushed against his chest, but he secured her with his steely arm around her waist. "Why are you doing this to me, Gavin?"

"Because I fucking love you, and I'm not lying," he answered, his breathing ragged and harsh. "Tell me right here and now that you don't love me, and I'll walk away. I'll walk away, and you'll never have to see me again." With his free hand, he tilted her neck back. He dipped his head and started feathering his lips against her temple, down her cheek, and along the curve of her jaw. Emily couldn't help it; a light moan left her lips. "You'll never have to feel me touch you again, Emily. You'll never have to hear my voice. You'll never have to wake up to me by your side again. Tell me right now that you don't love me, and I'm gone . . . forever."

Emily was shaking inside, but she wouldn't show it. If she let anything slip through, she would break down, and that couldn't happen. Though every fiber in her body wanted to believe him, she didn't. This was a carefully thought-out skit he was trying to manipulate her with. He was an actor on a stage, perfecting his skill, and Emily was his sole audience. Now it was her turn to send his heart straight into the crematory, where hers now lay.

"I don't love you," she said, lying through her teeth. That lie was literally ripping her apart. Her eyes dripped with tears as she stared into his. "I told you I needed to get you out of my system, and I did. That's all that night meant to me." Another lie.

However, there would be one truth that left her lips. "And I don't believe a word you've said."

Gavin winced and held back stinging tears. Her parasitic words—each one of them—sucked the air straight out of his lungs. She had taken his heart, ground it up, and turned it into crimson paste right before his eyes. Struck nearly fucking speechless, he stepped back and released her from his hold. "Thank you for the permanent scar," he whispered, his voice broken and defeated. Without another word, he shoved his hands in his pockets and walked over to his car.

Emily cupped her mouth, a wounded cry escaping her as she watched him pull into traffic, his tires screeching against the wet pavement. With her heart sinking in her chest, she waved a taxi over. Hands trembling, she pulled the door open, slid in, and let the driver know her destination.

Tonight, sleep wouldn't be either of their friends.

Tonight, loneliness, hurt, confusion, and pain would visit both Emily and Gavin.

19

Time

GAVIN TOSSED HIS phone on the couch next to him after it rang for the twentieth time. Dillon was fast becoming relentless at this point, and Gavin didn't give a flying fuck. Finishing the last beer in a six-pack, he mindlessly flipped through television channels. The cool liquid slid down his throat, working its way into his body. However, the only thing he could taste or feel running through his veins was Emily. No matter how hard he had tried over the last couple of weeks, Gavin couldn't remove her. Nonetheless, he kept his promise. Though it desperately took every bit of self-control, he didn't attempt to contact her. Still, that didn't stop her from bleeding through every coherent thought or haunting every sleeping nightmare Gavin had. Emily had morphed into an ache unlike anything he'd ever known.

The sound of the clock ticking away on the wall gained Gavin's attention. He glanced at it and pictured Emily walking out of the church, considering it was the evening of her and

Dillon's rehearsal dinner. Gavin had no desire to let Dillon know he wouldn't be attending. None of it fucking mattered. He didn't know how much more pain his heart could take, and showing up at the church or the dinner would surely sink him further. Groomsman or not, he wasn't going. In less than twenty-four hours, the woman he loved, the woman he saw a life with, the woman he'd thought would hold his child in her arms one day would no longer be Emily Cooper. She would be Mrs. Dillon Parker.

All of it was more than Gavin could handle.

Standing, he made his way into the kitchen with every intention of cracking into a second six-pack. It was then that a knock came at the door. After pulling the six-pack from the refrigerator, he padded over to open the door. Taken slightly off guard by his visitor, without saying a word, he walked back into the living room and settled onto the couch.

"You look like shit," Olivia noted, entering the penthouse. "I may be wrong, and tell me if I am, but I'm pretty sure you have the funds to buy a razor blade. Has the man worth millions gone bankrupt?"

"You've never been short in the humor department," he muttered, not looking in her direction as he continued channel surfing. "Shouldn't you be at the rehearsal dinner?"

After dropping her purse to the ground, she peeled off her coat and scarf. "As much as you should be," she quipped, flopping onto a leather chair. "You weren't at the church, and you seriously don't look dressed for the party. Come on, go take a shower, and I'll wait while you get ready. Oh, and I'll drive, since it's apparent you've been drinking."

Shaking his head, he plucked a bottle from the six-pack, popped the top off, and took a long pull. He didn't respond, but he gave her a look that was nothing short of threatening.

"What?" she asked in one of the most innocent tones he'd ever heard.

"Oh, give me a fucking break, Liv." He narrowed his eyes. "You know I'm not going."

She cocked her head to the side, her brown eyes wide. "Wow, Gavin, I thought you had a little more fight left in you. You're a powerful man in every aspect of your life except for when it comes to this? When it comes to Emily, you just throw the towel in, huh?" She gave a casual shrug and crossed her legs. "Hmm, I guess I don't know you as well as I thought I did."

"Fight left in me?" he bit out. Clicking the television off, he tossed the remote onto the glass table, its piercing sound making Olivia jump. He rose to his feet. "Why the fuck would I fight for someone who doesn't love me back? I'm fucked up over what happened. Believe me, you have no clue the ideas that have spawned to life in my head the past few weeks, kidnapping her being one of them. I'll love that girl until the day I fucking die, but I'm no fucking sap. Your friend's a little more warped than I imagined."

Olivia studied him for a moment as he paced. "Warped? You do realize who opened your door showing off pretty red panties the morning after you dropped Emily off, correct?" He shot her an icy look, but she continued. "She's ripped to pieces, Gavin. You have a long history of fucking women and leaving them. My friend's hurt because you fucked around behind her back. Did you expect a different reaction?"

Raking his hands through his hair, Gavin squeezed his eyes shut. "I didn't fuck around behind *her* back!" When he opened them, he could see the shock on Olivia's face, but he didn't give a shit. "You may be correct on not knowing me as well as you thought you did, but you do know the uncaring animal I've turned into the past few years. Why the fuck would I go to her job trying to get her back? Why would I pour my fucking heart out to the girl? For a piece of ass?" He chuckled, but that chuckle held no humor behind it. Digging into his pocket, he pulled his cell phone out and tossed it to her.

"Damn, Gavin."

"Damn nothing. Look in my contacts list. There's no shortage of ass eagerly available to me. It's plentiful. I make a phone call, and I can fuck for days if I want to. Gina came here drunk that night, telling me her father died. Yes, maybe I shouldn't have let her in. Yes, maybe I should've thrown her out onto the street like the animal she turned me into." Letting out a defeated sigh, he sat back down on the couch with his elbows on his knees as he gripped his hair. "But I didn't," he whispered. "I didn't, and now Emily's gone. The girl I love doesn't believe me because I was stupid enough to let the girl I used to love into my house. She fell asleep on my couch with her pants off. I didn't even want to touch her to get her out of here that night because she wasn't dressed. I didn't want my hands touching her because my hands had just touched Emily."

He lifted his head and looked directly at Olivia where she sat unmoving. "I love Emily. Fuck, I love her enough that I would do it over again—pain and all—just to hold her again. But I didn't do anything wrong other than let Gina in. So, no, Olivia, it has nothing to do with me being powerful or throwing in a towel. It has everything to do with the fact that Emily doesn't believe me, and most of all . . . she doesn't love me."

After a few seconds of noticeably trying to take in everything he had said, Olivia stood and sat next to him. She placed her hand on his shoulder. "She does love you, Gavin. She—"

"Come on, Liv," he interrupted, reaching for his beer. He finished it in one gulp. "She told me she didn't. Do you need me to quote her words? They're as fresh as fuck in my mind. Buzzed or not, it shouldn't be a problem."

"I know what she *told* you." She took the empty bottle from his hand and placed it on the table. "But I also know what she told *me* after you came to her that night." He went to speak, but she silenced him with a classic Olivia smash of her fingers against his lips. "She doesn't believe you right now, but she does love you. She said those things to you to try to hurt you the way she felt you hurt her. She's been a mess, Gavin," she whispered, her eyes soft. "Her nerves are shot. She's depressed, quiet, and throwing up over the whole situation. Even though she thinks she can remove you from her mind and fall back in love with Dillon, any time Dillon's not with her, she's crying . . . over you."

"You say she loves me, she's crying over me, and yet she's marrying him?" he asked, completely unconvinced.

"I know what you're thinking, but—"

"Oh, do you? Because *I'm* not even sure I know what the fuck I'm thinking right now," he said, rising to his feet. Beer wasn't doing its job at this point. Stronger. He needed something stronger. Stalking into the kitchen, he swung the cabinet door open, pulling out a bottle of bourbon and a shot glass.

Olivia stood up, crossing her arms. "Are you going to let me finish what I was saying, Dick?"

"I'm a cheater and a dick now? Sure, why the fuck not?" he replied, his tone thick with sarcasm. He filled the shot glass. After tossing it back, he smacked his lips together and looked at her. "What kind of shit are you handing me, Olivia? None of it makes any sense. Not one fucking iota of it does."

Moving to the kitchen, Olivia flipped her golden hair to the side and looked at Gavin as if he had ten heads. "What part don't you understand, Blake?" Now he returned the same look, but she continued. "Dillon was a safe bet when she moved out here with him. She stumbled upon you, and as much as she tried to fight it, the girl never stood a chance against you,

Gavin. Forget about the way you two met." Pausing, a light laugh escaped her lips. "You had her from the moment she saw you. Believe me, I had to hear all about Mr. Tall, Dark, and Fuckable Handsome." Gavin couldn't help it, but he drew up a curious brow at that statement. "After everything she went through with Dillon, you became her safe bet. But now that's been ripped from her. Unfortunately, you have her thinking Dillon is indeed the safer bet."

"Stop saying 'safe bet.'" He grunted as he poured another shot, still intrigued by the nickname he never knew about. Olivia sighed and rolled her eyes. "So let me get this straight." He leaned against the counter, a lopsided smirk on his face. "She's taking the consolation prize, which happens to be the prick who really cheated on her?" He paused and chuckled. Though his pain remained, the alcohol was quickly catching up to him. "Wait. Apparently, *I'm* the prick who cheated on her."

"Consolation prize?" she asked, her brows furrowed. "Is this a game to you, Gavin? She's hurting."

"Fuck no, it's not a game. It's my fucking life, and it's what should've been mine and Emily's life together." He chucked another shot down his throat, wiped his mouth with the back of his hand, and slammed the glass on the counter. "I'm hurting, too, but let me guess, you still think I fucked around behind her back. Go ahead. Tell me you don't believe me either."

"To tell you the truth, buddy, when I first got here, no, I didn't believe you," she answered, looking to her watch. She brought her eyes back to him. "But now I do."

"Oh, do you?" He smirked, almost laughing. "And why do you believe me all of a sudden, oh mighty Queen Olivia?"

She stared at him for a long moment and then grabbed her purse, coat, and scarf. She made her way to the door and turned back to look at him. "Because even when you were at your worst after Gina," she whispered, her expression pained, "you weren't as . . . fucked and tortured looking as you are right now." Swaying slightly, that smirk dropped from his face as he peered at her. "I love you both. You're my second brother, and she's the sister I never had." She let out a deep breath. "And it's killing me to see the two of you hurting the way that you are."

Tossing his hands through his hair, he perched himself on a bar stool. "What do I do?" he asked, his voice low and his heart sinking lower. "For the first time in my life . . ." He hesitated and looked at the floor. He slowly brought his gaze back to hers. "God, for the first time in my life, Olivia, I don't know what to do. She doesn't believe me."

Although he couldn't see it from across the room, Olivia's eyes glassed over. Looking back down at her watch, a timid smile crept over her mouth. "Then make her believe you, Gavin. You have less than twenty-four hours to change the course of both of your lives." She slung her purse over her shoulder and opened the door. "I hope I see you there." She stepped out into the hallway. Gavin watched her poke her head back in. "Oh, and if you do decide to go get our girl, do yourself a favor and shave. You're definitely a cutie, but honestly, I'm not digging the whole five-o'clock shadow thing you've got going on right now."

Gavin let out a deep sigh. "Anything else?"

"Yeah, as a matter of fact, there is," she replied, tapping her finger against her cheek. "Drop the whole jeans-and-sweatshirt thing you got going on, too. Love ya, my brother."

Gavin shook his head and watched her close the door behind her.

Time.

Tonight, time wasn't on his or Emily's side. Staring at the clock again, Gavin sat there for a few minutes. His mind rocked from the conversation. He sat there for a few more minutes, trying—and failing—to make sense of everything spinning through his head. Though his unease at the thought of never being with Emily again grew, gnawing at his stomach, the thought of showing up, only to get turned down, made him realize the decision he was about to make was for the best. There was no denying he needed her. He needed her like his veins needed blood and his lungs needed air. However, this time around, Gavin would rather suffocate than have to look Emily in the eyes and hear those venomous words again. No. He wouldn't go tonight.

And just like that, Gavin knew he'd changed the course of his and Emily's lives forever.

Teetering. Though a few weeks had gone by, Emily was teetering on a fine line between sanity and madness. She felt as though she were made of glass, and a small hammer—held in the hand of each man—was chipping away at her. She was sure that at any second she would shatter into a million jagged pieces. The larger pieces—representing Dillon—cut into her flesh. The smaller slivers—Gavin—stuck under her skin. Either way, both were slicing into her heart, leaving her a bleeding corpse of the woman she once was. She felt as though she were watching herself from a distance, no longer in control of her thoughts or the path she was walking. As she stared at her reflection, she couldn't deny the small sense of relief that had washed over her when she'd arrived at the church to see Gavin hadn't shown up—yet, her ache for him remained. A part of her knew she was being elusive. She was trying to fuse back together what'd been broken between her and Dillon even though a huge amount of their relationship had crystallized into dust. Still, she needed something to hold on to—and that something was a tiny glimmer of hope that she could bring her feelings for Dillon back to where they used to be. She needed to fall back in love with him.

However, she had become a very good liar lately, playing into her own game of staunch resistance to the obvious. She felt like the master of trickery because she knew she was trying to delude herself into thinking she could forget Gavin. Forget every stolen glance they had shared, every accidental brush of their flesh, and every moment they experienced together—right down to the second she knew she loved him. The force of will and string of lies she was trying to convince herself of would never be enough to keep her heart from splitting along the scars and stitches of the mess that was left. So tonight—as she stood staring at the hollow shell of the woman she had become, she wondered how far the delusion would get her into her marriage, wondered how long Gavin would haunt her every waking thought, and wondered how long she could fool herself. Trying to compose herself, Emily tore her gaze from her reflection when Fallon walked into the restroom.

"Are you all right?" Fallon asked, making her way over to her. "Or are you still feeling nauseous?"

Emily shook her head and cleared her throat. "No, I'm okay right now." She tucked her lipstick into her purse. "Is Olivia here yet?"

"She just texted me saying she'd be here in two minutes." She handed Emily her purse and walked into one of the stalls. "She had to stop somewhere after the church."

"Where did Trevor go?" Emily asked, placing their purses on the counter.

"When we got here, he realized he didn't have any cash," she called out. "He ran to an ATM."

Drawing in a deep breath, Emily flipped on the water and

started washing her hands. It was then that Olivia popped into the restroom. "Hey," she chirped, pulling off her scarf.

"Where did you have to go?" Emily probed and reached for a paper towel.

She plopped her belongings onto the counter and studied her reflection. She glanced at Emily. "I . . . uh, had to get cash."

"Why does everyone think they need cash while they're here?" Emily asked, quirking a brow. "Everything's paid for tonight."

"To tip the servers." Olivia shrugged. "You of all people should know that."

"Oh yeah, I guess I should," she answered absently, her voice trailing off.

"Your head's not where it should be. I get it." Emily gave Olivia a questioning look. "I know Dickhead hasn't noticed your act lately, since he's been consumed with working late again, but I have." Emily started to speak, but Olivia continued. "I have to admit I think him working late is bullshit. But, hey, you seem to believe him, so I guess that's all that counts, right?"

Emily let out an exasperated sigh. "Oh God, please don't start with me about this again, Liv." She plucked her purse from the counter. "Not now. I can't, and I won't."

"I'm just trying to make sense of all of this, Emily." Gently grabbing her elbow, Olivia stopped her from walking out. With tears welling in her eyes, Emily looked at her. "You're in love with somebody else—yet you're marrying another man. Stop. Honestly, just stop and think about what you're about to do." Emily stood mute and stared at her.

Biting her lip and noticeably uncomfortable, Fallon stepped out of the stall and washed her hands. She dried them and reached for her purse. "I'm just gonna leave you two alone. I'll see you guys inside."

"You don't have to do this," Olivia whispered, looking back at Emily after Fallon walked out. "Even if you don't believe Gavin, you don't have to marry Dillon."

"I love Dillon," she answered, looking down, her tone low.

Taking Emily's chin in her hand, Olivia lifted her face. "I have no doubt in my mind that you love him, Emily, but you're no longer *in* love with him, and to think that you can make yourself fall back in love with him is completely delusional, friend."

Emily swiped a tear off her cheek. "I can fall back in love with him." She stared at Olivia for a long moment and made her way over to the door. Turning around, she sniffled and shook her head. "I'm marrying him tomorrow, Olivia. You can support me or not—and I hope to God you can—but I'm doing it."

Emily swung the door open. Before her mind could even begin to compute the conversation that'd just taken place, her eyes locked on icy blues—those mesmerizing icy blues that caused her unimaginable heartbreak, confusion, and her now rapid breathing. Literally feeling frozen, Emily couldn't move as she stared at Gavin across the lobby of the restaurant. He looked more disheveled than she could've ever imagined, but it didn't stop her body from reacting to his sensually beautiful face. That breathtakingly pained face staring back at her. Almost instantly, she felt her heart drumming within her chest, felt the tiny beads of sweat crawl across every pore of her skin, and felt every hair on her body stand on end. Although guests from several different parties floated across the lobby, their eyes never unlocked. With his hands tucked into the pockets of his jeans, he made his way toward her, and Emily's breath hitched in the back of her throat. She faintly registered the sound of the restroom door closing behind her when Olivia emerged.

"You have to talk to him," Olivia said, placing a hand on her back.

Before Emily could protest, Gavin was standing right in front of her. With his cologne tickling her nose and his eyes intent on her, she was sure she was going to pass out.

"You look beautiful," he whispered, stepping closer. And, God, she did. Her wavy auburn hair falling over a white button-up blouse paired with a short red skirt and black knee-high leather boots had Gavin fighting for control. He was a fool to think he could've stayed away after what Olivia had told him, so this was his last-ditch effort to get her back.

Swallowing hard, Emily stepped away from him, her back pressing against Olivia's chest. "Why are you here?" She nervously tore her gaze from his, looking around for Dillon. "You have to leave."

A sad smile tipped the corner of Gavin's mouth, his voice low. "Well, I *am* in the wedding party. But I think it's apparent why I'm really here." He stepped closer. It was then that Emily smelled the liquor on his breath. "And no, doll, I'm not leaving until we talk. Do you understand me?"

Shocked, she didn't answer. In fact, she had no words at all. Emily simply stared at him.

Gavin flicked his eyes in Olivia's direction. "You'll keep an eye out for Dillon?"

Olivia nodded. "I checked on my way in. There's an empty room over here." She pointed to a door adjacent to them. "Make it quick, though."

Jerking away from Olivia, Emily narrowed her eyes. "You set this up?" Olivia gave a casual shrug. After pinning Olivia with a lethal look, Emily turned to Gavin. "I'm not talking to you." She scoffed as she went to walk away.

He caught her elbow. "Then I guess you're going to force me into making an announcement about the two of us right here at your party."

"You wouldn't do that," she huffed, pulling her arm away from him.

"Mmm, that you're incorrect about," he chuckled as his body swayed. He turned his attention to an older man walking past them. "Excuse me, sir," he called out, his voice booming.

The gray-haired gentleman—who thankfully wasn't with Emily's group—looked at him. "Can I help you?"

"Yes, sir. You see, I'm having a problem. I'm absolutely in love with this beautiful woman here," Gavin said, pointing to Emily. Her eyes widened in disbelief. "And she won't give me a few minutes to explain an extremely fucked-up misunderstanding. Do you have any suggestions as to how I should handle this?"

Appearing not in the least bit interested, the man shook his head and walked away.

"Fine," Emily whispered, her tone heated. "I'm giving you two minutes." Spinning on her heel, she pushed through the doors to the room.

Gavin looked at Olivia. "Keep him busy for as long as you can." She nodded. Upon entering the empty banquet room, Gavin found Emily staring at him with her arms crossed in obvious annoyance. In the darkness, lit only by the opulent moon beyond a massive window, he could see the roaring fire behind her green eyes. As he walked toward her, she backed away and nearly stumbled over a tower of stacked chairs.

"Don't walk away from me, Emily," he commanded, his voice low as he moved closer.

"Don't you dare tell me what to do," she spat with her chin tipped up in defiance. She continued to back away, the sound of her heels echoing throughout the room. She wanted to be impenetrable to his smell, his voice, and his face, but she knew the closer he got—under the cool gleam of those blue eyes—that would be impossible.

Undeterred, he continued his carnal pursuit until he had her backed against a table. Emily took a steeling breath as he slowly ran his hand over the curve of her jaw, up the side of her ear, to the nape of her neck. Biting his lip, he bent his head and stared at her, both of them breathing heavily. "When I wanted to call, I didn't, but I almost did. When I needed to see you, and Jesus Christ, I've needed to see you so fucking bad, I got in my car, and then I got back out," he whispered, smoothing his free hand down the side of her waist. "Tell me you love me, Emily."

"Fuck you," she hissed, her chest rising and falling.

He smirked, coaxing her face closer so it was mere inches from his. "Those pretty lips are hiding a lie." Gripping her waist tighter, he pulled her into his chest, the thrumming of their hearts colliding against each other. "You think you can just rid me from your thoughts? You can't. You're mine, Emily. Fucking mine," he growled.

Emily didn't think. She couldn't. It was impossible. Before she knew it, she threw her arms around his neck and jerked him down to her mouth. With her hands white-knuckled in his hair, she moaned against his lips. This wasn't a passionate kiss. No. This kiss brooked no room for argument, and it was equally angry and possessive on both parts. Hot, sweltering, pent-up aggravation transferred between them—yet love was there as they clung to each other. Lips still locked, Gavin picked her up and sat her on a table, spreading open her thighs while he pushed himself between her legs. Emily tried to catch her breath as he grabbed the back of her knees and hooked her legs around his waist. The sweet taste of alcohol in his mouth nearly intoxicated her. A deep groan rumbled in the back of Gavin's throat as his tongue swept over hers. The harder Emily tugged at his hair, the harder Gavin kissed her. The harder he kissed her, the further she fell—forgetting where she was and who she was, forgetting space, forgetting time, and forgetting how he'd hurt her so.

"Tell me you love me," he snarled, the words spoken into her mouth as his hand slipped under her skirt.

When he yanked her panties down, all Emily could concentrate on was the feeling of flames beginning to lick through her—and that feeling was threatening the last shreds of her self-control. His hand curved over her hot flesh. He slid two fingers into her syrupy wetness as his thumb circled her clit. Gasping, she tore her mouth from his, her arms clinging around his neck as her breathing flew past her lips, coming muffled into his shoulder. In all her anger, love, passion, and hurt, she bit down and sank her teeth into his skin. She wanted blood. She wanted him to hurt—wanted him to feel the same agony and pain she had felt every day since that devastating morning. Gavin groaned, and with his free hand, he fisted the back of her hair and tilted her head up, her back now taut as a bow. His eyes bored into hers. With his breathing heavy and his fingers still sliding in and out of her, his mind drowned in the sound of her panting. He crushed his lips over hers again.

"If I could, I'd rip my heart out to show you how much I love you." He nipped at her ear, and she nearly came on his fingers. "Fuck, I miss you. I love you so much, and you're killing me, Emily."

"You bastard, you don't love me. I hate you, Gavin. I hate you," she cried and tried to push him away.

He wouldn't let her, though. He snaked his arm around her lower back, pulling her to the very edge of the table, his fingers never stopping their delicious onslaught inside her pussy. Emily thrusted her hands back into his hair, a moan escaping her lips as her head fell back, exposing her neck in all its beauty.

Gavin took the opportunity and buried his face against her collarbone. He traced a wet, torrid line up her neck, nipping and sucking until his mouth was over hers again.

"I wish I could hate you—it'd be easier—but you have no idea how much I love you," he breathed, sucking her bottom lip and gently biting it. "And that's not hate you're feeling. You love me, goddammit. You're mad about something that didn't happen. Fucking hit me again. Fucking punch me if you need to, but stop saying you don't love me, because all you're doing is lying to yourself. You're tearing us apart."

Still clinging to his hair, she pulled her lips away from his. They were both fighting for air as they burned holes into each other's eyes. With one hand buried in his hair, she smacked him in the face with the other. The sound reverberated throughout the room. At the same time, a moan left her mouth as she felt Gavin's fingers slip out of her. Her body was left feeling torturously bereft by their absence. "I hate you," she cried out as her entire body braced itself for battle.

"No, you don't. You love me, and I love you," he growled through gritted teeth, glowering at her. He cupped her cheeks. "Hit me again if you have to, doll. Just do it. Fucking hit me and get it all out."

She didn't hesitate. She smacked him again, fury and confusion burning deep inside as angry tears spilled down her cheeks.

Pulling her by the waist off the table, he set her on her feet and crashed his lips over hers again. "Leave with me right now. Don't do this. Don't marry him," he pleaded, his words vibrating against her lips. Emily grabbed fistfuls of his sweatshirt, her eyes rolling back into her head as she sank into the familiarity of his kiss, smell, and touch. "We'll tell him together. I told you I wouldn't let you do it alone. Gina means nothing to me.

I shouldn't have let her in, but for fuck's sake, I didn't do anything with her."

Pain.

There it was again, sweeping as fresh as an open wound through her soul. It bled out with no sign of letting up. Whispering his sweet words of seduction while trying to veil the bitter taste of the ugly truth, he was trying to break her down into nothing but tiny particles of dust. Like a whip, the harsh reality of what he was trying to do cracked through her chest, disturbing her thoughts with its potency. Immediately, without conscious effort, the gates around the fortress of her shattered heart closed. The most important thing now was to protect the remaining pieces.

She shoved hard against his chest, pushing him away. Looking down, scrambling to pull her panties back up, she couldn't see the shock on his face. Without a backward glance, she headed toward the door. In a few quick strides, Gavin was at her side. Not intending to let her leave, he caught her arm and pulled her to a skidded stop. Swiping tears away from her hooded eyes, she looked up at him.

With his soul crying out for her to believe him, his expression creased painfully. "I've never felt so heartbroken and so in love at the same time. If you would've told me the day we met that you were going to break my heart—and that days, months, or even years would pass, that I would still be hurting like this—it wouldn't have stopped me from falling in love with you. But I would've done one thing differently, and loving you any less isn't it." He slowly brought his knuckles up to her face, wiping the tears away from her beautiful, confused eyes, his voice soft. "I wouldn't have let her in. That's the only thing I would've changed, Emily. I wouldn't have fucking let her in."

As her body trembled from head to toe, Emily stared at him, but before she could speak a word, the door flung open. Olivia poked her head inside. "Em, Joan is scouring the fucking restaurant for you right now," she whispered, her tone urgent.

Sniffling, Emily tore her gaze from Gavin, her heart grating to shreds in the process. Her mind was no less confused than when she'd stepped in there with him. Trying to calm herself, she took a deep breath, smoothed her hands through her hair, and walked out of the room. Gavin followed, his thoughts no less fucked up either. Emily looked at him as Olivia hastily handed her a tissue. "You have to leave, Gavin."

Shocked by her words, confusion and anger clouded his eyes. "I'm not going anywhere." He shook his head. "I'm in this wedding party, and I'm staying."

She glared icicles at him. "You're just trying to hurt me now."

"You know what?" he said, swallowing tightly. "Maybe I am. Maybe I'm trying to hurt you as much as you're hurting me. The saddest part about this whole thing is that while I was in there begging you to stay, I didn't fucking realize you were already gone. So, yeah, I'm staying, and I hope you fucking hurt through every second of it as much as I will. Deal with it."

After her mouth snapped shut from hanging agape, Emily spun toward the bathroom.

Olivia grabbed her arm. "No! You don't have time. You have to get in there right now, Em." She plucked the tissue from Emily's hand, licked it, and started wiping off the streams of mascara that were blanketing her cheeks.

Watching her intently, Gavin smirked. "Don't forget about the lipstick smeared all over her." Emily shot him a look. "I'm cool, right? There's no lipstick left on me?" His smirk turned into a full-watted smile. "I love getting kissed by women who *claim* they don't love me—makes my dick hard as a motherfucker."

Letting out a heavy sigh, Olivia handed Emily her lipstick.

"Oh my God, Gavin, now you're just being an asshole," Emily spat, reaching for the lipstick. She quickly slid it across her lips.

"Mmm, you haven't seen anything yet," he chuckled, tossing his hand through his unruly black hair. "I have a feeling I'm going to break my own record tonight." He went to walk away but turned back around. "And, if I recall correctly, I think I told you once not to bring any attention to those pretty little lips. Put the lipstick away or else I'll drag you right back in that room and really change your fucking mind." He slowly ran his tongue over his mouth while his eyes shimmered with insatiable lust.

Olivia raised a surprised brow as Emily's mouth dropped open.

Heart broken into pieces, he turned in a leisurely pivot, tucked his hands in the pocket of his jeans, and sauntered into the party room. Scanning the modestly sized space filled with thirty or so people, it didn't take him long to lock eyes with Dillon. Gavin grunted as he walked over to the bar and ordered a much-needed shot of tequila and a bottle of beer. He threw a $100 tip to the bartender and turned around to find Dillon behind him.

Swallowing down the need to beat the shit out of him, Gavin couldn't help but laugh. "Ah, and there he is—the lucky fucking groom." He tossed that much-needed shot down his throat, and out of the corner of his eye, he watched Emily float into the room. "And there's your beautiful bride." He gestured toward her with his head.

With a suspicious expression, Dillon stared at him for a moment and then turned around, motioning Emily over. If Dillon couldn't notice the way she nervously looked at them,

Gavin sure as hell did. When she approached, Gavin popped the top off his beer, arched a perfect brow, and bit his lip, making sure she heard the luscious smacking noise as he pulled it through his teeth. She glared at him.

"Are you all right?" Dillon probed. "You look upset."

"I'm fine," she replied, her voice monotone, her eyes never leaving Gavin's.

"Are you sure? You seem . . . off."

Drawing in a shaky breath, she finally looked at Dillon. "Yes."

After placing a kiss on the corner of her mouth, Dillon curled his arm around her waist and turned his attention to Gavin. "What's the deal, man?" he asked, giving him a quick once-over. "You never showed up to the church, and now you come to my rehearsal dinner looking like this?"

As Gavin watched Dillon circle his thumb against Emily's waist, seething anger, sharp as razor blades, shredded at his stomach. He flicked his eyes in her direction. "I'm having a problem with a woman right now," Gavin answered evenly.

"And? That doesn't excuse you showing up here looking like that," Dillon retorted.

With her pulse quickening, Emily could see the fire surging behind Gavin's eyes. "Dillon," she immediately interrupted, "does it really matter how he's dressed? Let's go sit down, okay?"

"Yeah, it matters. He—"

"Dillon," she interrupted again, her tone more insistent. "I'm not kidding. Let's just go sit." Dillon narrowed his eyes, and with that, she decided to bring her tone down a notch. "I don't feel good right now. Come on." She grabbed his hand.

"I'd listen to her if I were you." Gavin smirked, draping his arm over the bar. He took a long pull from his beer, nearly finishing it. "Just a guess, of course, but if you piss her off enough, she seems like the type that might smack a guy." Emily's eyes widened as he ran his palm over the spot where she had slapped him. "And I bet it'd sting like a bitch, too," he added, turning his back to them. His attention was focused on ordering another beer to help aid in his self-inflicted hell.

"What's your problem, bro?" Dillon asked, tapping him on his shoulder.

Gavin didn't turn around. "One, I'm not your bro, and two, I told you I'm having a problem with a woman."

"He's just drunk, I think," Emily whispered against Dillon's ear, her heart thundering in her chest. "Let's go talk to my sister and Michael."

After staring at the back of Gavin's head for a few lingering seconds, Dillon looked at Emily and gave a tight nod. Knees weak with relief, Emily silently released the breath she was holding. As they made their way through the party, she made eye contact with Olivia from across the room where she stood talking with Fallon. Shaking her head, Olivia looked at the floor and then back to Emily. It was then that Emily realized her and Gavin's situation had put all of their friends in a very bad spot—and for this, the unrest in her stomach grew. Trying to push her guilt aside, she plastered a smile on her face as she walked hand in hand with Dillon through the room, greeting their guests.

After Emily endured a few minutes of light conversation—namely with guests she barely knew—her eyes landed on her sister and her husband. Considering the torture the evening had shown thus far, Emily felt slightly at ease as they approached her and Dillon.

A wide, friendly smile spread across her brother-in-law's face as he pulled her in for a hug. "Where'd you run off to before, soon-to-be Mrs. Parker?"

Crossing his arms, Dillon cocked his head to the side after Michael released her. "Yeah. Where were you, actually? My mother said she looked everywhere and couldn't find you."

Emily opened her mouth to speak, her heart racing.

"Michael," Lisa chirped, glancing at Emily. Her hazel eyes showed a wealth of knowledge. "I told you she went outside for a breath of fresh air." Emily gave her a weak smile and mentally thanked her for the save.

Appearing confused, Michael ran a hand through his tousled brown hair. "Hmm, maybe you did," he laughed, holding up his martini. "It's quite possible that I've had one too many of these."

"Why'd you go outside?" Dillon asked, placing his hand on the small of her back. "I asked if you were all right before, and you said you were fine."

Smiling, Lisa reached for Emily's hand. "We girls can get a little . . . emotional before the big day." Feeling nearly lightheaded, Emily gripped her hand tighter. "Michael, why don't you explain to Dillon what we're looking to do with our retirement fund? I'd like to talk with my sister about the wonderful 'honeymoon' phase."

"Oh yeah," Michael said, turning to Dillon. Dillon peered at Emily for a second and adjusted his tie. "If we don't get our shit together, Lisa and I will most definitely *not* be retiring on an island somewhere." Hesitantly, Dillon dragged his gaze from Emily and gave Michael his attention.

Hands still locked, Lisa pulled Emily through the party, avoiding every possible guest that tried to stop and talk with her. Sitting at a small cocktail table in the corner, she gave Emily a sympathetic look. "What did he say to you?" Lisa whispered with panicked curiosity burning behind her eyes.

Emily rubbed her temples. "He keeps saying he didn't do

anything with her," she answered, trying to keep the stinging tears threatening her eyes from spilling out. "He just . . . I don't know."

Pressing her lips into a hard line, Lisa studied her with concern. "Emily, is it at all possible he's telling the truth?"

Slowly, Emily turned her head, her gaze immediately locking with Gavin's. As it did every time she stared at him, her heart raced and her breathing became uneven. Though he was talking with Trevor, standing with both elbows propped on the bar, his eyes were intent on hers. The sadness surrounding his presence was sickening, dragging her spirit down with him. Emily didn't know how long they stared at each other, but it felt like forever. She ran a hand through her hair, the need to believe his words growing to unbearable heights in her chest. Unwillingly, she tore her attention from his, bringing it back to her sister. "I'm so confused, Lisa," she whispered. "I keep seeing her open his door. She wasn't dressed. . . . She was so . . . beautiful."

Before Lisa could question the situation any further, Joan called to Emily from a few feet away. Emily's head snapped up, her body trembling. "There you are." Joan huffed, a questioning look molding her face. "I searched—"

"Yes, Joan," Lisa interrupted, rising to her feet. She reached for Emily's hand, and Emily stood with her. "We know. You searched high and low for my sister. She needed a breather. I'm sure you understand how nervous a bride can be the day before her wedding." She offered a smile that Emily knew to be as fake as they come.

Joan drew up a slow brow. "Of course I do," she flitted. Taking a sip of her white wine, she waved her hand in the direction of the U-shaped table in the middle of the room. "Everyone needs to take a seat now. The maître d' just notified me that the waiters should be coming around shortly to get everyone's orders." Without waiting for a response, Joan turned on her heel, her voice echoing throughout the room as she repeated her announcement to the rest of the guests.

Lisa rolled her eyes. "I swear if that woman dyed her hair any more blonde than it is, she could beat out the sun in its blinding effects." Emily pulled in a deep breath, shaking her head. Cupping Emily's cheeks, Lisa leaned into her ear. "I love you, little sis. I wish I could help you through this. The only advice I can offer is to go with what your heart's telling you." Emily stared into her eyes, thoughts of their mother swirling around her head. "It doesn't matter that tomorrow's the big day. You could postpone it until you figure all of this out with Gavin. The important thing here is that tomorrow represents the rest of your life. You need to know that you're spending it with the correct man. Don't feel stuck in a box. You know Michael and I will help you in whatever way you need, right?"

Grabbing her sister's hand, Emily nodded and started making her way through the crowd. With every step she took, the sound of a clock's pendulum swaying in her head reverberated through her ears.

Time was running out.

Tick . . .

Dillon's words to her a few hours before she took him back:

"Do you remember what your mother told us before she died, Emily? She told us to take care of each other. She told us to stick through whatever uphill battles life throws at us and to never give up on our relationship."

Tock . . . .

Gavin's searing pleas to her in the rain:

"You don't hate me. You love me. And, Jesus Christ, Emily, I

love you with everything inside of me, with everything I am, with everything I'll ever be."

Palms sweaty and body shaking, Emily took another few steps.

Ticktock . . .

As she tried to fight back tears, Dillon's voice kept pounding inside her thoughts:

"Let me fix it. I can fix it and make us better again. I can bring us back to where we used to be."

Ticktock . . . ticktock . . .

"Leave with me right now. Don't do this. Don't marry him. We'll tell him together. I told you I wouldn't let you do it alone. Gina means nothing to me. I shouldn't have let her in, but for fuck's sake, I didn't do anything with her."

Ticktock . . . ticktock . . . ticktock . . .

Feeling completely torn, it was all Emily could do to make it to her chair without passing out. Letting go of Lisa's hand, she sank into her seat at the head of the table, her eyes following Gavin as he moved across the room. He positioned himself diagonally from her, their view of each other as unobstructed as a full moon on a clear night. Draping an arm across Trevor's chair next to him, Gavin tipped his bottle of beer in Emily's direction with a lazy smile on his lips.

Shifting uncomfortably, Emily tore her attention from Gavin when Dillon sat next to her. As he leaned over to kiss her, her eyes flew back to Gavin, and if she wasn't mistaken, she could see his jaw tense. Swallowing hard, she quickly pulled away.

"What the hell is wrong with you tonight?" Dillon asked, his tone showing annoyance.

She cleared her throat. "Nothing. I told you I wasn't feeling well. That's all."

"I hope by tomorrow you'll snap out of whatever's going on

with you," he said, pulling his seat up to the table. "And something tells me you're fucking lying about not feeling well."

Emily's body rippled with an involuntary shudder at the thought that he could see right through her. Not saying a word, she reached across the table for her glass of water. Nervously sipping it, she tried to calm her racing thoughts. One of the waiters circling the room approached to take their orders, offering temporary reprieve from the conversation. She desperately needed a strong drink, but considering Dillon told her he hadn't consumed an ounce of alcohol since he'd returned from Florida, she decided to forgo it. Trying to keep her eyes from roaming to Gavin's, she kept her head down, staring at her hands in her lap.

"So," Dillon's cousin, Peter, called out to him from across the table, "one would assume that you and the Mrs. are going to start working on making some babies tomorrow night after the wedding."

Emily's head snapped up, her eyes darting to Gavin. Gazing at her, a tight smirk curled Gavin's lips. "They should have bucketloads of babies—and a green minivan, too."

Emily's mouth hung ajar as she watched him casually lean back. Downing the rest of his beer, he gave a shrug and exhaled a light laugh that didn't reach his eyes. Other than those who knew what was going on between them, the room broke out into quaking hysterics.

"Let's hope so, Gavin," Henry chuckled. "Joan and I want some grandbabies as soon as possible. If they could fill a green minivan with little ones, then that would make us all the happier."

"Well, I don't know about making babies just yet, but I know we'll have fun practicing," Dillon replied, tossing his arm around Emily's shoulder. Smiling weakly, she smoothed her hand down her neck, the perspiration on her body mounting by the second. "And the green minivan's not happening."

"Okay, enough talk about green minivans." Joan laughed. "Peter, since you're the best man, I'm sure you've prepared some sort of speech for the evening."

"Actually, Aunt Joan, I didn't," he replied, motioning one of the waiters over. "Just the one I've expertly prepared on index cards for tomorrow."

"Oh, come on, Peter." She leaned her elbows on the table, folding her hands under her chin. "You don't need index cards. Just get up and say something to our bride and groom."

"I'd be happy to make a speech for our wonderful bride and groom," Gavin chimed in, flicking his icy blue eyes to Emily. Emily stared at him, her heart nearly stopping.

"Nah, you don't want to make a speech, Gavin," Trevor interjected, the nervousness in his voice showing he was trying to salvage the situation. "You've never been good at them."

Rising from his seat, Gavin swayed slightly. He looked at Joan. "I took public speaking courses in college, so Trevor has no fucking idea what he's talking about. I'm pretty good at this shit."

"Killer save, Blake," Peter laughed. "I'm horrible at them, index cards or not."

"Okay, Gavin. Work your magic," Joan trilled, a beaming smile playing on her lips.

Sitting next to her, Olivia reached for Emily's hand and whispered, "Holy . . . mother . . . fucking . . . shit."

Emily quickly looked at Trevor, her eyes pleading. He shook his head and shrugged.

Pivoting, Gavin faced Emily and Dillon, his eyes immediately locking on hers. Trying to control her trembling body, she felt nearly on the verge of crying as she watched him reach for his beer.

"Mmm, what to say, what to say," Gavin whispered, staring at Emily. He planted his feet and leaned up against the wall, his head lolling slightly. "Well, let's start with the truth. That's a good idea, right?" he questioned, his voice louder. He looked around for a second at the abundance of smiling faces watching him. Pushing off the wall, he brought his gaze back to Emily's. "I was taught telling the truth was always a good thing . . . and the truth for me is that if I say I wish you and Dillon the best of luck . . . I'd be lying . . . because I fucking don't."

The smiling faces that had been plentiful dropped. Right after Joan let out a gasp, a thick silence descended throughout the room. Heart pounding and breathing shallow, Emily stared at Gavin, the pain in his eyes searing through every limb in her body. Feeling Dillon's hand clench her shoulder slightly, Emily turned toward him. His eyes narrowed like a snake's on Gavin.

Trevor cleared his throat and rose from his chair. "See, apparently alcohol is making the speech for Gavin right now." He nervously laughed. "Told ya he was never good at these things."

"Sit down, Trevor," Gavin mumbled, his eyes never leaving Emily's.

"Really, man," Trevor started. "I think—"

"Sit . . . down . . . Trevor," he slowly repeated.

Pushing his glasses up the bridge of his nose, Trevor hesitantly took his seat.

After a few moments of intently staring at her, Gavin moved his gaze across the room. "Really, people, it was a joke—a simple fucking joke. Of course I wish them luck. How could I not, right? Such a wonderful couple who's going to make bucketloads of babies." He chuckled, crossing his arms. "Maybe they'll make those babies in the back of a green minivan."

"Gavin," Henry politely spoke up. "Son, you might want to wrap this up. Dinner should be out soon."

"Yeah, wrap it the fuck up," Dillon said, his cold, steady voice reaching across the room. He clenched Emily's shoulder harder, his forehead wrinkling. "*Now,* Blake."

Emily's lips quivered. The room suddenly felt small as if the building was crashing in around her. With her heart stuttering, she looked at Gavin. His mouth turned up in one of the saddest, sweetest smiles she'd ever seen.

Raising his beer, Gavin fiercely rubbed a palm over his face. "Right, right, wrap it up. Okay," he said, looking around the room. "Everyone raise your glasses for the lovely bride and groom."

With uncomfortable tension churning in the air, friends and family slowly reached for their drinks.

Eyes intent solely on Emily, Gavin drew in a deep breath. "Here's to bottle caps, the Yankees and 'birds,' and most of all . . ." He paused, his voice lowering to a whisper. "And most of all, to a beautiful girl named Molly who refuses to believe the man who loves her—the man who loves her more than she'll ever know." He let out a light, condescending laugh. "Oh yeah . . . and to Emily and Dillon."

Doubt.

There it was. Though barely skimming the surface, it was there, making itself known, stirring every nerve in Emily's body. From somewhere deep within, her mind screamed that he might not be lying. Closing her eyes, she choked back a sob that threatened to crawl up her throat. Opening them again, she felt her face go white as Dillon slowly—so slowly—turned in her direction, his eyes anchoring her with something she'd never seen before. With a frown snapping between his brows, he quickly turned and pinned Gavin with a glacial look.

Rising from his seat, Trevor grabbed for Gavin's arm. "Come on, bro, I think you've had a little too much to drink for the night. I'm gonna take you home."

Still staring at Emily, Gavin jerked his arm away. "That's cool." He sniffed haughtily. "This party fucking sucks anyway."

Emily faintly registered the sound of Joan gasping again. Reaching for Emily's hand, Dillon stood up. "I think Emily and I will walk you out, Gavin." His voice was ominously low, with fury burning in his eyes.

Gavin glared at him a moment before turning to make his way out of the room with Trevor. Trying to suck in air that didn't seem to exist, Emily rose from her chair, tremors rolling off her body in waves.

Standing up, Olivia whispered, "I'm going out with you guys."

"We'll be right back," Dillon announced, his grip on Emily's hand tightening.

"Is everything all right?" Henry probed, also rising from his chair.

"Everything's fine, Dad," Dillon answered, walking past him.

Emily's sister looked at her with concern. She went to stand, but with two sharp shakes of her head, Emily mouthed for her not to. Reluctantly, she sat back down and whispered something into Michael's ear.

As Dillon dragged her through the lobby, Emily struggled to keep up, her palm sweaty against his. When they stepped out of the restaurant into the frigid air, her eyes locked on Gavin, but he wasn't looking at her. His focus was on Dillon.

Dillon snapped his head back and forth between Gavin and Emily. "Are you two fucking around?" he spit out through clenched teeth.

"No, Dillon," Emily breathlessly answered, her stomach rolling with fear and nausea. "Nothing's going on. Gavin's just drunk."

Gavin's blue eyes hardened to gemstone brightness, bloodlust surging through his veins. "You don't deserve her," he growled, stepping closer to Dillon until their faces almost touched. "Not . . . one . . . fucking . . . inch."

Before Emily's heart took another beat, Dillon cocked his arm back and connected a sharp blow against Gavin's mouth. Gasping, Emily pulled on Dillon's bicep as she watched Gavin slightly stagger back. A cocky smirk washed over his face when he regained his bearings. Stepping forward, he wiped his hand across his bloodied mouth, his smirk never wavering as his hate-filled eyes never left Dillon's. Dillon launched at Gavin again, but Trevor grabbed him and held him back. As if unaffected by any of it, Gavin stood as still as stone, glaring at him. With a huff, he spit at Dillon. His blood-tinged saliva landed on Dillon's cheek, slowly dripping down his face. Henry came rushing out of the restaurant, his eyes wide at the scene unfolding.

"You motherfucker!" Dillon yelled, struggling against Trevor and Henry's hold. "I'll fucking kill you, asshole!"

"Gavin!" Olivia let out. "Come on, I'm taking you home!"

Walking backward with Olivia tugging on his arm, Gavin stared at Emily. She could feel his cold and pain-stricken gaze slide over her. Reaching into his pocket, he pulled out a bottle cap and fingered it in his hand before flicking it at her. Emily felt it hit her chest, her heart constricting and clenching in the process. Averting her eyes down, as though in slow motion, she watched as it hit the ground, spinning recklessly in circles. It mimicked her every emotion. Although Dillon continued yelling and other patrons had gathered outside, the only sound piercing Emily's ears, like nails against a chalkboard, was the bottle cap clinking and clanking. It reverberated in her soul as a single tear broke loose, slipping down her cheek. Slowly lifting her head, Emily found Gavin staring at her. His beautiful face looked weary, broken, and defeated. He turned, and like a ghost vanishing through the air, he disappeared into Olivia's car. In that second, with her heart in her stomach, Emily was sure that this last vision of him would sear itself into her mind, haunting her forever.

As she watched the taillights fade into a distant glow amid Manhattan's chaotic traffic, she felt Dillon's hand wrap around her arm, his ironclad grip burning her flesh. Before she knew it, he was quickly leading her into the restaurant, with Dillon's father and Trevor behind them. Swallowing hard, Emily swiped her tears away, trembling from head to toe.

Once they entered the party room, Dillon let go of her and stalked over to the table. Yanking her purse from the back of her chair, he fished his keys from his pocket, his face fevered with anger. "Me and my fiancée are leaving," he barked out, making his way back to Emily.

"You can't just leave, Dillon," Joan retorted, her tone insistent as she looked around. She rose from her chair, sweeping her hand across the room. "You have guests here. It's apparent something's going on between you and Emily, but you need to tend to that later."

He shot his mother a cold look. "Like I said, we're fucking leaving."

Joan's eyes bulged and she went to speak, but Henry placed his hand on her shoulder, silencing her.

"I know what the fuck I'm doing tomorrow," Dillon spewed, pointing to himself. After grabbing Emily's hand, he pointed to the bridal party. "Do you all know what you're doing tomorrow?"

The crowd of family and friends stared silently at them, nervously shifting in their seats. Emily's sister went to get up. Once again, Emily shook her head, her eyes begging her not to do anything. Pursing her lips with worry, Lisa crossed her arms, her eyes narrowing on Dillon. However, she remained silent.

"That's what I thought." He pulled Emily toward the door. "We'll see you all tomorrow at eleven."

After retrieving Emily's jacket from the coat check, Dillon weaved them through the lobby, nearly running into other guests. Once they reached his car, Emily drew in a deep breath, trying to coax down her stammering nerves. Sliding into the seat, she bit her lip nervously as she watched him round the vehicle, the blazing look in his eyes triggering an upsurge of fear throughout her entire system. Getting into the car, he slammed the door and, without looking at her, he started the engine. Suffocating.

Emily felt as if she were suffocating as he curtailed out of the parking spot, his hands tightening around the steering wheel, his jaw clenching and unclenching. As thoughts of Gavin fired off in her head, she noticed they were heading in the wrong direction.

"I need to go back to my apartment," she whispered, the blood whooshing through her veins. It pounded and correlated with the throbbing pain in her chest.

"You're out of your fucking mind if you think I'm letting you go back to your place," he snapped, his eyes never leaving the road. Emily's heart seized and started racing as though it was about to burst right through her rib cage. "You're staying with me tonight," he added, his tone harder. "I'll bring you home in the morning to get your shit before the ceremony."

Fumbling for something to say, she stared at him but cowered back when he whipped his head in her direction, the fury in his eyes threatening to torch her into flames. For the remainder of the ride, she kept quiet, and by the time they pulled up to his town house, she was sure she was already sinking into the fiery pits of hell. Getting out of the car, he didn't utter a word as they climbed the stairs to his front door.

With her nerves trembling and skin crawling, Emily jumped when Dillon slammed the door. After ripping his jacket from his body, he loosened his tie, moved into the kitchen, and pulled a bottle of Jack Daniel's from the cabinet. He plucked a glass off the counter, filled it to the brim, and chugged half of it down. Brows knitted together and hostility brimming in his irises like burning coals, he motioned her over to him with his finger. Emily couldn't take in enough air as she slowly peeled her coat off and dropped her purse onto the sectional. She stared at him across the room, a cold spiral of fear running down her spine. "Come here, Emily," he said, his voice laced with a sickening calmness.

She swallowed, looking at him as he stared at her. Inhaling as her footsteps echoed against the marble floor, she cautiously inched her way into the kitchen, anxiety steadily building within her. Approaching him, bile rose in her throat when he darted his hand out, yanking her by the arm into his chest. Feeling his heart pound against hers, she didn't bring her eyes up to meet his. She couldn't. Something darker than fear had taken her over. Trying to catch her breath, she stared at his mouth, which had curled lopsided into a wicked grin.

Bringing his knuckles under her chin, he slowly lifted her face, looking into her eyes, his voice low. "You fucked him, didn't you?"

"No," she whispered, her voice weak, her muscles growing weaker by the second.

With his breath hot in her face, his tone remained the same but his eyes hardened. "And you expect me to believe that?"

"Yes," she answered, trying to keep her body from shaking.

Emily felt her stomach churn when he brought his other arm around her waist, kneading his fingers into the small of her back. He dipped his head, running his nose along her brow. She pulled in a sharp breath as he used the weight of his body to push her back, pinning her against the cold granite counter. With tears welling in her eyes, her heart tripled over as she stared at him.

His dirty-blond hair—usually meticulously styled—hung over his forehead. "You do know that if you fucked him, you mean absolutely nothing to him," he whispered, grazing his lips over the shell of her ear. "He'll fuck anything that opens its legs for him."

Though dread of what he'd said washed over her, and her heart felt exposed with torn open fresh wounds, she didn't reply as she tried to mentally push his words aside.

Burying his face in her hair, he pulled her tighter against his rigid chest. "Did you fuck him?"

"No, I didn't fuck him." Body still shaking, the whispered words slid from her mouth, her voice feigning innocence.

Slowly, he dragged his fingertips across her cheek and slid his thumb along her quivering lips. "Do you love me, Emily?"

Staring at him, she was confused by the question and unsure how to answer it. Her gaze reflectively dropped to the floor, her mind racing as she searched for something to say. "We've had a rough couple of months, Dillon," she whispered, bringing her eyes back to his.

He cocked his head to the side. "You didn't answer my question." He leaned in closer, his breath whispering against her cheek. One hand gripped her waist while the other cupped the back of her neck. "Do you love me, Emily?"

She swallowed and stared at him, a sob breaking past her lips. "I do love you, but I think—"

He cut her off, quickly bringing his fingers up to her lips, silencing her. Breathing heavily, her body trembled as he dropped his hands and placed them on the granite counter, caging her in like an animal. "Then prove it to me," he whispered, his face inches from hers, the smell of liquor oozing from his mouth. "If you didn't fuck him—and if you love me, Emily—then prove it."

She stared at him—body, mind, and soul shaking—as he slowly slid his fingertips down her arm. Reaching for her hand, he hastily led her to his bedroom. He snapped the door closed and started removing his clothing. The entire time, his eyes never left hers, their intent revealing an urgent need to reclaim her. "Take your clothes off," he ordered, his voice low as he approached her.

Standing completely naked before her, he breathed heavily, the sound hanging in the air. Emily stood rooted to the floor, unmoving—dying inside little by little.

"You *will* prove it to me." He framed her face with his hands. She looked away, but he cupped her chin, forcefully bringing her attention back to him. "Because if you don't," he whispered, leaning into her ear, "then I'll know you fucked him. And you want to know what'll happen then?" With her heart ricocheting in her chest, she nervously swallowed, her throat feeling as though sandpaper coated the lining. She shook her head. "You'll force me to hurt you both," he hissed, his hands fumbling to unbutton her blouse.

Standing completely still and silent, her instincts warned her to flee, but she couldn't. In the darkness of the room, the tears she was trying to hide tumbled down her cheeks. However, they fell silently as Dillon stripped her down to nothing—physically . . . mentally . . . and emotionally.

Pushing her onto the bed, he hovered over her naked body.

His face was peppered with anger, lust, and possession. Spreading her legs open, he sank himself inside her, and it was then the blackness of what Dillon had become enveloped her like a cold shadow. She knew in that very moment she was grasping on to something that would never be again. She could never love him the way she once had, and she could never love him the way she now loved Gavin. When her body had no more to give, she succumbed to the numbness that set in. Closing her eyes, she tried to shut herself down as he rocked into her harder, interminable pain pulsing through her head. She envisioned Gavin's blue eyes above her instead of the dark, vengeful ones staring back at her. Inhaling, she tried to picture that it was Gavin's hands groping her breasts, Gavin's sweat dripping onto her body, and Gavin's lips kissing her mouth.

Gavin . . .

Dillon grunted and collapsed all of his weight on top of her when he finished. Within a few minutes, he was fast asleep.

Hours. Emily lay there for hours, her mind replaying Gavin's words over and over. Feeling as though she had cheated on her own heart—the very heart that belonged in Gavin's hands—Emily slowly slid from the bed, her breathing shallow as her feet hit the ice-cold floor.

There would be no lace veils or vows taken tomorrow. No. There wouldn't be promises made or lies spoken. Gavin was correct. Her lips held lies, and those false truths had potentially ruined his and her future together. She loved him, and now she would go to him. She could only hope he would forgive her for doubting him and his love for her. As quietly as possible, Emily gathered her clothing and got dressed. She also gathered the nerve she so desperately needed to finally leave Dillon. She stood in the threshold of his bedroom, watching his sleeping form. As tears sprung in her eyes, she could feel her heart breaking and mending all at once. "Good-bye, Dillon," she whispered.

Almost tripping over her bare feet, Emily moved quickly into the living room and grabbed her shoes, coat, and purse. Trying to avoid making any noise, she slipped on her coat but kept her shoes in her hand as she tiptoed toward the front door. She reached for the knob, sucked in a deep breath, and slowly pulled it open. Though the door creaked, the sound echoing through the town house, her fear of waking Dillon was dwarfed by her incapacitating fear of losing Gavin forever.

The latter propelled her out into the cold winter air.

Ticktock . . .

The story of Emily and Gavin

continues in

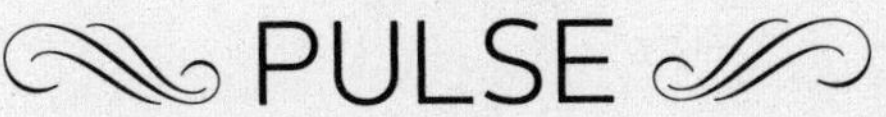

Book Two in the Collide Series

Available as an Atria Books e-Book

and available in print in

August 2014

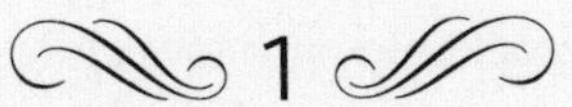

A Missed Last Encounter

EMILY LEANED HER head against the taxi window, watching the city lights of Manhattan with tear-soaked eyes. In a blur, the look on Gavin's face as he had walked away from her a few hours before rushed through her mind. The closer she got to his building, and the further away she got from her past with Dillon, the more she felt as though her sanity and heart were hanging by a delicate thread. She shifted restlessly and her gaze fell on the glowing green light of the digital clock. It was nearly one o'clock in the morning. A glimmer of hope flooded her body, and she squeezed her eyes shut, praying Gavin would take her back. As the taxi pulled up in front of his high-rise, she reached in her purse and pulled out a wad of cash. After handing the unknown amount to the driver, she swung open the door and stepped onto the sidewalk into the cold, late November air.

"Hey!" the Middle Eastern driver called. "You have to close the door, lady!"

Emily heard his words but paid him no mind. Her fumbling feet pushed her forward, kept her moving toward what she hoped would be a new start. A new future with the man she knew she couldn't live without. She pulled open the door and crossed the lobby. Sweat clung like decay across her flesh. With a trembling hand, she pressed the button for the elevator. Her nerves skyrocketed with love and anxiety. Once the elevator doors opened, she stepped inside and leaned against the wall, physically and mentally exhausted. As she tried to stop shaking, tears steadily fell. Unsure of Gavin's reaction, Emily struggled to pull in a decent breath.

She tried to tamp down the wicked emotions curling through her. The doors opened to what would either be a new beginning . . . or an end. Feet glued to the ground, she stood frozen for a moment, her eyes trained on the wall across the hallway. Vaguely aware of the elevator doors gliding closed, she became dizzy as she lifted her hand to hold it open. Slowly, she stepped out. Her vision tunneled as she turned toward Gavin's penthouse, and her mind spun out of control with every possible scenario. She strained to focus on his words from earlier, allowing her fear to wane as her feet led her closer. Her pace quickened with every step.

Once she reached his unit, her fears returned with a vengeance, anchoring heavy in her chest. With trepidation, she knocked on his door, each knock mimicking the fierce pounding of her heart. She wiped away tears as her body trembled from head to toe. The minutes ticked by with no answer, and she knocked again, harder.

"Please answer." She chanted the silent prayer while ringing his doorbell.

With tears trickling down her cheeks, she stared at the peephole, envisioning him staring back. The thought of him watching her stung and cut a path through her heart.

"Please," she cried, ringing the doorbell again. "God, Gavin, please. I love you. I'm so sorry."

Nothing.

Hands still shaking, she reached in her purse and pulled out her cell phone. She dialed Gavin's number. Eyes locked on his door, she listened to it ring over and over again.

"You've reached Gavin Blake. You know what to do."

Emily's heart clenched, tightened, and dropped into the pit of her stomach when she heard his voice. That sweet voice would forever haunt her if he didn't take her back. That sweet, pleading voice that had begged her to believe him. She hung up, dialed again, and listened once more. She didn't speak. She couldn't. Her frantic breathing would be the only message he would receive.

Words . . . she had none.

Emily pressed a hand to her mouth as the realization he wasn't forgiving her set in. For a few painful moments, she was silent. Then grief erupted in her chest. A torrent of tears flew down her cheeks. Her cries echoed throughout the hallway. She retreated and felt her back hit the wall. She stared at his door, the vivid memory of his face ingrained in her head. Searing pain surged and twisted in her gut as she slowly made her way into the elevator, her heart plummeting with its descent.

Shoulders slumped and spirit broken, Emily unlocked the door to her apartment. A small light above the stove cast a faint glow across the living room. Quieting her footsteps, so as not to wake Olivia, Emily made her way into her bedroom. Still shaking, a cloak of sadness enveloped her as she padded into her bathroom.

She flipped on the light and stared at her reflection. The green eyes, once vivid with hope, held no semblance of life. She ran her fingers over her cheeks, muddied with mascara. Her face looked pale. Even worse, her heart was stricken with loss. She flattened her palms against the cool marble surface of the sink, hung her head, and wept, gulping for air as pain so deep blanketed her soul. Regret in the most brutal form tightened like an unforgiving noose around her neck.

She tried to calm down by turning on the hot water and splashing her face. After reaching for a towel, she dried herself and shut off the light. Fatigue slowed her feet as she made her way to her bed, and she curled up on her side. Exhausted, she sank into the mattress, attempting to gain a few hours of sleep. But that wouldn't come.

No.

As seconds, minutes, and hours ticked by, Gavin's pained face and confused blue eyes invaded Emily's conscience. She drew in a shaky breath, rolled onto her back, and stared at the ceiling. Over the next few hours, swells of gut-wrenching pain rippled across her heart. She'd let him slip through her fingers.

Trying to ignore the ear-piercing sound of Blake Industries' private jet's engines firing up, Gavin wondered if Emily would remember things he'd never forget. Wondered how this was truly the end. He'd lost her. In less than seven hours, she would be Dillon's for good.

He tugged his suitcase from the back of Colton's Jeep, his heart sinking further into his stomach as he peered into the clear, cold night sky. Colton stepped onto the tarmac—his expression no more at ease than it'd been when Gavin came to him.

"You don't have to do this, little man," Colton yelled, tufts of his dark hair whipping around in the engines' fury. "Bouncing out of the city in the middle of the night won't bring her back."

Gavin wasn't sure if leaving would erase the mark Emily had seared into his soul. He also wasn't sure if he'd ever be free from the ache of needing her. The only emotion he truly fucking owned . . . he knew he had to get out of New York. Get the fuck out, and get far away from the ghost of Emily that would no doubt haunt him.

"I told you, I need to get off the grid for a while, Colton," Gavin argued, roughing a hand over his face. "I can't be here. Just take care of switching our stocks out of Dillon's hands."

Colton released a weighty breath and nodded. "I'll take care of it first thing Monday morning." He clapped Gavin's shoulder, his eyes softening. "You have to be good with all of this when you get back. Promise me you'll put Emily to rest while you're down there."

Gavin's chest palpitated at the sound of her name. "Yeah," he replied, his voice grave. "I'll try."

After a few moments of staring at each other, Gavin climbed the stairs to the jet. Turning, he watched his brother drive off the property of the small, private airport. Mind-fucked and in the deepest turmoil of his life, Gavin dug into the pocket of his jeans and pulled out his cell phone. Without looking at it, he tossed it onto the runway. It shattered when it hit the ground. Off the grid meant off the grid. No contact with anyone. No one trying to pull him from his pain, and no one trying to convince him his actions were destructive. After handing his bags to the flight attendant, the pilot came out to greet him.

"Good evening, Mr. Blake." The pilot, gray hair spilling over his forehead, firmly shook Gavin's hand. "Everything you've requested has been prepared, and we should arrive in Playa del Carmen in just over four hours, sir."

Gavin gave a weak nod and headed into his private cabin. He closed the door, and his eyes immediately landed on a mini-bar bottle of bourbon screaming his name. He gazed at it with contempt. Darkness seeped in around him. He peeled off his coat and tossed it onto the bed. Trying to stave off the evil angel invading his thoughts, he strode across the small space and reached for the mind-numbing amber liquid. Deciding to forgo a glass, he twisted off the cap and brought the bottle to his lips. The alcohol burned his throat, offering up not an ounce of reprieve from his pain.

It was then that Gavin knew there would never be a time in his life he wouldn't be aware of Emily's absence. Drunk or sober, she would riddle his heart and soul until the day he died. He loved her. Breathed her in as if she were the air around him . . . the air he would be deprived of forever. He put down the bottle, ran an exhausted hand through his hair, and attempted to cast visions of Emily's beautiful eyes staring back at him from his memory. He walked over to the window, peering out at the city below, and knew it didn't work. Nothing would. Neither soaking his pain in alcohol nor running from her could mend what he was feeling.

She was gone. As the twinkling lights faded with the jet's climbing altitude, Gavin's heart continued to mourn the woman he'd lost while his mind wondered how long he would be at her funeral.

Acknowledgments

WRITING IS AND always has been an outlet for me. When I sat down and first started writing *Collide,* I had no idea the road I was about to travel. I figured it would be easy enough to get my fingers to tap out some words, flesh out some characters, and build a relatively good story line. What I found instead was a painfully magnificent, torturous, beautiful, and emotional ride—all wrapped into one imperfect but perfect package. The mental attachment I endured having to essentially "become" my characters was neither something I was prepared for nor something that I will ever forget.

With that, I need to give my deepest thanks to my husband and my children for putting up with my many mood swings, many nights without a hot meal, and many days when mom or wife ceased to exist.

Joe, without your patience and support, none of this would have been possible. I swear that sandwich and Mustang will be yours one day. I love you, Big Daddy. Always.

Second to my husband and children is my sister-in-law, Cary. Oh, Cary, where do I begin? Your powerful insight and extreme positivity during the whole process surely saved a bit of my sanity—but definitely made you lose some of yours. The countless hours and many nights you spent on the phone listening to me yell, scream, and cry my way through *Collide* . . . let me just say . . . words, I don't have enough. Thank you for coming on this ride with me. Get your seat belt ready to do it all over again with *Pulse*.

As for the rest of you, please take a bow as I call your names.

Lisa Kates is my friend and one who I wish still lived nearby. I thank you for all the phone conversations as we daydreamed and talked about every chapter as I wrote it. Your honesty, although sometimes brutal, helped to shape Gavin into what he has become. Love and miss you, chick.

Gina, although many readers don't like the character that shares your name in this book, I will always love you, Chach!

Brooke Hunter, Lisa Maurer, Stephanie Johnson, and Teri Bland—my BCBWs—what can I say? Wow, you gals have made me laugh, cry, and really believe that there are readers out there who truly, one hundred percent, *unconditionally* love me and *Collide*. Each of you knew my fear going into this and talked me out of wanting to burn the manuscript. You saw me peak and dip and stayed with me during it all. You were there with pom-poms. No. Strings. Attached. I will forever love each of you for the support. I am amazed at the way our little reading and writing worlds have collided. Kismet. Here's to S.A. and Cali, babes!!!

To my graphic artist, Regina Wamba from Mae I Design and Photography: Wow. Just wow. Not only are you a one-stop shop for an author looking for photos, your design talent is simply amazing. Although I will always have a connection to *Collide*'s original cover, you knocked it out of the park with the second. I look forward to many years of driving you crazy as we discover new ways to make Kevin and Talia sweat it out for a hot cover!

To "Emily" from Right Now It's Your Tomorrow: A decision I made one day to contact you on your wonderful Facebook page led me to someone who helped me during the process of building Dillon (aka Douchepickle). Your page opened my eyes to exactly how many women deal with a narcissist on a daily basis. Your countless talks and direction as to where to take Dillon's personality helped me tremendously, and your advice is something that I will never forget. You're a strong woman, "Emily." You reach thousands of women, letting them know there *is* light at the end of the *very* dark tunnel they're in. That by itself speaks volumes of your character. I hope to one day meet you.

Author E. L. Montes, we're overdue for that Philly cheesesteak, girl. Thank you for your help and private messages. We've shared many, and each in its own little way has helped me. But, damn our boys, Gavin and Marcus. We need to stop them from fighting with each other.

To the very long list of book bloggers who simply do it for the love of reading: I can't say enough. You all know who you are. The constant "pimping" of my author Facebook page to your wonderful readers has helped me far greater than I could've ever imagined. In each of you, I have found friends that I hope to have for life. You ladies are spectacular, and I could never begin to tell you how much I've appreciated every single favor. Some of your blogs have brought me to women I am proud to call friends. I approached most of you as a very confused indie author, and you welcomed me with open arms, gave me advice, and rooted for me the whole time. Some of you are in college, and others have full-time jobs and families, but no matter what time of day I contacted you, you each were right there. You ladies humble me constantly.

To my first editor, Jovana Shirley, from Unforeseen Editing: Thank you for dealing with my panicky nervousness while editing *Collide*—as if the 2 a.m. private chats when I was trying to improve a description or sentence structure because of your recommendation weren't enough. You're just an all-around kick-ass woman to work with.

To my second editor, Cassie Cox: Thank you so much for teaching me a crisper way to write. You truly put wings on *Collide*'s second edit. I look forward to many years of working with you.

To my formatter, Angela McLaurin, from Fictional Formats: I feel like I struck gold with you! You're professional, sweet as candy, and you work quickly. Thank you for taking me on and bringing great ideas to the table as far as headers and page breaks. What are headers? Ha!

I would also like to thank my writers' group on Facebook. It has been awesome connecting with other authors who share the same love for writing as I do—and also share the same fear of putting ourselves out there for the world.

Last, and certainly by no means last, to my FictionPress readers: You were *Collide*'s first cheerleaders. Your following started in the first chapter and grew with each additional one that I posted. The countless e-mails telling me to continue *Collide* fueled me to no end. It drove me to where I am now. Because your words of encouragement inspired me to take the plunge, a thought that started with, "Hmm, let me write a story here and see if people like it," turned into something far bigger than I would ever have thought.

Had it not been for so many of you pushing me forward, I wouldn't be sitting here—on this Christmas night—typing an acknowledgments list for my first published book. There aren't enough words to describe how thankful I am for all of you.